HER SECRET ROGUE

RAKES & REBELS: THE ST. BRIAC FAMILY, BOOK 3

CYNTHIA WRIGHT

OLIVERHEBERBOOKS

Her Secret Rogue

The St. Briac Family, Book 3

Cover Design by Forever After Romance Designs

Published by Oliver-Heber Books

0 9 8 7 6 5 4 3 2 1

A lost rogue...

Dashing naturalist Anthony St. Briac has mysteriously gone missing in the Galápagos Islands and is presumed dead.

A noble lady on the run...

Radiantly independent Frederica Redfield aspires to do scientific research. Refusing her father's pleas to marry a wealthy old baron, she makes her escape.

A treasure-filled library...

In disguise as a male professor, Freddie takes a position in Anthony St. Briac's empty home, cataloguing his rare fossils. When, late one night, a threatening yet magnetic stranger appears in the library, her careful plans are thrown into disarray.

As Anthony and Freddie join forces to solve the mystery behind his near-fatal accident, passion flares white-hot. Yet can these fiercely independent lovers dare to risk their very hearts and discover the treasure of lasting love?

Rakes & Rebels: The St. Briac Family:

PROLOGUE

Galápagos Islands, Ecuador
HMS *Beagle*
October 8, 1835

*M*isty moonbeams streamed through a skylight in the cabin Anthony St. Briac shared with his friend, Charles Darwin on board the HMS *Beagle*. Blinking in the silvery light, Anthony tried to turn on his side, but his long legs were tangled in the gently swaying hammock. As he lay there, restless, an insect bite on his calf began to itch.

Was Darwin about to loom over him and announce it was time to get up? Anthony stifled a groan, remembering their plan to rise before dawn, row from their anchorage ashore to James Island, and remain there for several nights while the *Beagle* sailed off in search of enough fresh water to carry them through their looming voyage across the Pacific. Glancing over in the darkened cabin, Anthony was relieved to see that the brilliant young naturalist still slept contentedly in his own hammock nearby.

Anthony closed his eyes and drew a slow breath. He focused on relaxing his limbs. On nights like, this when sleep eluded him, it helped to imagine that he was back in England, either in Cornwall with his eccentric, rather wonderful family or in London, where he kept a home of his own. A pleasantly muddled memory drifted back, of riding his father's horse, Hugo, in Hyde Park ...years ago. It was early morning, long before the fashionable hour when the *Beau Monde* arrived to trot along Rotten Row. Anthony could almost smell the fresh meadow grass, see the golden light filtering through the leaves of the plane trees, hear the birdsong. Hyde Park was an oasis of green amid the bustling city. It was peaceful enough until he saw a young lady riding toward him, her slim back erect, the feathers on her hat bobbing slightly. Through the mists of time and sleep, he recognized the Honorable Frederica Redfield. No sooner had Anthony greeted her than she surprised him by bringing her horse alongside Hugo and declaring, "Perhaps you were not aware that I intend never to marry. I have no time for rogues like you."

It seemed then that she was shaking him. Laughing softly, Anthony murmured, "You are very bold."

The voice that replied was loud and male. "I'm glad you find me amusing! Now get up, St. Briac. We have a new adventure in store today."

Anthony returned to reality with a jolt. Opening his eyes in the shadows, he beheld Charles Darwin standing over him. "I was dreaming."

"I assumed so, old fellow. You have never spoken to *me* in that seductive tone of voice." His friend chuckled. "Missing someone?"

As he disengaged his tall, powerful frame from the hammock and rose, Anthony considered the question. In truth, he hadn't laid eyes on Frederica Redfield for a half-dozen years, and it wasn't as if their brief flirtation had come to anything. He hadn't even kissed her.

But, mused Anthony, perhaps that was the reason she occasionally appeared in his dreams …the frisson of desire lingered: that moment when Freddie *wanted* him to kiss her, to touch her, before she discovered that he'd been using her to unmask her father's crimes.

Darwin pulled a shirt over his head of thinning brown hair. "Do get dressed! Unless you've changed your mind?" Lifting a brow, he needled, "Perhaps you'd like to go back to sleep."

"Devil take it." Anthony reached for his own clothing. "I'm coming!"

Invariably, he agreed to accompany Darwin because he didn't want to miss a chance to discover something amazing. They had already unearthed countless natural treasures during their four-year expedition, traveling not only by ship but also walking and riding hundreds of miles in wild places like Brazil, Chile, and Tierra del Fuego. With Darwin, Anthony had collected fossils, bones of giant beasts, exotic insects, and had even discovered new species of animals. They had searched out the small ostrich-like rhea while riding with the gauchos who ruled Argentina's pampas. Along the way, the two men had learned to defend themselves with pistols, rifles, and knives while amassing crates of specimens to send ahead to their colleagues in England. It had been a grand, if grueling, adventure – and Anthony was changed forever. Glancing at his rough-hewn visage in a small shaving mirror nailed to the bulkhead, he saw a tanned, unshaven man who appeared transformed from a Regency buck into an uncivilized pirate.

Papa would be proud, Anthony thought with a wry smile.

Darwin propped himself against the bulkhead and pulled up his loose canvas pants. "Of course, Syms will accompany us," he said, referring to his young assistant, "as well as Mr. Bynoe. The servants will bring our gear and provisions. We shall erect a camp on the beach." He rubbed his hands together. "I am looking forward to having this extended time to examine the tortoises, lizards, and birds of James Island. Perhaps we will begin to understand the differences from one Galá-pagos island to the next."

Anthony nodded. There was no telling what they might unearth on James Island, and he had no intention of missing out on those moments of discovery. "I have been thinking about the birds. I trust you have been making careful notes about all you have captured on these islands, so we will know exactly where each bird was found." Pausing, he reached for his own small notebook and held it up. "I have."

Darwin's high brow furrowed. "I confess that my latest bout of seasickness has prevented me from recording those details as I usually would ..."

Before he could continue a voice interrupted them from the open doorway. "Good morning, gentlemen!"

Anthony looked over to see Terrance Buskin, a younger classmate from Cambridge University, who had recently been employed as a secretary for Nicholas Lawson, the Governor of the Galápagos Archipelago. When the men of the *Beagle* had visited Lawson on Charles Island, Buskin asked to join their party for the duration of their time in the Galápagos, announcing that he could serve as a guide of sorts.

"I trust you are hungry?" the young man now asked eagerly. "I've organized a proper breakfast for you both."

Darwin glanced over at Anthony. "Did I mention that Buskin volunteered to teach Cook how to prepare tortoise soup?"

"No, you did not." Anthony lifted both brows.

Terrance Buskin had rubbed him the wrong way since their days at Cambridge. It was difficult to explain, even to himself, why he could hardly bear to be in the same room with the solid, fair-haired Buskin. Although Terrance was helpful to the point of annoyance, Anthony's instincts told him the younger man was also quietly competing with him.

Just then, Anthony's stomach made a grumbling sound, loud enough for the others to hear.

Darwin gave a laugh and clapped Terrance on the shoulder. "Breakfast? Very thoughtful of you." Glancing over, he added, "And your stomach clearly agrees, St. Briac."

Anthony managed a smile. "Quite."

* * *

ON JAMES ISLAND, the servants pitched a tent on the beach, searching out a rare spot that wasn't riddled with burrows of the bizarre iguanas that roamed the volcanic island.

Working side-by-side, Charles and Anthony collected an array of flora, fauna, and rocks, even more than they had found on the other Galápagos Islands they'd previously visited. Darwin was aided by Syms Covington, the nineteen-year-old cabin boy and fiddler who had been trained as his assistant. Syms was especially adept at the necessary work of shooting and skinning the many birds and other small animals, freeing Darwin to concentrate on his copious notes.

The Galápagos Islands were an otherworldly assemblage of dormant volcanoes and stunted trees growing out of black, rocky ground. Everywhere Anthony looked, it seemed that he beheld large numbers of huge tortoises and iguanas and an abundance of birds.

On their last evening on James Island, the men

gathered at their beach camp while the servants cooked the meat of a giant tortoise for their supper. Anthony sat with Charles and Syms, as Terrance napped inside the tent. Despite the setting sun, the sand was burning hot.

Opening his collecting bag to reveal the day's specimens, Anthony withdrew two dun-colored birds. One had a thinner beak, while the other was smaller and had a thicker, rounder beak. They were the latest in a series of twenty-five similar birds.

"Look at these," he remarked. "It seems that each type we have discovered is different, yet all appear to be finches."

"I cannot agree," Charles replied firmly. "In fact, I daresay we have discovered two dozen entirely new species. Their plumage, beaks, and other notable attributes are somewhat different from any sort of finch we encountered in South America."

Anthony began to reply but thought better of it. Although he and Darwin might both be twenty-six years of age, his friend had greater experience in the natural world. Anthony was only on board the *Beagle* because Charles had asked Captain Fitzroy if he might bring his friend along as a sort of assistant. Leaning back on his elbows, Anthony smiled and surveyed the ugly, charcoal-gray marine iguanas who lounged on the volcanic rocks above them, powerful legs outstretched in the heat.

"No doubt you are right." He flashed a smile. "Again."

Charles laughed. "Fortunately, we have been sending crates of specimens back to England all along our voyage. Scientists like John Gould, the ornithologist, will no doubt have the answers we seek."

"And soon enough, we will be back on British soil."

Anthony said. "No doubt your reputation will precede us, my friend."

"I confess, it can't be soon enough for me. When we set sail, I never dreamed that four years later, we would still be so far from England. It's thrilling to realize we are about to begin the voyage home. It is my ardent hope that nothing delays us, and we may set foot upon English soil by next spring." He sighed. "Or sooner."

Anthony squinted at him in the golden-plum twilight. "You are homesick!"

"Of course. Aren't you?" Charles ate a last bite of tortoise meat and pushed the tin plate away. "The only thing I don't look forward to is listening to my sister Susan urge me to marry. Our years at sea have been a welcome reprieve from the strictures of daily life in England."

"Do you think you'll be able to bear those strictures after we return?"

"I suppose I won't have a choice. My father already believes I have only embarked on this voyage to avoid the responsibilities of manhood." Smiling, Charles gestured toward his canvas pants and open shirt. "Do you suppose we can continue to wear these comfortable clothes in London?"

"I would love to try. No doubt *my* father would approve." His voice was tinged with irony as he thought of the contrast between Darwin's stern parent and his own.

"Ah, yes," agreed Charles. "The famous Justin St. Briac. He has quite a reputation as a libertine and pirate."

"True, but I must say Papa has reformed during his years with my mother. At least as much as possible, considering his nature." The warm breeze and talk of home caused Anthony to feel reflective. "You have met him. He expected me to mold myself in his image when

I became a man, to fill my days with swordfights and the seduction of beautiful women. Papa found my interest in natural history both shocking and concerning." Anthony gave a short laugh.

"I seem to recall that you did follow in his footsteps as a seducer of women, especially during our visits to port cities." Charles uncorked a bottle of hard cider, took a drink, and passed it to Anthony. "Our parents could not be more different," he said ruefully. "Mine desires that I become a minister rather than a pirate."

"I had to assure Papa that he and I are more alike than he imagined. I too longed to sail away from the dull routines of everyday life ...I just want to have different sorts of adventures during my voyages." Anthony drank some of the cider and stretched his legs. "What will you do when we are back in England?"

"Beyond our work, I am not certain. Truthfully, I don't want to think about it yet." He sighed, and his sunburned face darkened. "What about you, St. Briac? Will you take a wife and seek a conventional profession?"

"A wife?" The very idea was foreign to him.

"You enjoyed your share of dalliances during our university years. Surely someone has sparked more ... tender emotions within your charming but cynical heart?"

"That sounds like something your sister would say to *you*." Anthony raked a hand through his disheveled black hair and allowed, "Well, perhaps. Very briefly. But the lady in question came to despise me, so it's not worth thinking about."

"Despise? That's a strong word. When did you last see this young lady?"

How odd, thought Anthony, that he was being made to think about Frederica again. First, there was that dream about meeting her in Hyde Park, and now he was fielding questions about her from Darwin …after all these years. "1829? Maybe even 1828. And really, it was nothing. No doubt she left an impression simply because she made it quite clear she never wants to set eyes on me again."

"Does this hard-hearted lass have a name?" Charles queried.

He shook his head, deflecting the question. "By now, she is doubtless married to a nobleman and has several children." Seeking to change the subject, he mused, "So many years have passed. I wonder if everything will seem very different when we return at last."

"I suspect that *you* will seem different to the people you left behind. They might not even recognize you, my friend." Charles's gaze touched Anthony's tattoo, barely visible inside his open collar. "And I suspect you will find it even more difficult to adjust to the constraints of polite society than I will."

"God, I despise that word: *constraint.*"

"Constraints will abound if you decide to court a young lady. You'll meet chaperones, gossips, and overbearing parents at every turn," Darwin predicted with a sidelong glance. "There will be none of the recent freedoms you've enjoyed." He waggled his thick brown brows. "For example, with Valeria Aguirre, in Chile."

Anthony frowned. "What of you? Don't they have a long list of expectations for you when you return home? If your sister Susan has anything to say about it, you'll be leg-shackled by next summer, I suspect."

Benjamin Bynoe, the surgeon's assistant, was loping toward them from the far side of the beach as Charles replied, "I admit I'm torn, but I don't think we have a choice, do we? We've had a long reprieve from proper society, and this grand adventure must come to an end. Serious work awaits us in England." He stifled a yawn. "Meanwhile, I am tired. At dawn, Syms, Mr. Bynoe, and

I will go by boat to explore a lake on the far side of the island, but I would like you and Buskin to head inland and make one last search for any birds or plants we may have overlooked. I can't help fearing that we missed an important clue."

Anthony managed to nod assent. He didn't look forward to spending several hours alone with Terrance Buskin, but he told himself it would be their last day in the Galápagos. When they weighed anchor, Terrance would hopefully stay behind with Vice-Governor Lawson. Soon enough the HMS *Beagle* would be sailing across the Pacific Ocean, bound for New Zealand – the first stop on their journey home to England.

* * *

"Look." Anthony pointed into a fissure of black volcanic rock where seven white, spherical eggs had been deposited. "Giant tortoise eggs."

The morning sun was beating down and Terrance Buskin paused to mop his pale, gleaming brow. "Good God. Ghastly creatures, aren't they?"

As if on cue, an enormous tortoise, weighing perhaps two hundred pounds, emerged from a thicket of scrubby bushes. Upon encountering Anthony and Terrance, it emitted a hissing sound and plodded off uphill, toward the greener center of the island.

"We can hope that fellow will lead us to a spring," said Anthony. "Darwin and I have been told that the tortoises walk for miles inland to reach a water source, spend a few days drinking, and then return to lower ground."

"Yes, yes," Terrance agreed, nodding.

"You doubtless know much more than we do, having lived on the islands."

"Not really." The younger man's broad face glis-

1

LONDON, 4 APRIL 1825

Olivia stepped inside the sweltering ballroom and felt as if a finch had been pulled on her.

The duke had assured her of a small salon.

Instead, she stood amidst the crush of the Season. The champagne punch flowed with no end in sight, as did the gossip, and the ballroom brimmed with every member of the *ton* currently in London.

How alone a person could feel in a crowd of people.

"Lady Percival," called a lady's perfectly cultured voice identical to every other lady's perfectly cultured voice in the room. "Or is it Lady Olivia now?" Soft giggles muted by raised silk fans floated on the air.

Before Olivia, an intimate circle of four couples radiated excitement, anticipating a gossip-worthy exchange, the ladies snickering in delight, the gentlemen shifting from foot to foot, discomfort evident.

"Lady Olivia will do," she replied, with a succinct snap in her voice, and immediately regretted it. She shouldn't be using that tone tonight, her first night back in society after a six-month absence. It could reveal anxious nerves. She'd believed herself prepared for the stir her presence would create, but her body told a different story. Her heart was a hammer in her chest, and sweat slicked her palms.

"We were just speaking of you, and now here you are." The chit's smile curved a smidgen too wide.

Her name was Miss Fox, and Olivia knew not a whit about her. She didn't keep up with her Debrett's.

"Your gown is ravishing. You must give me the direction of your modiste. A scandalous French one, to be sure." Sensing blood in the water, Miss Fox pressed, "It's so rare these days that you grace society with your presence."

A silence so taut a pin could puncture it, expanded, as the tight circle of couples awaited Olivia's response. No choice but to proceed as she meant to go on, she drew herself up to her fullest height and met Miss Fox square in the eye. "One must be careful about the company one keeps at a large and indiscriminate gathering such as this. It isn't as *select* as one might wish."

Her gaze swept up and down Miss Fox, and the vulpine smile fell from the younger woman's lips as the implication of Olivia's words hit her. No one could deny the fact that though she may be this Season's scandal, Lady Olivia Montfort still outranked Miss Anne Fox. "Now, if you'll excuse me."

Olivia didn't await a response before gliding away across the ballroom's polished mahogany floor to seek sanctuary in the ladies' retiring room. A single, bracing moment of peace and quiet should shore her up for this night.

She'd hardly exhaled the sigh that had wanted release all evening, when the outer door opened and closed with a muted, but distinct, click. She was about to peek around the screen when a firm, matronly voice rang out. "I say, she is lucky to be received in polite society, and you know it, Clarinda. But with a benefactor like His Grace at her disposal, well, who can refuse her?"

Olivia startled backward, breath suspended in her

chest, ears attuned to whatever words would come next.

"Now, Ernestine, His Grace isn't her benefactor. She is his daughter by law. Besides, Lady Olivia Montfort is the daughter of the Earl of Surrey. She isn't the sort of woman who needs a benefactor."

"*Was* the duke's daughter by law, you mean," Ernestine huffed.

"Yet," Clarinda began on a conspiratorial whisper, "it was the duke who backed her petition for divorce at the House of Lords."

"*From his own son.*" Ernestine lowered her righteous voice an octave. "*She* petitioned for the divorce, Clarinda. What is this world coming to that a wife can petition the *House of Lords* for a divorce? Then have the audacity to continue living beneath the roof of her divorced husband's father? I daresay, we may be near the end times."

That went to show what this battle-axe understood of these matters: the House of Lords hadn't the legal or ecclesiastical power to grant Olivia a true divorce. What they had was the power to set the marriage aside. It was called a *divorce a vinculo matrimonii*, and she was only the fourth woman in England to be granted one on the grounds of desertion.

Still, the gossipy duo was correct about one point: the duke had thrown his support behind her in the endeavor. In fact, he'd been the one to suggest it, promising to ensure that her daughter Lucy remained, if not legitimate to the exact letter of the law, a fully-fledged member of the powerful Bretagne family. She was the granddaughter of a duke, and no one would dare forget it.

The daughter of an earl herself, Olivia understood power and privilege, or thought she had, until the duke had chosen to flex his ducal muscle on her behalf and the might of the dukedom was revealed to her in its full glory and scope. It was a magnificent and awe-inspiring thing, that sort of power, and she'd never felt so humbled in her life as when it worked on her behalf. With nary a whimper of contradiction, the House of Lords had acceded to his directive in the matter. Still, she understood that if Percy hadn't been a younger son, or if their daughter had been male, the outcome wouldn't have settled so satisfactorily in her favor.

"But, Ernestine," Clarinda's voice lowered a conspiratorial octave, "Lord Percival Bretagne was alive these last twelve years. Can you believe it? We mustn't be too hard on the poor chit."

"The woman spent a decade running around with those artistic, bohemian types while her husband lay dead in Spain."

"But he *wasn't* dead in Spain," Clarinda insisted.

"What sort of *proper* widow spends her time in *those* circles? I daresay," Ernestine continued as if Clarinda hadn't spoken. Olivia imagined brows lifted to the ceiling in damning hauteur.

"But the girl wasn't a widow at all."

"Girl?" Ernestine spat.

"Well, no longer a girl, I suppose." Clarinda paused while another "humpf!" sounded from Ernestine. "But when she lost that boy—"

"You mean her husband, Lord Percival?" Ernestine interrupted.

"What a sweet love match they made in her first Season. Rumor has it she nearly went mad from the grief, poor dear."

Olivia's fingers curled into tight fists, the nails digging into her palms. They discussed her as if she was some sort of revolutionary bent on rending the very fabric of society in two.

Perhaps she was. Except that hadn't been her intent at all.

When her sister Mariana had returned from Paris

six months ago and revealed that she'd seen—and spoken with!—Percy, an avalanche of dread had nearly crushed Olivia, making it difficult for her lungs to draw air, suffocating her.

Percy was alive.

"He was His Grace's favorite, they say," Clarinda said.

Olivia couldn't deny the truth of those words. Percy had been everyone's favorite.

Except hers. At least, by the time he'd died. And most definitely by the time he'd rejoined the land of the living as, of all things, a spy, and the full weight of the truth crashed down on her: Percy had *chosen* to stay away—from her, from their daughter—for the last twelve years.

He'd been better off dead as far as she was concerned, which was why she needed to press forward with her plan to move house. Someday, he would arrive in Town, and when he did, he wouldn't find her still housed beneath his father's roof. She would eat glass first.

An unladylike huff of frustration escaped her. This morning, her plan had hit a snag. The duke's solicitors refused to assist her without his express consent. He would help her, of that she was certain, but she'd wanted to purchase a Mayfair townhouse herself and present it to him as a *fait accompli*. This final step toward independence was hers alone to take.

Yet, with no other option open to her, she'd had to petition her father's solicitors for their services, even though her father and mother would remain in Italy for another season and have no ability to back her request any time in the near future. When she'd set out on this course six months ago, she'd had no idea how much male assistance a woman needed to become free and independent. Galling.

"Speaking of His Grace," Ernestine began, a ribbon

of girlish excitement twirling through her words. The door opened, and a roar of bright gaiety rushed in. The gossipy duo were exiting the room. "Have you seen him tonight? He is one eligible bachelor."

"At five and sixty?"

"An unmarried Duke of Arundel is eligible at any age, Clarinda."

The door shut behind the pair, and the outside world again dulled its pitch to a quiet muffle. Olivia stepped out from behind the screen and paused before a gilded Baroque mirror. Even its warm, reflective glow couldn't mask the fact that her face spoke of devastation, like it had been scrubbed raw across a washboard. This wouldn't do.

She leaned over the washstand and dabbed her skin with its cooling water. Hands to either side of the basin, she closed her eyes and inhaled deeply, clearing her mind on a long exhale. This salon was no place for her past.

Another glance in the mirror revealed the red splotches mostly gone. Only a hint of pink remained, which could be taken for too much heat at a crush like tonight's. Emotion could darken the sky blue of her eyes into stormy gray in an instant. She opened them a little wider into a semblance of their usual selves. The clouds receded.

Social armor intact, she stepped to the door, pushed it wide on a gust of festive cacophony, and her seventeen-year-old self danced before her on the happy notes of violin strings underlain by the grounding drone of cello and bass; the sporadic shrill giggle here and there, punctuating a witty remark like an exclamation point; the rustle of silk and superfine as guests wove in and out of each other, seeking good conversation, good gossip, and good champagne. All underscored by the dull, monotone din of the crowd as the light from a thousand candles glittered overhead, tiny prisms of chandelier crystals dancing to the subtle rhythm of the string quartet.

How her seventeen-year-old self had loved the controlled chaos of a party. Although there was pain on one side of this memory, she experienced the pleasure on the other side of it.

Her lips curved into her first genuine, if subdued, smile of the night. The past didn't have to be all guilt and hurt.

How that girl would be giddy over the sight of this full-to-capacity ballroom, at the possibilities hidden within it. A tidbit of choice gossip. A chance to roam a room unchaperoned. A stolen glimpse of a handsome-beyond-compare boy with the deepest brown eyes in the wide world...

Oh, how Ernestine and Clarinda had conjured the past tonight. She longed to rush home and lie with Lucy, her daughter's breath soft and regular in the cadence of sleep. Then she would steal away to her studio to ready the sketches she would present to her art master on the morrow.

But the present beckoned, and she must pretend to enjoy herself, smile pasted onto her face. She lifted her chin a notch and feigned indifference. She would be an ice queen, not the soft, gay girl this room had seen over a decade ago.

It was too soon. Hardly a fortnight had passed since Parliament set aside her marriage.

For the people populating this room, life maintained a smooth, unwavering trajectory from birth to death. They couldn't comprehend how her fate had diverged so dramatically from theirs. Six months ago, she'd been an unremarkable widow, if a little eccentric given her involvement with the arts. But they'd understood her.

Now? She was a real, live divorcée, little more than a new species on display at the zoo.

Across the crowd, she spotted the duke's signature shock of silver hair and began making her way toward him through the ever-changing maze of ever-sweaty *ton*. She could hardly remember a time when she'd seen more of society's luminaries assembled in one place.

Who was tonight's honoree? She hadn't been attentive to the details when the duke had requested her presence tonight.

"Olivia!"

She turned toward the first welcome voice of the night, her sister's. "Oh, Mariana, what a relief to see you."

Upon their presentation at court, "Milk and Honey" was the moniker the Regent had bestowed on the Earl of Surrey's twin daughters, Ladies Olivia and Mariana, in reference to their respective, un-twinlike appearances. Olivia's clear, milky complexion had been the perfect complement to Mariana's tawny hair and eyes.

"Lady Olivia," Mariana purred, not unlike the intonation of a jungle cat settling in for a feast of minced rat. She indicated the rather pugnacious-looking man at her side. "Sir Edwin was inquiring about The Progressive School for Young Ladies and the Education of Their Minds."

"Oh?" Olivia smiled and began to back away. No good ever came of crossing Mariana when her lioness purr coupled with that particular glint in her eye.

Most gentlemen of the *ton* regarded The Progressive School for Young Ladies and the Education of Their Minds to be a complete waste of time and resources for the needless education of daughters who were best married off as soon as could be decently managed. It was clear as day that Mariana was spoiling for a row.

"I'm uncertain how I can be of more help than my sister. If you will pardon me—"

Mariana slipped her hand into the crook of Olivia's

arm, securing her to her side. Olivia was caught. "Sir Edwin," Mariana began, turning a dazzling smile onto her prey, "has difficulty believing our daughters' feeble female brains are capable of progressing mathematically beyond tallying the number of stitches on a sampler."

Olivia heard in Mariana's tone the familiar stirrings of a righteous and one-sided debate. Sir Edwin would have no hope of getting a word in edgewise once Mariana warmed to her subject.

Herein lay the difference between herself and Mariana: Olivia was no crusader. While she believed that her daughter needed a *male* education—the very reason she and Mariana had founded the school, after all—she had no interest in converting the Sir Edwins of the *ton* to her way of thinking.

The *ton* simply wasn't ready for The Progressive School for Young Ladies and the Education of Their Minds. And it wasn't Olivia's mission in life to make them so.

"Sir Edwin," Olivia conceded, "I suggest you bring your daughter for a visit if your curiosity has gotten the better of you."

Sir Edwin's nose darkened into an unattractive shade of aubergine. "I can assure you that curiosity about such a school does not in any way outweigh my good judgment. Curiosity, indeed." The man harrumphed. "More like turning my daughter into a curiosity with these outlandish—"

Olivia was spared the remainder of Sir Edwin's scold when his voice died away and the volume of the room hushed to a dull murmur. Her eyes shifted from Sir Edwin's florid face and followed the collective gaze.

At first glance, it appeared to be nothing more than the announcement of yet another couple standing at the top of the ballroom's grand staircase. A closer examination revealed that the pair was no couple, rather a man and a girl a few years shy of her debut.

The girl was both the man's opposite and his equal at once. Where she was dark, he was light. Where he towered impressively, she stood modestly. Their connection, however, was apparent in the intangibles: a similarity in their composure and in the quiet way they took in the scene before them.

Mariana pulled Olivia close. "It appears the night's gossip trump card is being played. You, dear sister, are old news."

Olivia tore her gaze away from the new arrivals and lent an attentive ear to her sister.

"The newly minted Right Honourable Jakob Radclyffe, Fifth Viscount St. Alban," Mariana whispered. "Rich as Croesus and tonight's guest of honor. A shipping heir, if the gossip is true."

Olivia couldn't resist the tug of another glance. They were an impossibly gorgeous and arresting pair. His golden head of hair was the finest mixture of red and sun-kissed blond she'd ever seen, which contrasted sharply with the girl's hair, the deep, complex black of a crow's wing. It would be a challenge for any painter to get the colors right, especially a novice like herself, but she would love to try.

She heard someone say, "She's his daughter. Haven't you heard?"

Mariana squeezed Olivia's arm. "Oh, the gossips will have a field day with this."

Olivia nodded once, taking Mariana's meaning. The girl's parentage, specifically on her mother's side.

The resemblance to both her Asian and European ancestries clear, the girl's features came together in flawless synthesis: a heart-shaped face, a full rosebud mouth, and the most beautiful eyes Olivia had ever beheld, oval but angled in the exact same line as high cheekbones sharp enough to cut glass, appearing to be not brown, but the changeable gray of a black pearl. It was as if Nature had taken the best from both lines of descent to illustrate for the world its capacity for perfection.

The ladies formed a tight, exclusive circle, and whispered snippets of conversation flurried around Olivia.

"Rumor has it that the mother is Japanese," she overheard.

"A servant, do you think?" came the scandalized reply.

"And he acknowledges her?"

"Oriental women have secrets, don't you know?" came a giggly whisper from her left.

"Which ones did they teach him?"

"Wouldn't mind finding out," came a sly response.

The giggles grew bolder, and the crowd roared back to life as the string quartet swept bows across strings and played on with renewed vigor. The clamor to gossip about this new and intriguing development eluded Olivia, even as it possessed everyone around her.

Unable to take her eyes off the viscount's face composed entirely of angles and shadows, she felt a twinge of something she couldn't identify and quickly dismissed the feeling as nothing more than simple curiosity.

Why on earth would she feel anything more? The man was nothing to her.

"Have you ever seen such a pair?" came Mariana's whisper in her ear.

"I think not," was all Olivia could speak through parched lips.

"Come, let's waggle an introduction from the duchess."

As Mariana pulled in one direction, Olivia leaned in the other and slipped her arm free. "I'm afraid not tonight. I have a splitting headache." At Mariana's bewildered expression, she continued, "You can fill me in on all the details at my soirée in a few days."

"Promise?"

"Yes, sister."

Without further hesitation, Mariana was off on her mission, leaving Olivia on her own, a strange relief at her sister's departure stealing through her. Recently reunited with her husband, happiness radiated off Mariana in waves. Olivia wouldn't weigh down Mariana's newfound joy with her problems and anxieties. In this way, she knew she wasn't alone, for she had a full life and a supportive family, but she was alone in her choices and the path she wanted to forge. It was simultaneously exciting and terrifying.

Her gaze again stole toward the staircase where Lord St. Alban stood quietly surveying the room. Except his eyes weren't quiet. They were absolutely fierce, only softening when he bent his head to make a comment to his daughter. The girl nodded once while staring straight ahead and drawing her embroidered silk reticule close to her chest. Deliberately, protectively, he placed a hand at her elbow. His message was clear: his daughter was a peer of this room as much as he.

The fearsome display of love elicited a confusion of emotion within Olivia, strange and alarming. She couldn't help thinking of Lucy and Percy, of how he hadn't been that father to her, and a hard knot twisted inside her chest, even as a warm shiver purled down her spine.

Instinct urged her to run as fast and as far away as her feet could carry her from this scene. After the scandalous six months of gossip she'd provided the *ton*, confusions of emotion were best left unexplored and avoided at all costs.

She would make her excuses, kiss her good-byes,

and forget all about the unsettling Right Honourable Jakob Radclyffe, Fifth Viscount St. Alban. By tomorrow morn, she would be settled and ready to begin her independent future, decidedly free from all confusions of emotion.

tened. "I've been working in an office most of the time, assisting Governor Lawson. I confess I feel my talents are wasted there, and I crave an opportunity to put my education as a naturalist to good use! I know that I am capable of great things if given a chance."

Anthony nodded, but his attention was fixed on the tortoise. He quietly followed it through the brush until he had a good look at the pattern on huge animal's shell.

"What is it?" Terrance was at Anthony's elbow, panting slightly.

"I've just realized that the pattern on this tortoise's shell is quite different from those we saw on Charles Island." He paused, considering. "I think the tortoises on each island we have visited might have uniquely different shells. The question is, what does it mean?" As he spoke, Anthony reached inside his canvas bag and withdrew a slim blue notebook. Lifting the pencil that was attached to it by a chain, he scrawled his thoughts in the little book.

"Really," said Terrance, "you and Darwin are riveted by the dullest things."

Anthony laughed, but his thoughts were far away as he jotted notes.

Tortoise shells different on each island. Why?

Discuss with Charles – what is the connection?

Different birds – could they all be finches, altered to fit their surroundings?

Deciding to talk to Darwin about his suspicions later, Anthony put the little book back in the canvas sack with the small assortment of leaves, birds, and insects collected that morning. Up ahead, the trees were taller and denser, and the tortoise had come to a standstill next to a group of other tortoises. They all had similar patterns on their shells, noted Anthony.

"Let's see what has attracted them," he said to Terrance.

At the top of the hill, the trees gave way to an opening. Reaching the row of tortoises who hesitated on the brink, Anthony saw that they teetered on the edge of a precipitous embankment. Far below, what appeared to be a freshwater spring sparkled. It was the first such body of water Anthony had seen on the Galápagos Islands.

He looked around at the tortoises. "No wonder you've all made this journey to the center of the island," he said to them. Over one shoulder, he told Terrance, "It seems they must lumber inland to drink their fill before returning to the open land near the beaches. I'll go down to have a closer look; perhaps this isn't even their preferred spring. The water might be salty, like the ponds we found on Charles Island. Are you coming?"

Terrance took a step backward. "The cliff is very steep," he said doubtfully.

"I've done my share of climbing on cliffs and rocks in Cornwall. This should be easy enough." As he spoke, Anthony pulled off his canvas shoes and rolled up his pants. "Hold onto my collection bag, won't you?"

Handing the cloth bag with his precious notebook and specimens to Terrance Buskin, he turned and began to descend the sandstone cliff, grasping a thick root while reaching down with one bare foot for purchase on the slippery rocks. The familiar thrill of danger sent Anthony's blood pulsing through his veins. He savored each moment.

Unable to resist the temptation to take a greater risk, Anthony again lowered his right foot, farther this time, reaching down into thin air. The root he clung to tore slightly, and his heart lurched. He brought his foot back up to safety and paused, considering where to transfer his hand next. There was another jagged bit of rock below the fraying root. He moved his hand to the rock, fitting his long fingers around the pointy curve, glad to feel the heft of it.

From the grassy edge of the cliff above, Anthony thought he heard Terrance say something, but the other man's voice was muffled by the breathing of the tortoises and the gurgle of the water below.

Glancing down, Anthony saw that it was farther to the spring than he had realized. No wonder the tortoises were still above, watching, rather than attempting to reach the water.

He held fast to the cliff with one hand and reached down once again with his foot. There was a ledge of sorts a few feet lower. Was it too far? The muscles in his left thigh contracted, hard as steel, as he bent his supporting leg and stretched out the toes on his right foot, reaching down, searching for the cursed ledge.

At that very moment the rock began to crumble in his hand before it broke off entirely. Anthony could only stare in disbelief, scrabbling at the cliff for something, anything else to hold onto.

A blinding flash of terror came at him like lightning. He was falling fast, sideways into space, stopping only when the back of his head struck something sharp and hard as iron.

The world went black.

CHAPTER 1

LONDON, ENGLAND, SEPTEMBER 1836

Frederica Redfield blinked back unshed tears as she stood in the entry hall of her grandparents' Grosvenor Square home, surveying the assortment of trunks that contained all of her possessions. Although the morning was sunny and fair, a chill crept over her, and her hands were cold as ice.

"Mistress, are you unwell?" a soft voice inquired from the stairway.

Grandpapa's faithful housekeeper, Mrs. Bell, emerged from the library. The old woman's plump face wore a compassionate smile that only intensified Freddie's heartache. "I cannot say I am well, but I will certainly carry on."

"Lord Justmore would be very proud of you," Mrs. Bell said gently.

"He was fond of telling me that no matter what challenge came my way, I would prevail. Those words are precious."

Frederica looked through the doorway of the vast, memory-filled library. After her grandmother's sudden death five years ago, Freddie had called a halt to her second London Season. She had been grateful for the reprieve from the marriage mart, glad to escape her father's efforts to marry her off to a suitor who would be wealthy enough to pay his debts, and glad to move to Grosvenor Square and care for her dear Grandpapa, the Earl of Justmore. He had been blind, thus dependent on her grandmother for some time, and so Freddie took her place.

During the ensuing years, she spent nearly every waking hour inside the earl's long neglected library. Her grandfather's spirit would always linger there, in his favorite tufted leather chair where he sat, listening to Freddie read aloud and discuss her progress as she lovingly organized his vast collection of books. Today she couldn't bear to look inside that beloved room. The scent of old books and tobacco, the texture of the worn leather bindings, the burnished rays of sunlight spilling across Grandpapa's cluttered desk ...all of it brought a wave of sadness.

"I suppose you mean to go to Viscount Redfield's house now," murmured Mrs. Bell.

"Yes, Papa is expecting me. It is my only choice at the moment." Her heartbeat accelerated. "Carter has gone for the barouche. He will take me home and bring my trunks as well."

Mrs. Bell bit her lip. "I know it isn't my place to offer an opinion, but I'll say it all the same. I am sick at heart that his lordship could not leave his estate to you rather than his nephew. As far as I know, Sir Harold Middleton has never set foot inside this house!" Frowning, she added, "I think his lordship was so happy during those years you were here with him, he forgot about the dreadful arrangements that were made long ago."

"Grandpapa's estates were entailed, as you well know, Mrs. Bell. He had no sons, his only daughter had died, and so his property passed to the son of his younger brother." She tried to smile. "Perhaps Sir

Harold will prove to be a perfectly nice man. I do hope so."

"If he were, he would have insisted that you stay here and have this house," Mrs. Bell muttered. "He has inherited a title, wealth, and more than enough other property for himself without pushing you out of your rightful home. It's not right."

"It isn't as if I will be on the street. I do have another home …" As Frederica spoke, she thought about Redfield House, where she would return today. Mama had brought the residence on Park Lane to her marriage, and many times before her accidental death, she had told Frederica that one day it would be hers. This memory was somewhat reassuring.

"I still don't like it," insisted Mrs. Bell.

Just then, the knocker sounded at the front door, startling both women. "Please, send whoever it is away, Mrs. Bell." Frederica swallowed. "Unless, of course, my cousin has arrived early."

Drawing a stoic breath, the housekeeper trundled over to open the heavy portal.

"Good morning, Mrs. Bell," came a voice from Frederica's past. "My daughter and I were out for a stroll and couldn't resist the impulse to pay a call on our friend, Miss Redfield."

A young female spoke, calling out, "Hello, Freddie!"

"Good day, my ladies," said Mrs. Bell in a firm voice. "I'm sorry to tell you that Miss Redfield is not receiving callers this morning."

Frederica hurried forward, her heart swelling. "Of course, that does not apply to these two ladies, Mrs. Bell."

Standing in the entryway in a halo of soft morning sunlight was Mouette St. Briac, her ebony hair accented by glints of silver. By her side stood a beauty who Freddie realized must be Mouette's daughter, Emeline. She was, it seemed, nearly a woman now.

Reaching out, Mouette said warmly, "Dearest Frederica, it has been far too long since we have seen you. We have come up from Cornwall to spend several weeks with my parents across the square, and they informed us of your grandfather's passing. Lord Justmore was always very kind to me when we met over the years. I hope you don't mind …I had to come to offer our condolences."

Suddenly conscious of her drab black gown, Frederica nodded. "Thank you for those kind words. I have been so preoccupied in recent years, caring for Grandpapa and helping him organize his sprawling library, I may have become something of a recluse. Seeing both of you reminds me that I have missed the company of good friends."

"I encountered your father some months ago, and of course, I asked after you. Lord Redfield informed me that you had been living here since the death of your grandmother," Mouette confided.

Frederica cringed inwardly at the mention of her father, for he had long carried a torch for Mouette and tried to make trouble in her marriage. "Yes, that's right, I've lived here for almost five years."

"How lucky for you!" Emeline exclaimed suddenly. "You were able to escape the marriage mart before some horrid creature *purchased* you for a sum your father could not refuse." For emphasis, she widened her thick-lashed violet eyes.

"Emeline!" cried Mouette, rounding on her daughter. "You are shockingly impertinent."

The girl nodded happily. "Guilty as charged, Mama." She paused, dimples winking. "However, I prefer to think of myself as forthright, like my friend, Freddie."

Mouette's gaze swept the entry hall, taking in the

assortment of trunks and the general air of gloom. "We will not take any more of your time, my dear. It appears that you may be ...going away?"

"I am. My great-uncle's son, Sir Harold Middleton, has inherited my grandfather's estates. He arrives later today." She managed a grim smile. "I must return home to Papa."

"Oh, my." Mouette bit her lip.

"Don't worry, I shan't let Papa coerce me to wed, even to help him settle his debts." Frederica told them. "In any event, I am five-and-twenty, far too old for the marriage mart."

"But what will you do?" queried Emeline.

Straightening her back, Frederica replied, "I have abilities and talents, fostered by my grandfather. I loved the painstaking, absorbing work I did with him. The hours flew by, and I felt such a sense of accomplishment. It is my dream to be a scholar at the British Museum, helping to catalogue natural history wonders being uncovered all over the world. In recent years, I fancy I've had more experience at that sort of work than the men who seek employment at the Museum." Seeing Mouette's faintly doubtful expression, Frederica added, "Perhaps you think such a dream is impossible because I am a female. But the world is changing every day! Look at the accomplishments of great women like Mary Anning. How I dream of studying the fossils she has unearthed! I mean to join the scholars who assemble the pieces of the puzzle, solving the mysteries behind those magnificent discoveries."

"Brava!" exclaimed Emeline. "I too am utterly fascinated by Miss Anning's discoveries!"

"We will certainly be cheering for you," Mouette assured Freddie. "Remember that you have friends if you need us, and we are near at hand. Do not hesitate to call on me at any time, should you need help."

"Of course. Are you speaking of my aspiration to be employed by the British Museum?"

"I wish I were." After a brief pause, Mouette said, "Let me be plain. I am not certain your father will share your conviction that you are no longer marriageable. And my dear, you are a splendid female, possessed of both striking good looks and a uniquely fine mind."

"My looks do not signify." Freddie shook her head. "I shall do everything possible to hide whatever good looks I might have. I want nothing to do with men or the horrid restraints they wish to impose on women like me."

"Clearly you are a fighter." Mouette held her gaze. "But in the weeks to come, pray do not forget that you have friends. You are not alone."

Tears pricked Frederica's eyes, the first she had allowed herself since the night her grandfather died. "How kind you are. I am very grateful."

"I understand more of your current challenges than you know," Mouette said cryptically.

With that, she straightened her stylish bonnet of raspberry silk and turned back to the partially open door.

Frederica surprised herself by catching Mouette's wide sleeve. "Wait. I cannot let you go without asking about your son, Anthony." She felt her cheeks grow warm. "I knew him a little, years ago. Grandpapa heard that Anthony had joined his friend, Charles Darwin, on board the *Beagle*. I suppose they have returned from their adventures by now."

Mouette's beautiful face went white, and she closed her eyes for a long moment. "The *Beagle* has not yet returned, but we received word from Captain FitzRoy some months ago that ..." She paused, swallowing. "They spent five weeks exploring the Galàpagos Archipelago, near Ecuador—"

Unable to restrain herself, Frederica clasped her hands and interjected, "How fascinating that must have been! I can only imagine the discoveries they have made, as naturalists, during such a voyage. Just the sort of things I was speaking of earlier." As she spoke Frederica saw a shadow pass over the older woman's face. "What is it?"

Mouette closed her eyes for a long moment. "My son was lost while exploring on the Galápagos Islands, on the very last day before they set sail for New Zealand. That is all we know."

Frederica's heart seemed to stop. "Lost? But—"

"He has …vanished without a trace."

"It's all a lot of nonsense!" Emeline burst out, bright spots of color on her cheeks. "My brother is far too clever and strong to come to any harm. I have no doubt *whatsoever* that he is perfectly fine, and one day soon we will all laugh about the fright he gave us."

Stunned, Frederica reached for Mouette's gloved hand. "Emeline is right. This must be a terrible mistake!"

Drawing a shaky breath, Mouette managed to nod. "Of course. We all pray that is the case." She began to turn away, then stopped and looked back, her eyes shining. "Surely every mother feels thus, but I find it impossible to imagine this world without my Anthony in it. He is too vital—too splendid!"

"Indeed," whispered Freddie, remembering Anthony St. Briac's magnetic charm and dark good looks, which he wore with ease. Unbidden, the memory came to her of the night she discovered him in her father's study. The air between them had fairly crackled with desire, and she could still remember the way he had stared at her mouth in the shadows. How she had ached for him to take her in his arms and teach her the mysteries of kissing! She had been but eighteen years old then, thrust unwillingly into her first Season, the embodiment of innocence.

And Anthony's attentions had ignited her girlish passions to a shocking degree. Her nipples tingled even now at the memory. But that night, he had *not* kissed her, for she discovered that he had crept into her house for quite another reason: to recover Mouette's portrait. Furthermore, his notorious father, Justin St. Briac, was hiding behind the sofa, and Freddie had quickly realized that even the intimate moment between them had been mere acting on Anthony's part.

In truth, all his attentions had been counterfeit, part of a bigger plan to enlist Frederica's aid to bring down her father. Seven years later, the memory still caused her cheeks to burn with humiliation …while sending a traitorous current of arousal through her body. It was a part of her she thought was buried, but it seemed Anthony St. Briac still had the power to awaken her, though he might only be a ghost.

And, dead or alive, Frederica continued to despise him with every fiber of her being.

"I suggest you both stop looking so glum," Emeline said sternly. "He is coming back."

"Of course, he is." Frederica spoke with conviction, yet the back of her neck prickled as she walked outside with the two women. The sight of Grosvenor Square, sun-dappled in the golden September morning, made her sigh. "I shall miss this place."

"My Raveneau grandparents live directly across the square." Emeline pointed through the trees to André and Devon Raveneaus' handsome corner home of red brick.

Mouette put a hand on Frederica's shoulder and reminded her, "I beg that you remember, you will always be welcome there."

CHAPTER 2

Frederica silently turned the knob and, inch by inch, eased open the door to her bedchamber. Holding her breath, she listened, straining to decipher the muffled male voices that drifted up the stairway.

Why did she feel panic begin to flutter in the shadowed recesses of her memory?

Since returning to her father's home a week earlier, Papa had been on his best behavior. He ordered Cook to serve her favorite dishes, he called Frederica by the pet names from her childhood, and he never mentioned his previous plan for her to wed a man who would not only pay his immense debts but also continue to support his lifestyle as Viscount Redfield.

Reluctantly, Freddie thought back to the end of her first Season, when Baron Cobleigh, one of the richest men in London, had begun his relentless efforts to woo her. Her father had been overjoyed, despite her protestations that Cobleigh was not only far too old but also possessed of stick legs and an enormous paunch. Her suitor's favorite form of flattery was to assure Frederica that she was 'fine breeding stock'. She shuddered now at the memory. Coming so soon after her humiliating experience with the duplicitous Anthony St. Briac, Baron Cobleigh's attentions had made her even more eager to seek refuge with her grandfather.

Eventually, to Frederica's relief, Cobleigh had married another, and she had forgotten about him.

Until today. There was something about the second voice that made her feel ill with dread. She told herself she was imagining things, even as she heard her father call her name.

"Frederica!" He was on the stairway. "Will you kindly come down and join us?"

After a long moment, she stepped into the corridor. "Papa, if you don't mind, I would rather not. I am quite fatigued today."

He came into sight on the top step, and the hard set of his features told her that she had no choice. "You, fatigued? Nonsense, my girl. Make yourself presentable and come downstairs to the drawing room."

* * *

SQUARING HER SLIM SHOULDERS, Frederica entered the room, praying that her imagination had been playing tricks on her.

"Ah!" exclaimed a chillingly familiar voice. "A vision appears."

To her horror, she beheld Baron Cobleigh sitting on a velvet chair near the fireplace.

"How good of you to join us," Papa was saying, beaming as if this were an occasion for celebration.

Cobleigh rose and tottered forward on spindly legs, his stomach straining against the pearl buttons of his waistcoat. He stopped before her and bent low, the crest of his balding head just below her nose. "My dear lady, I could not stay away. In truth, I confess I have thought of you every day since we were forced apart by your obligation to care for your grandfather."

She blinked. "My lord, are you not wed to another?"

"Ah, yes, I was." Sighing, he gazed at her breasts and added, "However, Lady Cobleigh is no longer with us."

"I do not take your meaning." Freddie felt as if she were trapped in the middle of a bad dream.

Her father appeared next to them, and one glance told Frederica that he was not her ally. Instead, Papa chimed in, "My dear, I thought you would have heard ... tragically, Lady Cobleigh did not survive childbirth, nor did their baby daughter. As you might imagine, this past year has been exceedingly *lonely* for his lordship."

Trying to extract her hands from the baron's clammy grip, Frederica said, "Indeed, I am very sorry to hear of your loss, my lord. How fortunate you are to have good friends like my father to help you through this difficult time." With that, she managed to free herself and step backward. "I will leave you two men to enjoy your visit."

"But – but—" spluttered Lord Cobleigh.

Ignoring her father's stormy countenance, Frederica lifted her skirts as she hurried toward the door. "Good day, gentlemen."

* * *

FREDDIE COULDN'T SIT STILL. She felt trapped in her bedchamber, but it would be a much worse trap if she should venture back downstairs. Cobleigh was hunting her like a deer in the forest, and her own father was assisting him. It was sickening.

A knock sounded at her door, followed by a stern voice. "Frederica Redfield, open to your father."

She felt enraged by his demand that she submit to his will. "Go away, Papa! I am not receiving callers."

"Do not take that tone with me, impertinent minx!"

This was too much. Striding across the room, Frederica threw open the door and faced him. "I am no minx, sir. I am a woman of five-and-twenty years." She met his angry stare unflinchingly. "I already know what you have come to tell me, and I shall spare you the effort. I will not marry Baron Cobleigh."

"Hear me out!"

"No, I will not. I was not brave enough to tell you exactly how I felt when he first offered for me. I went to Grandpapa instead. But years have passed, and I am not afraid to speak my mind." Her heart was pounding madly with the force of her emotions. How liberating it was to say these words to Papa! "I have plans for my life and they do not include marriage, especially to that odious creature."

"I suppose you still think you may seek employment at the British Museum!" sneered her father.

His sarcastic tone wounded her, but only for a moment. "If you aim to demean me, to make me doubt myself, you will not be successful!" She touched slender fingertips to her breastbone. "My belief in myself is rooted in my very soul, Papa. You cannot shake it."

"The devil fly away with your *belief in yourself!*" His eyes blazed. "I have it in my power to make you marry Baron Cobleigh, and one day you will thank me for it."

Frederica paced across the room, pausing before the tall cheval mirror. "Dash it, I do not understand why he is set on me!" She paused, momentarily distracted by her own reflection. Before her stood a young woman with simply dressed hair of golden brown, clad in an unadorned gray gown. She was a bit too tall for the taste of most men, small-breasted and slim but for the curve of her hips. Clear delphinium-blue eyes were her best feature, Freddie thought, and Mama had always said that the stubbornness of her chin was quite forgotten when she smiled.

Today there would be no smiles. "Why does his lordship persist so? I am no beauty, I am taller than he is, and I am quite on the shelf! Furthermore, I do not like him." She turned again to face her father. "I beg you, Papa, do not encourage him another minute."

A range of emotions played over his features that were like hers in many ways. Freddie could see that her father wanted to rage at her some more, but he realized that would get him nowhere. After a long moment, his expression softened, and he approached her.

"Ah, little puss, you have ever been headstrong. Perhaps that is what causes Baron Cobleigh to want you so. He likes the chase."

"Well, I do not like it. Not a bit."

"Are you not a little tempted by the notion of being a wealthy and titled woman? You were born of nobility, and well you know it. Your own children should carry on that noble bloodline."

"No, thank you," she said simply, meeting his eyes. "I have no desire to marry anyone."

Papa lifted a big hand to pat her glossy curls. "I have been an indulgent parent, especially since your mother's passing, but today I must ask you to put your own wishes aside." He drew near, his big chin quivering just enough to give her pause. "You see, my situation is more desperate than you know."

"Desperate?" Her stomach turned. "What are you saying, Papa?"

Beads of sweat dotted his upper lip. "I am …in the basket."

Her heart seemed to stop. "What exactly do you mean?"

"I am stony broke. On the rocks. You must wed Cobleigh; it is the only way out. His lordship has promised to rescue me, to pay my creditors and secure the mortgage on this house—"

"Mortgage!" Frederica gasped. "But Papa, this house came to you from Mama. It was part of her marriage settlement. A gift!" *And Mama promised that one day it would be mine,* she cried silently.

Her father took out a handkerchief and dabbed at his lip and brow. "You must understand, I had to do it. There was no other choice! I had to do something to save this property for you, my only child."

She stared in disbelief. Was he trying to paint himself as some sort of hero, to suggest that he had mortgaged this house for *her* sake? Bile rose in her throat. "I wouldn't have believed you were capable of this."

"I own that I have made mistakes ..." His face was red.

"*Mistakes?* Papa, your debts were deep enough before I went to live with Grandpapa, but instead of endeavoring to make things right, you knowingly spent and gambled funds you did not have. It makes me sick to hear that you could have mortgaged this house that Mama brought to us!" Frederica had to pause for breath, her heart racing. "Would you have me give my body and my very life to that creature because of your appalling deeds?"

"My dear girl, you have no choice."

Frederica burned with outrage. "I will not do it."

Her father clenched his fists, trembling. "You are ungrateful and selfish!" Marching to the door, he whirled and withdrew a key from his pocket, waving it in the air. "You will stay in this bedchamber until you agree to wed Lord Cobleigh, do you understand? Take all the time you need, Frederica. I will wait to hear you speak the words I *must* hear."

With that, her father closed the door and turned the key in the lock.

* * *

FREDERICA PACED, her mind whirling, for what seemed like hours. At dusk, a timid knock sounded at the door, followed by a maid's voice.

"Ma'am, I have a tray with your supper. Shall I bring it in to you?"

The thought of food made her sick. "No, just put it outside the door." No sooner were the words out of Freddie's mouth than she remembered her situation. She could not open the door to fetch the tray herself because she was a prisoner. Papa's strident voice echoed in her ears: *My situation is more desperate than you know!*

How could it have come to this? Frederica had a hundred questions, but none of that signified tonight. She was trapped unless she agreed to wed Lord Cobleigh ...but she simply could not and would not let that happen.

As night fell, she packed a small portmanteau with valued possessions, including two books by authors she had come to revere: naturalist Alexander von Humboldt and geologist Charles Lyell. And in the back of her cupboard, Freddie found a third book wrapped in a chemise. A smile touched her mouth as she found space in the portmanteau for *The Wicked Highwayman*, a rather naughty romantic adventure that was her secret pleasure.

Almost at the last moment, Frederica remembered a small velvet box she'd hidden among her gloves while packing to leave Justmore House. Drawing it out of the drawer, she pushed at the button clasp and held the open box near the candlelight. There, nestled in a bed of worn satin, was a stunning gold ring consisting of one large oval diamond edged with small sapphires. Before he died, Grandpapa had presented it to her.

"This ring belonged not only to your grandmother but also to the last five countesses of Justmore," he said, holding her gaze. "I want you to have it, darling girl. Think of it as security. It is not part of my estate, but a private gift to you to use as you see fit. Do you take my meaning?"

The ring was far too grand for Freddie's taste, but she had accepted it gratefully and hidden the case inside an old glove. Now she stared at the glowing jewels and took a deep breath. *Security*, Grandpapa had said.

She might well need it in the days to come, she realized, and tucked the ring in again with her other possessions.

With that, Frederica closed the portmanteau, tied up her skirts, and blew out the candle. Crossing to the windows overlooking a narrow strip of trees, she gazed out at the great elm that Anthony St. Briac and his father had climbed to enter her father' study seven years ago. The memory of that night made her heart sting anew with a mixture of anger and arousal …and an unexpected sense of deep sadness that a man so magnetically alive could be lost on the other side of the world. Lost and quite possibly dead.

No time for any of that now! Freddie reminded herself sternly.

Straightening her spine, she pushed open the window and leaned out to survey the heavy, moon-silvered branches that twined below. Could she do this?

Of course, she could!

Carefully, Frederica tossed the portmanteau down to land in the crotch of the tree before climbing out, reaching over to grasp a branch with both hands, and boldly swinging herself away from her prison to freedom.

CHAPTER 3

*M*ouette St. Briac couldn't help smiling as her husband dealt another hand of loo to the family group gathered round the sitting room table. Beeswax candles flickered in wall-mounted sconces, adding their golden light to the convivial mood, and Daisy the corgi snored softly on her nearby cushion. Everything felt perfect until Mouette thought of her absent son Anthony. A little arrow seemed to pierce her heart as she remembered all the times he had sat next to his little sister, playfully sabotaging Emeline's efforts to win whatever game the family was playing.

At moments like these, Mouette forced her thoughts away from Captain FitzRoy's terrible message: *I regret to inform you that your son is* LOST. The words were seared on her heart, but she had found many ways to distract herself from the unacceptable.

Mouette knew perfectly well that *lost* was simply a less final word for *dead*. However, until someone could prove otherwise, she and Justin and the rest of the family had entered into an unspoken agreement to behave as if Anthony was still somewhere across the world, enjoying an array of exotic adventures.

"It's your lead, *chérie*," Justin said, after everyone had made their bets. One glance at him told her he guessed what she had been thinking. Almost as an afterthought, he turned over the top card in the remaining deck to determine trump: hearts.

Mouette focused on her three cards. Smiling, she put down a knave of diamonds. Justin reached under the table to squeeze her thigh through her skirts. "Thank God I never had to face you in a gaming hell," he whispered.

"Are you passing Mama a card?" exclaimed Emeline from across the table.

"No, it's more personal than that," Justin said and arched a black brow above his eye-patch.

"Honestly, Papa," she said, and shook her head in mock dismay. "Must you?"

"I am merely reminding your mama that I adore her," he murmured.

To Mouette's left, her own father glanced at his cards before casually placing the queen of diamonds over her knave.

She pretended to gasp. "You would do that to your own daughter?"

André Raveneau raked a hand through his thick white hair and sent her a roguish smile. "You would do the same to me, *chérie*. In any case, I have a feeling your own offspring may triumph over both of us. She has a killer instinct at the gaming table."

"It is quite true, I do." Emeline grinned, nodding. "Anthony taught me."

Mouette's mother, Devon, played next, exchanging her three cards for the extra hand known as the "miss." Wrinkling her nose, she put the four of diamonds on the table and announced, "Well, this was worse than the hand Justin dealt me!"

Everyone looked at Emeline. Mouette delighted in her only daughter, conceived in white-hot passion when Mouette and Justin were only pretending to be married. It didn't seem possible that she could truly be seventeen years old! Almost a woman. Blessed with glossy ebony curls and a face as expressive as it was pretty, Emmie was already attracting glances from London's fashionable young men. God help them when they tried to get past her formidable papa.

"As usual, Grandpère is right. I shall be victorious tonight." Emeline pointed at the growing pile of chips in the middle of the table. "And, I have plans for my winnings."

Mouette exchanged amused glances with Justin, who leaned closer to murmur, "Something extravagant …from the fossil shop, no doubt."

Emeline extracted her card and held it up with a flourish, drawing out the suspense. She was just about to reveal it to the others when the mood was broken by a loud tapping at the door below them. Daisy the corgi jumped to her stubby feet and began to bark, rushing out to the head of the stairway.

Devon stood up immediately. "Who could be calling at this hour?"

"Grandmama, do sit down," protested Emmie. "The butler will see to it. I am about to play the winning card!"

"I think Cedric has already retired for the evening," Devon said, looking distracted as the lion's paw knocker struck the door three more times, and Daisy returned to alert them. "Whoever is at the door is quite insistent. Perhaps they are in distress."

Justin stood next. "Or drunk. I will go." Glancing at the excited corgi, he commanded, "If you stop barking, you may accompany me."

André pushed up from the table, and Mouette felt proud to see how lithe her father remained at six-and-eighty. "It's not your house, St. Briac," he said to Justin. "I will go."

"*D'accord*. We will both go," Justin replied.

Rap-rap-rap! Daisy frantically circled the table before herding the two men out of the sitting room and down the wide staircase.

"Fiddle," complained Emmie, triumphantly waving the queen of hearts in front of Mouette and Devon. "I was about to lay down this excellent trump card, claim the trick, and make myself quite wealthy."

"How nice," Devon murmured, clearly not listening. As the sound of raised voices drifted up the stairs, she rose and started toward the doorway. "Who on earth could that be?"

* * *

WHEN THE DOOR to the Raveneau home in Grosvenor Square swung open at last, Frederica's racing heart skipped a beat. *Thank God! Now she would be safe.* Before her stood two compellingly handsome men, haloed in the entry hall's soft light. Before they spoke, she realized they were not servants at all, but Mouette's father and husband.

"How may we assist you, mademoiselle?" The somewhat younger man, who wore a rakish patch over one eye, spoke with a French accent. At his side squirmed an excited fawn and white corgi, a strawberry-pink satin bow tied around her fluffy neck. The dog opened her mouth as if to bark but refrained after one warning glance from her master. "I am Justin St. Briac," he continued, "and this imposing gentleman is Captain André Raveneau."

"I am so very sorry to disturb you," Frederica said, her voice shaking. "But I had nowhere else to go."

André Raveneau, who remained an arresting figure despite his great age, smiled at her, and she noticed the thin white scar on his jaw. "You must come in and tell us what is wrong." He reached for her portmanteau and was kind enough not to comment on the fact that she had appeared uninvited, with luggage.

No sooner had Frederica stepped into the lamp-lit entry hall than St. Briac approached, taking a closer look. "Why, you are Mademoiselle Redfield, *n'est-ce pas?*"

"Yes." She fought a mad urge to burst into tears. "I am Frederica Redfield."

"*Sangdieu,*" he breathed and glanced meaningfully at his father-in-law. "The lady is Viscount Theodore Redfield's daughter. I trust you take my meaning?"

Frederica knew he referred to all the trouble Papa had caused in this family with his schemes to steal Mouette away from her husband. "Sir, you must believe that I am nothing like my father."

Footsteps sounded on the stairs, and Frederica looked up to see Mouette and her mother, Devon, descending quickly with Emeline following in their wake.

"Oh, my dear!" exclaimed Mouette as she reached her side. "You have come, just as I said you must."

To Frederica's immense relief, the woman embraced her. "Thank you," she managed to say, her voice choked.

"Let us go upstairs. Have you eaten supper?" When Freddie shook her head, Mouette spoke to Emeline. "Please ask Arabella to prepare a hot meal for our guest."

Frederica was swept by a reassuring sense that she was in the right place, with friends, and perhaps everything would truly be all right. After divesting her of her cloak and bonnet, they settled her on a tufted green sofa in the sitting room.

Looking around the elegant yet inviting room, Freddie spied the mahogany game table with chairs randomly pushed back and chips and cards scattered over it. "I have interrupted a game," she said.

"Yes, we were playing loo," Devon replied, "but I had terrible cards."

"You arrived just in time to save us from defeat at Emeline's hands," added Justin, flashing a smile. "Our daughter is a very bad winner."

"Indeed," agreed Mouette. "She gloats."

Emeline herself entered then. "Arabella promises to send up a tray. She is warming some soup and a piece of pigeon pie."

Justin poured a small glass of cognac and presented it to Frederica. "It appears that you might need this."

"Indeed." Mouette, seated just a few inches away on the sofa, spoke in a reassuring tone. "When you are ready, I hope you will tell us what has happened to bring you here tonight."

Justin and André offered to leave the ladies alone, but Freddie shook her head. "I have nothing to hide. I've been ill-mannered enough to burst in on your evening, so you all may as well know the reason why." She sipped a bit of brandy as everyone took seats and waited.

"Is it Theo?" asked Mouette.

"Yes. I left because of Papa, but there is more." Freddie tried to imagine that she was watching herself speak from a distance, which made it much easier to hold her emotions at bay. Gradually, she told her story, beginning with the first time Lord Cobleigh had tried to court her, long ago, before she went to live with her grandfather. "I knew then that Papa had gotten into debt ..."

She saw Mouette and Justin exchange a glance. "So did we," said Mouette. "Theo was already in dire straits when we were here in London some years ago, but I imagine he was able to patch things together for a time by selling the emerald."

"Oh, that's right," murmured Frederica, and fixed her gaze on Justin St. Briac. "When you reclaimed the portrait of Madame St. Briac that Papa had hidden, sir, you left an enormous emerald in its place!"

St. Briac shrugged. "It was one of many such gems, gathered during my years at sea. I never missed it. I admit I was filled with contempt toward Lord Redfield at that time, but I never wanted to inflict any suffering on you, my lady. I hoped the emerald would allow him to carry on and perhaps be a better person, for your sake."

"No doubt it did help for some time," she allowed, "but a year later, Papa was urging me to welcome the attentions of Baron Cobleigh."

"That old toad?" Mouette cringed. "How awful."

"My father was always determined that I should marry someone with a title, and by then he was set on a fortune as well. Of course, I refused. Aside from every- thing else, I decided long ago not to marry. I mean to be an independent woman."

Emeline applauded this statement. "How brave you are!"

"I do not mean to disparage men," Freddie hastened to add, glancing toward her hosts, "but I have no desire to spend my life catering to the needs and wishes of a husband who cares not a whit for me. Fortunately, Grandpapa invited me to stay with him, as you all know, and there I remained for these past five years, caring for him and cataloguing his fascinating library. I found my calling, I think, and became determined to do similar work at the British Museum." As she spoke, she saw surprise on the faces of her listeners, but in the next moment they were all nodding approval.

"I perceive that your father did not encourage you in your aspirations," said Devon.

"Indeed, he thought I was deluded," Frederica confirmed. Pausing, she sipped the brandy,

welcoming the warmth that loosened the tension in her body. Slowly, she told them about the scene with Baron Cobleigh that afternoon, her escape upstairs to the bedroom, and finally the visit from her father.

"Papa finally confessed that the real reason I must agree to the marriage was because his lordship had promised to pay his debts, maintain his lifestyle in the future, and ...secure the mortgage of Redfield House. He said I had no choice." Unexpected tears stung her eyes. "He told me that I would remain locked in my bedchamber until I agreed to marry Baron Cobleigh."

This was met by a chorus of shocked disapproval from Mouette and her family.

"You must stay right here with us," cried Emeline. "We will keep you safe!"

Mouette nodded thoughtfully. "Of course, there is no question of that, but I don't believe you can remain in this house. Theo would find you soon enough, and we don't want that."

"We must contrive a solution that will allow you to move about at will, unnoticed," agreed Devon.

Emeline clapped her hands triumphantly. "I know! We can hide Freddie at *Anthony's* house! Dozens of crates and barrels filled with artifacts are waiting there for someone to examine and catalogue. No doubt Anthony would wish to choose this person himself, but of course he has been unavoidably detained." She paused before adding firmly, "Who better to do this than Freddie? It is a perfect solution! Then, when my brother returns, everything will be in order for him."

Frederica saw the others exchange glances, their eyes clouded with pain. It seemed that only Emeline remained convinced that Anthony St. Briac was still alive. After a long moment, Justin spoke.

"It is a good idea, *ma petite*." He touched the girl's shoulder. "Someone must examine the artifacts Anthony sent home during those five years of exploration, and I agree that Frederica is just the person to begin."

The thought of spending her days hidden safely from her father, examining fossils and other amazing discoveries from the far reaches of the world filled Freddie with wonder. "I would be honored."

"It does seem a fine solution, but it isn't that simple," said Mouette. "As a single woman, Frederica certainly cannot stay alone in Anthony's house. A skeleton staff remains there, looking after things—"

"Clearly, we must contrive a *disguise!*" exclaimed Emeline. She jumped to her feet and Daisy began to bark. "Why not transform Frederica into Frederick?"

"Goodness, I should adore that." Freddie sank back against the cushions and smiled for the first time that day. "How much easier my life would be if I were not a female."

"It is a mad idea…yet also quite brilliant," conceded Mouette.

André Raveneau cleared his throat. "My wife has some experience with this sort of masquerade," he said laconically.

"I do," Devon admitted, sending him a loving glance. "But one hopes Miss Redfield will have more success at it than I did. Fortunately, she is quite tall, which will help. We can choose her disguise from the chests of boys' clothing I've saved from our son and grandsons."

Mouette nodded thoughtfully. "We still must find a maid or housekeeper to join Anthony's staff, someone who can be trotted out for appearance's sake, as a chaperone, if Frederica is discovered."

"And I will help in any way I can," announced Emeline.

"I will agree to all of this, and I have a maid in mind," said Freddie, thinking of her beloved Mrs. Bell, "but honestly, I don't care a fig for rules of propriety. I am five-and-twenty years of age, and apart from the odious and persistent Lord Cobleigh, the *ton* doubtless regard me as hopelessly on the shelf." She nodded, and her smile widened. "I find that liberating."

Mouette squeezed her hand again, and their eyes met. "I understand. Who can blame you? But won't you need some means of support in the future …in case your plans for the British Museum don't work out?"

"My grandfather left me something that should help if it comes to that. I have it with my things." Before she could rise, Justin brought the portmanteau to her on the sofa. Unfastening the clasps, Frederica looked inside and brought out the glove that concealed a small cube-shaped object.

They all stared as she opened the tiny velvet box and withdrew the diamond and sapphire ring. It was a dazzling sight, sparkling in the candlelight.

"*Mon Dieu,*" murmured Justin. "It is exquisite."

"That ring will provide you with a lifetime of security," said André, "provided you can bear to part with it."

Freddie's smile widened. "It is good to hear you say so."

"But do not think of it now," Justin cautioned. "All your needs will be met at Anthony's house and of course, you will be remunerated for cataloguing our son's discoveries."

"I am immensely grateful to all of you." As Freddie spoke, she felt almost euphoric.

"But *we* are the grateful ones," said Mouette, blue eyes agleam with tears. "Providence sent you here tonight. Anthony packed each precious artifact that now waits inside his home on Charles Street. I would not want anyone else to touch them but you, dear Frederica ...and somehow, I feel that he would agree."

CHAPTER 4

"*Y*ou are almost ready. I can't believe my eyes!" Emeline put a hand to her mouth to stifle laughter. "I vow, if I didn't know you were a female, I would be quite convinced."

Standing in the lovely bedchamber overlooking Grosvenor Square, Frederica surveyed her reflection in a cheval mirror. She wore a handsome but outdated suit of clothing that once belonged to Mouette's brother, Nathan, who now lived on the island of Barbados. The coat and trousers of navy-blue superfine were set off by a striped waistcoat of gray kerseymere, all of which fit convincingly because Emeline had helped tie strips of linen to flatten her breasts.

When she was ready, the dashing André Raveneau himself had appeared to tie her starched white neck-cloth in a simple Corsican style that would be easy to replicate. Freddie's long, golden-brown curls were braided and pinned up under an equally outmoded beaver hat, pulled low on her brow.

Turning to Emeline, she queried, "Why do you say I am *almost* ready? What do I lack?"

"Mama is concerned that although your face is nicely angular, your complexion is too soft, with no sign of whiskers." Emeline tilted her head to the side, considering. "Furthermore, you cannot go on wearing that hat indoors, and what will happen when you remove it?"

"Dash it." Freddie bit her lip. "I hadn't thought of that. It's all rather overwhelming!"

Just then Mouette entered, carrying a fancy yellow box. "I have come to the rescue," she said cheerfully. "Gwynn, my dear maid, managed to procure a wig and a mustache! I haven't even seen them myself."

They gathered round to peer inside the box. There, like the pelts of dead animals, reposed a wig of rather curly gray hair and a small, darker gray mustache.

"Oh!" Freddie grimaced. "How very peculiar they are."

"Yes, they are rather, aren't they?" replied Mouette, appearing torn between amusement and dismay. "I believe an elderly goat donated the curls for the wig."

Emeline looked doubtful. "Won't Freddie look very odd with gray hair?"

"Some men go gray at a young age." Mouette smiled warmly at Frederica. "In truth, I fear you would look much odder *without* these accoutrements. Your feminine beauty will be quite obvious unless we contrive to camouflage it."

Freddie felt her cheeks grow warm. She had never thought much about her looks. Surely, she could not hold a candle to the exquisite Raveneau women, yet it was wonderful to hear someone reference her *beauty*. She beamed at Mouette. "If you say so. I trust you, dear madame."

With the help of her friends, Frederica donned the rather wild wig that mingled coarse, wavy strands of white, black, and gray. It wasn't until Emeline had glued the false mustache to her upper lip that Freddie finally turned back to the mirror.

"Wait!" cried Mouette, reaching back into the yellow box. With a flourish she produced a pair of silver-rimmed spectacles. "You'll need these as well. They will disguise your long eyelashes and lend you a scholarly air." Settling the glasses on Freddie's slim nose, she gave her a mischievous smile. "Now you may look."

The reflection she beheld in the mirror was that of a slim, pale, rather odd-looking young man with wild, curly gray hair and a dark mustache. "I cannot recognize myself!" Freddie exclaimed in delight. "The spectacles are the perfect touch. I do look quite scholarly, and just peculiar and eccentric enough that people should not be inclined to approach me."

"I have some curling papers and pomade you might use to tame that wig from time to time," mused Mouette. "I know a few dandies who use them."

"If you wear the beaver hat in public, the strangeness of your hair will not signify," declared Emeline. Coming closer, she peered at Frederica. "Does it itch?"

"The wig? No." Laughing, she added, "Not yet at least!"

Mouette looked more serious. "There are a few other details we must address. Do you still want your name to be Frederick while you are in this disguise? I only worry a bit that it might be too close to your real name, if you should encounter anyone who knows you."

"A valid point," Freddie agreed, "but I think a greater danger is that I might not remember my new name at some crucial moment. It will be tricky enough to pretend to be a man, night and day, without bringing a new name into it."

"Point taken. What about your voice? Are you able to deepen it, at least a little?" asked Mouette.

"I will try," Freddie said gruffly. "Will this do?"

"Very nicely!" approved Mouette. "Fortunately, you

will be alone in Anthony's house most of the time." A shadow crossed her face as she spoke her son's name.

"I am very eager to be there, isolated from the world, and I assure you that I will treat all of Anthony's discoveries with the utmost respect and care."

Mouette reached out to clasp both her hands, smiling. "We should be on our way soon. I have packed a portmanteau with a few more of Nathan's clothes. Are you ready to depart?"

"Yes! However, I would first like to speak to Mrs. Bell who has been my grandparents' housekeeper for at least three decades. She was my great support during the last five years, and since you suggested I have a chaperone of sorts, I thought I might beg her to come with me to your son's house." Freddie sighed. "Unless, of course, Sir Harold will not allow it. Truly, I am not certain how matters go on there. Sir Harold may have realized what a treasure Mrs. Bell is, but I did want to ask ...just in case."

Looking doubtful, Mouette replied, "Hmm. I feel a bit concerned that your father might be able to discover your whereabouts through Mrs. Bell."

"I can assure you that we may trust her implicitly. She loves me." As she spoke, Frederica went to the window and gazed across Grosvenor Square toward the familiar red brick façade of Justmore House. The realization that a nephew who had no previous ties to her grandparents' beloved home was now its owner made her heart ache. "Perhaps I could go to the tradesmen's entrance to avoid attracting attention."

A moment later, Frederica saw a familiar green landau roll to a stop in front of Justmore House. She gave an involuntary little cry, and Mouette and Emeline were by her side in an instant.

"What is it?" Mouette asked in alarm.

"Papa." Freddie's voice was choked. She watched as

his tall figure emerged from the carriage, made his way to the entrance, and lifted the heavy knocker. When the door opened, her father went inside. "Papa never visited Justmore House when my grandfather was alive, and I lived there. He is only there now because he is looking for me." The notion that he was so close, just across the square, sent a cold chill of dread down her back. "I am not afraid of him! But he is my father, and I am his daughter. I shudder to imagine that Papa might have the *right* to imprison me in his house until I agree to marry the man of his choosing."

Mouette frowned. "I'm not at all certain he does have that right, especially at your age—"

"Worse things have happened to women in England," Frederica said grimly. She shook her head then and straightened her shoulders. "Clearly, I cannot go there to speak to Mrs. Bell, nor should I tarry here."

"You are safe under this roof, and thankfully you are now well disguised," Mouette assured her. "However, we will send you off to Anthony's house in Charles Street without delay. I shall ask Justin to accompany you, for I must linger in Grosvenor Square until Theo has gone so that I may speak to your friend, Mrs. Bell, for you."

"I will accompany Papa and Freddie!" exclaimed Emeline, her cheeks bright with excitement.

Frederica, who rarely allowed herself to weep, felt a surge of emotion. Heedless of her false mustache, she embraced the two females in turn and kissed their soft cheeks. "I adore you both."

Drawing back, Emeline giggled. "Sir, you are very bold to take such liberties!"

* * *

ANTHONY ST. BRIAC's townhouse was located in a charming bend in Charles Street. Painted a deep shade of butterscotch, the two higher stories featured bow windows that opened onto black wrought-iron balconies. Neatly trimmed green boxwood filled a planter near the entrance, and a glass lantern hung from the arched portico. For Frederica, it was love at first sight.

"I was expecting it to be the one next door," she said to Justin and Emeline, pointing to the plainer, adjacent building of charcoal gray trimmed in white. "I like this house so much better! It is …fanciful."

The trio walked to the front door and Justin lifted the knocker. "*Oui*. My son is half French, you know. He has a whimsical streak." In the next moment, his bemused smile faded, as if it had just come back to him that Anthony was lost and likely dead, a world away on the Galápagos Islands off the coast of Ecuador.

"Do not look like that, Papa," Emeline said firmly. "You know as well as I do that Anthony is coming home."

"I do know that." Even as the dashing former pirate wrapped a reassuring arm around Emeline, he sent Frederica a glance that tore at her heart. "How could it be otherwise?"

The mahogany paneled door swung open to reveal a portly, balding older man clad all in black. As soon as he recognized Justin, his somber expression was transformed by a smile. "M'sieur St. Briac! It is very good to see you."

Justin nodded and turned to Frederica. "This is Quincy, my son's butler. During Anthony's long—" He broke off but recovered more quickly this time. "During his absence, Quincy has become, for all intents and purposes, the steward, for he looks after virtually everything except the housekeeping. We have let the rest of his staff go on to other positions elsewhere."

Quincy bowed. "It is my privilege to remain here, m'sieur."

Justin led Frederica into the narrow entry hall and closed the door. She was relieved to be safely indoors, for part of her now feared that her father might appear on the street at any moment, shouting her name.

"Quincy, this fine gentleman is Professor Frederick Loudon," announced Justin, saying aloud for the first time the name Freddie had invented. "He will be living here for the time being to begin cataloguing all the artifacts that young Mr. St. Briac has been sending home from his travels."

The butler's gray eyes widened. "Welcome, sir," he said to Freddie. "You must tell us how we may serve you."

"Professor Loudon will be spending his days in my son's library, laboring alone," Justin said firmly. "However, I am counting on you and Meg to see to it that he is comfortable, well fed, and looked after. I expect you to anticipate his needs rather than the other way round. Do you understand?"

"Yes, m'sieur," Quincy intoned. Turning, he gestured toward an open doorway and a young, doe-eyed maid emerged, a feather duster clutched in her hands. "Meg, did you hear what m'sieur has said?"

The fair-haired girl bobbed a curtsy, gazing at Frederica under her lashes. "Welcome, my lord."

Justin seemed amused by this. "Meg, Professor Loudon is not a lord. I believe 'sir' will do."

Freddie smiled and summoned the husky voice she'd been practicing. "Thank you both for your welcome. I am only here to catalogue the specimens that Mr. St. Briac has sent back during his travels."

The two servants exchanged glances before Quincy addressed Justin. "All of them, you said, m'sieur?"

"That's right."

"In that case," the butler said to Freddie, "you may be staying for a very long time."

With that, Meg gestured with her feather duster toward the nearby doorway, and they all walked the short distance to look inside what appeared to be a magnificent library. Freddie's gaze went immediately to the tempting array of books lining the walls, but many of the shelves were blocked by crates. It was then she realized that scores of wooden boxes and casks in towers of four and five covered nearly all of the jewel toned Kuba rug.

Frederica blinked but did not gasp.

Flinging out one long arm toward the crates, Quincy turned to look at Freddie. "Our master sent these almost weekly for four years. Some of them have a certain odor of decay I will not attempt to describe further. In time, we began to worry that the chests would fill the entire house."

"But no more shipments have arrived?" Emeline asked.

The butler sighed deeply. "Indeed. Not since word came that our master had gone missing."

Justin's fiery tone caught Frederica off-guard. "*Mon Dieu!* The only thing that stops me from going to those cursed islands myself and searching every inch of them is the knowledge that the *Beagle* is due back any day. I must gather more information from M'sieur Darwin and Captain FitzRoy before I embark on such a long voyage."

"Mama needs you," Emeline said softly.

His nostrils flared. "That is the other reason I haven't left yet."

"And of course," the girl added resolutely, "Anthony is doubtless on his way home. It would be terrible if you should unknowingly pass at sea!"

Just then, there was a knock at the door and Quincy

trundled off to answer it. A moment later, Frederica heard Mouette speaking, followed by the welcome sound of Mrs. Bell's voice.

There was barely time for Freddie to panic about Mrs. Bell exposing her charade before the two women appeared on the library threshold.

"Professor Loudon, look who I have brought to join the staff here," exclaimed Mouette while drawing off her ivory kid gloves.

Freddie feared that their masquerade was about to end before it had even properly begun, for although one might order servants to forget a secret, the odds that they would keep quiet were extremely slim. However, she managed to meet Mouette's gaze and even smile.

"Ah, thank you, Madame St. Briac. You have brought Mrs. Bell ..." Freddie began.

"Yes!" Mouette interrupted. "It is indeed Mrs. Bell. She may be known to all of Mayfair as an extraordinary housekeeper, but of course she was once your *nurse*. Who better to look after you here?"

"Very true," Freddie agreed uncertainly.

Mrs. Bell surprised her by turning to Quincy and Meg and proclaiming, "I've known this lad since he was in leading strings. I can cook all his favorite foods, and I am acquainted with all his rather peculiar tastes."

Quincy and Meg exchanged glances, apparently relieved that they would not be required to cater to the rather odd professor's needs after all.

"I will look after Frederick," Mrs. Bell continued. Coming closer, she gave Freddie the tiniest of winks. "Why, I can even cut his hair, so he won't have to leave this house to seek a barber."

Freddie involuntarily raised both hands to her disheveled gray wig and managed to laugh. "Mrs. Bell to the rescue, as ever."

When Mouette had dispatched Quincy and Meg to prepare a tea tray and the servants had disappeared down the corridor, she turned to Frederica. "Well done. I feared someone might say the wrong thing, but both of you were superb!" Drawing Mrs. Bell forward, Mouette continued, "It was this wise lady who suggested we say she was your nurse long ago. That way, if anyone should remember that Mrs. Bell has been employed at Justmore House, they need not necessarily connect her to Frederica Redfield."

"Brilliant," Freddie murmured. "My head is spinning."

Mrs. Bell put an arm around her. "I cannot tell you how relieved I was when Madame St. Briac arrived and explained your plight to me. I've been miserable since that awful Sir Harold arrived. I will never get used to the idea that he is now the Earl of Justmore! His undeserving *lordship* has no use for me, and it was just a matter of time before he would have hired a new housekeeper and put me out on the street."

"How shocking." Freddie shook her head in dismay. "I now see that Grandpapa should have provided for you, Mrs. Bell. Thank goodness you are here now."

The old woman beamed. "It was a pleasure to tell that stuffy man I was leaving. And now I am here and quite thrilled to be part of this daring masquerade!" She touched Freddie's mustache and chuckled. "I vow, I am not certain I would have recognized you."

"Good," Justin interjected. "That is what we hope."

At that moment, the servants arrived with the tea tray and Quincy spoke to Mrs. Bell. "If you will come with me, ma'am, I will show you your room."

This announcement caused Freddie to pause, her teacup in mid-air. "I hope Mrs. Bell's quarters won't be very far away from mine."

She could see that the butler found this request very

odd, coming from a grown man, but he betrayed only a flicker of surprise. "If you like, she could have the servant's room directly below you. There is a small back staircase leading between the floors. Would that do?"

"Perfectly," Freddie confirmed in her deepest voice.

* * *

AN HOUR LATER, the St. Briacs had departed, Mrs. Bell was getting herself settled, and Frederica was alone in her new rooms. To her surprise, she found that she was the only occupant upstairs, where the private bedchambers were located. Although she sensed that utter exhaustion was lurking close at hand, she couldn't lie down just yet.

Her rooms of green and muted gold were tastefully decorated enlivened by creative touches that caught her eye. The Sheraton mahogany furniture was handsome, perfect for a man, but the rich green walls were scattered with striking framed watercolors of birds and animals. Was that a hawk, or something else altogether? And what about that odd animal that resembled a badger wearing chain mail? As she scrutinized the paintings, Frederica saw the initials in each lower corner: ASB.

Her breath caught. Anthony had made these watercolors! Suddenly, she felt him all around her and her heart began to race. A map of South America was framed above the fireplace mantel. There was a book on the bedside table: *Principles of Geology* by Charles Lyell ...the very same book Freddie had cherished enough to bring with her when she climbed down the tree and escaped from her father's house.

She stared at the bed and felt heat spread over her body. Was this where Anthony had slept before he set sail on the *Beagle* five long years ago? It must be. Suddenly, it seemed she could smell his masculine essence and feel the heat of his lips on the back of her hand, kissing it as he had done during their long-ago interlude in Hyde Park. He had looked up at her under his thick lashes, his dark eyes filled with a mad, potent allure she could not resist.

For just a moment, Frederica had forgotten how much she *despised* him. He had used his effortless charm to wear down her defenses and enlist her help in recapturing the portrait her father had hidden. When she finally realized it had all been an act, she had felt like an utter fool. Her face burned anew at the memory.

It was a bitter lesson in the game of love, a game she was resolved never to play again.

Carefully, Freddie peeled off her low boots and stretched out on the counterpane. Closing her eyes, she imagined *him* lying here, on this very pillow, staring up at the crown molding. Her nipples tingled traitorously under the linen strips that flattened them against her chest.

Of course, Freddie was very sorry Anthony was likely dead, but if he were alive, it would be perilous for her. He had casually crushed her heart like a rose petal under the heel of his boot, and it was better that she would never see him again.

CHAPTER 5

*D*ays later, Frederica was in the library as usual, still unpacking and cataloguing the first crate of specimens. She had spent much of the morning moving the containers so that she might access Anthony St. Briac's desk, where she began to arrange the various fossils and artifacts and write her detailed notes. So engrossed was Freddie in her work that she scarcely noticed Meg standing in the doorway with a tray of fragrant breakfast dishes.

"I don't see a place to set this down," said the maid, looking around the library.

Freddie crossed to clear off an inlaid side table. She had to remind herself that she was supposed to be a man, and so it was only right that she should then relieve Meg of the heavy tray. "You and Quincy were right," she told the girl with a meaningful glance at the scores of crates and barrels. "At this rate, I will be at it for at least a dozen years."

The maid nodded, smiling shyly. "Would you truly stay that long?"

"I suppose we must take it a week at a time, eh?"

Freddie thought, not for the first time, that if Anthony St. Briac had perished on the Galápagos Islands, his parents could hardly maintain this house indefinitely. The prospect of it being closed up and sold off to someone else brought a twinge of sadness. Even as a young man, Anthony had created a home that spoke his name everywhere one looked.

"Isn't it tragic?" asked Meg, crossing to a bookshelf laid bare that morning when Freddie shifted more crates around. She reached out and withdrew a small miniature that had been pushed back into the shadows. "Master Anthony could have had the world at his feet, if only he had taken more care."

Freddie had just bitten into a warm hot-cross bun, one of Mrs. Bell's specialties, but she stopped chewing as Meg approached with the framed image. Freddie's stomach did a little flip as she took the frame in her free hand and brought it closer.

The artist had captured Anthony St. Briac in exquisite detail. He seemed alive in the small portrait, clad in riding clothes and sitting on a low stone wall, one booted foot casually propped on his other lean, buckskin-sheathed thigh. It seemed that she could reach into the painting and touch his tousled black locks. Anthony's smile was open, filled with an easy, knowing charm that Frederica remembered all too well. At his side posed a tri-color corgi who wore a smile as raffish as his master's.

Meg pointed at the dog. "That's Robinson, God rest his soul. He belonged to M'sieur and Madame St. Briac but visited us often. These two were as close as they could be. Master Anthony had such a way with Robinson!" Tears filled the maid's eyes. "I like to think they are together now."

To Frederica's horror, she felt her own eyes well up, and a sob rose in her throat. Somehow, she managed to cough instead and quickly handed the miniature back to Meg. "Very sad, indeed. Meg, I am surprised to hear you reminisce about a time before Mr. St. Briac sailed off on board the *Beagle*. Is it possible that someone as young as you remembers that?"

"Oh, yes, sir! Pa was the coachman here. We were alone in the world since my mum died of smallpox, so the master brought me in as a kitchen maid when I was only twelve. This house was full of life in those days. Master Anthony liked to have his friends about. Some were quite scholarly, and they would talk long into the night, but the master had other sorts of friends as well." Meg gave Freddie a conspiratorial wink. "If you take my meaning."

"Oh, yes," Freddie said gruffly. "I can well imagine." She felt an annoying sting in the region of her heart.

Just then, the knocker sounded at the door and Quincy appeared in the stair hall, on his way to see who was calling. As he passed the wide doorway to the library, he sent Meg a stern glance.

"I was just serving the professor's breakfast," she said defensively, then looked over to give Freddie a smile that might have been flirtatious. "I will leave you to your labors, sir, but if I can be of any assistance, do not hesitate to ring for me."

When Freddie was alone, she stood staring for a long minute at the miniature. She wanted to put it away again, to hide it from view, but felt compelled to look at the lifelike portrait just a few moments longer.

"You needn't bother to announce me, Quincy. Professor Loudon and I are old friends," declared a familiar feminine voice, and a moment later Emeline appeared on the library threshold. "Ah, there you are, sir! I've come to tell you that the *Beagle* has returned at last, and we have had word from Charles Darwin. They will visit this very afternoon at three o'clock. You must join the gathering."

"I?" Freddie shook her head in disbelief. "I don't think it would be right."

"But you have begun the process of examining and cataloguing Anthony's discoveries. Surely you will have questions of your own?" Emeline came closer and tugged at Freddie's coat sleeve. Softly, she added, "I rather feel as if you are part of the family now. You should be with us. Please say yes." When Freddie did not immediately agree, she added, "I feel certain that they will bring word that Anthony is safe, and on his way back to England, perhaps on another ship."

"Really? But, my dear, wouldn't they have written as much to your parents if that were so?"

Emeline's beautiful face clouded momentarily before she shook her head. "Actually, I suspect that Anthony himself will *appear* today, with Mr. Darwin! It would be just like him to do something dashing like that to surprise us. When he was at Cambridge, he often traveled home without any warning at all, when we least expected him." A radiant smile lit her face. "When I was growing up, Anthony brought a spirit of celebration with him each time he came through the door! Those were magical times."

Frederica wished she could believe such a joyous surprise was in store for Emeline today. "One can certainly hope," she managed to reply.

"Say you will come back with me. Please! If you are worried that Anthony won't want you staying in his house, I can assure you that all of us will explain to him, and I know my brother will understand."

Realizing that Emeline might need the support of a friend in case tragic news was in store, Frederica sighed. "Although I would rather stay here in solitude, I will come. I owe you too much to refuse."

Emeline threw her arms around Freddie and kissed her cheek, nearly dislodging the false mustache.

"Thank you, dear friend!"

* * *

As Frederica strode along Hill Street, freed of a corset and layers of petticoats, she felt a heady sense of liberation. She could walk as quickly as she pleased in her men's trousers without impediment or censorious glances from passersby.

"I rather like this masquerade," she whispered to Emeline. "Especially in contrast to the constrained life one must endure as a female."

"I have been fortunate to be born into a family populated with adventurous females. My grandmother stowed away on Grandpère's privateer ship, the Black Eagle, after her village in America was attacked during the Revolutionary War. I think she wasn't much older than I am now, and Grandpère was a wicked rogue." Emeline grinned and lifted her brows suggestively. "Isn't it a thrilling tale?"

Freddie looked over at her young friend and laughed. "My escapade pales in comparison. Madame Raveneau was very daring!"

"She still is," Emeline said firmly.

"I suppose I should relax and try to enjoy being out in the open. After all, I may not have many opportunities to wander the streets of Mayfair in the coming days ...or weeks."

No sooner had Frederica uttered those words, smiling, than Emeline reached over to grip her arm for just an instant. "Don't stare ...but isn't that your father, Viscount Redfield, walking toward us?" In a hushed voice, she continued, "He is wearing a tall Aylesbury hat."

Suddenly Frederica felt as if she were in real danger. Her pulse raced, and she knew an urge to turn and run. Instead, she dipped her head slightly, grateful for the spectacles and false mustache that helped conceal her features from his view. Glancing up through her lashes, Freddie quickly picked him out from the crowd on busy South Audley Street. Papa was headed straight toward her, his head cocked as he listened to a companion who resembled his man of business.

Her mouth went dry, and she could hear the thud of her own heart. Looking over toward Emeline, she saw that the younger girl was pale. Freddie offered her arm, and when Emeline did not immediately take the cue, she took the girl's hand and put it through the crook of her elbow.

"Gaze at me as if we are in love," Freddie ordered through gritted teeth.

Papa was coming closer; now he was only a few yards away. Frederica felt perspiration dampen her underarms. If only there were a shop she could dart into, but every door they passed led to a private residence.

Emeline rested her head on Freddie's shoulder and sighed. "Oh, sir, I vow I have never known another man like you."

As they drew even with her father and his companion, Freddie held her breath and watched him from the corner of her eye. She could feel her face flushing as he focused on her for a moment. Was he about to shout her name, to grab her by the arm? Just as it seemed her heart might burst, his gaze shifted to Emeline, who looked particularly fetching in a strawberry-pink gown with a green silk sash. Her ebony curls gleamed beneath a matching bonnet, and her lovely face was radiant as she held fast to Freddie's arm.

The men continued on in the opposite direction, and Freddie's sense of imminent danger began to lessen. When Papa and his friend had turned the corner, she allowed herself to pause before the pillared façade of Grosvenor Chapel.

"Good lord," Frederica said with a nervous laugh, "that was a very close call!"

"It was a terrifying moment indeed."

"Yet, how enlightening to realize that he didn't even notice me in my male disguise," mused Freddie. "All Papa seemed interested in was stealing a look at you!"

"Perhaps we should endeavor to make you even uglier," teased Emeline.

Before Frederica could reply, the bells in the chapel tower chimed three o'clock. "Oh my, we shall be late," Emeline exclaimed. "Do hurry! I am convinced that we shall discover my brother lounging in the drawing room, waiting to surprise me. He'll be wearing a jaunty smile and will scold the others for not believing all along that he would be coming home."

With that, the girl started off quickly toward Grosvenor Square and Freddie rushed to keep up.

* * *

THE MOMENT CEDRIC opened the door to them, Frederica guessed the mood inside was not one of celebration. The butler looked shaken, and his eyes were damp and bloodshot.

"We will show ourselves up," Emeline told him and hurried past.

Freddie felt a cold knot of dread settle in the pit of her stomach. As they drew closer to the sitting room entrance, she heard the sound of weeping.

"Mama," whispered Emeline in disbelief. The girl stopped where they were, one hand covering her mouth, and when she would go forward, Frederica caught her skirt and held her back.

"Wait," she mouthed to Emeline.

Through the wide doorway, Frederica saw Mouette perched awkwardly on the tufted green sofa. Her beautiful face was streaked with tears, and her mother, Devon, sat beside her, endeavoring to hold her near. Justin St. Briac paced back and forth like a caged tiger, his face stormy, while André Raveneau waited nearby, as if hoping to calm or comfort his son-in-law.

Facing the sofa, two young men Frederica didn't recognize were sitting on silk-upholstered chairs. They exchanged pained glances, as if wishing they could be elsewhere.

"*Sangdieu!* I expected you to bring me answers," Justin shouted. "My son could not simply vanish, as if someone put a damned spell on him."

"Mr. Darwin, I beg you to enlighten us," Mouette said brokenly.

One of the men nodded and leaned forward, affording Frederica a view of his thinning brown hair, high dome of a forehead, and bushy brows. She drew in a breath, realizing this must be Charles Darwin, the young naturalist who had already begun to make such a name for himself. Glancing at Emeline, she received a nod of confirmation.

"I wish I could tell you exactly what happened to Anthony," Darwin said in a low voice. "Captain FitzRoy and I wrote very little initially because we hoped to gather more information over time. The captain, incidentally, sends you his deepest condolences. He would be here today but for his duties now that the *Beagle* has come into port in Plymouth."

"When exactly did our son go missing?" St. Briac challenged, looming above the two visitors.

Darwin swallowed uncomfortably and took a sip from his cup of tea. "In truth, it was a full year ago—"

Justin interrupted with a string of French epithets. "We did not have FitzRoy's letter until summer! If I had known, I would have sailed to the Galápagos myself, but instead I waited because the *Beagle* was due in port at any time, and we expected more information." He looked as if he would like to murder his visitors.

Beads of sweat dotted Darwin's wide brow. "I can only apologize for the delay getting word to you! We were committed to sail to New Zealand the very day after Anthony went missing. Captain FitzRoy wrote to you then, but his letter must have gone astray, doubtless on one of the British warships that often carried our mail. I am sorry to say it happened often. One of the letters I sent my own sister never arrived at all."

"And why the devil did it take a year for the *Beagle* to sail back to England?"

"We began our return voyage when we left the Galápagos, but there were many stops and delays en route. It was highly frustrating, for FitzRoy had a host of tasks to complete during our voyage, and in recent weeks we even had to sail *back* to Brazil so that he might take an additional longitudinal measurement in Bahia." Pausing, Darwin seemed to sense St. Briac's impatience and finished in a rush, "In any event, I am quite certain there was nothing you could do if you had sailed to James Island."

St. Briac stared, a muscle twitching in his jaw. "Just tell us what happened that day. All of it."

"Your son was an exceedingly valuable addition to our party. He made discoveries of his own," said Darwin. "And of course, as you well know, Anthony and I were close friends since Cambridge. This tragedy has shaken me to my core."

Mouette turned her face into her mother's shoulder.

Darwin's companion spoke up. "I was with him the day he went missing," the young man said, and all eyes turned his way. As if assuming that they had forgotten his earlier introduction, he added, "My name is Terrance Buskin. Anthony and I were acquainted at Cambridge, and more recently I was employed as a secretary to Nicholas Lawson, Vice Governor of the Galápagos Archipelago."

Frederica stared at him, thinking Buskin was one of the most nondescript people she had ever seen. He was of medium height and stocky build. His fair hair was colorless and straight, his eyes bulged slightly, and his complexion was sallow.

"Terrance joined us on the *Beagle* when we reached James Island," Darwin explained. "On that fateful day, I had to go with FitzRoy in search of a quantity of water to store for our long voyage to New Zealand, so Terrance and Anthony set off on one last expedition inland."

All eyes were fixed on the pale Terrance Buskin. He took out a handkerchief and mopped his brow. "It was really an uneventful day. We made our way inland, searching for a group of tortoises who had traveled inland in search of fresh water. Anthony was very interested in the tortoises and their habits, and he wanted to investigate further."

"And?" demanded St. Briac.

Everyone seemed to have stopped breathing, including Frederica as she and Emeline watched, frozen like statues, from the hallway.

Terrance blinked several times. "I wish I could tell you more, but I cannot. We separated for a bit, and when I returned to the place where we parted, Anthony had simply disappeared without a trace." Before Justin could shout more questions, he put up a hand and added, "I can assure you, I called his name and searched. At first, I assumed he had simply wandered off in a different direction. That would have been like him, to do so without saying anything to me. A few hours passed before I realized something was truly amiss."

"Could he have been attacked by one of the giant tortoises?" cried Mouette. "Or bitten by a snake?"

Leaning forward, Darwin spoke to her. "The tortoises are not savage in the least," he said gently. "When we returned at dusk from our daylong errand and learned what had happened, all the *Beagle*'s crew joined in the search, by torchlight, but there was no sign of Anthony. After our night of searching, Captain FitzRoy concluded that he must have had an accident on the cliffs and ...fallen into the sea. It seems the only logical explanation."

"Yes," Terrance agreed sadly. "I too fear that must be what happened."

Mouette pressed both hands to her flushed, tear-stained cheeks and sank back against her mother. "This is a nightmare!"

Darwin nodded and looked around the room at Anthony's family. "I confess I held out hope ...until today. I prayed that there might be an explanation for his disappearance, that he would have sent word home to you, and you would tell me that my friend had survived." Swallowing again, he added, "It fills me with sadness to realize that he has not."

The two men rose then, insisting that Anthony's family should not hesitate to contact either of them if they could be of service. "I will return to my own family tomorrow, in Shrewsbury. As you might imagine, I have countless crates of specimens to unpack, examine, and catalogue, but if you should need me, you must write, and I will travel back to London."

Terrance Buskin gazed sympathetically at Mouette. "I wish I could have brought you very different news. I shall remain here in London, ready to assist you in any way."

"There is only one kind of assistance we desire," St.

Briac said harshly. "If either of you can bring me my son, please do not hesitate to do so."

After a long, charged moment of silence, Darwin cleared his throat. "Before we go, I should mention that you will find Anthony's personal effects in the stair hall. That is to say …we have brought his portmanteau from the ship."

"Oh, that reminds me," said Terrance Buskin. It was then that Frederica realized there was a small, battered valise next to the man's chair. He reached down for the bag and opened it. "When I was searching near the cliffs on that dreadful day, I did find one item belonging to Anthony." Buskin held up a battered canvas shoe. "He was wearing this the last time I saw him."

Mouette recoiled as if the man had produced a serpent, and Emeline began to weep. Freddie gathered her into her arms, her own heart aching. Somehow, the single shoe felt wrenchingly final.

Even though it had seemed that most of Anthony's family had realized he was probably dead, they had been clinging to hope, the kind of hope that had allowed them to carry on with their day-to-day lives.

Today those hopes had been crushed. Now, in the space Anthony St. Briac had occupied so vibrantly, there was only a chilling void that stretched into eternity.

CHAPTER 6

Frederica sat in her usual chair at Anthony's library desk and slowly unwrapped another specimen, enjoying each moment of anticipation. As the object was revealed, she caught her breath. It appeared to be a long tooth, cracked and discolored. Could it be the fragment of a tusk? Or perhaps it was a bone shard. Measuring it, she saw that the fossil was nearly six inches in length.

Amazing! If only she could hear the story behind the discovery of this relic.

Freddie then noticed a small piece of paper in the wrapping cloth she had set to one side. "September 1832. Punta Alta, Argentina."

Turning to her notebook, she wrote the dimensions and a description of the fossil, adding Anthony's own date and the location of his find. For a long moment, she paused to gaze at the confident strokes of his pen and her throat grew dry. Despite her own personal resentment toward the man, she felt a renewed pang of sadness knowing Anthony St. Briac would never touch these artifacts or embrace his family again.

As Freddie pondered this sad truth, her false mustache began to itch, and she absently rubbed at it with the tip of her forefinger.

"Professor?" Quincy spoke from the doorway. "A gentleman called Mr. Terrance Buskin is here. Shall I show him in?"

Freddie blinked, realizing she had been so lost in thought that she hadn't even heard the bell. "Oh! Yes, certainly." She rose from the desk, straightened her cravat, and waited, but the butler continued to stand in the doorway, looking at her. "Is there something else, Quincy?"

He gave a nervous cough but inclined his big head slightly and touched his own upper lip.

Freddie put a hand up to her false mustache and realized it had gone askew when she scratched it. Her cheeks flamed as she pressed it back into place and said gruffly, "Ah, thank you, Quincy. You may now show Mister Buskin in."

The barest hint of a smile touched the butler's lips as he nodded and turned away. There wasn't time for Freddie to wonder about his thoughts because moments later, Terrance Buskin appeared on the library threshold.

As he introduced himself, Buskin's pale blue eyes scanned the crates, casks, and barrels that filled the room. "I am a naturalist, and I was with Anthony St. Briac on the last day of his life," he informed her. "I have come to help with the artifacts he sent home before his death."

Freddie found it jarring to hear Anthony's demise spoken of in such final terms, but a more immediate challenge was presenting herself to this stranger in her new male identity. Praying that she looked convincing, she said, "My name is Professor Frederick Loudon." Squaring her slim shoulders, Freddie strode forward, hand outstretched. "I am an old friend of the St. Briac family, and they have sent me to unpack and catalogue their son's discoveries."

Terrance Buskin looked at her with frank curiosity. "I see. You'll need help of course."

"Actually, I do my best work in solitude."

"Be that as it may, you don't look terribly strong, old fellow. No doubt you could use someone like me with a good pair of shoulders." Reaching out, he gave Freddie's arm a reassuring pat. "And actually, Charles Darwin prefers that I oversee this project."

"Indeed?" Freddie blinked behind her spectacles and tried to sound authoritative. "Justin St. Briac, Anthony's father, has asked me to do that."

"With all due respect, Mr. Darwin maintains that someone from the expedition should be involved so that nothing important may be overlooked. That would be a tragedy after Anthony gave his life for these specimens, don't you agree, professor?"

Something in Terrance's bearing told her he would not be put off. "However, let us compromise. You may assist me. Will that suit you?"

Buskin was nodding as he eagerly started forward, stripping off his coat. "Indeed, sir. That would be excellent."

With that, he found the small crowbar Freddie had been using and applied it to a crate of his own. For the first time, she saw Terrance Buskin flush with excitement as he pulled off the slats and peered inside.

* * *

As the days passed and more fossils, flora, fauna, insects, and geological specimens were unwrapped and catalogued, Frederica's passion for her work mounted and she rarely left the library. Anthony himself had placed colored numbers on each piece, and there were instructions for unpacking them in a specific order. When Freddie occasionally discovered notes and sketches made in Anthony's own hand, she felt a wave of awe mingled with grief.

"How tragic it is that St. Briac is not here to do this work himself," she said to Terrance Buskin as they worked side-by-side one afternoon in the library.

He was standing at one end of the large desk, peering through a magnifying glass at a bird with a small, pointed beak. "Hmm? Oh, yes, terrible, terrible." After a moment, Buskin seemed to recall himself. Looking her way, he spoke again. "My dear professor, we can only strive to carry on Anthony's work in his stead. It is what he would have wanted."

Freddie cleared her throat. "Indeed. It is my honor to do that very thing."

"What do you have there?" Terrance inquired in a friendly tone. He set down his stuffed finch and sidled over to her.

They both wore special gloves and were scrupulously careful with each item that they touched. Freddie picked up the long, narrow jawbone she had been examining and showed it to him. "It is the mandible of an animal neither St. Briac nor Darwin could identify." She pointed to the handwritten notes containing exact measurements and a description of the precise location where it had been discovered. On a separate page were Anthony's excellent sketches of the fossil. "He speculated that it might belong to an ancient mammal resembling a sloth."

"Fascinating!" Buskin marveled.

Freddie stared at the sketches that included a sloth like the one Anthony imagined was related to the fossil. "How talented was Mr. St. Briac," she mused. "His drawings and paintings hang throughout the house."

Glancing up at Terrance Buskin, she asked, "Do you sketch as well, sir?"

"Not a bit. Most children draw better than I." He rolled his eyes. "I must confess, I always felt that St. Briac was blessed with more than his fair share of gifts. The rest of us could only look on, quite awestruck." For a moment, it seemed that a shadow passed over his face, but then Buskin was smiling and brandishing his magnifying glass. "Would you allow me to study that specimen?"

It was not really a question, so Freddie nodded as he reached for the fossil with its two remaining teeth and returned to his side of the desk. The rest of the afternoon slipped by until Mrs. Bell appeared with a tea tray accompanied by thin slices of fruitcake.

Quite suddenly it came to Freddie that she was hungry and very tired. "Our work is so absorbing that I sometimes forget to eat," she confessed as she poured tea for both of them.

"My good fellow, you've been at it for days! You must be exhausted." Buskin beamed and passed her the fruitcake. "Sit down and enjoy your cake. Why not turn in early? I will carry on for both of us."

* * *

TIRED TO HER BONES, Frederica took Terrance's advice and retired while he still labored in the library. She instantly fell into a deep sleep, and the bedroom was cloaked in blackest night when she awoke hours later. Her heart was racing.

Suddenly, a hushed voice came to her out of the pitch darkness. "Mistress!"

Pushing herself up to a sitting position, Freddie discerned a dim figure amid the deep shadows. Panic was quickly replaced by relief. "Oh, Mrs. Bell, it's you! Where did you come from?"

"Up that back staircase that winds between my chamber and yours." Mrs. Bell paused, and Freddie could hear her labored breathing. "I heard a noise in the library! I would have gone for Quincy, but he is quite old, isn't he, and I was afraid the intruder might hear me and – and kill us all!"

Freddie could feel her wits returning. "What time is it?"

"'Tis long past midnight, mistress!" Mrs. Bell approached the bed, her voluminous nightgown glowing white. Her silver braids were concealed under a large, old-fashioned nightcap.

Freddie was already climbing out of bed. Fumbling in the darkness, she lit a lamp and crossed to Anthony St. Briac's dressing room. After donning trousers and a cambric shirt, she selected a handsome dressing gown of claret velvet and tried it on. Although it was too big for her, the cut of the shoulders disguised her own slim torso, and she tied a belt at the waist to adjust the length. One glance at her reflection in his cheval glass nearly caused her to laugh aloud. Her goatshair wig was in wild disarray and her mustache needed straightening again. However, no one would mistake her for a woman, especially when she added a final touch.

"What do you mean to do, mistress?" asked Mrs. Bell anxiously.

Freddie opened a drawer in Anthony's tall chest and withdrew a polished, inlaid wooden case. Lifting the lid, she chose one of the silver-trimmed dueling pistols inside and held it aloft. "I mean to capture our intruder and discover exactly what he is about!" she whispered in defiant tones.

The housekeeper gave a loud gasp and began to

wring her hands. "Oh, mistress, I beg you, do not do so!"

"Don't worry, I'm certain it isn't loaded. In any event, I haven't a clue how to use this thing - but the intruder won't know that." She put a hand on Mrs. Bell's arm before starting toward the door. "Perhaps the villain will take one look at me and make a mad dash for the door."

The two of them exchanged rather desperate smiles before Freddie tucked the pistol into the folds of her dressing gown and stepped out into the dark corridor. Pulling the door shut behind her, she crept to the landing and leaned over the banister, listening. Her heart was racing like a runaway curricle.

A faint glow shone under the library's double doors. Hearing a slight noise, Freddie thought her heart might burst. She told herself that the so-called intruder must be Terrance Buskin. Perhaps he had been so immersed in his work that he had stayed on, losing track of time! It was the only explanation that made sense.

Clutching the pistol with one hand and lifting the long folds of her dressing gown with the other, she felt her way down the stairs. Thankfully, her eyes had begun to adjust to the dark.

When Freddie reached the bottom step and crept toward the library doors, she nearly lost her nerve. What if the intruder had a pistol—or even a dagger!—of his own? The notion that she could be in mortal danger sent a wave a terror through her.

Frederica drew a deep breath and thought of the marvelous treasures that were stored behind the library doors. She had come to feel as attached to them as if she had discovered them herself, and she also felt bound to protect the specimens on behalf of Anthony St. Briac, who had lost his life while amassing the impressive collection.

Straightening her shoulders, Freddie tried to make herself taller. Her hand shook a little as she reached out to silently push one of the doors open a few inches and peer inside.

A single candle flickered atop Anthony St. Briac's handsome desk. In the soft glow, Freddie saw that the black-caped intruder was turned away from her. He stood in front of the desk, head bent, his attention fixed on the long piece of fossilized wood he held in one gloved hand. The man was tall, lean yet powerful, with wide shoulders and a head of tousled ebony curls.

Abruptly, he turned to face her. A thrill of fear skittered down Frederica's spine as she realized this menacing stranger was definitely *not* Terrance Buskin. The deeply tanned intruder wore a close-trimmed black beard. His eyes blazed into hers through the shadowed space between them.

"Who the devil are you?" the man demanded in a deep, sardonic voice. To her alarm, he started toward her, appearing for all the world to be intent on doing her serious harm.

Frederica clenched her teeth and forced herself to stop trembling. Gripping the pistol, she extended her arm and aimed the weapon at his broad chest.

"Stay where you are!" she challenged in her best imitation of a threatening male. "Do not come any closer or I will shoot!"

CHAPTER 7

Scowling, Frederica continued to point the pistol, but the black-clad intruder merely arched a brow and advanced on her, seizing her wrist through the velvet dressing gown. It took every ounce of her self-control not to cry out as his grip tightened. After several moments, she was forced to release the weapon, panting in surrender.

"Who are you?" he demanded again, looming over her.

Even as the man bit out the words, he stared at her in a way that made Freddie grateful for her spectacles. Her forearm throbbed, and she had to remind herself that she must behave as a man and not accuse him of mistreating a female. Besides, he was now holding her pistol in his free hand. It might not be loaded, but the villain could certainly use it to bludgeon her.

"I live here!" Freddie challenged in her deepest tones. "But I owe you no explanation. You are the trespasser! Now, get out before I summon the watch."

To her consternation, the stranger gave a harsh laugh. "This is my house. If anyone is trespassing, it's you, my good man." With that, he reached over and fingered the claret velvet of her sleeve. "By Lucifer, you're even wearing *my* dressing gown!"

Stunned, Freddie took a step backward and blinked at him. Was it possible that this could be Anthony St. Briac, returned from the dead? He was so changed from the slim, dashing, witty young man she had known seven years ago that for a moment she felt dizzy with confusion.

"Gammon," Freddie declared bravely. "You are an imposter."

"On the contrary, I am Anthony St. Briac," he replied with calm assurance.

"Impossible. The real Anthony St. Briac was lost on the Galápagos Islands a full year ago."

He leaned forward, dark eyes burning her senses. "I have been away, but now I have returned. You are in my house." His powerful fingers squeezed her wrist. "Now it is your turn. Explain yourself."

As he spoke, Freddie heard an echo of smooth baritone she remembered from years ago, now rough-edged in a way that reminded her of his pirate father. He was more powerful than she remembered, his shoulders broader, his face and hands sun-darkened, and his features chiseled. Even his nose was quite different; bent rakishly out of alignment.

Her thoughts whirled. If this man really was Anthony St. Briac, she could not reveal her authentic identity to him, or he would surely put her out. Not only was it unthinkable for an unmarried woman to reside in the same house with an unmarried man, but Anthony would not want her here. Her heart sank as she realized he doubtless would not want Professor Frederick Loudon underfoot either, but she had to try.

In a cajoling tone, Freddie exclaimed, "My good sir, your family will be overjoyed to know you are alive and safely returned to London! How they have worried, nay – *mourned* – for you." As she spoke, she felt his grip on her arm relax, and a gentler emotion seemed to flicker in his black eyes. Seizing the opportunity, Freddie freed her hand and extended it to him. "My name is Professor Frederick Loudon. Your parents engaged me to unpack and catalogue the many crates of specimens you sent back from your long voyage with Charles Darwin."

St. Briac looked wary as he briefly shook her hand. "Indeed?" He paused and flicked a glance over her. "That does not explain why you are wearing my dressing gown."

Freddie's throat was dry. "Madame insisted that I stay here to save myself the trouble of traveling back and forth from my own lodgings, and—"

He cut her off. "And where might your lodgings be?"

Caught off guard by this question, she felt her cheeks warming. "A good distance away, in Russell Street," she lied, then rushed ahead "Truly, I have been working here night and day, and since you were …absent, Madame felt this arrangement would be best. As for this," Freddie pointed to the dressing gown that thankfully covered her from neck to toes. "I donned it in haste, when the housekeeper alerted me that there was an intruder in the house."

"You said your name is Professor Loudon?" St. Briac tested the name, sounding doubtful. "I've never heard of you."

"My good sir!" Freddie blustered. "May I suggest that you have been away for many years? My credentials are impeccable. I am not only a naturalist but also have extensive experience cataloguing items for a private library. Your parents agreed that I am the ideal fellow for this grand undertaking." Gaining momentum, she dared to add, "And now that you are back, I shall gladly devote myself to assisting *you*."

As Anthony stared at her, Frederica saw the exhaustion in his eyes. "We shall postpone this discussion until tomorrow," he said. "For now, I must sleep. I assume Quincy is still employed as my butler?"

To Freddie's horror, the man crossed into the library and pulled a velvet cord she had never noticed, partially concealed behind the draperies. "But, sir, it is the middle of the night. Quincy will be sleeping!"

"No doubt he has been waiting seven long years to hear that bell," remarked Anthony.

Those words proved utterly true when, mere minutes later, Quincy rushed in from the back of the house, cheeks hectic with color, fumbling to close gilt buttons over his considerable girth. When his eyes fell on St. Briac, Freddie feared the elderly butler might faint.

Quincy rubbed his eyes. "My lord, how can this be? Am I seeing a ghost?"

"Nay, it is I," Anthony said. He approached the old man, flashing a familiar, irresistible smile, and Frederica was suddenly convinced of his identity.

"But ...how?" whispered Quincy.

"I will tell all to you on the morrow, but for now I must have some sleep. I've been missing my own bed more than you can know."

Freddie caught her lip between her teeth and exchanged glances with Quincy. "Sir, you should know that I have been using your rooms."

"All the others needed a good deal of freshening," the butler hastened to add. "That is to say, there had been no guests in this house since your departure on the *Beagle.*"

Anthony waved him off. "Never mind. I don't care. I could sleep on this deuced carpet tonight." He then seemed to take pity on the crestfallen Quincy. "However, the blue bedchamber will do. There is time enough tomorrow for me to reclaim my own rooms."

"Of course, as you wish, sir," the butler replied. "But where is your baggage?"

He gave a harsh laugh. "On the *Beagle*, I surmise. I was left for dead with only the clothes on my back. Any meager belongings I have acquired since then are here." As Anthony spoke, he reached for the large canvas bag that lay beside his desk.

There was so much Freddie longed to ask him, but all of it would have to wait until tomorrow. As he hefted his bag and strode toward the stairs, St. Briac glanced her way.

"I'll deal with you in the morning." He paused, distracted. "I beg you to remind me ...what name did you give?"

"Loudon." She straightened her shoulders. "Professor Frederick Loudon."

"Ah, yes." The fleeting glint of amusement in his eyes gave her an unsettling qualm.

"I shall vacate your rooms at dawn, sir, and make myself available to converse with you at your earliest convenience."

Anthony had already disappeared into the shadowed stair hall, but his wry voice drifted back to her. "Splendid, professor."

* * *

FREDERICA WAS CARRYING a candlestick when she entered her bedchamber. After a few moments she saw a door at the far corner of the room open an inch or two.

"Mistress?" The whisper was so faint, anyone but Freddie might not have heard.

She hurried across to the door, holding her candle aloft, and said softly, "Mrs. Bell?"

"Yes, mistress." The door opened further, and

Freddie saw the housekeeper standing on the landing of the servant's corner staircase, a shawl wrapped around her sloping shoulders. "I couldn't leave until I knew you were safe."

Freddie's heart began to race anew as the sheer consequence of tonight's events came to her in a rush. "Oh, Mrs. Bell, you cannot imagine what has happened. Anthony St. Briac is not dead at all but returned to this very house." To her surprise, tears threatened. "I am, of course, very glad he lives, but what shall I do?"

"Will you not tell him the truth and hope that he understands your plight?"

This very notion made her feel ill. "I must think. But please protect my secret until I can decide on a course of action." A sudden thought made her reach out to the housekeeper. "And, Mrs. Bell, you must not come up this way again! Mr. St. Briac will reclaim these rooms tomorrow and he must not know we have used this staircase."

Mrs. Bell's pursed lips were exaggerated in the flickering candlelight. "Oh, mistress, I must say you have got yourself into a pretty pickle!"

"I know." Freddie sighed deeply, nodding. "I fear I won't sleep a wink tonight."

* * *

EVER SINCE SHE had taken refuge in Anthony's house on Charles Street, Frederica had been careful to lock the bedroom door before retiring just in case someone happened to come in and see her without her mustache or wig. However, that course of action was no longer an option. She certainly couldn't bar Anthony St. Briac from his own rooms!

And so, on this night, Freddie went to bed in full disguise, but when she awoke in the middle of the night, her wig was askew, her mustache lost in the covers. Her breasts, still wrapped tightly against her chest, ached for release.

Freddie's heart raced whenever she thought of him sleeping in another room, just down the corridor. The entire situation felt like a bizarre dream. One part of her was elated that Anthony was not dead after all, yet selfishly she could not help feeling panicked about what would happen next.

Lying in the darkness, her mind went round and round. The more she considered Mrs. Bell's suggestion that she reveal herself to Anthony, the more impossible it seemed.

Yet equally impossible was the prospect of carrying on with her charade, even if he did agree to let "Professor Loudon" remain under this roof, which was highly doubtful. Why, after so many years of absence from London, should Anthony allow a stranger to live in his house for the sole purpose of helping to catalogue the specimens from the *Beagle* expedition?

Every option for her future now seemed to end in one word: *impossible*. When tears gathered in her eyes, Freddie turned her face into the pillow and vowed that, somehow, she would find a way forward.

Falling at length into a fitful slumber, Frederica dreamed that her father was coming toward her again on the street. Drawing near, he reached out and ripped the mustache from her lip, accusing, *"You!"* With that, Freddie turned and ran, her wig flying off, cravat coming undone and spooling away, the buttons on her coat opening to reveal her female shape beneath. Still, she ran, lungs burning, as Papa shouted, "Stop, stop, little wretch!"

* * *

ANTHONY OPENED one eye and slowly surveyed his surroundings. For five long years, he had awakened in a hammock on board a ship or in a variety of rustic shelters in exotic lands. A handful of times he had slept in a real bed, courtesy of a willing female, but none had felt like this.

The bedchamber was bathed in the golden glow of early morning. Sheets, fresh and soft as silk, floated against the hard contours of his naked body. The forest-green counterpane was vaguely familiar. Had he chosen it, long ago? Slowly, the events of last night returned to him and he remembered that he was back in London ...in his own house, but not in his own bed. That exceedingly odd professor had appropriated Anthony's rooms.

He closed his eyes again. Memories teased his mind. Something compelled him to bring his right hand to his nose and inhale. Very faintly, Anthony detected the scent of meadowsweet, apparently left during the few moments when he and Professor Loudon shook hands.

Deuced peculiar.

Rolling onto his stomach, he told himself to think of something else. He wondered if any of his former paramours were still in London and at liberty to see him. One opera dancer in particular, Marianne Chambers, would be a welcome companion under sheets like these. Heat surged to his loins, and he hardened against the feather tick, remembering how she loved to pleasure him with her mouth. God, how long it had been since he'd spent a full night with a lusty female like Marianne?

He'd been careful during his years on the *Beagle*, especially in cities like Buenos Aires and even in remote villages in the Andes. His mother had taught him that females were not playthings to be used for his pleasure, so Anthony had endeavored to be discerning, considerate, and truthful when the opportunity for a brief romance had presented itself.

Now he was home, though, and the years of travel were behind him. For an instant, he imagined Marianne's warm, luscious body next to him under the sheets. Her mouth opening to him, her breast swelling against his palm, the sound of her moan, the welcoming slickness between her thighs.

He wrapped long, sun-darkened fingers around his stiff cock and let the ache of anticipated release spread through his loins. Damn but it was good to be home ... and alone at last.

Adjusting his grip, Anthony began to stroke himself, and his head of unruly black curls dropped back on the pillow.

However, barely a moment later, his solitary pleasure was cut short by a scratching sound at the door. Anthony could scarcely believe his ears.

"Sir." This single word was followed by apologetic throat-clearing. "Forgive me for disturbing you."

He nearly barked at Quincy to go away, but it came to him that countless matters doubtless required his attention now that he had returned. God only knew what problem might have cropped up this morning. And of course, myriad crates of specimens waited for him in the library ...and he must visit his family.

With a harsh sigh, Anthony sat up and drew the sheet up in folds over his male parts. "Come in!"

The elderly butler entered, and despite his master's unfriendly greeting, he broke into a wide smile and threw open the draperies. "I hope you will pardon me for saying so, sir, but this might be the happiest day of my life."

"Did you come in here just to tell me that?" Anthony blinked against the morning sun and sent Quincy a glare he'd learned from his own father: bad-tempered on its face but tinged with affection. "You could have at least brought coffee. And a bath." Rubbing one bearded cheek, he added, "And a razor."

"Oh, yes, sir. I mean to send all of those up straightaway." Quincy cleared his throat. "Before I order your bath, I should inform you that Mr. Buskin has arrived."

Anthony hoped he hadn't heard correctly. "Speak plainly, man. I haven't the patience for riddles today."

"Mr. Terrance Buskin, your devoted friend from Cambridge, has been helping Professor Loudon examine and catalogue all your specimens. He arrives here early each day and departs late."

"Who told you he was my friend?"

"Why, Mr. Buskin said so himself." The butler lifted his furry white brows, waiting.

"Hmm." Even as Anthony lounged back against the pillows, he was struck by a worrying thought. "I hope Professor Loudon hasn't seen Buskin yet today."

"No. The professor is late to come downstairs today, but of course it wasn't an ordinary night, was it?"

"No." Brows aloft, he added, "I'm in devilish need of coffee. See to that, won't you? And ask Professor Loudon to come in—before he greets Mr. Buskin."

Quincy blinked. "In here?"

"Right. I want to talk to him."

"Do you mean to stay ...as you are?"

"Would the professor be offended if I did?" Anthony arched a brow, amused. "I've been on a ship, and worse, these past five years. I've quite abandoned the niceties of polite society."

Seemingly at a loss, Quincy cleared his throat and mumbled, "One imagines so."

Anthony's smile flashed. "You'd be shocked by the things I've seen."

"No doubt." The butler began to back out the door. "I'll see to your requests now, sir."

"Splendid. And should you have a few scraps of breakfast in the kitchen, you might gather those for me as well."

"Immediately, sir."

"Oh, and one more thing." Anthony sharpened his gaze before adding, "I don't want you or Meg to speak of my return to anyone – yet. Not Terrance Buskin, not even my parents. Understood?"

The butler looked taken aback, but he nodded. "Completely, sir. You may rely on our discretion."

When Quincy had gone, closing the door in his wake, Anthony raked a hand through his tangled hair and lay back to wait for Professor Loudon's knock. The day ahead promised to be more entertaining than he had imagined.

CHAPTER 8

*P*ressing her horsehair mustache into place, Frederica took deep breaths and told herself to be calm. The unexpected summons from Anthony St. Briac probably meant nothing.

Her earlier indecision about whether to reveal her true identity to St. Briac had been resolved by Quincy's announcement that Terrance Buskin had arrived. Because today was Sunday, she hadn't expected him to turn up, but he clearly required no day of rest.

Any personal disclosures she might make would have to wait until Buskin had gone.

As she prepared to leave Anthony's own rooms, she closed her portmanteau. All her male clothing, on loan from Devon Raveneau, was packed up so that the master might reclaim his bedchamber. At the last moment, Freddie retrieved the dressing gown she had been wearing the night before, taking it with her in case Anthony needed it.

Out in the corridor, she saw the door open to the blue bedroom. Meg emerged, cheeks flushed. When she saw Freddie, she quickly glanced down as if to conceal her impure thoughts.

"Good morning, professor! I just took breakfast to my master. He expects you."

It was rather maddening to realize that Anthony seemed to undo each female he encountered. Thank goodness he thought Freddie was a man.

The door was slightly ajar, so she knocked once and peeked inside. "Mr. St. Briac?"

"I am right here." His voice was husky with sleep.

Even before Freddie saw him, warmth tingled between her legs. When she entered and looked toward the bed, she beheld Anthony St. Briac reclining against snowy pillows in all his male glory, the breakfast tray balanced precariously next to him on the bed. His wide, hard-muscled chest was exposed to her gaze, its light covering of dark hair narrowing to an arrow that traveled south past his navel. What it pointed to was thankfully left to her imagination, for a rumpled sheet was drawn up to Anthony's hips. As Freddie met his hooded gaze, it came to her that his entire body exuded sex.

Of course, all she knew about *that* was centered around a fictional but very wicked highwayman.

"I apologize if I have arrived precipitously," she said in the deepest voice she could manage. "It seems you were not truly prepared to receive guests."

"Ah, professor. May I call you Frederick?" Anthony inquired, taking a large bite of one of Mrs. Bell's hot-cross buns. He moved slightly and Freddie glimpsed a small tattoo of what appeared to be an exotic lizard, coiling up the side of his strong neck.

Shocked, she could only nod mutely in reply to his question.

"I hope you are not offended by my appearance. I've had a devil of a time the past several months. Now that I am finally home, I want only to sleep, eat, and bathe." He seemed to wink, faintly, and added, "Then, once I reunite with my family, I can move on to …more carnal pleasures."

She attempted a suggestive chuckle, as she had heard her father and his friends do, and returned his wink. "Perfectly understandable, sir."

"Quincy tells me Terrance Buskin is here, in the library. I understand that he has been coming here daily to help you catalogue the specimens I sent home throughout the expedition."

Freddie watched him eat the last of the bun, then lick a bit of icing from one fingertip. "That's true. He came here and said that Charles Darwin himself insisted he be in charge." She straightened her padded shoulders. "I agreed that he might share the duties with me."

"Buskin has no right to share anything at all that has to do with me." He stared at her. "Frederick, I must ask you not to inform anyone that I have returned, especially not Terrance Buskin. I will tell you plainly that I have reasons not to trust him. I want to see what he is about before I reveal myself. Do you understand?"

A thrill raced through Freddie's body. "Yes, sir! I mean, yes, Anthony. How may I be of assistance?"

"Go downstairs and engage with Buskin just as you normally would but keep my words in mind. Meanwhile, I will bathe and dress. We will meet again later, and you can report anything you have learned." After a brief pause, he added, "As much as I long to reunite with my family, that joy must be postponed for now. I suppose, after five years, I can wait a bit longer."

"If they had any idea that you were alive and back in London, we could not keep them away," said Freddie.

"That's why they must not know, at least not yet. I suspect Buskin may have other motives for wanting to help with my specimens. Let us discover what he is about, then we'll consider the way forward."

To Frederica's horror, St. Briac threw off the sheet. Before she could react, he swung his long legs over the side of the bed and rose to stand in front of her. Heat flooded her face. Averting her eyes, she thrust the dressing gown out to him. "I believe you'll be needing this!"

He took his time shrugging into the garment and sent her a sardonic smile. "My good fellow, I perceive you have been spending too much of your time locked up with scientific books. That's well enough, but you don't want to turn missish. You could do with a few liberating weeks on board a ship with a crew of rowdy seamen, as I have done. Soon enough, nothing would shock you."

Anthony took his time closing the front of the dressing gown, and she had to suppress an urge to cover her eyes. "Thank you for the suggestion, but I must decline," Freddie mumbled, turning toward the door. "While you dress, sir, I shall meet with Mr. Buskin in the library."

* * *

SAFELY OUTSIDE THE BLUE BEDROOM, Frederica leaned against the closed door and drew a deep breath. If Anthony was purposely trying to shock her, he couldn't have been more successful. She brought both hands to her hot cheeks, praying she hadn't been beet-red while standing before him. *Missish*, he'd said! Anthony must already think her an excessively odd man, the last thing Freddie needed was to be seen blushing furiously each time she came into his presence.

He is a scoundrel! she told herself, silently repeating the sentiment just in case her secret self didn't fully believe it. It seemed he had no scruples, speaking that way to a respectable fellow scientist.

Memories of the long-ago night Freddie had discovered him in her father's study returned in a confusing rush. She had burned for him to kiss her, touch her intimately, press his hips to hers. If he had done so, she would have released all her pent-up desires, and doubtless would have let Anthony have his way with her. Thank God she'd discovered his true, nefarious reason for being there before any of those things had happened. Yet even as she remembered, Freddie shivered with the memory of him kissing her hand, his mouth trailing fire over her fingertips ...

Stop! she warned herself.

That night, years ago, had imprinted a powerful lesson in Frederica's heart. Men could not be trusted, no matter how irresistible their smiles and words might be. She had been on the verge of making a terrible mistake in that darkened study, but Freddie was not the kind of woman who forgot so painful a lesson. And now that their paths had crossed again and Anthony believed her to be a man, he was casually suggesting that she act like him and partake of vice and depravity. No doubt he would invite "Frederick" to accompany him to one of the unmarked houses where painted lady-birds would vie for the honor of retiring to a private room with Anthony St. Briac.

It seemed the man had no morals! Shuddering, Freddie told herself to be grateful he didn't know her true identity. How could she have entertained any notion of telling him the truth of her plight, hoping that he would allow *Frederica Redfield* to hide in his house? Even if he did so, feigning kindness, it would be only a matter of time before he would scheme to have his way with her, taking her virtue and then discarding her like a bit of muslin.

Even as Freddie started down the stairs in her male attire, her mouth set in determined line, she felt dampness pulse between her legs. It was as if Anthony had put a wicked spell on her ...but she resolved that he would never know.

* * *

STANDING SILENTLY in the doorway to the library, Frederica watched Terrance Buskin. Light streamed in through a long window and spilled over the handsome desk where Buskin occupied his usual place at one end. He was squinting through a glass at a small, stuffed bird that he held in one gloved hand. When he lowered his arm, she didn't see the bird on the desktop.

"Good morning," Freddie said, and started toward him.

"Ah, there you are, professor! I began to wonder if you were out today." He peered at her through spectacles in need of polishing.

"I had a few other matters to attend to," Freddie said. "Did I miss any exciting discoveries?"

"Oh, no. Just a lot of dull bits of petrified wood in this latest crate."

Nodding, she crossed to the desk and noticed that one of his coat pockets bulged slightly. In the jovial tone she adopted as the professor, she asked, "Was that a bird I saw in your hand a moment ago?"

Terrance blinked twice and his pale face flushed slightly. "Oh, this?" He reached into the pocket and withdrew the dead little bird. It was stone-brown with darker spots and a razor-sharp beak. Before she could ask why the specimen was in his pocket, he chuckled and said, "It belongs to me. A finch from Galápagos. I brought it from my own collection, simply to compare it to one I thought I'd seen here."

Quickly then, he put it back in his pocket, but not before Freddie noticed the tiny green tag on the bird's leg. The number on it was written in Anthony's distinctive hand. Why was Terrance Buskin lying to her? Had he been stealing Anthony's specimens all along?

Freddie quickly reminded herself not to jump to conclusions. Smoothing her mustache, she smiled. "I was rather surprised to hear that you were here on a Sunday. Do you never stop working, Mr. Buskin?"

"Perhaps I have been inspired by you, sir – so dedicated to your labors here that you have moved in."

"Sadly, the house is empty. I only reside here at the suggestion of Mr. St. Briac's parents, and I am saved the trouble of traveling to and from my own lodgings."

"You are unmarried, then?" His pale blue eyes were watching her.

"I am devoted to my work." Shrugging, Freddie added, "In any event, I am hardly the sort of fellow the ladies flock to."

"I do see your point."

She wanted to laugh at this but opened the desk drawer instead and busied herself taking out notebooks and other paraphernalia.

"There is another reason I came here to work on a Sunday," Terrance Buskin said. He glanced up at Freddie as if he had just remembered this piece of news. "I've been invited to present a paper at the Geological Society."

"Good God!" exclaimed Freddie. "Is that so? My felicitations, sir. What sort of paper?"

He gave a little bow. "I'll own I am very pleased. They have asked me to speak a fortnight hence, at their next regular meeting, about my groundbreaking study of the giant Galápagos tortoises."

"I didn't know you had been studying the tortoises there, but I recall that you were with Anthony St. Briac on the day he went missing." Freddie strove for a casual tone. "I am very curious to know what you've discovered."

"Oh, I naturally cannot discuss my theories, gathered during my time as secretary to Governor Lawson. You understand, of course, professor. I was developing them long before the *Beagle* came to the Galápagos Islands." He paused. "But if you are interested in attending, I will see to it that you have a seat of honor."

Freddie bit her lip. "Attending?"

"As a respected scholar of natural history, you are *doubtless* a member."

She wished that were possible. Her father belonged to the Geological Society, but of course women were not allowed to even cross the threshold. To Freddie's way of thinking, such backward institutions ought to be banned.

When she didn't immediately reply, Buskin stepped closer and put a hand on her shoulder. "Never mind, it doesn't matter, sir. Not everyone can be a member. I shall request an invitation for you and have it sent round." Clearly, he was enjoying his favored status. "And now I must pack my things and be on my way. You can well imagine how much work I must do to create a presentation worthy of the Geological Society. I will endeavor to make time for my work with you, but I may not be able to return here until the meeting is over. If it comes to that, I hope you can manage without me."

Freddie reached out to shake Buskin's clammy hand. "Of course, it will be difficult to carry on alone, but I shall strive to do so."

* * *

THE INSTANT the front door closed behind Terrance Buskin, Frederica turned and hurried up the stairway.

On the top step, she remembered that Anthony had returned to his own rooms. The door was ajar, and sunlight from the tall windows slanted out into the corridor. As Freddie paused there and lifted her hand to knock, her heart began to pound in a way she found extremely annoying.

"Is that you, Frederick?" Anthony called from a distance. "I am in my dressing room. Come."

Good God, what if he were in the bath – or worse, strolling around completely naked? Steeling herself, Freddie pushed the door open and headed toward the mahogany-paneled dressing room attached to Anthony's bedchamber. To her relief, she found him standing with Quincy in front of a tall cheval mirror, tying his neckcloth with deft, sun-darkened fingers.

"It's coming back to me," Anthony said dryly. "Have the styles changed in the past five years, Frederick?"

She gulped. "To be perfectly honest, sir, I don't pay much attention to such trivial matters."

"That's right, you are a scholar." He looked amused. "In that case, I shall consult my dashing father ...as soon as I am able to meet with him."

Quincy cleared his throat. "You must engage a proper valet, sir, who will devote himself to your clothes and grooming needs. And, as you have doubtless realized, you'll also need to hire more servants to help Meg and me. It was only possible for us to manage these past years because we were alone in the house."

"I will let you know when it is possible to do so," said Anthony. His gaze moved to rest on Freddie. "What do you think of my transformation?"

"I might not have recognized you, sir," Freddie said, unable to suppress a smile. She was glad to be standing in a shadowed area, where she hoped her thoughts were hidden from view.

Anthony's trim beard had gone, along with the unruliest of his curls. She wanted to stare, to drink in his face and form. Everything about him had changed since their first meeting seven years ago, and yet she now recognized the man who had awakened her deepest longings.

His handsome face was more chiseled now, his once-classic nose bent slightly to the left. How had he broken it? Anthony's black eyes were more guarded, and the charming smiles of his youth were tinged with irony. Although clad in the refined clothing stored in his dressing room, he exuded an air of restrained power. He was taller, his shoulders broader, and Freddie was aware of lean thigh muscles outlined against his kerseymere trousers.

"As soon as I am able to go out, I must visit my tailor," Anthony remarked. "Nothing quite fits any longer." After a slight pause, he added, "One suspects it may be true of life in general."

"Five years is a very long time," Freddie agreed pensively.

"Indeed."

Anthony was watching her, and she had to concentrate to remember who she was supposed to be.

"That will be all, Quincy," he said suddenly. "Professor Loudon and I have business to discuss."

"As you wish, sir."

When the door closed behind the butler, Freddie suddenly felt vulnerable. "I came to tell you what I learned from Terrance Buskin."

Having untied his neckcloth, Anthony started arranging it again, watching the results in the mirror. "And?"

Freddie said gruffly, "He has been invited to speak at the Geological Society's next meeting." Her eyes met Anthony's in the mirror. He stopped tying the neckcloth, waiting until she continued, "Mr. Buskin informs me that he has been making a groundbreaking study of giant tortoises on the Galápagos Islands."

Anthony's eyes were dark flames. "You are roasting me."

She blinked, offended. "By no means, sir! I am merely repeating what Mr. Buskin said to me. He will be devoting himself to his preparations for the next several days, so we may not see him here."

A shadow passed over Anthony's features. "I may be forced to murder him," he muttered, then straightened and gave her a faintly devilish smile. "But enough of that. If you will join me for supper tonight, I will enlighten you further."

Freddie had been about to tell him about the stuffed bird in Buskin's pocket but decided it could wait until supper. "I do have one or two other matters I'd like to discuss. And do you mean that you will tell me what happened to you and where you have been this past year?"

He nodded. With a few deft movements, he finished tying the snowy neckcloth in a style that set off his tanned jaw to perfection, then turned to survey Freddie from head to toe. She prayed she wasn't blushing under his regard.

"Quincy's admonishment that I hire a valet makes me wonder if *you* shouldn't have one as well, Frederick." There was a glint of mischief in his eyes that only increased her feeling of wariness.

"As you have doubtless noticed, I am unencumbered by vanity," Freddie said, and took a step toward the doorway.

"But, my dear professor, you are still a healthy male. Surely you would enjoy a romantic liaison as much as the next fellow. One must use a bit of ingenuity to attract the ladies." He arched a brow. "I perceive that you could do with a proper haircut and some new clothes."

Picking up the scissors he had just used to trim his own locks, Anthony came toward her. "I have hidden talents as a barber. If you will allow me ..." His hand reached toward her hair.

Freddie stepped sideways and put both hands up to her untidy goatshair wig, heart racing. "No! I like my hair just as it is." A feminine note of panic had crept into her voice.

"If you insist. But I also have some clothing for you, a few things that no longer fit me. Your own suit is sadly out of date." His gaze flicked over her. "In fact, if you were an older man, I might suspect you had owned it for at least two decades."

Dear God, Freddie wondered wildly, how could she contrive to get away? If only someone would knock at the door! "You jest, sir, but I did inherit this suit from an uncle. It fits well enough."

"But no, it won't do at all," Anthony countered. Turning, he withdrew a stack of fine linen shirts from a polished shelf. "Here we are. Try one on, just to be certain. I'll be glad to hold your coat."

Freddie felt beads of sweat dampen her false mustache. As Anthony reached to help her out of her coat, she stepped backward, burningly aware of the hidden linen strips that bound her breasts. "Really, I don't need any shirts."

"No?" He inclined his head, devils dancing in his eyes. "What about trousers, then? Several pair are too snug for me, but they're cut far better than the ones you are wearing. Come now, let us see if I am right."

She felt her face growing warmer and warmer. "I would rather not."

"Old fellow, there's no cause for modesty. We're both men after all." He was staring at her in a way that made her blood run cold. "Are we not?"

Freddie stood up straighter. "It's just that ...I am rather set in my ways."

"Ah." In two steps, Anthony closed the distance between them, and she found herself backed up against one of the paneled walls. He reached for one of her hands and lifted it to his nose. "That must explain some of the highly original habits you favor, Frederick —like meadowsweet soap."

As Anthony St. Briac pressed his nose to her soft palm and inhaled, she wished the floor could open and swallow her up.

Still holding fast to her hand, Anthony lifted one brow and queried, "Or should I say ...*Frederica?*"

CHAPTER 9

$\mathcal{A}$nthony savored the moment as Frederica stood
before him, paralyzed, her unforgettable delphinium-blue eyes blazing behind those ridiculous
spectacles. At last, she pulled her hand from his and
turned to flee, but he easily moved to bar the dressing
room doorway.

Shaking his head in mock dismay, he remarked,
"You surprise me, Miss Redfield. I have never taken you
for the sort of female who runs away from conflict."

She straightened defiantly and demanded in her
own voice, "How did you know?"

"You have sadly underestimated my powers of observation. I suspected it was you immediately, and
when I saw the good professor in the morning light, I
was certain. I must tell you, though, that next time you
masquerade as a male, you should not use your favorite
soap."

Frederica bit her lip behind the farcical mustache. "I
am not certain I understand."

"I remember your scent, from our long-ago encounters." He couldn't resist injecting a hint of seduction
into his tone. "Do not say that you have forgotten."

"Sir, I fear your memory is muddled. Perhaps you

have confused me with another of your many female conquests. You and I had no encounters of *that* sort."

Her manner was so stern that he had to laugh. "Do you have any notion how ridiculous you look, delivering that set-down in a false mustache and wig?" Anthony reached out and peeled off the offending mustache which appeared to be made of horsehair. "Where the devil did you get this? And that grotesque wig?"

"Your own mother brought them to me!" Freddie exclaimed. She touched the coarse gray locks that stood out, helter-skelter, from her small head. "This wig is fashioned of goatshair, I believe. Your mother and sister were the architects of my disguise, so you may lodge your complaints with them."

"What were they thinking? They couldn't have imagined that I would be fooled."

"Perhaps you have forgotten, sir, that everyone believes you are lost, which is a gentler way of saying *dead*. No one ever imagined that I would have to fool anyone but Quincy and Meg." Freddie glanced in his cheval mirror, looking slightly offended. "I thought it was quite a convincing disguise. Your friend Terrance Buskin does not seem to question my identity as Professor Loudon."

Anthony snorted. "He is hardly a person of great mental acuity. And cease calling Buskin my *friend*."

"I'll gladly do so if you will let me out of here."

He stood aside and gestured for her to precede him into the bedchamber. "Do me the honor of staying long enough to tell me what the devil this is all about. I understand that you disguised yourself as a man, with the help of my own family, but I must know the reason."

"I would rather not say," she replied stiffly.

"Yet I must insist, Miss Redfield." It was rather disturbing, Anthony thought wryly, to feel twinges of desire toward someone who was gotten up as an ill-favored man. "You have chosen to carry out this charade in my home. Before you take your leave, I deserve an explanation."

He lightly took Frederica by the elbow and led her to the pair of rosewood chairs. With a deep sigh, she sat down in the one nearer the door and watched as he poured canary wine for both of them.

"I suppose you mean to put me out on the street tonight," she said suddenly. Defiance mingled with anxiety in her voice.

He gave her the wine and watched as she sipped. "My dear, if anyone discovers that you are staying in the same house with me, you'll be ruined."

"But I have a chaperone," she said. "Mrs. Bell, my grandfather's housekeeper. Your mother insisted that she accompany me here ...just in case."

Thoroughly confused, Anthony sat down in the other chair. "Start at the beginning and tell me what precipitated this mad scheme." He wanted to demand that she remove the rest of her disguise but realized that the servants still thought she was Professor Frederick Loudon.

"If I am to leave here tonight, I must begin packing immediately. I really don't have time for this conversation."

"You are very difficult!" Anthony scowled. "All right, you shall remain here for one more night, but I hate to think what your father would say if he knew." Drawing a harsh breath, he added, "I will warn you now: Viscount Redfield will not coerce me into a forced marriage!"

Outraged, she cried, "Neither shall I, sir! In fact, as I told you years ago, I will never be coerced into *any* sort of marriage, so you may rest easy." Frederica paused. "In truth, that is how this misadventure began. You see,

I am hiding from Papa. He locked me in my bedroom because I refused to wed Baron Cobleigh—"

"Wait." He held up a hand. "You aren't referring to that old toad who wanted you years ago, before I left with Darwin? I thought he gave up and married someone else."

"You are correct on both counts. Unfortunately, his young wife died along with their baby daughter." Frederica went on to explain how she had gone to live with her grandfather, where she had virtually become his assistant, cataloguing his entire priceless library. "I learned so much during those years! And, as time passed, I assumed I was safely on the shelf, and no other man would care to marry me."

Anthony watched her as she spoke, mentally stripping away her male disguise to discern Frederica's own looks. She had never been a classic beauty, yet there was something about her that had always stirred him in a way he couldn't forget. Still slim as a willow, she held herself erect, her bearing confident. He reckoned Freddie must be five-and-twenty by now, and he found her more appealing than ever. How interesting that she had kept her young vow to remain unmarried.

"A fortnight ago, my dearest Grandpapa died," she was saying.

"I remember Lord Justmore very well, and I am sorry to hear of your loss."

"Thank you. His nephew, Sir Harold Middleton, inherited everything including the Justmore title. Upon his arrival in Grosvenor Square, I was forced to return home."

Anthony's attention was wandering. Before she could continue, he leaned forward in the chair. "You don't really need those spectacles, do you? Take them off."

"What?" Frederica said in surprise.

"Let me see your eyes."

Casting a dubious glance his way, she obeyed.

He flashed a smile. "*That's* why you have been wearing those cursed spectacles. You knew your eyes would betray you." He was charmed to see pink tint her cheekbones. "That color, those lashes ...stunning."

"You, sir, are a rogue. You revealed your true nature to me years ago, when you and your father broke into our home, and you trifled with me in order to gain access to your mother's portrait." She was sitting up very straight again, lips pressed into a disapproving line, breasts rising and falling against the front of her men's waistcoat.

"Trifled?" His lips twitched.

"Indeed." Before he could press her to elaborate, Freddie continued, "We digress. I was telling you about the day I returned home to Redfield House. Papa locked me in my bedchamber, insisting I must agree to wed Lord Cobleigh. I packed a few things and climbed out the window, down a tree—"

Anthony broke in, "Do you mean the same tree I ascended long ago to gain entrance to your father's study?"

"Exactly." She favored him with a bold smile. "The great elm's branches spread over to my bedchamber as well. At any rate, once I had reached the street, I made my way to your grandparents' home in Grosvenor Square."

"Really! And why did you go there?"

"Your mother and sister visited me at Justmore House on the very day I had to leave. They were so kind. I knew they would offer me refuge." Frederica leaned forward and looked into his eyes. "I think I provided a welcome distraction from their sadness about you. As time passed following your disappearance, everyone except Emeline feared the worst."

Anthony's heart clenched. "I must find a way to see them, to let them know. It's just that the situation with Terrance Buskin is serious. I must discover what he is truly up to before I can let anyone know I am alive, here in London." He sighed. "It isn't that I don't trust my family, but if they know, the chances increase that word will slip out."

"I'm certain they would keep your secret!"

"Oh, yes, no doubt. But accidents happen, and the walls have ears in a large house like that." He drank the rest of his wine. "Please, finish your story."

"I was very honest with your family. When I told them about Baron Cobleigh and my father, they determined to help hide me. We realized that I could not stay there, but eventually this plan revealed itself to us. You see, after my years in Grandpapa's magnificent library, I have dreamed of a position at the British Museum. I love to study and organize historical documents and specimens like the ones you have sent back. So, we contrived to create Professor Frederick Loudon."

When he tried to imagine the scene with his entire family, including his beloved Raveneau grandparents, a wave of regret and sadness broke over him. It had been a devil of a year, terrible beyond imagining. Although many of his memories were lost, Anthony couldn't shake the gut feeling that Terrance Buskin was behind all of their suffering, especially his own.

Realizing that Frederica was waiting for him to respond, he said dryly, "Your plan was ingenious, but clearly it did not allow for my return." He watched as her expression became wary. "You must realize you cannot stay here. It is out of the question."

"But why?" Suddenly she came down on one knee beside his chair and reached for one of his hands. "No one has discovered me up to this point. I will continue as Professor Loudon, quietly doing my work in your library. I will never leave the house! You will scarcely know I am here."

"It is impossible. One misstep and your good name would be ruined."

"Dash it, I don't care a fig for my good name!" she cried. "Kindly listen now. I am now the only person who knows you are alive and back in London. If you mean to remain hidden, undetected by Mr. Buskin, I can investigate on your behalf! In my disguise as Professor Loudon, I will attend Buskin's presentation at the Geological Society, thus protecting you from discovery while you assemble your evidence against him. You must agree, it is a perfect solution for both of us!"

He blinked, tempted, but slowly shook his head. "There are other people I trust who can watch Buskin and find out what he is up to."

"None of them are acquainted with this situation in the way I am." Frederica paused, eyes widening. "I have not had a chance to tell you this, but Terrance Buskin stole one of your stuffed Ecuadorean finches today! He was examining it, and when he thought I wasn't looking, he put it in his coat pocket. I asked him plainly if he had taken it, but he assured me that the finch belonged to him." She gave a little snort. "As if he were in the habit of carrying them about in his pocket!"

As Anthony listened to her, anger mounting, he felt the first flashes of a headache. The spears of pain had plagued him since his accident, especially when memories began to circle and sting his mind. *Damn Terrance Buskin.*

He realized that Frederica was still speaking. "You see, no one else would perceive the meaning of his activities better than I."

Rubbing one temple, Anthony said, "Buskin's theft of my finch does not surprise me. He would stop at nothing to usurp my discoveries, especially now that he believes I am well out of the way." He saw that she was holding her breath in anticipation and gave a quick shake of his head. "However, your well-being is a different matter. My dear Miss Redfield, you claim not to care about your reputation, but time will doubtless change your mind. I think you do not understand the problems you would create for yourself if you were discovered here."

Frederica narrowed her eyes. "You speak as if your only concern is for me, but I suspect you have a more personal reason for sending me away." Rising partway, she pointed at him. "You doubtless think that my presence would put a damper on your evening *activities*, which you are eager to resume. I suppose there are many beautiful Incognitas who would come here for a price, and the last thing you would want is a dull professor hanging about."

Anthony wanted to laugh. "How do you know the word *Incognita*?"

"It refers to a refined prostitute, does it not? Just because I have no such experience of my own, that does not mean I am a green girl who is easily shocked, sir." She wrinkled her nose as if detecting an offensive smell. "I can assure you that I will stay well out of the way when you have *guests*. I shall sleep on a cot in Mrs. Bell's room."

"You are very good at making plans," he observed, torn between exasperation and amusement. "Let us proceed hour by hour, shall we? You may remain here tonight, and tomorrow we will revisit this conversation."

"All right. I suppose that is fair enough."

"Thank you," he said dryly.

"And now that I have bared my secrets, it is your turn, sir. You promised to tell me what happened and where you have been since you were reported to be lost and quite probably dead."

Anthony was enchanted by her forthright personality. He wanted to catch her hand and draw her onto his lap, despite her goatshair wig and trousers, but of course that wouldn't do. Instead, he met her gaze and smiled in a way that had undone countless females.

"Miss Redfield, I seem to recall a time when you said we should dispense with the formalities and address one another by our Christian names." He paused before adding, "I believe it was in Hyde Park. You had sent your groom back to fetch your riding crop so that we could be alone."

He was pleased to see her flush. "That was long ago, before I discovered your character flaws."

Anthony splayed a hand over his heart. "You wound me …Frederica."

"If you think I can be so easily distracted, you are mistaken." Her voice rose as she continued, "You said that you would enlighten me, and I am very anxious to hear every word!"

Before he could reply, a knock came on the bedchamber door and Anthony heard a shockingly familiar female voice call out to Frederica.

"My dear Freddie, I hope you don't mind. I have come to surprise you!" the visitor exclaimed from the other side of the paneled door. "I had to tell you about my momentous decision!"

In the next instant, the door swung open, and Anthony's little sister, Emeline, burst into the bedchamber.

CHAPTER 10

Glimpsing Emeline from his rosewood chair, just beyond the place where Freddie sat, Anthony felt a powerful jolt of emotion. There had been many times over the past year when he'd thought he might never see her again, never tease her, embrace her, offer her unsolicited advice as she grew older. And now, in typical Emmie fashion, she had arrived back in his life unannounced.

Frederica jumped up. If she meant to hide, it was too late. In that moment, her form blocked Anthony's chair from Emeline's sight.

"I simply couldn't wait another moment," Emmie declared, breaking off as she stared at Frederica in surprise. "Why, you have lost your lovely mustache. You look positively naked. Do put it back."

Anthony saw Frederica reach furtively back toward him, so he brought the furry thing out of his pocket and slipped it into her hand. A moment later, her mustache was back in place.

"Is that better?" Freddie said.

"Barely. It is quite askew!" Emmie scolded fondly.

In the next moment, his sister was coming toward them, clearly intent on setting her friend's costume to rights. Anthony made a futile effort to become smaller in the fragile rosewood chair. The very air seemed to change at the moment she saw him. Wincing, Anthony glanced up and saw that Emeline had gone white. Raw shock and disbelief transformed her lovely face.

"No!" she gasped even as Frederica moved away from them.

He started to rise, but his sister quickly flung herself onto his lap, embracing him and weeping. For long moments, she could not speak, so Anthony held her close, marveling at how much she had changed since the day he'd sailed away on board the *Beagle*.

"Don't cry," he murmured, patting her ebony curls as he had done so often when she was a little girl. "I've come back. Is that cause for tears?"

Emmie clung to him tighter, burying her face in his neck. "I dreamed once that you were alive, that you came home, and I threw myself into your embrace and felt the warmth of your neck. But when I awoke, you were gone."

He tightened his arms about her slim form. "I promise you, this time I am quite real."

"I have known all along," she asserted, drawing back at last to gaze at his face, tracing its contours with damp fingers. "I alone believed."

"I appreciate that," Anthony said with irony. "Look at you. When I left you were still a little girl, but now you are very nearly ..."

"A woman," she agreed proudly. "Behold!"

He laughed as she straightened and swept a hand downward to indicate the curves outlined by her pretty blue gown. "I already have many would-be suitors, but of course Papa cannot know. He would want to kill them all."

"You are a beauty. I don't doubt that you're a great social success."

Emeline wrinkled her nose. "I don't care a button for any of that. It is all very silly, and I have more important things to do."

Anthony set her on her feet and stood. "Indeed. I perceive you are the mastermind behind Miss Redfield's plot?"

The two females exchanged conspiratorial glances and laughed. "One of them," Emmie allowed.

"Your brother means to put an end to Professor Loudon," said Frederica.

"I don't doubt it. I shall argue for clemency, but first you must tell me everything. Anthony, when did you return? How did you discover Freddie? And, most importantly, what happened to you and where have you been?"

He couldn't help thinking, if only for a moment, that life had been easier to manage when he was all alone on the other side of the world. But then his heart seemed to crack open, unbidden, and he smiled at his little sister.

Before he could attempt to reply to the torrent of questions, Frederica suggested, "Let us sit down together and call for some refreshment." She led the way to the small inlaid table near the window and gestured for each of them to take a chair before ringing for Meg. Then, looking at Emeline, she added, "Before we forget, the servants still don't know my true identity. Your brother only arrived very late last night, so it's all been a bit chaotic."

"Indeed," Anthony confirmed. "Miss Redfield tried to shoot me."

Frederica sent him a dark look. "I assumed you were an intruder. You certainly resembled one!" Turning to the amazed Emeline, she added, "Your brother was unshaven, his hair wild and long, and he looked immensely dangerous."

Emeline glanced curiously between them. "How thrilling! I assume Freddie was not successful in shooting you."

"Not in the least," he said mildly. "Of course, you must remember that I thought she was a man, so I showed admirable restraint, I believe." Anthony went on to tell his sister what had transpired since the episode with the pistol. "Because Miss Redfield and I had been …acquainted several years ago, I soon suspected her true identity."

The girl nodded. "Oh yes. I never would have attempted to fool *you* with the Professor Loudon disguise."

"Thank you. I am relieved to hear it."

"Oh, Anthony, I am so excited for you to come home and show Mama and Papa and all the family that you are *alive!* In fact, I feel quite guilty to be sitting here chatting when they are still grief-stricken. Why didn't you come home this morning to reunite with all of us?"

"In truth, as much as I want to be with my family, I cannot tell them yet that I am here. I think I know who is responsible for my near death and the ensuing year lost from my life, but if I am to entrap the villain, he cannot know I am alive." Anthony wasn't ready to say Buskin's name aloud to anyone but Frederica.

Emeline stared at him. "I can understand your plan, but you must tell our family you are alive. They have all suffered too much already!" She stood up. "Let us go now. I don't care for any refreshments, and I could not sit still another moment when I imagine our parents only a short distance away, in ignorance of the truth."

"Emmie …" For the past year, he had been razor-focused on finding the person behind his terrible ordeal. Now, when it seemed that vengeance was at hand, Anthony could not afford to take any chances. "I cannot tell them yet. Trust me."

"Truly, you have no choice." Emeline started toward the door. "Papa is about to travel to the Galápagos Islands to search for you himself!"

Anthony could only blink in disbelief.

"He has wanted to go ever since we learned you were missing," his sister continued, her hand on the doorknob. "But he and Mama hoped Mr. Darwin would bring good news. Now Papa insists that if you are out there, somewhere, he will find you."

Emmie was gazing back at him just the way their mother did when she wanted him to surrender to her wishes. "All right!" Anthony put his hands in the air, palms up. "I will see them, but first I must think of a way to do so completely in secret …"

* * *

THAT NIGHT, thick clouds blanketed the moon and stars, and fog swirled in from the Thames, creating a perfect backdrop for intrigue. Anthony stood in the shadowed mews behind his home and waited to hear the sound of carriage wheels on the cobbles. He wore a greatcoat and an Aylesbury hat with the brim pulled low.

"I think I should stay behind," came Frederica's soft voice near his shoulder. "I will be intruding on an emotional family scene."

Anthony glanced over, marveling anew at how unrecognizable she was in her mustache and spectacles, tall beaver hat, and flawlessly arranged neckcloth. "I thought you might be past all that, having already interrupted a Raveneau family game of loo. When you said they not only didn't mind your intrusion but invited you up to join them, I knew you would be welcome tonight." Anthony could not read her expression in the darkness. "Besides, I dread telling this story, and I only want to recite it once."

She was watching him as he spoke. "All right, then. If you insist."

At that moment, Anthony heard hoofbeats and turned his head to watch for his parents' familiar green landau. Instead, he saw a fine black town coach, pulled by four handsome chestnuts, rounding the corner. It was Emeline who peeped out the window and ordered in a conspiratorial tone, "Get in!"

As much as he wanted to be with his family again, Anthony flinched from the intense scene ahead. He would never admit it, but one of the reasons he wanted Frederica there was to cushion him from his parents' strong emotions.

And, quite possibly, his own.

A footman appeared to let down the steps and open the door for Anthony and Frederica. His heart seemed to stop as he followed her into the darkened interior of the coach. They took seats next to Emeline and, as the door shut and the horses started forward, Anthony forced himself to look into the stunned faces of his parents.

"As you asked," Emeline said, "I have told them only who would be joining us tonight. Nothing else."

The enclosed space heightened all his senses. Their mingled scents were keenly familiar, and even the sound of his mother's breathing recalled memories older than his comprehension.

"My beautiful boy," Mama whispered brokenly. Her eyes filled with tears as she stretched out both hands to him. "Emmie told us we would see you, but it still doesn't feel real."

His father was nodding with an expression bordering on disbelief. When he spoke, there was a catch in his voice. "I was only one day away from sailing to the Galápagos myself. I had to know, one way or the other, if you might still be alive."

"I know, Papa. That is why I agreed to show myself to you." Anthony released one of his mother's gloveless hands and reached out to touch her cheek, wiping away a tear with the edge of his thumb. "How have all of you been? I received a few letters while on board the Beagle, but of course nothing for this past year. What of my brother Charles?" he asked, referring to his older half-brother, born to Mouette and Sir Harry. "Is he still studying architecture in Italy?"

His father looked tense. "Your family are much better now that we know you are alive. Yes, Charles is living in Rome and studying classic architecture." He leaned forward. "But tonight, it is your story we want to hear."

Pain radiated from the center of Anthony's chest. He could see that Mama yearned to embrace him, but the jostling motion of the cramped coach made it impossible for him to rise and take her in his arms.

Looking between his parents, he said, "I thought this moment might never come."

"Oh, my dear," his mother said, "how you have changed. I'm not certain I would have recognized you on the street." No sooner had his mother spoken the words, than he saw that she wanted to take them back.

"Changed? In what way?"

"I think you are …much harder." She sighed and gave her head a little shake. "But pay no attention to me. No doubt these past five years have changed all of us."

"Especially me," Emeline chimed in. "I have grown so much! And now we are eager to hear your story. Freddie included no doubt!"

Beside him, he felt Frederica's nod. As the coach slowly traversed the winding, lamp-lit streets bordering St. James and Piccadilly, its interior seemed to shrink. There was no handle on the inside of the door, no possible escape for Anthony. Pain flashed a warning in his head.

"Indeed," he said. "Since all of you arranged for Miss Redfield to adopt this disguise and live in my house, I have promised her a full explanation of my whereabouts. That is why she is here tonight. Quite honestly, I couldn't bear to go over the events of the past year more than once."

"Oh, my son," Mama whispered brokenly.

"*Eh bien*," said Papa. "We are all listening. Kindly begin at the beginning. We have heard from Darwin and the others what events led up to the day you went missing. What exactly happened?"

Anthony nodded. For the thousandth time, he reviewed the events of that terrible day and then spoke of them aloud: the Galápagos tortoises who were heading inland for water, the notes he took while gathering more samples, and the annoying presence of Terrance Buskin.

"When we came upon the tortoises looking down from a precipice to what appeared to be a spring below, I decided to climb down to sample it for myself." With an effort, Anthony kept his voice even. "Every other body of water we had found turned out to be salty, so this was potentially an important discovery. I descended an embankment, more dangerous than it looked from above. At one point, the rocky ledge I was holding onto simply crumbled away in my hand. I fell back and downward, and I believe I struck my head. That is my last memory for some time."

Anthony felt the force of his mother's gasp. The air inside the coach seemed to thicken, and for an instant he couldn't breathe. Next to him, Emeline held fast to his arm.

His father spoke next. "Terrance Buskin and Charles Darwin both came to us recently, after the return of the *Beagle*. Buskin said you two were separated and claims he didn't realize you were truly missing until much later that day. The entire crew searched the island, we were told, by torchlight for most of the night. They found no trace of you, and everyone agreed that you must have fallen from a cliff into the ocean."

Anthony pressed his fingertips to the side of his head. Was it possible that his disjointed memories of that day were faulty?

"No. Buskin should have told them! He was standing there, holding my notebook, when I began to climb down. He knew perfectly well I wasn't on any damned oceanside cliff!" As he spoke, Anthony felt a flicker of doubt. Hadn't Buskin still been there?

"What happened next?" His father leaned forward, one brow arched above his silk eyepatch. "After you fell."

"I don't know." Anthony clenched his jaw. "I don't *know!*"

Frederica was watching him. He was calmed by her presence, despite the disguise. She said, "Perhaps if you simply tell us what you do remember, that will help your memories to come together."

"Yes," agreed his mother. "We shall not interrupt you."

Anthony drew a breath, resolving to face this challenge one minute at a time. "I awoke a day or two later. I was lying on a filthy, stinking mat in a very rough dwelling. I later understood that it was on the highest point of James Island, constructed by the Spaniards who'd been sent from Charles Island to dry fish and salt tortoise meat." He paused, loathe to relive that time when he had been convinced he was dying. "For days, I awoke only intermittently. I didn't know who I was or what had happened to me. The two men who slept there spoke only Spanish, but I knew enough from my months in South America to communicate with them. Eventually I realized I was not going to die. They told me they had come upon me floating in the spring, my head against the rocky edge, which apparently spared me from drowning. I rather suspect that they made the effort to recover my body because they thought I was dead and possessed something of value. I'm not certain how the devil they managed to get me out of there—using a sling of some sort, I believe."

"Thank heaven they did!" cried Emeline. "Did you have other injuries?"

"My right ankle was badly swollen. A fracture, I think. I was able to wrap it tightly, and after a few weeks, I could bear weight on it. It is much better now." Anthony then touched the side of his head. "However, I continue to be plagued at times by headaches."

His father looked grim. "The hovel where they took you must have been far enough inland that Darwin and the others didn't reach there in the course of their search. What happened next? How long were you there?"

"I couldn't say. Months, I suppose. I lived on little else besides dried fish." Seeing his mother's stricken face, Anthony decided to omit the worst of his ordeal. "Eventually, most of my memory returned and I grew stronger. I discovered that we were the only people on the island, and I made a camp near the beach and waited for rescue. Of course, there is very little shipping traffic in the Galápagos. After a fortnight, I heard from the Spaniards that a whaling ship was anchored off-shore, and I rowed out and begged to join them. Since I had no money, I had to earn my passage."

"Oh, Anthony!" exclaimed his mother. "And you were still suffering from your injuries!"

He shrugged and patted her hand. "Fortunately, I was strong and healthy before the accident. I left the ship in Concepcion, Chile, which had been decimated by an earthquake the year before. I had made a …friend there during the *Beagle*'s previous visit, and so I remained for some weeks." For reasons he couldn't explain, Anthony did not want to mention in front of Frederica that his "friend" was a beautiful artist. Valeria had offered comfort and care at a time when he badly needed it. "When I was in Concepcion, I sent a letter to you in Cornwall, but I now realize you never received it."

Both parents were shaking their heads. "I know from experience that many letters go astray when ships are carrying them," said his father.

Next to him, Frederica spoke up. "How in the world did you get from Chile back to England?"

He gave her a rueful smile. "Every ship I encountered was headed in the other direction, toward Australia. Eventually, I decided to travel by land to Brazil. I joined a group of men bound for Botafogo, a bayside hamlet near Rio de Janerio where the *Beagle* had anchored early in our voyage. A few weeks ago, I finally found a trading ship that brought me home to England."

"You make it sound much simpler than it was, no doubt," said his father.

"In truth, I would like to forget everything that happened after my accident." Leaning back against the leather squabs, he drew a deep breath, relieved that this interview was over. "You all deserved to know how I was lost and where I have been. I have told you as much as I care to."

Laughter drifted to them from outside the clubs of St. James, and Anthony felt an odd pang. Once, he had been among the carefree young men who aspired to be libertines and dandies, but those times now felt very distant. What sort of life lay ahead for him?

Frederica broke the silence. "As I understand it, you believe that Terrance Buskin was somehow responsible for your accident."

He shrugged. "I don't think he caused it, but my memory is that he was there, watching, when I fell. His actions since then are highly suspect, and now he appears to be stealing my discoveries." Anthony saw that his father was nodding agreement in the shadows. "That's why he can't know I am alive. Miss Redfield formed an acquaintance with him during her masquerade in my home." Pausing he flicked up a brow at his family, the co-conspirators. "She wishes to remain there—"

Frederica interjected, "Yes! I will help to entrap Terrance Buskin in a way no one else possibly can."

"If Miss Redfield is discovered, living in my home, she would be ruined," Anthony continued. "I am naturally hesitant to take this risk, but she insists ...and perhaps this is a special situation."

"On both sides," agreed his father. "You two will aid one another."

"Exactly so." With that, Anthony looked over and saw that Frederica's blue eyes were hopeful behind her spectacles. He allowed a smile to play about his mouth. "All right then, I surrender, Miss Redfield. You may stay ...for now, at least."

CHAPTER 11

*W*hen Frederica opened her eyes the next morning, a wave of euphoria swept over her. Last night's chilly mist had given way to bright sunshine and, outside her window, the trees in Anthony's back garden were turning saffron, orange, and gold. Chiffchaffs and warblers hopped from branch to branch, seemingly delighted by the brilliant blue skies.

Freddie threw back her covers and went to the window, smiling at the little birds. For the first time since Grandpapa's death, her spirits soared. Not only had Anthony agreed that she might remain here, but she also felt free to remove her disguise in the privacy of her bedroom. Now that Anthony knew her true identity, he had instructed the servants that only Mrs. Bell would attend to Professor Loudon's needs.

What a treat it was to rise and remain in her high-necked, snowy nightgown, to leave her hair in a long braid down her back, to begin unpacking in the blue bedroom as if she intended to stay there indefinitely. She resolved to make it her own private sanctuary.

Of course, Freddie had very little to unpack—only the few garments she had hastily taken during her escape from Papa's house. The rest were men's clothing, chosen by Mouette and Devon for Professor Frederick Loudon.

Looking inside the battered portmanteau she had tossed down from her Redfield House window, Freddie saw treasured books. Two had been gifts from her grandfather: *Principles of Geology* by Charles Lyell and *Views of Nature* by Alexander von Humboldt. The third, still concealed in the folds of a chemise, was *The Wicked Highwayman*. During her years with Grandpapa at Justmore House, the novel had been her one guilty taste of romance. She now glanced down at the worn volume and thought of all the hours of fantasy she had enjoyed in its pages. Her lips curved in a mischievous smile.

Leaving *The Wicked Highwayman* in its hiding place, she removed the other two and held them in her slim hands.

Her reverie was broken by a knock at the door. Expecting Mrs. Bell, who brought her breakfast tray each morning at just this time, Frederica called, "Come in."

The door opened a few inches. "Good morning. I brought you some items you may need."

Shocked, Frederica looked up and beheld Anthony St. Briac peeking into her bedroom. Overnight, his rakish good looks seemed to have become even more potent.

"Oh!" She held the books to her bodice as if to conceal it from his view. "I thought you were Mrs. Bell. I am not presentable yet." She looked around. "I should at least don a wrapper."

"Nonsense," he scoffed lightly. "You are covered from chin to toes by that voluminous garment."

Freddie glanced down and saw that he was right, yet she was also very conscious that she wore nothing at all underneath her nightgown. His very nearness caused her nipples to pucker against the soft cambric fabric, and she instinctively pressed the books closer. Realizing what was happening, Frederica reminded herself, she was no green girl, but five-and-twenty years of age. Furthermore, she had no use for the endless unwritten rules that governed a female's behavior!

"You are quite right, sir," she replied. "Come in."

Anthony did have the good grace to leave the door ajar as he entered. She was amazed to see him looking so refreshed, eyes alert and black hair appealingly disheveled. He wore some of the clothing she had seen in his dressing room before his return: snug buff trousers, a charcoal striped waistcoat over a shirt set off by a deftly tied, starched neckcloth.

"How civilized you have become," she observed with an irrepressible smile.

"I can assure you, Frederica, that beneath this veneer of respectability, I remain the same disreputable scoundrel you recently threatened in the library."

Something in his tone sent a delicious chill down her spine. Just hearing him call her by her Christian name added to the feeling that they were engaging in forbidden behavior.

"I have no doubt of that," she replied. "Indeed, I have heard that many rakes are experts at tying a neckcloth."

"Have you?" Drawing near, he glanced down at the snowy folds of his own cravat. "In truth, I was not certain it would come back to me after five years spent exploring distant jungles and oceans." Before she could reply, Anthony brought something out from behind his back. "I believe you left these behind in my dressing room?"

Freddie wrinkled her nose when she saw that he was holding curling papers and a familiar porcelain jar of pomade. "Your mama gave me those. She thought they might help Professor Loudon to tame his unruly locks."

"If my hair resembled that wig, I would use them

too." Devils danced in his dark eyes. "No doubt you will need these the next time you are in disguise."

"Well, perhaps." She had to set down the books in order to accept the pomade and curling papers, and as soon as she did, Anthony claimed one of the volumes and scrutinized the gold-embossed cover.

"Charles Lyell!" he exclaimed softly. "Darwin and I both obtained copies of this book shortly before the *Beagle* set sail. It is a masterpiece. How did you come to have a copy?"

"Have I not told you that I have a longstanding interest in the natural sciences? I read Lyell's book more than once while I was living at Justmore House, and Grandpapa made a gift of it to me. When I fled my father's home, I could only bring this small portmanteau, but I made space for these two cherished volumes."

She could feel him watching her closely, taking in every word. "I would be very interested to hear your views about both these books, and I would be glad to show you my own collection. I possess everything Alexander von Humboldt has ever written."

"I have been able to admire your library," Frederica replied. "It is remarkable for a man as young as you were before you set off on the *Beagle*."

"Yes ..." He opened her copy of Lyell's book and smiled at the sight of the little notes she had inserted between the well-worn pages. "I forget that you have been rattling around my house unattended and even slept in my bed."

Freddie felt her face grow warm. Suddenly she was keenly aware that she bore no traces of her alter-identity this morning. No wig and mustache, no waistcoat and trousers, no strips of linen flattening her breasts. They were alone together, looking at one another as they had years ago, when he had made her feel alive in ways that she could never quite forget.

"I can assure you, I treated your possessions with the utmost respect," she said softly.

He gave a wry nod. "Since you believed me to be dead, I would expect nothing less. I hope you don't mind terribly that I have returned from the grave."

The air around them seemed to pulsate. Freddie couldn't put her finger on what was happening, but she suspected Anthony of casting some sort of rake's spell on her. No doubt he did this regularly, so he didn't even have to think about it. Her heartbeat accelerated. When, for an instant, his gaze dropped to her mouth, heat throbbed at her very core.

Those intimate stirrings were quickly replaced by a stab of panic. If she allowed herself to succumb like a moth to the flame, all would be lost. Freddie's very future depended on remaining in this house, safe from her father and his dire, determined plans for her.

Anthony reached out and grazed her cheek with one dark finger. "Why such a worried face?"

Just then, a voice called from the corridor, "Good morning!"

There was Mrs. Bell, her lace cap slightly askew as she pushed the door further open with one hip and entered carrying a breakfast tray. She stopped short at the sight of Anthony. In a moment, he had taken the tray and was setting it on a table near the window.

"Ah," he told Frederica approvingly, "they've given you brioche. It's a recipe from our family steward, Baptiste. How I missed his pastries during my years away from England."

Before she could reply, Mrs. Bell spoke sternly. "Sir, I must request that you leave now. I am here to guard my lady's reputation, and you should not be in this room, especially with her in this state of undress."

Anthony flashed a smile guaranteed to melt the resistance of harder women than Mrs. Bell, but she did not appear to soften in the least. "Thank you for your words of advice, ma'am," he said.

"I have known my mistress all her life. She may be grown now, but that changes nothing as far as I am concerned."

"Very admirable," Anthony agreed soberly. To Frederica, he added, "I look forward to seeing you later, in the library, when you see fit to join me …to continue cataloguing my specimens, of course."

She could only nod, rendered speechless by the scene she'd just witnessed. When Anthony was gone, Freddie turned to Mrs. Bell.

"How bold you were! One hopes Mr. St. Briac will not take offense and turn us out into the street."

"Nonsense!" Color stained the housekeeper's apple cheeks. "I need not curtsy to that rogue! St. Briac is not *my* master. I am here for one reason only, to look after my mistress. I will not abandon you to the likes of him!"

Pulling apart the warm brioche, Freddie spread jam on a piece and smiled. "I can look after myself with that man."

"Can you?" Mrs. Bell snorted. "Anyone can see that you fancy him just by looking at your pretty, blushing face."

"I certainly do not fancy him!" she protested. "But I will remember your observation in future and be sure to wear my full disguise in Mr. St. Briac's presence."

* * *

IN THE DAYS THAT FOLLOWED, Anthony grew increasingly restless to escape the confines of his own home. The greater his temptation to get closer to Frederica Redfield, the more he wanted to put distance between them, yet he could only blame himself for the plan to keep his presence in London a secret. Returning to his old haunts, where he might find distraction in gaming, drink, and the company of willing females, was not possible.

Not yet at least, Anthony thought with a sigh.

"Oh, look at this!" exclaimed Frederica as she used a crowbar to pry open yet another crate.

They were together again in the library where the two of them spent most of each day unpacking the containers Anthony had sent home over the past years. He vividly remembered writing each label himself.

Frederica, clad in her disguise which seemed more ridiculous to him with each passing day, stood at the table they had recently positioned beside his desk. She had just unwrapped a small, fossilized jawbone and now held it up to the light for him to see. "The label says *Monte Hermosa – Cavia*. What does it mean?"

He rose from the desk and joined her. "Farola Monte Hermoso is in Argentina, south of Punta Alta, in the bay of Bahia Blanca. We went ashore there four years ago and discovered a trove of fossils in the low cliffs above the beach. While we were camped there, a ferocious storm struck, and there were moments when it seemed we might not survive."

"Oh, my!" She gazed at him, her mustache slightly askew as usual. Anthony reached out to straighten it. For an instant, his fingertip grazed the edge of her upper lip, and she glanced away, blushing slightly. "It seems you faced many threats to your life."

He shrugged and picked up the hard, dark-red fossil. "I think this may in fact be an ancient relative of the little tuco-tuco, a rather sweet burrowing rodent. We kept a few as pets on board the *Beagle*."

Just then, a knock sounded at the front door. Anthony had devised a plan with the servants, whereby they would ask any callers to wait in the entry while they checked to see if Professor Loudon was available. Anthony would then have enough time to slip out of the library and up the stairs. If the caller happened to be Viscount Redfield, whom Frederica feared might track her down, they were instructed to say that no one was home

Meg hurried past them toward the front door, and Anthony straightened, listening. When he heard a man's muffled voice his senses sharpened.

"I think it is Terrance," whispered Frederica. "What if—"

As Anthony heard Meg speaking, he started toward the door, planning to quickly turn a corner and be on the stairs.

"No, no!" Buskin was speaking in jovial tones, followed by the sound of footsteps. "Do not trouble yourself. I need no introduction."

Turning back, Anthony saw Frederica pointing rather wildly toward the desk. She quickly sat in the chair and gestured for him to crouch down in the small open space in front of her. It seemed he had no choice but to obey. He had just squeezed himself into the opening where Frederica's legs were meant to go when they heard Terrance Buskin entering the library.

"Ah, my dear professor ..." Buskin's voice drifted closer until Anthony sensed he was standing close enough to the desk to hear his rather heavy breathing. "Here you are, in the same spot where you and I have enjoyed so many long days of scientific study."

"What an unexpected surprise it is to see you today," said Frederica in her gruff professor voice.

Anthony's awkward position became more problematic with each passing minute, for there was not enough space for both his tall, powerful body and her long, slim legs. When Frederica tried to free her left knee, so it wasn't pinned by his shoulder, he suddenly found her legs on either side of his crouching form. There was no place to put his head except between her trouser-clad thighs. Above him, Frederica was still speaking to Terrance Buskin.

"Won't you take a chair, sir? I would rise to shake your hand, but I have injured my …" She coughed. "…foot."

If the situation hadn't been so fraught with peril, Anthony would have laughed.

"Indeed?" Buskin sounded extremely concerned. "How did that happen?"

"I, uh, accidentally dropped the crowbar on my toes."

Anthony was finding it increasingly difficult to breathe. In an effort to expand his chest even slightly, he turned his head to the left and found his cheek resting on Frederica's warm right thigh. He inhaled her subtle meadowsweet essence. Inches away in the shadows he glimpsed the most intimate part of her body, hidden behind her snug trousers. For a long moment, Anthony could only stare. If she were going to be completely convincing as a male, she should wear something to fill out that area. A rolled-up stocking might do. In the meantime, he found himself imagining what was under the kerseymere fabric, and as he did so, his heartbeat accelerated and his cock stiffened, aching. There wasn't even space to reach down and readjust himself.

As if she felt something as well, Frederica squirmed in her chair. Anthony felt a bit desperate as he tried to remove his head, but there was no place else to put it. The rest of the tiny space under the desk was filled with his crouching body and Frederica's lovely legs.

If he didn't know better, he would swear that he could feel heat emanating from her body. A devil's voice urged Anthony to nibble slightly at the inseam of her trousers, but somehow his better self prevailed.

"Perhaps I should examine your foot, professor," Terrance Buskin suggested in solicitous tones. "My father was a physician, so I fancy that I have some medical experience."

"Oh, no, that won't be necessary," Frederica replied quickly. "But do sit down and tell me what prompted this visit."

"I have brought your invitation," he announced dramatically. "My presentation will be at the Geological Society's next meeting at Somerset House."

Anthony closed his eyes in an effort to shut out the proximity of Frederica's nether regions, to stop himself from thinking about what he would really like to do between her shapely thighs. *Scoundrel! You haven't even kissed her*, he reminded himself sternly.

"It promises to be a monumental afternoon," Buskin was droning. "Nearly every member of the Geological Society will be in attendance. Even Charles Darwin himself has promised to come. Of course, that will be a great honor for me since he has become quite famous since returning to England."

"Ah, Darwin, how interesting," Frederica said, "But no silly females I hope?"

"No, no!" He sounded shocked. "Society rules preclude females setting foot inside the premises."

"Excellent," barked Frederica in her best professorial voice. "In that case, I will be honored to attend. Thank you so much for stopping by."

In the background, Anthony heard Meg pipe up, "I'll show you out, sir."

Long moments ticked by as Buskin took his leave and then, abruptly, Frederica pushed back her chair and rose. Anthony was dislodged from her lap, and when he looked up, he saw that she had pressed both hands to her rosy cheeks.

"You!" she cried. "How dare you?"

Surprised by this irrational outburst, Anthony unhurriedly clambered out from under the desk and dusted off his trousers as he rose to his full height. "You know perfectly well that I had no space to move, no choice about anything that happened once you forced me into that cramped hiding place."

"But you …" Looking confused, shook her head. "It was …indecent."

"Was it?" Anthony bit back a grin. *Aha, so she felt it too!* Slowly, he studied a speck of lint on his coat sleeve, brows aloft. "If you were more experienced, my dear, you would realize that I exhibited great restraint."

Frederica gasped, but before she could reply, Meg reappeared in the doorway. They both turned and saw that she was staring in surprise, mouth ajar. In the next moment, the girl tried to smile.

"Oh, pardon me …I thought I just heard a woman's voice."

Frederica transformed back into Professor Loudon before Anthony's amused eyes. "A woman, you say? No, no, not a bit!"

Meg nodded uncertainly, backed out of the room, and disappeared from sight.

"Disaster narrowly averted!" Pressing one hand to her heart as if to calm its frantic pace, Frederica whispered, "We forgot ourselves completely. Not that Meg is any threat to our plans. She is quite devoted to me." With a wan smile, she added, "To the professor, I mean."

Anthony glanced heavenward and muttered, "By Lucifer, I hope you are right."

CHAPTER 12

*A*s soon as possible, Frederica made an excuse and fled to her bedchamber. Closing the door, she leaned back against its paneled surface and struggled to contain her confusing emotions. Her senses swam. Her breasts ached under their linen bindings, not in pain, but with a need that traveled downward to her most intimate places. Heart racing, Freddie slipped one hand into her trousers and tentatively touched herself among the soft curls at the apex of her thighs.

She was wet, swollen, pulsing ...yearning. Oh, if only she could find a way to close off this part of herself that was so responsive to even a smile or a glance from Anthony St. Briac. It had ever been thus, Freddie reflected, from the very moment he had swept her into a waltz at the Countess of Penhurst's ball, seven long years ago.

She squeezed her eyes shut, imagining that he was holding her in his arms again, but in a different way. The urge to press herself against his hard body, to at last feel his knowing touch, his *kiss,* was almost more than she could bear.

Her mind forced its way back to those early weeks of their acquaintance when she had felt herself falling in love with Anthony. How many nights had she lain awake, filled with innocent dreams of kisses and romantic promises. When it was finally revealed that Anthony's attentions were prompted not by feelings for Freddie but, instead, by a scheme to recover the painting of Mouette, hidden in her father's study, Freddie had known a crushing sense of disillusionment.

And yet here she was again, lusting after an older, harder, even more irresistible version of Anthony St. Briac! Had she learned nothing from the past? In truth, Freddie was angrier with herself than him. She well knew the risks—yet today in the library, when he had been crouching under the desk, his face against her thigh, she had known a wild desire to sink her hands into his thick, glossy hair and press him to her sex, to let him strip away her men's trousers and show her all that she had been missing.

All these vivid thoughts brought such a surge of arousal that Freddie unbuttoned her trousers and sought the pulsing source of her need, touching herself rhythmically, panting softly in the stillness of her room. How much simpler life had seemed before, when she lived an isolated life and the man who stirred her thus had been a fictional highwayman! Freddie could put him away each time she closed the book, but that was impossible with Anthony.

Anthony! Blinking back tears, Freddie found release at last ...but true satisfaction eluded her.

* * *

ON THE MORNING of Terrance Buskin's presentation at Somerset House, Frederica was standing at the mirror in her bedchamber fussing with her neckcloth when a voice spoke from the doorway.

"Do you have a moment?"

Her heart skipped a beat. She and Anthony had worked together in the library, but sometimes he would lose himself for hours in his fossils, examining every detail with a magnifying glass, and studying old notes before making new ones. Once, his sister had slipped in the servant's entrance and the two of them put their heads together all afternoon, talking and sketching. Before Emeline left, she announced that their father planned to escort "Professor Loudon" to the presentation at Somerset House. This prospect was reassuring yet slightly intimidating to Freddie, for Justin St. Briac seemed bigger than life.

Turning toward Anthony, Frederica smiled. "Yes, please, do come in."

As much as she had tried all week to maintain a safe distance from Anthony, she was very glad to see him today. After all, the plan to entrap Buskin had been a joint endeavor, and she wanted his guidance for the day ahead. In many ways, Freddie was merely going on Anthony's behalf.

As he entered her bedchamber, he inquired, "Would you rather confer with me more publicly? I could attend you in the library."

His tone was so polite that Freddie's heart ached, but she reminded herself that this was her doing. She was the one who had lashed out at him in those moments of emotional confusion after the ...desk incident.

"No, no. Nothing of the sort."

Anthony came close and scrutinized her neckcloth. "Let me do that for you. If it is tied properly, there will be no question that you're a man."

When he reached out to grasp both ends of the starched fabric, Freddie felt a frisson of delight. She watched his fingers, his face. Anthony's black brows knit in concentration as he deftly tied, tugged, and twisted. Finally, a smile lit his handsome countenance. "Success."

Frederica was wearing a high-necked, green-striped waistcoat from Anthony's own wardrobe, tightened in back to fit by Mrs. Bell. Unbuttoning the first two buttons, he pulled a loop of the neckcloth through just enough to add a slightly dashing flair.

Standing back, Anthony ran his gaze over her, one brow arched. "Excellent. Very convincing. But ..." He broke off and shook his head.

"What is it?"

"Nothing. Never mind."

"No, I insist that you tell me. What were you thinking?"

He raked a hand through his tousled locks. "I was just wondering ...where have you put them?"

She cocked her head. "Put what?"

Color faintly touched his sculpted cheekbones as he raised both hands and splayed them over his own chest in imitation of her curved breasts. "Do you wish me to say the words?"

Under the strips of linen binding Freddie's breasts, her nipples tingled and tightened as if endeavoring to get his attention. Reminding herself that her response was hidden from him under many layers of fabric, Freddie replied, "I have bound them, sir."

"Please, say no more." He held up a hand in mock dismay. "That sounds cruel."

Seeking a distraction, Frederica took her spectacles from a side table and began to polish the lenses with a handkerchief. "I hope you will tell me again everything that I must note during the coming hours. Of course, I have never been inside the Geological Society so no doubt I shall be awestruck by the library and the collections of fossils, shells, and rocks."

"Did you not promise to be my eyes and ears today?" His light tone held a serious undercurrent. "Normally, I would ask my father to spy for me, but as you have stated so forcefully on other occasions, you understand what to listen and look for so much better than he ever could."

"Yes, of course. I have not forgotten."

"Good." Anthony led the way to the window overlooking the back garden which today wore a cloak of gray mist. The two of them stood far enough away from the doorway that, if someone should enter, their conversation could not be overheard. "I had a notebook, a log of sorts, with me on that last day, before I fell. Its current whereabouts are a mystery." His jaw tightened. "I kept one each year of our voyage, sending them home one by one, with the rest of my artifacts. The last notebook, however, was with me on that day."

His manner was so deadly serious that Frederica put a hand on his coat sleeve. "Could it have fallen with you?"

"I think not." A grim smile touched Anthony's mouth. "Before climbing down to inspect the water, I asked Terrance Buskin to hold my notebook." He leaned close enough that she inhaled the subtle, masculine scent of his soap. "Everything I had observed throughout 1835 was in that notebook. Among other things, it contained all my private observations and speculations about the Galápagos Islands. I made a decision not to share them, even with Darwin, until we could return to England and consult with other experts —as I assume Darwin has already begun to do with his own collections."

Absorbing the meaning of his words, she said, "Would Terrance Buskin dare bring *your* notebook to the meeting today?"

Anthony shrugged, but his black eyes were hard. "I

believe he left me for dead, assuming I either died from a blow to the head or by drowning. Who else would recognize it?"

"Charles Darwin, perhaps?"

"He could scarcely keep track of his own logs. I doubt that he paid any attention to mine."

The deep, French-accented voice of Justin St. Briac drifted up the stairs.

"Your father has come to fetch me!" Freddie exclaimed, adding quickly, "What does the notebook look like?"

Anthony sketched a size in the air and added, "It is covered in midnight-blue leather ...but I think you are probably right, he wouldn't be careless enough to keep it with him. What interests me more is the content of his lecture. I expect you to take careful notes, professor."

She grinned and replied gruffly, "I shall do my best to comply, sir."

As Freddie turned toward the door, Anthony caught the tail of her frock coat and pulled her back toward him. Her heart leaped as she looked up at his handsome face. For one thrilling moment, it seemed that he might kiss her, but instead he reached down and readjusted her false mustache.

"Have a care, my dear," Anthony remarked, looking amused. His forefinger slid sideways to graze her cheek. "That peculiar aspect of your disguise could be our undoing."

* * *

FREDERICA SAT BESIDE JUSTIN ST. Briac as he drove his fine cabriolet the short distance to Somerset House. The equipage, drawn by a single chestnut gelding, was made for only two passengers, and Anthony's father was able to navigate the crush of vehicles on Piccadilly with ease.

Originally the Duke of Somerset's magnificent Tudor palace had stood on this site overlooking the Thames, but over the last fifty years this grand, colonnaded structure had been constructed in its place. The public building was home to an assortment of royal societies and exhibitions, and the Geological Society's rooms were in the block adjoining King's College.

As the cabriolet drew up outside, a sudden wave of panic swept over Frederica. Perhaps she had gone pale, for Justin St. Briac glanced over at her and arched a brow above his eye-patch.

"Are you unwell?" he inquired.

"Until this moment, I have been quite caught up in the excitement of this adventure, particularly since the Geological Society forbids women to attend its meetings," she said, wrinkling her nose.

"Emmie can talk of little else," Anthony's father agreed. "All the women in my family were outraged when Mary Anning brought her fossils to London in 1829 but was not permitted to present them to the Society herself."

"Yes, I am engaging in quite a piece of subterfuge, on behalf of all females." Freddie nodded, but her smile was distracted. "Sir, I have just remembered that my father may well be in attendance. Do you suppose he would recognize me?"

Justin stared at her for a long moment then shook his head. "I do not think so. Your disguise is exceptional, but to be safe, I shall endeavor to block you from sight whenever possible." He gave her an encouraging smile. "In any case, even if Viscount Redfield does recognize you, he can hardly carry you off in the presence of so many other people. And you may depend upon me to protect you from any threats.

That is why Anthony asked me to accompany you today."

"Is it?" she murmured, surprised.

"*Assurément,*" Justin said as the groom descended from his perch and waited for them to alight. "Shall we now go forth and enjoy this adventure, Professor Loudon?"

It was a short walk to the Geological Society's entrance in the east wing of Somerset House. Inside, they passed by cabinets lined with rocks, shells, and fossils, while Justin explained that the foreign collections were upstairs. She longed to pause and study all the specimens, but Justin murmured that the meeting would soon begin.

It seemed that most of the other men had already arrived and were inside the comparatively small room set aside for Society meetings. As they crossed the threshold, a whey-faced gentleman with tiny spectacles greeted St. Briac by name and turned to Freddie with an inquiring look.

"Sir Miles, allow me to present Professor Frederick Loudon," said Justin. "He has been assisting my family with the collection of specimens sent home by my son, Anthony ...before his disappearance." As he spoke, Justin gestured to Freddie to show her invitation, but the be-spectacled gentleman seemed uninterested.

"Such a sad business," rejoined Sir Miles, his voice rising with curiosity. "Have you any news? Any notion at all what might have happened to him?"

"No, nothing yet."

"Mr. Darwin himself is here today," confided Sir Miles. "Perhaps he will know more."

"Perhaps," agreed Justin, a slight edge to his French-accented voice. "Ah, Charles Babbage is arriving. We will go and find our seats." He nodded to Sir Miles and led the way toward the neat rows of chairs.

Frederica kept her head down and followed him, her heart beating wildly. Everyone seemed to be dressed in nearly identical black frock coats and gray trousers. Each blurred face glimpsed from the corners of her eyes seemed, for one terrible instant, to be her father.

Touching Justin's sleeve, Freddie whispered, "Do you see him?"

He glanced all around the room, the picture of nonchalance. "In fact, I do. Redfield and Cobleigh are sitting together near Darwin and Charles Lyell, at the front of the room. Your father is looking rather gaunt. Perhaps your absence has caused him a few sleepless nights."

After an instant's dizzy panic, Frederica sternly reminded herself that she did *not* faint.

"I suggest that you sit down here," Justin continued in an undertone. He pointed to a chair at the end of the last row, blocked from the view of most by two very large men who sat just ahead. "I will mingle for a few minutes, just to exchange greetings and hopefully prevent them from approaching us later and getting a closer look at you." Sardonically, he muttered, "I find these meetings a dead bore, but I come for Emmie and my nieces, Louise and Camille, who are also mad for fossils, rocks, birds, and so on. When the Society finally admits women, my obligation will end, thank God."

"Perhaps we shouldn't sit together," Freddie whispered. "If Papa feels even a flicker of recognition when he sees me, your presence might heighten his suspicion."

St. Briac shrugged his broad shoulders in a way that reminded her of Anthony. "You may be thinking too much, professor. However, if it eases your mind, I will agree to sit one place away from you."

With that, he dropped his gloves and hat on the designated chair and went off to endure the company of the stuffy Society members. As soon as she was alone, Freddie shifted restlessly, feeling like a sitting duck. Perhaps if she walked around a bit, she might be able to learn something valuable. Wasn't that why she had come?

Noticing the cabinets lined with British rocks on the near wall, Frederica rose and began to study them, grateful to turn away from the assembled men. If her father should look her way, he would only see a slender fellow's back and unruly head of graying hair.

"Professor, there you are!"

She smothered a gasp at the sound of Terrance Buskin's voice. Looking around cautiously, Freddie saw that he was seated at a table inside a nearby anteroom marked PRIVATE! MEMBERS ONLY. Pages covered with writing were spread before him, while next to his left elbow a slim notebook lay open.

A notebook! The very sight of it caused the tiny hairs at the back of her neck to rise up. Could it possibly be the one Anthony had lost the day of his accident? Perhaps, as he suspected, it was not lost at all, but stolen by Terrance Buskin.

"Do come in, Professor Loudon," he invited, half rising from his chair.

Freddie glanced right and left as if expecting one of the members to realize she was a female in their midst and raise an alarm. Did she dare tempt fate by entering this private room? A thrill ran through her. Behind her large horsehair mustache, she smiled.

When had Frederica Redfield ever backed down from a dare?

CHAPTER 13

"*I* am gratified that you were able to attend," Terrance Buskin said as Frederica crossed the threshold. "I will be speaking first. Because my lecture will consist of theories, rather than any real conclusions, I will not speak at length. Adam Sedgwick, who will discuss some of his latest findings in Welsh rock strata, will be today's main speaker. No doubt you will wish to partake in the general discussion at the end of the meeting."

"I look forward to it," Frederica said in her professor voice. She sidled closer to the desk, nodding, while stealing glances at the papers spread before him. "My good fellow, surely you are not still writing your presentation?"

Buskin glanced down and nervously began to assemble the various pages of his speech. "No, no, not a bit, sir. I was merely perusing my notes one last time, just to be certain I hadn't overlooked something."

"Ah." Freddie dared to lean closer, squinting at the notebook that lay open on the far side of the desk. Just as she managed to focus on the handwritten notes and sketches, Buskin snatched it up. She met his eyes and tried to smile. "That log looked fascinating! Did you make the drawings yourself?"

"Hmmph," he mumbled.

Before she could get a good look at the cover, he had mixed it with other materials, opened a worn leather satchel, and pushed all of them inside.

Just then, a voice spoke from the doorway that sent a cold chill down Freddie's spine. "I say, Buskin, this is no time for idle conversation. You will be introduced in five minutes. Are you ready to take your place?"

"Yes, yes, Lord Redfield," Terrance Buskin replied. "I was just gathering my things."

Freddie froze, praying her father would not come closer, would not speak to her. All her life she had stood up to him, unafraid, but now the stakes were much higher. Her heart stood still as he walked up behind her.

"I do not believe I have met your guest, sir," Papa said in his smooth, deep voice.

Did she dare turn around to face him? Freddie's palms were damp as she stalled, fumbling for her handkerchief, pressing it over her lower face, and loudly coughing into it.

"This is Professor Loudon, my lord," Buskin said. He gestured toward Freddie, who mumbled apologies and continued to turn away from her father, noisily clearing her throat and coughing again.

"Another time, perhaps," Papa said from a distance. "We are all eager to hear your lecture, Mr. Buskin." And then he was gone.

Freddie wanted to laugh with relief. She knew better than anyone how much her father hated illness of any sort. In the weeks before Mama had died, he had avoided going into her room or getting too close to her. Every time Papa appeared in the sickroom door and made an excuse to Frederica, her regard for him had eroded further, and now she felt pleased to have used his dread of illness to slip past him today.

"Are you quite well, professor?" Terrance Buskin was saying as he started toward the door.

Freddie coughed one last time, for good measure, pressing her mustache firmly into place. "Perhaps I breathed in a bit of dust. Nothing to worry about. You go on."

"You must come with me." Buskin took a key from his pocket. "Private room, you know. I must lock the door when I leave."

Reluctantly, she followed him out of the anteroom, sending one last longing glance back at the satchel he had left behind on the table. She told herself it was just as well he had a key, for it doubtless would have been folly to try to linger behind and open it when so many things could go wrong.

Better to wait and plan with Anthony ...a prospect that sent a joyous burst of anticipation straight to her heart. Returning to her seat in the Geological Society's meeting room, Frederica found that she could hardly wait to see him, to tell him everything that had happened, to hear his reactions and, perhaps, to feel the heated magic of his touch again.

She flushed slightly, realizing that such thoughts were coming more often every day. Yet what harm could there be as long as she kept them secret and never, ever acted on them?

* * *

ONCE TERRANCE BUSKIN'S speech ended, it was all Frederica could do to sit still through the rest of the meeting. Any other time, she would have found Andrew Sedgwick's revelations about Welsh rock strata deeply interesting, but today she only wanted to hurry home to Charles Street before she could forget any-thing Buskin had said.

Two hours later, Frederica was at last following in Justin St. Briac's wake, emerging from the shadowed rooms of the Geological Society into the open air of Somerset House's quadrangle.

Unable to repress an excited smile, she looked up at the elder St. Briac and whispered, "I must say, I thought that would never end. I can hardly wait to share every-thing I learned with Anthony."

"I'm delighted that this long afternoon has proven worthwhile," he replied dryly. "When I saw you inside that anteroom with Buskin, I feared I might have to rescue you from yourself."

On the street, his dashing cabriolet was visible, the groom waiting by its side. Justin and Freddie wound past the Society members who continued to chat in the open courtyard until they encountered Charles Darwin.

The shade of his coat and trousers nearly matched his sparse brown hair. Darwin still retained a slight sunburn after his years south of the equator, and al-though his smile was warm, he looked thin, as if the long voyage had taken a toll.

"Good day, M'sieur St. Briac," Darwin said, ex-tending his hand. "When I saw you in the meeting, I hoped we would have an opportunity to speak." His tufted brows drew together. "Listening to Terrance Buskin's inconclusive speech, I could only think that it should have been Anthony presenting *his* findings. I cannot tell you how many times I have wondered what he was writing in his notebook—and what he was thinking—during those last days on the Galápagos Is-lands." Darwin sighed. "He was tight-lipped, promising only that we would discuss his theories after he had an opportunity to organize them upon our return to England. We planned to catalogue our findings together, here in London ..."

Justin nodded soberly, giving a good imitation of a grieving father. "I appreciate your kind words more than you know." Gesturing toward Freddie, he said, "I would like you to meet Professor Frederick Loudon. He has devoted himself to unpacking and cataloguing the specimens Anthony sent home during the *Beagle*'s voyage."

Darwin blinked and shook Freddie's hand. "Have you indeed, sir?"

"Yes," she replied in a husky voice. Suddenly she felt very self-conscious, as if he could see right through her disguise. "It has been my honor."

"I hope to examine them all one day." To her relief, Darwin turned back to Justin. "Do not doubt that I am keenly aware of Anthony's absence every day. He is not forgotten! If I can be of service to you, m'sieur, I beg you to reach out to me. I am staying with my brother Erasmus at 43 Great Marlborough Street. In the coming weeks, I intend to consult with my new friend, Charles Lyell, and other scientists about the many discoveries made during our voyage."

"*D'accord*," nodded Justin. "I will remember your address, sir. *Merci*."

* * *

AFTER BIDDING JUSTIN ST. Briac *adieu* in the mews behind the Charles Street house, Freddie hurried through the small back garden. Meg was outside, beating a rug, when she rushed past, too impatient to stop and pretend to be Professor Loudon. Once, she reached down with both hands as if to lift the skirts she was not wearing. It was becoming harder and harder to remember her disguise, or to care about it.

Inside the house, Freddie made her way to the library where she found Anthony sitting at his desk, a magnifying glass in one hand, a stuffed, gray-and-white finch in the other.

"I must speak to you, sir, in private," she said, her tone midway between her own and the one she had adopted for her alter-ego. For good measure, she tugged at his sleeve and hissed, "Immediately!"

Anthony lifted both brows. "I was about to go upstairs to retrieve an ornithology text I was reading last night. Perhaps you would care to accompany me?"

"Yes!"

He led the way upstairs without another word. However, once they were inside his bedchamber, he closed the door and turned to face her.

"You should be more careful, I think. At any moment, it seemed you might forget and speak or behave as Frederica. I trust my servants, but anything is possible."

She wanted to tell him that she was growing bored with this charade but realized that would not be wise. Instead, she promised, "I will endeavor to be more mindful, but it will be such a relief when you can come out in the open again."

"Perhaps, but have you forgotten that you are also in hiding from your father?"

Freddie paced across the spacious bedchamber, pulling off her mustache and spectacles. "I wish I could forget! He was there today, with the hideous Baron Cobleigh!"

She saw that Anthony was watching her with a pensive expression. "We will have to find a real solution for your problem, I fear. You can't spend the rest of your life, hiding here in this disguise."

His words made Freddie's heart stop for an instant as the future came clearly into focus. Once Anthony resolved the problem with Terrance Buskin and could openly resume his life, he certainly would not want a female disguised as a man lurking about in his house. Of course, he would want to return to his rake's habits. To revel in them! No doubt he dreamed nightly of lying with a willing woman; perhaps someone from his past. One could only imagine what carnal pleasures he would enjoy with that female.

The reality of Freddie's situation pressed down on her. She was there on borrowed time, but at least she still had the diamond and sapphire ring Grandpapa had thoughtfully given her. When the moment of truth arrived, she and Mrs. Bell would slip away and begin a new life in the country.

All these thoughts only intensified the sense of urgency generated by the afternoon's adventure. "Please, let us talk about that later. Don't you want to know what happened today at the Geological Society?"

"You are in such a fevered state, I am almost afraid to ask," Anthony replied in ironic tones. His neckcloth was loosened in a way that made him look especially appealing, and now he backed up and leaned against the side of the bed, arms crossed over his wide chest.

"You shall be in a fever as well when you hear this!" Freddie pronounced triumphantly. "I only ask that you attend me." With that, she began to pace back and forth in front of him.

He nodded. "I am in suspense."

"Good. But first I must remove this horrid wig. It has been itching since midway through Mr. Sedgwick's speech." Impatiently, Freddie drew off the goatshair wig and unpinned her curls. The sensation of her own long locks spilling loose over her shoulders was heavenly. "Ah, that's better."

"Perhaps you shouldn't remove anything else in my

presence," Anthony suggested, the merest hint of a wicked smile touching his mouth.

Freddie met his dark eyes, remembering how he had gazed at her in her nightgown, and felt a frisson of warm arousal. "Yes, well, as I was saying ..." For a moment, she couldn't remember anything at all. "After your father and I arrived at the meeting, I saw an opportunity to look around. Stealthily, you know."

"Ah."

"Also, I wanted to turn my back to the others, especially my father and Lord Cobleigh, to avoid detection. I wandered along the perimeter of the meeting room where the British rocks are on display, until I spied a little room. Inside, sitting at a table, was ..." She paused for effect. "Terrance Buskin!"

Anthony's face darkened. "Go on."

"His speech was laid out in front of him, and there was also an open *notebook*." She stepped closer to Anthony, smiling proudly. "Of course, I did my best to see what was on the pages, but it was too far away, and everything was upside-down. However, I was able to make out several small *sketches*!" She caught his sleeve. "I immediately remembered one morning here in the library when Terrance Buskin disclosed that he had no talent for sketching, unlike *you*. I specifically remember because I perceived that he was secretly jealous of you. When I saw the notebook today, I tried to ask him if he had made the sketches, but he immediately started putting everything into his satchel. I couldn't even get a look at the cover of the notebook."

Anthony reached for Frederica's hands. "You are a wonder!"

Dazzled by his smile and the warmth of his touch, she exclaimed, "There is more! I feared all was lost when my father came in to summon Buskin, but I managed to escape recognition. I returned to my seat and listened to every word of the speech."

"Amazing," he approved, drawing her closer.

"Terrance went on at length about Galápagos tortoises and the fact that the tortoises on each island had unique patterns on their shells. He also spoke about the various birds, speculating that they may have all been finches that adapted to the specific islands where they lived. Although he didn't present any definitive conclusions, there was quite a bit of whispering in the audience during his lecture."

Anthony's expression hardened. "Those are exactly the observations I wrote in my notebook that day, just before I fell from the rocks. Of course, it's *possible* that Buskin developed his theories on his own, or even in discussion with Darwin during the voyage home. The only way I can prove his guilt is by finding my notebook in his possession."

"Oh, Anthony, it is chilling to think what he may have done! Stealing your ideas may be the least of it."

"Indeed." Glancing away, he said, "But I have no intention of letting him get away with it."

"I will help you!" Her hand went to his wide shoulders.

"No, Frederica. It could be dangerous, and I will not put you in harm's way. You've already done enough."

The air between them was charged in a way she didn't fully understand. "I am an independent woman, fully capable of making these choices for myself." When he didn't immediately look at her, she stood on tiptoe and met his gaze.

"You are mad," he said huskily.

"Perhaps." Frederica pressed her body against his. For years, she had ached to discover Anthony's touch, his kiss, and now she might do so ...if she dared. All her senses were heightened. Through his clothing, Anthony was both hard and warm, and she inhaled the clean scent of his shaving soap. Her arms twined around his strong neck and then she was kissing him, helplessly pressing her lips to his mouth, as a storm of need broke inside her.

CHAPTER 14

$\mathcal{A}$nthony's hands gripped Freddie's hips over the fabric of her trousers, and for an instant he paused. It almost seemed he might put her from him, but then he was kissing her back, his tongue coaxing her lips to part and let him in. This was something that had never occurred to Freddie when she imagined kissing, yet the sensation of his tongue stroking hers was beyond thrilling.

Freddie was a woman of five-and-twenty, yet it seemed she'd had no clue what she'd been missing. Sparks kindled and spread through her body, until she was on fire with need. Her breasts ached for Anthony's touch. Did she dare? Yes, why not! She didn't seem to be able to stop her fingers from fumbling at the fastenings of her shirt.

"This clothing …it's all wrong!" she heard herself say.

Anthony, who was doing something madly pleasurable to the sensitive shell of her ear, made no reply, but his hands cupped her bottom and brought her in closer contact with the hard ridge that strained against his trousers. This just increased her need. Spreading open the front of her shirt, she found the edge of the linen bands knotted just below her breasts.

"Help!" she croaked.

For an instant their eyes met, and she saw that Anthony was on fire as well. Although he shook his head *no*, his fingers quickly undid the strips of cloth, and her aching breasts were freed. In that moment, it seemed that all the nerves in her body were concentrated in her nipples. She didn't know what it was she needed so desperately, but clearly Anthony did. With one movement, he lifted her by her bottom, turned, and set her atop his bed.

"No," he muttered and shook his head again, but in the next instant he was bending her back, her shirt falling away from her shoulders as he kissed his way down her throat and over one swollen breast. Each touch of his lips seemed to burn her sensitized flesh.

Freddie sank her hands into his hair and pressed herself closer. Her heart was racing beneath his mouth, and when he brushed his warm, wet tongue over her nipple, she gasped. *Please don't stop!* Had she said it aloud? Anthony fastened his mouth over the tightened peak and began to suckle, all the while circling with his tongue in a way that brought Freddie to the edge of a climax she had only ever achieved alone before, with her own fingers. She heard herself whimper.

He gently squeezed her breast while his free hand tantalizingly explored her bared midriff, the curve of her hip. She opened her thighs beneath him, and he pushed more insistently against her through the layers of their clothing, letting her feel just how much he wanted her. Wild sensations surged at her core. She desperately needed ...*more*.

When Freddie wedged a hand between them and tugged first at her trousers, then his, Anthony suddenly raised his head and stared into her eyes. Expecting him to kiss her again, she parted her lips and arched closer, but to her surprise, he covered her mouth with his hand.

"For God's sake, don't do that," he bit out.

"What – what is it? What's wrong?"

To her utter astonishment, he pushed himself away from her and strode across the room, raking both hands through his disheveled locks and shaking his head. "I've been drugged, I think, but now I'm coming round and see clearly that what we have been doing is —" He broke off and threw his hands in the air.

"Is *what?*" cried Freddie. Face flaming, she scrambled up and drew her shirt together.

He glared at her. "Unconscionable!"

"I can't imagine what you mean. Don't you do this all the time with women? This, and much worse? Why is it unconscionable if you do it with *me?*" Freddie discovered that if she stuffed the tails of her shirt into the front of her trousers, her hands were freed to gesticulate at Anthony. "I think you must be mad."

"Mad? Me?" Sparks flashed from his black eyes. "I am not the one strutting about London in a wig made of goatshair and a ridiculous horsehair mustache!"

Suddenly Freddie couldn't get away from him fast enough. Head held high, she marched to the door in her stockinged feet, her own glossy hair swirling around her shoulders, not caring who might see her when she emerged from Anthony's bedroom.

Gripping the door handle, she flung back at him, "I've known for years that you were a scoundrel, Anthony St. Briac. Yet in a weak moment, I gave you another chance. Unconscionable, indeed!"

* * *

WHEN THE DOOR slammed behind Frederica, Anthony sank into a chair and pressed his fingertips against his eyes. Pain stabbed his temple, then blessedly it receded. Meanwhile, his body continued to thrum with raw lust, and his cock ached, unsatisfied.

How the devil could I allow that to happen? He had been so careful, guarding against even touching Frederica! Yet minutes ago, he had been on the verge of making love to her, over and over again! It was dangerous enough to have a female of her breeding living under his roof, but he had sworn that if he allowed her to stay, Frederica would never know that he was drawn to her in ways even he didn't fully understand.

For a moment, he wondered what she had been thinking during their brief yet highly carnal interlude. More than once, Frederica had denied any wish to marry, yet clearly, she had powerful needs as a woman, seemingly pent up during her years at Justmore House with her grandfather. Had those few stormy minutes with him been simply a case of lust for her ...or could Freddie, like many other women in Anthony's past, have feelings for him?

Deeply conflicted, he rose from the chair. He wasn't the sort of coward who lost his head with a chit and then avoided seeing her afterward, and in any case that wasn't possible. Frederica was living in his house, sleeping in the bedchamber across from his! There was nothing for it but to go to her and talk about what had happened. Wasn't that the advice he had always given his tempestuous parents when they quarreled?

After straightening his clothing and retying his cravat, Anthony crossed to the cellaret, splashed brandy into a crystal glass, and drank it down. If anyone deserved a bloody drink, he did!

Opening the door to his bedchamber, Anthony immediately encountered Mrs. Bell, exiting Frederica's room with an empty tea tray. Her normally merry countenance was pinched with disapproval as she bustled past him with scarcely a nod.

When Anthony knocked at her door, Frederica called, "Come in," in a wary voice. Entering, he saw her sitting at the little writing desk by the window, clad in a simple rose-and-cream morning dress with bishop's sleeves. Her golden-brown curls were drawn back in a cluster at the nape of her neck, and her demeanor was remote.

Anthony couldn't help asking, "You weren't worried that someone else might see you like that?"

"I find that I am tired of pretending this afternoon," she replied, sipping from a cup of tea. "I thought I would remain here until my reckless mood passes."

Touché, he thought. "May I sit down?"

Gesturing toward a small bench several feet away from her, Frederica nodded. Her cheeks grew flushed as she watched him, and he had a sudden vision of her face as she responded to his kiss and begged him to free her breasts.

Do not think of that, he warned himself. It was a relief to sit down and hide his traitorous male parts from her sight.

"I would ask you to be brief," Frederica said, coolly polite. Her expression told him she had had quite enough of his company for one day.

"I came to beg your pardon." When she didn't reply, he cleared his throat and added, "For what happened … in my room."

"I am not certain I understand. For which part are you sorry?"

Anthony wished his father were hiding behind the curtain to whisper the right answer to him. "I regret that I lost my head. I swore that if you stayed here in this house, I would behave as a gentleman." His voice trailed off as he noted that her deep blue eyes were flashing. Had he insulted her? He was about to add that he had taken advantage of her, but perhaps that would only dig him into a deeper hole.

"I see." She pressed her soft lips into a hard line. "I perceive that we have misunderstood one another."

Intensely curious, Anthony was about to ask what she meant when Frederica rose from her chair.

"It seems I must beg your pardon, sir, for losing *my* head as well," she said. "We were together in your bed-chamber. I was not a victim, and neither were you. Shall we agree to forget it ever happened?"

Of course, that was what he thought he wanted, but when she put it like that, it felt like a punishment. "Yes, of course. Fine." Anthony stood to face her, hands fisted at his sides.

Head high, Frederica led him to the door. "We have much more important business to attend to, after all, do we not? I would like a holiday from Professor Loudon for the rest of this day, but tomorrow let us decide how to trap Terrance Buskin." As she showed him out, she continued to speak in a tone both frosty and cordial, as if she were bidding goodbye to the dustman. "Perhaps we might speak again at breakfast."

"I suppose so," Anthony agreed. No sooner had he passed into the corridor than Frederica firmly closed the door behind him. He stood there alone, his thoughts in a whirl. Could she truly be so indifferent to him? If not, what the devil was happening? He knew he should be immensely relieved that she hadn't wept or accused him of assaulting her or insisted that she was ruined, and he must now be leg-shackled to her for life ...but somehow her cool indifference seemed worse. At least he had experience dealing with tears and recriminations.

Remembering the many incomprehensible dramas

he had witnessed between his own parents, Anthony shook his head. *This* was exactly the reason he was determined to maintain a safe distance from the wedded state.

In fact, if he hadn't just returned from sea, Anthony would be sorely tempted to seek out another lengthy voyage to far-off lands. The longer the better!

CHAPTER 15

*A*s soon as Anthony was out the door, Freddie paced across the room to the window, wishing she could scream. It had taken every ounce of her self-control to pretend she felt nothing, yet the truth was that during her interlude with Anthony in his bed-chamber, she had bared herself to him in every way. Had he believed her when she tried to take it all back?

She knew that he liked her. Perhaps they were even friends. But she also knew she was there because he had taken pity on her. He wasn't the sort of man to put her out in the street. Perhaps Anthony even felt desire toward her now, but Freddie was convinced that she was merely a convenient substitute for the women he would seek out once he was free to do so.

Otherwise, why push her away?

Freddie wrapped both arms around herself, feeling trapped like a bird in a cage. Her instinct was to flee, but as she considered this possibility it came to her that the cage was her own heart. Her memory whirled back to the night she and Anthony had first waltzed to-gether, seven long years ago at Lady Penhurst's ball. It seemed now that the moment he had first touched her, and she looked up into his merry eyes, she had been lost. Anthony might not be that same lighthearted youth, but Freddie had changed as well. The one thing that hadn't changed was her secret, burning passion for him. It had announced itself today but must now be repressed.

It would take all her strength to make that happen …at least until Terrance Buskin was exposed and Anthony was free to live his life publicly. Freddie's eyes stung as she crossed to her bureau, took out the tiny velvet case, and opened it. Inside gleamed the diamond and sapphire ring Grandpapa had given her. One day it would buy her passage to an independent future, far away from this house and all the terrible, wonderful feelings Anthony St. Briac ignited in her heart.

* * *

As Anthony saw it, he had two choices tonight. He could either drink himself into a stupor or escape from this deuced house. Remaining sober, with Frederica just paces away, felt impossible. Even the thought of unpacking more specimens in his library could not spark his interest.

As soon as darkness gathered, Anthony donned a caped greatcoat and a Wellington hat with the brim pulled low over his brow. Downstairs, he looked for Quincy, but was told by Meg that the butler had gone out.

"There are just the two of us, you know, sir, even to do the shopping," she said, frowning. "Mrs. Bell only wants to serve Professor Loudon, it seems."

"Right, well, that's fine. The professor is here to help me, and I want his needs to be met." Anthony gave the girl a distracted smile. "I have a brief errand to attend to, Meg. I will return later in the evening."

"But – sir!" she exclaimed. "Is this wise? Perhaps you

should wait for Quincy. He would doubtless go in your place."

"Don't worry," Anthony said. "This is a call only I can make."

Outside, he traversed the garden path leading to the mews, feeling liberated. He kept his head down until he reached the gate, and then looked back just once, up toward Frederica's window. Unexpectedly, he saw her standing there wrapped in a shawl, gazing down. Their eyes met for only an instant before she turned away and disappeared from his sight.

Anthony walked the relatively short distance from Charles Street to Grosvenor Square, where his Raveneau grandparents had kept a home for more than a half-century. He kept to the lesser-traveled alleyways and mews, stepping into a shadowed doorway whenever someone came his way. Once, on Adams Row, he saw a man coming toward him whose silhouette resembled Viscount Redfield. There was no niche to conceal himself in, so he simply stopped to check his timepiece, head bent in the shadows. His pulse raced as he waited for the man to pass by, and eventually the fellow did, without speaking.

Alone again, Anthony reminded himself that even if it had been the viscount, Redfield posed no threat to him. Although his lordship was a member of the Geological Society, it was highly doubtful that he had any connection to Terrance Buskin. Anthony's heart squeezed as he realized that his visceral fear was not for himself, but for Frederica.

Minutes later, he went through the stable gate into his grandparents' walled garden. Memories from childhood swirled around him as he passed under a familiar arch that, in springtime, dripped with wisteria. At the servants' entrance, Anthony paused to knock. After a moment, Arabella, the Raveneaus' tall, plain housekeeper opened the door and peered out at him.

He put a cautionary finger to his lips and stepped inside. The woman emitted a little squeak of surprise, growing even paler than usual. "It cannot be! Why, you are …"

"Dead?" Anthony grinned. "I'm not, but please don't tell anyone yet. May I rely on you to keep my secret?"

Dazzled she nodded. "Oh lord, sir, your parents will be over the moon!"

"They know," he confided. "I've come to see my father tonight. Where is he? I should like to see him without attracting further attention."

Picking up her oil lamp, Arabella gestured for him to follow her through the kitchen. "Your mother and father have taken your grandmother out to a play at the Adelphi Theatre. Your sister Emeline has gone as well, but M'sieur Raveneau remained behind. I'll vow he would want to see you, young sir!" She spoke with the assurance of a servant who had been there so long that she was virtually a member of the family herself.

Anthony glanced toward the worn worktable where a maid was picking through a basket of apples. Smiling at her, he took one and put it in his pocket for later. "Yes, I would like very much to see my grandfather, although I cannot stay long."

"Of course, M'sieur Raveneau is in his private study. You know the way, but—" Arabella touched the sleeve of his greatcoat. "I trust he knows you are alive? If not, the shock might do him in!"

"I think you may underestimate my grandfather," Anthony said dryly. "But, yes, he knows."

With that, he left her, pausing only to take off his greatcoat and hat and drape them over a chair in the stair hall. Outside the door to André Raveneau's study, he saw his beloved grandfather sitting at the same desk he had used as long as Anthony could remember. He was writing by the light of a bronze oil lamp, his head of thick white hair bent as he worked.

When the two men made their farewells five years earlier, just before Anthony sailed away on the *Beagle*, it had occurred to him that he might not see his grandfather again. He had been, after all, more than eighty years old. Yet, here he was, clearly older, perhaps even a trifle frail, yet still an impressively magnetic male animal.

At that moment, as Raveneau reached over to the inkpot, he lifted his head just enough to catch a glimpse of Anthony. He straightened and quickly took off his silver-rimmed spectacles.

"*Mon Dieu*, can it be? Ah, Anthony ..."

The sound of his grandfather's voice husky with emotion brought tears to Anthony's eyes. Raveneau pushed to his feet and came around the desk to meet him.

"Grandpère," Anthony murmured as they embraced, "I am sorry I could not come sooner."

"Bah!" Drawing back, Raveneau gave him one of his legendary smiles. "Never mind that. When I was your age, I was too much the libertine to be constrained by familial obligations, and I suspect your St. Briac father was just the same. Maybe worse! I would expect nothing different from you, Anthony."

"But I love my family," he protested. "More than ever, since I thought I might never see any of you again."

His grandfather gently touched his back. "Let us sit together and talk. You have doubtless heard that your parents have carried my bride off to the theatre? I don't suppose you can wait for them." As he spoke, Raveneau moved to the cellaret and poured them each a small glass of ruby-red port.

Anthony accepted the port and followed his grandfather to the sofa of tufted forest-green velvet near the window. As they sat down, he heard a loud yawn and looked over to see a fluffy fawn-and-cream corgi sprawled on a pillow near the door. The dog seemed to smile at him before rolling onto its back, stretching, and making low, sleepy noises.

He blinked. "That is not Robinson." Not only were the markings of this corgi different, but it was much more subdued than Robinson, who would have charged forth to meet him the moment he entered the kitchen, barking as if he were a highly paid house watchman. It came to Anthony then that Robinson, who had joined their family when Anthony was a little boy, must have died during his five-year absence.

"*C'est vrai*," confirmed Grandpère. "Sadly, Robinson is no longer with us, but you will recall that he lived to a great age. This is Daisy, his daughter. Your sister Emeline chose her from the litter of puppies, and then she gave her to *us*." He arched a brow for emphasis.

As if to reinforce this point, Daisy trundled over to them and put her front paws up on the sofa in a silent demand to be lifted up. "You should be able to jump up on your own," Raveneau suggested in ironic tones, but she continued to stare. When he complied at last, the corgi climbed heavily onto his lap. "My beautiful wife feeds her too much. Daisy is especially fond of salmon. And cheese."

Anthony laughed, then sighed. "How I have missed all of you. And this house." He looked around his grandfather's study, taking in the familiar sketches and paintings of Raveneau offspring. The wall above the desk was dominated by a magnificent oil painting of the great Captain André Raveneau's privateer, the *Black Eagle*, responsible for the capture and destruction of countless British ships during the American Revolutionary War. "You and Grandmama fell in love on that ship, didn't you?"

Following his gaze, Raveneau smiled almost wistfully. "*Oui.* Your grandmother stowed away on the *Black Eagle* more than a half century ago. How enchanting she was! At the time, I pretended she was a great annoyance, but I now concede that I loved Devon from the first. She bewitched me." He slanted a mischievous smile at Anthony. "Fortunately for all of you, *n'est-ce pas?*"

"What a life you have led, Grandpère," Anthony remarked, shaking his head in wonder.

"Quite true. And you also have the passion for seagoing adventures in your blood." As he spoke, his long fingers slowly stroked Daisy's fluffy neck, and her tongue lolled. "I hope you have enjoyed your freedom, for one day a female will turn all your plans on end."

Anthony glanced over in surprise and saw that his grandfather was watching him with shrewd silvery eyes. He managed a derisory laugh, though the back of his neck prickled. "Do you mean that as a blessing or a curse?"

"I think you know the answer." They were silent for a moment, then Raveneau said, "I am eager to hear all about your voyage with Darwin and this past year, when you were lost, but I sense tonight is not the right time. Your parents tell us you are hoping to entrap the man behind your recent suffering?"

"Yes. I hope to do so before week's end. In fact, I planned to visit my friend Charles Darwin this evening, to speak to him about this matter. Papa has his London address, I believe, but since he is not here, it will have to wait."

Raveneau shook his head. "I may be able to help you. When your papa returned from the Geological Society meeting, he mentioned that Darwin is lodging with his brother, Erasmus, in Great Marlborough Street. Do you want me to go upstairs and see if I can find the paper in their rooms?"

"No, I am acquainted with Erasmus Darwin. I know exactly where he lives." Elated, Anthony set down his empty goblet and leaned over to lay a thankful hand on his grandfather's shoulder. Daisy offered her opinion of this intrusion by giving him a narrowed, sidelong look and emitting a low growl.

"She is very possessive," remarked Raveneau with mock dismay. "*Vraiment,* I never would have imagined that I could be part of such a situation as this—with a *dog.* Your grandmother approves, so I indulge her."

Anthony laughed and rose to his feet. "Daisy is quite different from Robinson, yet just as comical, I believe."

"Indeed."

"My apologies for leaving in such haste, but the evening advances." He reached down to clasp his grandfather's free hand. "I beg you, Grandpère, do not disturb Daisy in order to see me out. I hope to resolve this matter very soon so that we may all be openly together again."

"Until then, have a care. Perhaps those dueling lessons you enjoyed years ago with your papa will soon prove beneficial," his grandfather remarked. "Meanwhile, I wish you well tonight with Darwin."

Anthony was halfway to the door when his grandfather spoke again, his tone studiedly offhand. "Ah—I nearly forgot to ask you, how fares Miss Redfield?"

He stopped and slowly looked back over one shoulder. "Miss Redfield?"

"Why yes." Raveneau slowly scratched behind the corgi's foxlike ear. "Frederica was here, you know. She told us all what had transpired at Redfield House that caused her to leave so precipitously. I know all about the scheme to hide her at your home in disguise." His eyes were hooded in the shadowed light. "How is that working out?"

Anthony coughed. "Her presence greatly complicates my life, as you might imagine."

"Indeed, I do." A knowing smile touched Raveneau's mouth. "It is almost as if she has stowed away under your very roof, *n'est-ce pas?*"

CHAPTER 16

During Anthony's short walk from Grosvenor Square to Great Marlborough Street, he felt increasingly reckless. At times he forgot to keep his head down or turn away from passersby, and he found himself yearning to be free again ...to ride in Hyde Park or stroll into a club and be greeted by old friends.

His thoughts turned to Frederica, who now chafed against the restrictions of her secret identity, and he felt new sympathy for her plight. Indeed, if he must lie low in order to unmask Terrance Buskin for the liar and thief he was, the trap would have to be sprung before he did something rash and ruined the element of surprise. And after that, a solution would have to be found for Frederica's future. Clearly, it was not going to work for them to be together in the same house, no matter how they each might insist that it could be done.

Erasmus Darwin's modest lodgings were located on a perfectly respectable but darkened stretch of Great Marlborough Street. When Anthony lifted the knocker, he wondered what he would do if Erasmus himself opened the door. Long moments passed before he heard footsteps and the door swung open to reveal

Syms Covington, the fiddler-turned-cabin boy who had been at Charles's side throughout the voyage of the *Beagle*. Tonight, the loose canvas trousers and white shirt previously worn by the lanky young man were replaced by an ill-fitting suit of brown broadcloth.

"By Jupiter!" Covington gasped. He immediately began to rub his eyes as if he were having a vision. "It cannot be you, sir!"

Smiling, Anthony reached out to him. "It is I, but I must beg you not to shout." Even as he spoke, a shadowy silhouette appeared in the doorway to the parlor.

"Good God." Charles stood there holding a sheaf of papers in one hand, his mouth agape. "Is this possible?"

"Indeed, it is I." Doffing his hat, Anthony went forward to embrace his comrade. "How good it is to see you both!" He stood back to look between the two men's shocked faces. "And what of your brother, Erasmus? Is he at home?"

"No," said Darwin faintly. "Ras is away at the Mount, visiting our family."

"I am relieved to hear it. Before I go on, I must ask you both to say nothing about this to anyone. I still hope to discover exactly who might be responsible for my ...disappearance."

"I knew it," Syms said darkly. "You came to harm."

Wide-eyed, Darwin muttered, "I can scarcely believe you are real. Come in, my friend, and tell me all."

Anthony obeyed, following him into a dimly lit, cluttered parlor. A coal fire burned in grate, infusing the stale air with the faint smell of smoke. At one end of the room, next to a pile of specimen crates, Darwin had transformed a long table into a desk, now covered with stacks of papers, various fossils and shells, and one large, stuffed armadillo.

"Ah," commented Anthony with fond irony, "I feel completely at home."

Charles ignored this. "Sit down." He pointed to the sofa, and Syms cleared away a jumble of coats, hats, and pillows to make a place for their guest to sit.

"Syms," said Anthony, "I perceive you have traded life at sea for a permanent position with Darwin?"

"Aye, sir." The young man beamed and gestured toward a small table near Darwin's. "I even have a desk of my own."

"Syms has been invaluable, sorting and cataloguing all my specimens as we unpack them," Charles confirmed before sending his assistant off to get wine. "But, St. Briac, it is you I want to hear about. Tell me all, this instant. What the devil happened to you back on James Island?"

After a year of separation from his friend and the expedition they had so enthusiastically undertaken together, Anthony felt slightly disoriented by this reunion. So much had happened to both of them since their last conversation on that iguana-filled Galápagos beach.

"It is a very long story," Anthony said.

Syms reappeared with a bottle of Bordeaux wine and a modest cold collation.

"Drink," Darwin ordered, "and eat something. Start at the beginning, when you and Buskin set off to explore more of inner James Island." He paled at the memory. "How many times have I thought about my last glimpse of you, when you turned to wave goodbye as we parted on the beach. I'll own, in the days that followed, I came to believe I would never see you alive again."

Feeling the wave of darkness come over him, Anthony drank half his glass of wine and leaned back against the sofa. "I wish I could tell you that I remember exactly what happened." Methodically, he forced himself to lay out the facts, as he had that night in the coach with his parents. The fall, the blow to his head, waking up in the Spaniards' rough dwelling on the highest point of the island.

"We searched for hours!" Charles exclaimed in despair. "But I suppose we didn't go that far inland." He paused. "If only the *Beagle* didn't have to sail that next day. Good God, I didn't even realize those men were living there. What the deuce were they doing, so far from the sea?"

"Salting tortoise meat," Anthony supplied with a grim smile. "I didn't regain consciousness for at least a day, perhaps longer. I think they expected me to die, but I must be grateful they made a sort of sling for my body and carried me up out of the rocky spring where I had fallen." He paused. "My father told me that Terrance reported we were separated, that he didn't realize I was missing until much later in the day. But I don't remember it that way at all."

"Do you think it is possible that he saw you fall and knowingly abandoned you?" Darwin's voice was hushed, as if he were suggesting the impossible.

"Exactly so, but of course I cannot prove it. I sustained a blow to the head and for some time I barely knew who I was. My memory returned, but who can say if it is reliable concerning the events of that day?"

"Tell me the rest. How the deuce did you get back to England?" Leaning over, Charles poured more wine into both their glasses.

Every time Anthony tried to condense the story, his friend broke in with questions and demands for more details. He told of working aboard a whaling ship to earn his passage to Chile. "Do you remember the artist I enjoyed a brief romance with when the *Beagle* was at anchor at Concepcion?"

Charles exchanged a telling glance with Syms. "Remember?" He snorted. "All of us were deeply envious of you, St. Briac. I suppose you took *refuge* with the beauteous Valeria?"

Syms, seated at his desk examining an assortment of fossilized barnacles, interjected wryly, "Aye. Mayhap she nursed you back to health?"

"As a matter of fact, she did!" laughed Anthony, but his smile quickly faded. "It was an interlude of peace in the midst of the year's turmoil. I sent a letter to my parents from Concepcion, but I now know it never arrived. I hoped to find a ship returning to England, but every one that passed was headed toward Australia. Eventually, I joined a group traveling overland to Botafogo, Brazil, and gained passage home with a trading ship. I shared quarters with a lot of unwashed seamen and a loquacious young Brazilian stowaway, bound for England to search for his father. It seemed the voyage home would never end." Anthony paused. "I didn't guess my family believed I was dead, especially since I'd written to them."

"You must have arrived back in London shortly after we visited the Raveneau home." Darwin stared off into space for a few moments, as if conjuring up the scene. "You know, Buskin insisted on coming with me. He said he felt he ought to speak to your parents because he was the last one to see you alive."

"Bastard," muttered Anthony. Thank God he had reached the end of his tale. Feeling some of his tension unspool, he reached for a piece of cheese from the plate Syms had assembled. Suddenly he was hungry. "The real reason Terrance wanted to meet my parents, I think, was to wheedle his way into my house. He'll stop at nothing to claim credit for my discoveries now that he thinks I am out of his way."

"What exactly do you mean by that?" Charles inclined his balding head, and Anthony could see the wheels turning in his mind. "Do you think he was responsible for what happened to you?"

"I am quite sure my fall was accidental, but I had given Terrance my notebook to hold onto. I'd been making notes in it just before I decided to climb down to see if the water was fresh or salty. After I fell, Buskin assumed that if I hadn't been killed by the blow to my head, I would drown. How easy it was for him to walk away and pretend he didn't know what had become of me. He kept my notebook and took my place on the *Beagle*, sailing with you to London. He has been coming daily to my house, supposedly to help catalogue my specimens, but in reality, he has been stealing them for himself. He has already given one speech based on *my* findings!"

"Good God!" Darwin cried again. "I can see it all happening exactly as you describe. If only I had known." His voice broke as he paused to shake his head. "What a devil of a coil. How can we expose his crimes?"

"I don't think there is a way to bring him to justice for walking away from me when I lay unconscious in the water. Unless he admits it outright, it is impossible to prove exactly what happened." Anthony clenched his jaw for an instant, then inhaled to dispel the white-hot rage that threatened him. "I am more focused on my notebook, which I believe is in Buskin's possession. Everything he said in his speech to the Geological Society came from it."

"How can I help you entrap him?"

The ghost of a smile flickered across Anthony's mouth. "There is someone who is helping me. A lady. She is in hiding from her father, who would force her to marry against her will. My parents installed her at my house, before I returned, where she has been unpacking and cataloguing my specimens."

Darwin's blue eyes narrowed. "Might she be in disguise as a man?"

"I cannot say. I have sworn to protect her secrets."

"I believe I may have met this person, in your father's company at Somerset House!"

Anthony shook his head and repeated, "I cannot say."

"Hmm!"

"Suffice it to say that this lady is very brave and resourceful. I think that together, we can spring a trap on Terrance Buskin."

"By Jove! I wish I could see it! I beg you to tell me how I may assist you."

"I hope you will think about Terrance Buskin's weaknesses. Perhaps, during the long voyage back to England, you noticed foibles that will aid in his capture. I plan to steal back the notebook, but I would additionally like to compel him to confess to some of his crimes at the very least."

"Hmm." Charles ate a piece of pickled salmon and scratched his head. "I confess to paying as little attention to Buskin as possible."

Across the room, Syms Covington cleared his throat. "I have a thought."

"What is it?" Anthony encouraged.

"Well, when we were on board the *Beagle*, I became aware of Mr. Buskin's fear of spirits. Ghosts. Once there was a strange wind that came through the poop cabin, where you used to sleep, sir. When I said, rather in jest, perhaps it must be your ghost, haunting the ship, I feared the man might faint dead away, like a lady!"

Anthony laughed. "I wish I could have seen it!"

"After that," Syms confessed, "I couldn't resist doing it again. Once I even borrowed one of Mr. Darwin's stuffed finches, the same sort you caught and preserved as well, Mr. St. Briac. I put it in his hammock ...and when he crawled in to sleep and discovered it, I said it had belonged to you. He was so terrified, I thought he might throw himself overboard!"

Darwin joined in Anthony's laughter. "You never said a word to me about this!" he accused his servant.

Syms flushed slightly. "I thought you might not like what I was doing, sir." He met Anthony's gaze. "I always had a bad feeling about Mr. Buskin. Never trusted him."

Anthony nodded and, as the clock struck ten, he set aside his plate. "Neither did I, but I told myself I was being petty, that perhaps he merely annoyed me because he is such an obsequious toad-eater."

"I fear I was too preoccupied with science during our voyage to pay much attention to Buskin," confessed Darwin, a trifle shamefaced. "But of course, rocks, beetles, and fossils have always interested me more than people."

"Don't worry. As long as you remain a bachelor it doesn't signify." Anthony patted his friend's shoulder and rose from the sofa. All he could think of now was returning home and sharing everything he had learned with Frederica.

"Odd that you should mention my single state. As it happens, I have begun giving serious thought to marriage," murmured Charles as he stood. "But that is a subject for another time. You have more pressing concerns, my friend."

"On the contrary." Anthony shook his head. "I have been remiss not to inquire about your life since returning to England. What fortunate lady has stirred your heart?"

Darwin went over to his desk and held up a sheet of foolscap. "Oh, there is no lady!" He smiled uncertainly. "But the process has begun ..."

Approaching, Anthony saw four words boldly written across the top of the page: *This is the Question.* Under this title were two columns, listing the benefits and drawbacks of marriage. How like Darwin, who would doubtless prefer to hunt beetles than woo a lady!

Leaning closer he read the first entry: *A wife would provide children and a companion in old age, an object to be beloved and played with – better than a dog, anyhow.* Under the "Not Marry" heading he saw: *Not forced to visit relatives.*

Anthony couldn't suppress a laugh. "A process indeed. I look forward to hearing more when next we meet."

"I would be grateful for your advice, St. Briac," Charles said, looking relieved. "You have a great deal more expertise with the fair sex than I."

"I should be delighted to assist." He pointed to the first entry. "To begin, I would urge you not to compliment any lady by telling her she is better than a dog."

Darwin looked momentarily puzzled, then he chuckled. "By Jove, I shall remember that."

Reaching across the desk to shake his friend's hand, Anthony added, "I have just one more question. Do you happen to know where Buskin is living?"

"I'm no good at those sorts of details." He looked over at Covington. "You have an address for Mr. Buskin, don't you, Syms?"

"Of course!"

Anthony was relieved to see that Darwin's able assistant was already writing it down for him. "That is a great help. I hope to pay a visit to his lodgings tomorrow night, but first I must contrive to lure him away from home."

Syms Covington interjected suddenly, "What if Mr. Darwin sends him an invitation?"

Charles glanced over in surprise, his tufted eyebrows drawing together. "What sort of invitation?"

"Mayhap I spoke out of turn," the younger man said, flushing. "I only thought, because you offered to help, sir, that Mr. Buskin would not refuse a summons from you."

Anthony took a chance and offered, "That plan would be so much better than anything I might devise."

"In that case," Charles said, "I shall do so. What if I invite him to come by at eight o'clock for supper and a look at a few of my prize specimens?"

"Excellent." Anthony felt euphoric. "I cannot thank you enough!" As they walked toward the door, he added, "Oh, and one more thing. If either of you has the opportunity, you might mention a rumored sighting of my ghost. I'd like to set the mood for what's to come."

Syms, who had gone to fetch Anthony's greatcoat and hat, laughed. "I'll own I can hardly wait for tomorrow night!"

CHAPTER 17

*J*ust as she had tucked her men's shirt into the waistband of her trousers, a knock came at the door. Freddie glanced over at Mrs. Bell. Who could it be at seven o'clock in the morning?

Frowning suspiciously, Mrs. Bell crossed to open the door a few inches. "Sir! What business do you have here?"

Freddie was annoyed to feel her heart speed up at the sound of Anthony's deep, amused voice filtering in from the corridor.

"My dear Mrs. Bell, I have brought a breakfast tray. I must discuss an important matter with Professor Loudon—in private."

"Private?" The housekeeper sent Freddie a questioning glance.

"It's all right," she assured her. "As I have told you, Mr. St. Briac and I are engaged in a bit of subterfuge to bring a villain to justice."

"Hmm." Mrs. Bell opened the door and Anthony walked past her with a tray laden with covered dishes. "I'll leave you two, then, but know I'll have my ears open, sir."

"I shall be on my best behavior, ma'am." His tone held an undercurrent of amusement.

When they were alone, Frederica felt her pulse accelerate. How to behave with this man given yesterday's shocking events? Not only had she revealed her physical passion for him, but she'd also pushed him away by saying many harsh things she might come to regret. She wanted to extinguish all her strong feelings, but too many sparks would not be snuffed out.

Anthony placed the tray on the small table near the window and sketched a bow. "Breakfast is served, my lady."

Freddie tried not to notice how intensely attractive he was, a dark roguish wolf among the sheep of the civilized London. He held her chair for her, then took away the covers to reveal dishes of ham, warm raisin buns, apple compote, and coddled eggs. As he poured chocolate into her cup, Freddie watched his tanned, deft fingers and remembered how he had cupped her naked breast and lowered his mouth to her nipple.

"It looks ...delicious," she stammered, feeling her cheeks heat.

"You've forgotten a few parts of your disguise," Anthony observed as he took the chair opposite hers.

"I did not forget. You interrupted me." Freddie put a hand up to her hair, pinned into a loose Apollo knot atop her head. "Besides, I was in no hurry to put on that awful wig and mustache. I must say, I am sick to death of them."

Anthony nodded, smiling, but his gaze lingered on her chest. "I was referring to something else."

Instantly, her breasts tingled. "Oh my!" She looked down and saw the curves outlined against her soft cambric shirt. Reaching for a large napkin, she tucked it into her collar. "There. That will do for now."

Anthony was watching her with hooded eyes as he took the other chair. "I couldn't wait to see you today."

The center of her being warmed at his words, but Freddie reminded herself that she had sworn to maintain a safe distance. "I surmise you have news of some sort about our plans for Terrance Buskin?"

"I went out last night."

This news caught her off-guard, for she had tossed and turned, wondering what Anthony was doing, imagining that he too was lying awake ...perhaps thinking of her. But instead, it seemed that he had lost no time in escaping.

"Wasn't that very risky?" Freddie asked.

"Perhaps, but I had to get out of this house." His dark eyes met hers for one telling moment before he continued, "I wanted to speak to Charles Darwin. Being very careful, I went first to my grandparents' home, hoping to get Darwin's address from Papa. Only Grandpère was in, but I welcomed the chance to re-unite with him."

Watching his face, Freddie sensed again the powerful bond of love Anthony enjoyed with his relatives. Bittersweet emotions squeezed her heart. Did he realize how fortunate he was to have such a large, close family? Perhaps one only noticed love when it was lacking.

"Your grandfather Raveneau is one of the most impressive men I've ever met," Freddie said. "It must have been wonderful to see him again."

"Yes, and he was able to tell me where I could find my friend Charles. I went there next."

"What a reunion that must have been," Freddie smiled, remembering Darwin's ashen face when he visited Anthony's family to tell them their son was truly lost.

"Indeed." Anthony set down his fork and leaned forward. "Charles not only told me Buskin's address, but has agreed to invite him to dinner tonight, clearing the way for me to find and recover my notebook."

So, this was the exciting news he had been eager to share. "That's wonderful."

"You don't sound as enthusiastic as I had expected," Anthony remarked. He ate another bite of ham before continuing, "I thought we agreed on that plan?"

Freddie couldn't help replying, "We did, but I did not expect you to do it by yourself. Was I not going to help you?"

"I think it would be too dangerous."

"That is one more reason why you shouldn't go alone."

Setting down his fork, Anthony leaned forward, holding her gaze. "I had time to think last night, and I concluded that I did enough damage when we …were alone yesterday. As you pointed out, I am a scoundrel."

Freddie struggled inwardly to conceal her emotions. "Did we not agree to forget that ever happened?"

He nodded, watching her. "Yet it seems I must remember, or risk doing it again." His hand reached toward hers. "Frederica, how could I put you even further in harm's way by allowing you to join me tonight in what might prove a perilous outing? If anything should happen to you, I would be forced to fall on my own sword."

Freddie nearly laughed. "Literally or figuratively?" Before he could respond, she gave his outstretched fingers a no-nonsense pat and quickly drew her own hand away. "There is no call for dramatics! If I were the sort of female who allowed men to make decisions for me, I would be betrothed to Lord Cobleigh today."

Anthony's dark brows flicked up. "Thank you for that timely reminder."

"Now, please tell me what transpired during your

visit with Mr. Darwin. Then we must make our plans to recover your notebook."

Leaning back in his chair, he related the entire tale of his visit with Charles Darwin and Syms Covington, including Syms's revelation that Terrance Buskin had believed Anthony's spirit was haunting the *Beagle* during the return voyage. Freddie clapped her hands as she imagined Buskin's terror upon discovering the stuffed finch in what had originally been Anthony's hammock.

"Of course, he probably didn't believe in ghosts until then," she exclaimed. "His fear sprang from guilt."

"Exactly." He began to put the dishes back on the tray as if preparing to leave.

Frederica narrowed her eyes slightly. "Now we must make our plan. What time will Terrance join Mr. Darwin for supper?"

"You are very tenacious."

"It is one of my great strengths," she agreed, smiling.

"And headstrong."

"So my father likes to say. Why is it that *men* are never accused of being headstrong?"

Anthony gave a rueful laugh. "If we were dueling, you would have just flicked off my buttons with the point of your rapier." Shaking his head, he added, "All right, then, I surrender. You will accompany me tonight. Let us make that plan."

"Wonderful!" It took all her self-control not to throw herself into his arms. "It will be just the adventure we've both been needing."

* * *

STORM CLOUDS WERE BREWING that evening as Anthony and Frederica prepared to leave his house in Charles Street. Their plan was set, but when she appeared at his room at seven-thirty, Anthony opened the door and drew a harsh breath. Freddie stood before him wearing a long, forest green cloak, its hood drawn close about her face. Seeing no sign of her luxuriant hair, he assumed she must have pinned it up out of sight.

"What's this all about?" He frowned. "What have you done with Professor Loudon?"

"I am tired of him," she replied.

"Come in here before Quincy or Meg see you."

When he had pulled her inside and closed the door, Frederica threw up her hands. "I am at the end of my tether. I never want to put on that ghastly wig again! I am simply fed up with pretending to be a man."

Brows aloft, Anthony sighed. He didn't blame her a bit, yet something about this declaration sent a chill down his spine. If Frederica was done being Professor Loudon, didn't that mean she must also be done hiding in his house, in disguise? He regularly told himself he didn't want her there any longer, and he knew her scheme had never been sustainable. Yet …he was growing used to Freddie being there. Nettling and stirring him up in a hundred disturbing ways.

"Your feelings are understandable," he said evenly, "but I think you would be better able to carry out our plan if you are dressed as Professor Loudon, especially if something happens to me and you are discovered."

Frederica stared back at him, eyes alight in a way that made him want to open the front of her cloak and take her in his arms, to feel her warm curves pressing into the hard planes of his body. *Stop, idiot.* He smothered a silent groan.

"I was afraid you would say that." Freddie wrinkled her nose. "And I suppose I must agree."

To his surprise, she reached up to her throat and pulled at the silk bow that fastened her cloak. Anthony nearly laughed aloud, for under the cloak she had been wearing trousers and a knee-length frock coat of gray wool. Her own curls were pinned close against her head.

"You are a minx," he said fondly.

"Thank you." She made a mock curtsy. "I still refuse to wear that awful wig again unless it is absolutely necessary." Freddie reached into the pocket of her frock coat and withdrew a much smaller mustache. Smiling, she stuck it onto her upper lip and confided, "I gave it a trim."

"Excellent," Anthony said, laughing.

"I happen to know that you have an entire wardrobe of hats, sir, and I am expecting you to lend me one that will completely cover my own hair."

He went into the dressing room, returned with a beaver hat in the Collegian style, and pulled it down over Frederica's glossy curls.

She reached into her pocket again and produced the silver-rimmed spectacles. "There. Will I do?"

Anthony gave her a lazy smile. "If you keep to the shadows, I suppose so," He pressed his forefinger against the edges of her considerably smaller mustache. Her rosy lips parted for an instant and he felt an involuntary stab of arousal. "I must say, however, your disguise becomes less convincing each time I see it."

Her cheeks pinkened. "That is because you now are so aware that I am *not* a man."

"Yes, I am." *All too aware,* he thought ruefully. "Let's be away. The sooner this escapade is ended, the better I will feel."

CHAPTER 18

By the time Anthony and Freddie arrived by hackney coach outside Terrance Buskin's modest lodgings in Morwell Street, frigid raindrops were spitting from the black clouds clustered overhead.

Just before they emerged from the equipage, Freddie caught Anthony's sleeve and reached into her coat pocket. "I think you might benefit from a small disguise as well," she whispered, all too aware of the warmth of his powerful body against hers on the narrow seat. She opened her hand. "I saved half of my mustache for you."

Anthony also wore a beaver hat, its brim pulled low over his brow, but Freddie reasoned he was such a striking figure that it seemed likely people might notice him. Any small change in his normal appearance would be helpful.

"How thoughtful," he replied with heavy irony.

"Let me put it in place for you."

As Freddie centered the mustache on his upper lip, she inhaled his faintly spicy, masculine scent. It made her long to kiss him, to taste him, and she blushed again, grateful for the darkened interior of the hack.

"Your solicitude is touching." The corners of Anthony's mouth twitched under her fingertips. "You are certain it isn't askew, as yours so often is?"

She gave him a light push. "Trust me."

"A daunting prospect."

The driver, having been overpaid, didn't seem to mind the delay. When they had emerged onto the street, Anthony leaned in to ask the scruffy fellow if he would return in half an hour.

"I will, if ye pay now, milord," the driver replied, staring curiously at the mustache that hadn't been there when Anthony had first gotten into the hack.

Anthony looked at the man askance, then reached into his pocket. After putting several coins in the driver's outstretched hand, he walked back to join Freddie on the raised pavement.

"I doubt he will return, but one can hope," he said. "We may need to make a quick escape from the vicinity."

Looking around, Freddie was very glad she had not come as a female. There were no ladies in sight on this out-of-the-way street, and the antiquated streetlamp flickered weakly.

"Perhaps you were right," she said to Anthony. "It is better for me to be a man tonight."

His sidelong glance was amused. "I am struck by your ability to shift between sexes almost at will."

They were in front of Terrance's lodgings. After knocking, Anthony consulted his watch.

"Damn. It's past nine o'clock." He broke off as the door swung open to reveal a pudgy, white-haired man with bleary close-set eyes.

"What d'ye want?" His breath stank of spirits.

"Good evening, sir," said Anthony. "My assistant and I are here at the behest of the Earl of Rutford, calling on Mr. Buskin."

"'E's gone out."

"His lordship has bid us wait."

Just then, a chorus of drunken laughter rose from the nearby parlor and the landlord glanced longingly toward the doorway. "I'm busy. Come back tomorrow."

"We don't wish to disturb you, sir, but his lordship insists," Anthony said smoothly. Even as he spoke, he held out a gleaming gold guinea. "The earl also wishes you to forget you ever saw us. If you do so, he will send another reward for your cooperation."

Eyes bugging out, the landlord snatched the coin. "Aye, sir. I never saw a thing. Besides, Buskin owes me rent." With that, he turned and hurried back to rejoin his friends.

Alone in the dim, musty entryway, Freddie and Anthony exchanged smiles. "That was shockingly easy," she whispered.

"For the moment," he agreed.

Freddie caught his sleeve. "But *who* is the Earl of Rutford?"

"Devil if I know! Come on. We haven't a moment to waste."

They hurried up the narrow stairs. Reaching a dimly lit corridor, Freddie saw that six doors opened off of it. Softly, she wondered, "How do we know which room belongs to Terrance?"

Anthony merely laid a forefinger over his mouth and started toward the first door. Leaning in, he listened, and Freddie could hear a mumbled female conversation inside. They crossed the hall to the second door. No sound came from within, so Anthony knocked. A moment later, the door swung open to reveal a pair of curly-haired, adolescent boys. They stared at him, wide-eyed.

"Our ma went out," the taller one said.

"Never mind. Sorry to disturb you." Pausing, he added, "Do you boys happen to know which room belongs to Mr. Buskin?" When they exchanged glances, Anthony gave them each a shilling.

The taller boy blinked at the coin and pointed down the corridor. "There."

"The Earl of Rutford thanks you, young man."

As Freddie followed Anthony to the designated door, heart racing, her sense of apprehension grew. She tried not to think about the countless things that could go wrong.

Anthony put his hand on the knob and twisted to no avail. "Curse it," he muttered.

Wildly, Freddie wondered why they hadn't thought of this, but in the next moment, Anthony had brought out an assortment of metal lock picks. Without a word, he gave them to her to hold.

She watched, palms damp, as he very casually glanced around and tried the first pick ...without success. Holding her breath, Freddie handed him a thin, hooked pick. What if someone appeared while they were breaking into Terrance's rooms?

As if reading her mind, Anthony glanced back over one broad shoulder and whispered, "I told you it would be dangerous, but you would not listen."

"I am not afraid." She put up her chin.

An instant later, Freddie heard a faint click, and Anthony turned the doorknob. Adrenaline surged through her veins as they entered the pitch-black room. She wrinkled her nose at the mixture of unpleasant smells, and it came to her that Buskin must be preserving and stuffing dead birds in the same room where he slept.

Anthony's eyes seemed to adjust quickly to the dark. He felt his way to a table, and a moment later a gaslamp, turned very low, gave them light.

"Oh, my." Freddie looked around in dismay. There were bird skins and various uncleaned tools of taxidermy spread out on one table, while another was scattered with papers, books, and other notes. In one corner stood a narrow, unmade bed, and it appeared that most of Terrance's clothing was tossed over a nearby chair. "I am quite shocked. He was so neat while working in your library!"

"Buskin is one of those people who presents himself to the world as a paragon, yet behaves as he pleases when no one is looking," Anthony said grimly. Without another word, he moved to the table and began sorting through the jumble of papers.

Freddie joined him, painfully aware that Terrance could walk through the door at any moment and discover them. "Perhaps I should go out into the corridor, so that if he returns, I can warn you?"

He sent her a quelling look. "Absolutely not. I don't want you out of my sight."

Swallowing, she nodded. Although she didn't like to give Anthony the idea he could order her around, Freddie found that she was beginning to trust him in a way she didn't completely understand. Together they carefully sorted through papers, looking for Anthony's blue notebook. They had already discussed the possibility that Terrance had changed or disguised it in some way, and she saw that Anthony was examining every single piece of paper in case he found his own handwriting or drawings on it.

Nearly a half-hour later, they were finished, and Freddie's heart sank as she realized their search had been unsuccessful. Anthony consulted his pocket watch and frowned. "It is past ten o'clock. Although it's unlikely, I suppose Buskin could return at any moment."

Freddie followed him over to the table where Terrance had stuffed birds and other small animals. Anthony retrieved a few of his own stolen finches, then took from his pocket a specimen with black feathers and an exceptionally thick beak. A tag tied to one tiny leg read *Geospiza Fortis, male, 15.01.1836* ...the words printed in Anthony's own distinctive hand.

"I caught and stuffed this ground finch after the accident, when I was living with the Spaniards," he explained. "It's one of the few specimens I brought back to England with me. I wish I could see Buskin when he finds this and reads the date on the tag." A wicked smile touched his mouth. "Even if we don't find that notebook, it's almost enough to know that coward will believe I am haunting him from the watery grave where he left me to die."

Freddie shivered. She looked around the room, her heart twisting at the thought that they might have to go away empty-handed. She went to the bed and looked among the rumpled bedclothes, even peeking under the pillow and mattress. Nothing. She had just straightened and begun to turn away when her gaze touched on a brown leather satchel, only half visible under a heap of clothing on the nearby chair.

Instantly, Freddie remembered the day at the Geological Society meeting when she had been in the private room with Terrance Buskin. He had picked up the notebook and papers and jammed them all into a satchel just like that one!

Across the room, Anthony was opening books and shaking them. "It's not here." His low voice was edged with frustration. "Buskin could return at any moment. Come on, we must leave while we can." Looking across at Freddie, he added, "I was mad to let you come with me."

"Wait!" she whispered hoarsely. "Look at this!"

"Frederica..." His tone was a warning.

Heart pounding, she pulled the satchel out from under the pile of clothing and fumbled with the fastenings. Was it possible that Terrance had left the valuable notebook here, seemingly forgotten since that day at the Geological Society? Anthony had crossed to stand beside her, watching, and she prayed she hadn't gotten his hopes up for nothing.

"This is the satchel he had with him at Somerset House," she explained softly, her fingers shaking as she worked at the second clasp. "When I asked about the notebook, he hurriedly put it in here."

Anthony took the satchel and had it open in an instant. The pause that followed was charged with energy. One by one, he pulled out crumpled papers ...and then, a slim notebook with a dark blue cover. When he opened it and Freddie saw the pages covered with Anthony's own handwriting and sketches, tears stung her eyes.

"Oh God," she breathed, gripping his arm with both hands.

"Indeed." Anthony's jaw was set in a hard line as he thrust the notebook into the front of his heavy coat. "Now, let's be away."

Quickly, he extinguished the light. They had only taken a few steps toward the door when voices reached them from the corridor. One of the boys was speaking.

"Indeed, 'twas the Earl of Rutford, come looking for you, sir!"

"But I don't know the bloody Earl of Rutford!" a man's voice answered.

Freddie's heart threatened to burst. "It's him!"

* * *

ANTHONY TURNED AROUND, looking for a hiding place, but none existed. There was not even an armoire that they could squeeze into together. Across the room, there was one tall, dingy window. Pulling Frederica in his wake, he was there in a moment and threw open the sash.

It was storming outside, and rain was blowing sideways across the building. Anthony wanted to shout epithets. Leaning out, he saw that there was a tiny wrought iron balcony surrounding the window, not even deep enough to stand on.

For an instant, he considered simply facing Terrance Buskin, and Frederica seemed to read his mind. "No!" she hissed. "We've come too far to stop now." She peered outside. "We can drop down from the balcony." She was already putting on her gloves.

Anthony nodded shortly. "I will drop first, so I can catch you. Agreed?"

"Oh, all right! I will wait for you."

She went out into the dark, forbidding night, grasping the top edge of the iron railing and throwing one trousered leg over the side. Even in that adrenaline-fueled moment, Anthony knew a warm pulse of admiration for Freddie's indomitable courage. Quickly, she climbed down and clung to two of the railings, her legs dangling toward the ground.

Anthony was right behind her, closing the window before he followed her. They hung suspended in the lashing rain, side by side. When Freddie turned her face, he saw that she was beginning to struggle to hold on.

Suddenly time disappeared and Anthony was back on the Galápagos Islands, teetering on the edge of the crumbling cliff. Icy pain speared the side of his head, born of the primitive memory of letting go and falling into a black void. His heart clenched with terror, as if the end were near. That's what it had been like that day when he fell through space, just before his head struck the rock ...the black jaws of death, yawning wide below him and swallowing him whole.

"Anthony!"

Through the sheets of rain, he saw Freddie staring at him, and her wildly questioning face jolted him back to reality. The stabbing pain receded into the past. He had promised her. He would not die.

"Hang on!" Anthony heard himself shout. "Wait!" And then he opened his freezing hands and hurtled toward the ground.

Freddie was nearly in tears. Her gloved fingers, clinging to the thin metal bars, were numb, and it seemed she could not hold on one instant longer. Had she been mad to trust Anthony St. Briac, knowing what she did about men? Her heart thrashed with panic that extended far beyond this moment of danger.

"I'm here!" His deep voice carried up to her on the wind. "Let go, Frederica!"

Oh God, those were the hardest words. But holding on, even one more second, was impossible. As a peal of thunder shook the iron railings, Freddie let go and plunged toward the earth...

CHAPTER 19

When Freddie plummeted into Anthony's waiting arms, the force was enough to send them both tumbling backward. She found herself on top of him, soaking wet, in the midst of a prickly boxwood hedge. Had she crushed him? He gave a muted groan.

"Are you hurt?" Freddie asked urgently.

Anthony was already scrambling to his feet. Grasping Freddie's waist, he lifted her up as well and set her on the grass.

"Come on," he shouted over the wind and rain.

She barely had time to grab hold of his cold, wet hand before they were running the short distance under an elm tree to the brick garden wall. To Freddie, the barrier looked insurmountable, but Anthony pushed her up the wall, ordering her to use the thick vines of a climbing wisteria to gain purchase on the bricks. When she had safely reached the top, he followed her and dropped lightly down to the street below.

"Hurry!" he commanded and held up his arms. "Jump."

The longer she delayed, the better the chance that

Terrance Buskin might look down from his window and see her, perched under the sheltering branches of the elm. So, Freddie leaped down from the wall and Anthony caught her again, staggering slightly, and held her tightly against him for an instant. Then they were running together toward the drab hackney coach waiting round the corner.

Not bothering to greet the scruffy driver, Anthony flung open the door, and they both threw themselves inside, the sound of their breathing filling the chilly, confined space.

"Miser'ble night," grumbled the unshaven old man. "I nearly didn't wait."

Handing the man an additional crown, Anthony gave him an address a short distance from Charles Street and sat back next to Freddie. They were both drenched to the skin, and she began to shiver as the hack rolled forward into the stormy night.

"You were right," she said in conspiratorial tones.

"I was?" Anthony bent closer, chilly and damp, yet radiating an inner fire that warmed every corner of her being. "Tell me more."

"You were right when you said I must not wear skirts." His irresistibly masculine face was just inches away. Freddie longed to touch him, wished he would kiss her.

He peeled the false mustaches from their upper lips and said seductively, "I like it when you say I've been right. Let's go home and you can tell me again."

* * *

HOME, Anthony had said. The word reverberated inside Freddie as they came into the quiet house and started up the stairs together. Of course, even if Anthony meant anything by that—which he most certainly did not—it would be folly to entertain anything beyond this shared adventure.

When they paused on the landing, Freddie saw him wince. "You're limping!"

Anthony glanced down. "It's just my ankle. The one I broke when I fell on James Island."

"It's my fault you hurt it again. I fell on you and knocked you down," she whispered.

"That's *not* what happened. I caught you." Sending her a wry glance, he continued up the stairs. "Make haste, before your stern Mrs. Bell appears to interrogate me."

When they reached his door, Frederica paused. "I should look at your ankle."

His brows flicked up. "Be my guest."

Inside his bedchamber, Anthony gathered linen towels. He handed a few to Freddie and began to strip off his wet clothes. "Your ankle?" she asked, her voice breaking.

"I am in greater discomfort from the cold and wet. We both should get out of these clothes and into something dry." Opening his coat, he reached inside and withdrew the blue notebook, which appeared undamaged by the night's rigors. He set it on a side table and met her eyes. "I am eager to look at this more carefully, but not just yet."

Freddie suddenly felt teary. "Thank God it is still dry and in one piece."

While unbuttoning his shirt, Anthony disappeared into his dressing room and returned with the claret velvet dressing gown she had been wearing the first night he returned home, when she surprised him in the library. Holding it out to her, he said with a hint of mockery, "I believe you already are well acquainted with this garment."

She scarcely knew what to do. Pretend it didn't

bother her in the least that he had begun to undress? He was stripping off his shirt now, revealing a broad, hard-muscled chest lightly covered with crisp black hair. As he toweled off, Freddie murmured, "I'll just step into your dressing room and change, if you don't mind."

Something in his amused glance suggested that he knew everything she was thinking and feeling. "You are welcome to do whatever pleases you."

Her entire body felt warm and sensitive as she went into the darkened space and hurriedly peeled away her sodden garments. As she rubbed her bare skin with a towel, it came to her that she was alone with a sinfully handsome man in his bedchamber and both of them were undressed!

Yet hadn't she spent years defying convention, rebelling against the rules decreeing that women of quality remain pure and aspire to make an advantageous marriage? Yes, but it was one thing to rebel under her grandfather's roof and another to do so in the bedchamber of Anthony St. Briac.

For years, Freddie had struggled to suppress her feminine longings. Now, as she slipped her arms into the heavy velvet dressing gown, warm blood coursed through her veins. Every secret part of her was alive and eager. She might be unschooled in the ways of intimacy and passion, but who better to teach her than Anthony?

His voice interrupted her reverie. "Frederica, I hope you haven't gotten lost amidst my vast wardrobe."

She laughed, her tension dissolving, and emerged from the dressing room. A fire was burning now in the grate, illuminating the room with its cozy glow. Anthony sat on the edge of the bed, wearing an open, dry white shirt, a fresh towel draped over his lap.

His gaze roamed over her. "Charming. I'd nearly forgotten how well you wear my dressing gown."

"You are teasing me." Freddie wagged a finger at him. "We both know I look ridiculous."

"Hardly." Suddenly there was a warm edge to Anthony's voice that sent a current of arousal through her body.

Freddie looked at his bare, powerful legs and remembered that she had insisted on examining his ankle. Adopting a no-nonsense tone, she approached the bed. "How does your ankle feel?"

He shrugged his wide shoulders. "A bit sore, as usual, but I never think of it."

She tried to pretend he was her grandfather, whose various aches and pains she had often ministered to over the years. "Hmm. Let me take a look."

Anthony extended his right leg, and Freddie cradled his foot in her pale hands. Her mouth went dry. She touched his ankle, which looked slightly swollen. "Oh, I am so sorry I've hurt you. We should wrap this."

"You didn't hurt me. All my injuries are due to Terrance Buskin, including any that happened tonight."

"But if you hadn't tried to catch me—"

"My dear, I didn't try." He arched a black brow. "I succeeded."

"Yes, of course, but ..." She tried to swallow. "Let me get something to wrap your ankle."

He leaned forward and his hand caught her wrist. "Later."

Freddie's heart beat wildly as he slowly brought her closer until she was standing between his knees. *What are you afraid of, you goose?*

"We must talk."

"Talk?" she squeaked.?

"Yes." His breath was warm on her cheek. "You are

in a very compromising position, Frederica. How do you feel about that?"

Oh, drat him for saying it out loud. "I …" Freddie felt warmth throb between her legs. "I am aware of that."

Anthony nodded slowly. "I would not want you to regret anything that happens between us." His voice was a caress. "What do you want to do?"

I want to put my hands on your splendid face and feel its warmth. I want to lean forward and touch your mouth with mine, to feel your fingertips on my body … She swayed toward him silently, seemingly unable to speak.

"Tell me, Frederica," he murmured.

"Please call me Freddie." She sounded intoxicated.

"Of course. What do you want, Freddie?"

"I want …" *Oh, lord.* Feeling as if she were plunging off a cliff, Freddie boldly whispered, "You. I want you."

For an instant, his eyes closed, revealing the sooty crescents of his thick lashes. She stared at his crooked nose, the chiseled lines of his cheekbones and jaw, the lizard tattoo peeking from his open shirt. Surely, a man like this was beyond her touch. As Anthony encircled her waist with one arm and reached with his other hand for the sash of her dressing gown, Freddie spoke again.

"Just to be clear, I have no illusions, I mean, I do not imagine that this signifies any serious intentions. On your part." She cleared her throat. "Or mine!"

"No?" he asked mildly.

"I mean only to remind you that I am not some schoolroom miss, and I do not imagine that you are …"

"I am—what?" Inches away, his sensual mouth curved gently. "Be easy, sweet. You may speak freely to me."

Freddie took a deep breath. "In love! I mean to say, I do not imagine that you are in *love* with me! And of course, I am not in love with you!" She gave a nervous laugh. "You may be assured on that score." To her further chagrin, she felt her face growing very hot.

"I see." His hand reached to cradle the curve of her cheek. "Would you like me to kiss you?"

Closing her eyes, she nodded, waiting, aching. After a long moment, his lips brushed hers and Freddie heard herself groan, and then she was in his embrace. She parted her lips to him, kissing him back, her arms twining about his strong neck. Her tongue sought his, and for a bit she sensed that he was allowing her to vent to her own hunger. How good he tasted! Freddie scarcely noticed when Anthony lifted her onto the bed. He lay back and she straddled his lean, powerful body, pushing open his shirt so she could feel the muscled contours of his chest. As she continued to kiss him, Anthony easily reached up to pull the sleeves of the dressing gown off her slim arms. Bared to the firelit air, Freddie could hardly wait for his touch. When he covered both breasts with his warm palms, she shuddered with pleasure and a primitive need she had never imagined.

"You are beautiful," Anthony whispered.

It was a mad thing for him to say, yet she reveled in the moment, as if they were sharing a dream. "Thank you, sir." Freddie laughed a little as her mouth clung to his.

"Are you done yet having your way with me?" His voice was husky. "I want to fulfill your desires, if you'll let me."

When she stopped kissing him and sat back, she felt a jolt of sensation as their bodies met. She was wet and pulsing, fitting against the shockingly aroused length of him. "Oh, my."

Anthony moved ever so slightly against her, creating a delicious friction, and her hips instinctively answered his. He didn't ask her permission this time. In one movement, he turned her back into the pillows and removed the last of their clothing. Freddie looked up into his face and, as their eyes met, she felt something intangible shift inside. Her hand went up to push back his disheveled curls, still damp from that night's adventure.

"I'm going to make love to you," Anthony said.

Part of her resisted that word *love*, for of course this had nothing to do with love, but she couldn't help sighing. When his mouth found hers again, exploring for long, hungry moments, then burned a path down the side of her neck and throat, Freddie stopped thinking. His tongue, swirling on her nipple was what she had dreamed of night and day since the last time he had done these things. *Yes*, the pull of his mouth, nudging her tantalizingly close to the edge of release.

His hands traced the slim line of her back, ribcage, the curves of her hips and then her bottom. "I've wanted to touch you this way," he whispered. One fingertip trailed fire along the cleft of her bottom until he turned on one hip and nudged her thighs apart. Freddie shamelessly opened to him, her climax already building. She was slippery, ready in a way she didn't fully understand, and his knowing fingers stroked and touched, circling the bud where sensations buzzed like lightning.

"Show me what you like, sweet." Anthony brought her hand over his and she moved with him, slower, faster, gasping. When he carefully pushed two long fingers inside her, in and out, touching a sensitized place deep within, she moaned.

He paused for an instant. "Am I hurting you?"

In response, Freddie arched against his hand, her need swelling, throbbing. She sobbed aloud when, at last, her orgasm crested and slowly uncoiled in excruciating waves of pleasure that shook her to the core.

As the tremors gradually subsided, she wanted to touch him as he had touched her, to taste him all over, but Anthony was on top of her, kissing her again, and she sensed that now his release was at hand. Lithe and strong, he rose up on an elbow and reached down between them to guide himself to her entrance. His gaze caught hers. Suddenly Freddie knew a jolt of apprehension, for she had heard terrible stories about the loss of one's virginity. Yet Anthony came into her so gradually, even teasingly, that she yearned for all of him, dimly aware of a burning sensation. Her hips rose up and suddenly he was fully inside, filling her in a way that made her feel deeply complete.

Slowly, he began to move, and Frederica joined in the timeless rhythm. It was as if they had spiraled into a new heart-pounding adventure, one that she never wanted to end. She clung to his shoulders, her face in the crook of his neck, as she met his thrusts. When at last he tensed, then shuddered, she felt the power of their connection, body ...and soul. Tears burned her eyes as his heart pounded against her breasts. *This is different, special*, she thought. *It must be!*

In the afterglow, Freddie lay still joined to Anthony, and he reached back with one hand to draw the covers over them. As she felt him dozing off, a secret part of her hoped to hear him vow, "I love you."

But of course, the words did not come.

CHAPTER 20

Rain rattled the windowpanes as Anthony came slowly awake. Frederica lay curled in his arms, one pale hand on his tanned chest. The fire continued to burn brightly, so it seemed he hadn't been sleeping very long. Lifting the covers, he looked down and saw the smear of blood against the white sheets.

I must be mad! He smothered a groan.

Not only had he deflowered her, but there was also a possibility he'd gotten her with child. He hadn't even had one drink, so drunkenness could not be blamed for his reckless behavior. No, the source of his intoxication seemed to be one stubborn, spirited, invincible lady: Miss Frederica Redfield. In the golden shadows, Anthony studied her sleeping face. Others might not think her a beauty, but she stirred him like a goddess.

Her voice rang in his ears. *I do not imagine that you are in love with me! And of course, I am not in love with you! You may be assured on that score.*

Well, good.

Frederica was made of strong stuff. He'd known that about her since their first meeting, and she had proved it over and over during those early encounters seven years ago, when he'd felt his heart turning inside-out in a most inconvenient way.

During the intervening years when Anthony had been away on board the *Beagle*, it seemed Frederica had only grown braver and more self-reliant.

But how to reconcile all of that with this soft and passionate woman in his bed?

"Hello …"

Anthony looked down to see that her eyes were open, and she was watching him.

He gathered her closer. "How do you feel?"

Frederica seemed to know what he meant. "I am a bit sore now, but do not imagine that you hurt me. It was quite the opposite."

Her slightly naughty smile made him laugh. "You are the most unique female I have ever known." He thought back to one of their first encounters, when they met to ride together in Hyde Park. Frederica had sent her groom on an invented errand so she might speak freely to Anthony, and she had admitted as much to him with charming frankness.

"You know very well that I have no use for the rules of conduct for so-called ladies. Perhaps I should have been born a man." As soon as those words were out, she bit her lip and laughed. "Oh, no, that's not right. Tonight, I am very glad to be female."

As she fitted herself to him, Anthony's arousal mingled with a heady sense of joy he had never felt before. Kissing Frederica was ambrosia, and as her hands roamed down his back, exploring each plane and muscle, he forced himself back to reality.

"Let me get a damp cloth for you, sweet," he murmured, raising his head. "Don't go away."

As Anthony threw back the covers and climbed out of the warm bed, Frederica sat up. "I will admit, I am quite ignorant about all of this."

"I should have thought it through. I was a bit mad." Turning back from his washstand, he lifted a brow and added, "Mad with wanting you, my dear."

"How thrilling. That is the sort of thing that I never thought to hear from a man." She gave him a dazzling smile. "Thank you."

Anthony came back to the bed, aching to make love to her again, but instead he gave her the cloth and went to tend the fire.

"Although I don't want to talk, I suppose we must," he said at last.

"In bed?" Frederica lifted the covers and gestured for him to join her.

"Your servant." Anthony poured them each a small glass of port and walked back naked to join her. Frederica watched him approach with open wonderment, her eyes roaming over his body.

"You are very bold, my lady," he said, handing her a tiny goblet.

"I simply have no patience for concealing my thoughts or ..." She broke off, color washing her cheeks. Had she been about to add *feelings*?

"I must say, I like that about you immensely," he said, saving them both from a more sensitive discussion. Anthony climbed into bed beside her, and they sat back against the pillows, sipping the port.

"Perhaps we should talk about Terrance Buskin," suggested Frederica after a moment. "What shall we do next? I am very eager to be done with this masquerade."

"So you have mentioned." Her warm, beautiful breast grazed his arm in a most distracting way. Anthony's breath caught, but he forged on. "Shall we summon Buskin, and my ghost could then appear to him?"

Frederica nodded, eyes sparkling. "Excellent! But I think we should have a witness. Your father, perhaps, or even Emeline?"

"Yes, that's a good idea. I will consider it further in the morning."

He gazed at the rosy peak of her breast and watched it pucker, begging for his mouth. Their eyes met; he sensed her breathing quicken. All his devils urged him to make love to her again. There were so many ways they could pleasure each other without further risk of conception. The very thought of tasting her intimately, of feeling her arousal build until she moaned and writhed, brought him to a state of aching hardness.

Frederica licked her dry lips. "I should return to my own bed."

Of course. Of course, she should! Still, it hit him like one of the thunderclaps that shook the night sky. "Right," he agreed hoarsely.

"Not only do we both need sleep if we are to capture Buskin tomorrow, but there is the matter of Mrs. Bell."

"Yes. Very sensible."

Leaning upward, she touched her lips to his. "It's not that I *want* to go, but Mrs. Bell is doubtless already wondering where I was last evening. If she rises early and goes to my bedchamber, it would be quite disastrous."

Mrs. Bell could go to the devil as far as Anthony was concerned, but he kept this sentiment to himself. "Quite understandable," he said with a sober nod. "But now you must remove yourself from my sight before I succumb to temptation and do something wicked." His voice turned husky. "Again."

He got out of bed and went to slip into a dressing gown of gray-and-black brocade. When he reemerged into the bedroom, Frederica was standing there covered from neck to ankles in the claret dressing gown.

"Do you mind if I wear this?" she asked. "Just to return to my rooms?"

"Not in the least. I would urge you to keep it, but doubtless Mrs. Bell would not approve."

She flushed slightly. "It isn't that I'm afraid of her, you know. I just ..." Breaking off, she swallowed. "I don't know."

Charmed by her frankness, Anthony drew her into his embrace. "In truth, neither do I. For now, I suggest that we deal with Buskin."

"Yes," Frederica nodded against his shoulder.

He lifted her chin and kissed her with more tenderness, even wonderment, than passion. Had they crossed over into some new dimension? Anthony had been with many women over the years, but none of them had caused him to feel so unsettled. Disoriented.

"Goodnight then." Frederica stepped back out of his arms.

Feeling a bit like a schoolboy, he nodded. "I will see you – or perhaps I should I say, Professor Loudon – tomorrow."

She wrinkled her nose, then sighed. "Perhaps, with luck, it will be the last time."

But then what? Anthony wondered. It seemed that they had reached a crossroads in more ways than one.

He watched her open the door, peek out, and slip away down the corridor, melting into the shadows. Turning back to his own bed, he thought it had never looked so empty.

* * *

THE STORMY NIGHT gave way to a clear, bright dawn. Freddie awoke early and rang for a bath. As she washed herself, she was acutely aware of her tender intimate parts, reminding her of the glorious interlude in Anthony's bed. In the light of day, it all felt rather like a dream ...and perhaps that was for the best. It would be a memory she could hold close in the years to come, when she was living and working as an independent woman.

Mrs. Bell knocked when Freddie was nearly dressed as Professor Loudon. As she put the finishing touches on her neckcloth, she called to the housekeeper to come in. Any hope she had that her absence had gone unnoticed disappeared as soon as she saw Mrs. Bell's pursed lips.

"And where have you been?" the old woman asked, setting down a tray of chocolate and warm buns. She put her hands on her ample hips as she waited for a reply.

Freddie pressed her newly abbreviated mustache into place and looked around for her spectacles. "I have been here, sleeping, bathing, and now dressing," she said with a friendly smile.

"I won't mince words." Mrs. Bell crossed to stand before her, and Freddie saw the spots of color on her cheeks. "I came to speak to you last night, and you were not here. Then, later, I heard voices coming from Mr. St. Briac's rooms …above my quarters. I will admit, I stepped into the stairway, and I heard you." Blinking nervously, she added, "Laughing with him, in his bed-chamber."

It had seemed such a good idea for Mrs. Bell to sleep in the valet's room, attached to Anthony's via a hidden staircase, but now that he was back, everything had changed. "I think we should find other rooms for you, Mrs. Bell," said Freddie.

The housekeeper put a hand on her arm. "You are like a member of my family, mistress, and I feel responsible for your wellbeing."

Freddie nodded. "That means more to me than you know, but perhaps you forget that I am five-and-twenty. I am determined to chart the course of my own life. You must trust me to do so." Lowering her voice, she added, "You know what I have endured from my own father. I simply will not be constrained by another person, not even you."

"But *that man* ..."

From the doorway, an amused male voice interjected, "Mrs. Bell, were you about to utter my name?"

Freddie's heart jumped as she turned and saw Anthony entering the room. He wore riding clothes: a midnight-blue frock coat over a waistcoat of palest yellow and buff breeches, and his ebony locks were appealingly windblown. How splendid he was! He gave the housekeeper a smile designed to melt her resistance, then turned to Freddie.

"You are looking very, ah, scholarly this morning, professor."

Freddie felt herself blush to the roots of her hair. Burningly conscious of Mrs. Bell's disapproving stare, she adjusted her spectacles. "I anticipate a full day of work in your library, sir."

"Let us go down, then." Anthony picked up the breakfast tray and sent the housekeeper another magnetic smile. "We won't even have to ring for breakfast, thanks to our good Mrs. Bell."

Freddie went with him out into the corridor. When they reached the top of the stairs, Anthony paused and met her eyes.

"How are you feeling this morning?" he asked softly.

Before she could reply, Meg came into view on the landing below. When she saw that Anthony was holding a tray, she hurried up to take it from him.

"Mister Darwin is here to see you, sir," said the maid. "I bid him wait for you in the library."

"Ah, thank you, Meg."

As they followed her retreating figure down the

stairs, Anthony glanced at Freddie. "I had come up to tell you about Darwin's planned visit."

Their eyes met and she mouthed the word *Witness?*

Lowering his voice, he said, "Indeed. I took a message to him early this morning. Charles then sent a servant to bring Buskin to meet him here."

Freddie's heartbeat accelerated. So that's why Anthony was wearing riding clothes; he had gone out again, this time by daylight! "You are courting danger."

His brows flicked up. "Not for long, I hope."

CHAPTER 21

*E*ven though she had met Charles Darwin before, Freddie seemed to truly see him for the first time as she and Anthony entered the library. Sitting at Anthony's desk, surrounded by books, fossils, rocks, and stuffed birds, Darwin held a large bony claw in one hand and a magnifying glass in the other. Light streamed in through the tall window dividing a wall of bookshelves. It bathed the young naturalist in a golden glow as he bent over the specimen, his thinning brown hair falling forward, eyes obscured by bushy brows.

"Charles," Anthony said as they drew near, but Darwin appeared oblivious to anyone or anything except the large, fossilized claw. Only when Anthony put a hand on his shoulder did he finally glance up.

"I didn't know you had found this," Darwin said, shaking the claw in the air.

"You are as absentminded as ever," laughed Anthony. "You did know! We discovered several pieces at the same time, at Punta Alta, remember?" Turning to Frederica, he added, "We believe it is part of a giant, ancient armadillo. Charles found some bony plates and other bits, all together, on the beach. We recognized it immediately, for only the week before, some local gauchos had fed us a dinner of armadillos roasted in their shells."

As disgusting as that sounded to Freddie, she was captivated nonetheless by the conversation between the two men. They reminisced about their adventures in Argentina for several minutes, ending with a good-natured demand from Darwin. "See here, St. Briac, I insist that you give me this specimen. It belongs with the teeth, thigh bone, and other pieces I have assembled!"

"Of course," Anthony nodded agreement. "I was about to offer it to you."

Darwin blinked under his tufted brows, as if surprised that it had been so easy. In the next moment, he seemed to notice Freddie for the first time. Pushing errant locks back from his brow, he put down the magnifying glass and extended his hand to her.

"My apologies, sir. I didn't see you standing there! But we've met, haven't we?"

"Yes, at the Geological Society at Somerset House. I attended Buskin's speech with Anthony's father," Freddie replied in her gruffest voice. "I'm Frederick Loudon. Very good to see you again, Mr. Darwin."

As they shook hands, Anthony said, "This is the person I told you about, Charles. My parents engaged Professor Loudon to begin unpacking and cataloguing my specimens even before I returned to London."

"Oh, yes, of course ..." Darwin's cherubic lips quirked as he exchanged glances with Anthony. "*That* person."

Freddie blanched. *He knows!* She turned narrowed eyes on Anthony, but he would not look at her. As the mantel clock struck nine, Freddie realized that this must be a topic for another time.

"I understand that you two have a great deal to talk about, but have you noticed the time?" she asked, remaining in character as Loudon. "If Terrance Buskin is expected soon, I hope you have already formed a plan."

"That's his job." Darwin pointed at Anthony. "I'm just here to offer my help if needed."

"I don't think it will be that difficult," Anthony said coolly. "I suggested to Charles that, when Buskin arrives, he should say you two wanted to show him what has miraculously turned up." Stepping behind the desk, Anthony opened a drawer and took out one of the stuffed finches Freddie had seen him steal back from Terrance Buskin's lodgings.

Darwin blinked at the very unprepossessing bird. Only a few inches long, its feathers were drab tan and pale gray, and its beak was small and thin. "Ah, an excellent example of our tool-using woodpecker finch!" he breathed.

"Indeed," nodded Anthony. "I actually captured this specimen on the day of my accident. It was in the bag I asked Buskin to hold ...minutes before I fell." Eyes agleam, he added, "Last night, I repatriated it, so to speak."

"Oh, my," uttered Freddie. "If he remembers where this bird came from, it will be positively chilling."

"Especially with the new addition of one of my own labels, written in my hand." Anthony bent to make a handwritten tag, which he attached to the tiny finch's leg with a bit of string. Straightening he gave her a knowing smile. "Believe me, Buskin will recognize this bird immediately. In fact, once he realized it was gone last night, I'll wager this tiny fellow haunted his dreams, if he managed to sleep at all."

"I hope you are right!" Freddie paused to watch Anthony carefully position a cactus needle in the finch's beak.

"It uses the needle as a tool—to probe tree bark for insects," he explained.

"How fascinating," murmured Freddie.

"Woodpecker finches can improvise an array of tools, which they hold in their beaks," explained Darwin. "They hunt mainly for arthropods."

Freddie felt proud that Darwin used the scientific word *arthropods*, assuming she would know its meaning. Just then, however, the mood was broken by a knock at the front door. Her heart jumped.

Anthony pointed to the finch with its new tag. "Put it right in the middle of the desk. Say that you discovered it when you came downstairs this morning and immediately alerted Mr. Darwin." He smiled grimly. "I will do the rest."

She obeyed, her hands shaking slightly, and watched as Quincy passed the library on his way to the front door.

"Shh," cautioned Anthony. Quickly, he crossed the room and reached above a row of books to touch the back of the shelf. To Freddie's astonishment, the bookcase swung inward, and Anthony passed inside. A moment later, the room was as before.

"I wonder if I am dreaming," she whispered to Charles, forgetting to disguise her voice.

He seemed unaware of her slip. "As I recall, this house has a few secret rooms and staircases. When Anthony heard, he couldn't resist buying it."

Voices carried to them from the entry hall, and a few moments later Terrance Buskin came into the library. He was followed by a dark-haired man Freddie recognized as Darwin's cabin boy, Syms Covington, one of the *Beagle* party who had visited Grosvenor Square bearing sorrowful news for Anthony's family.

Terrance, usually so pale and dull, appeared transformed. His color was hectic, he had mis-buttoned his waistcoat, and his white-blond hair appeared uncombed. "What is happening?" he demanded.

"My good man, are you quite all right?" inquired Darwin as he approached Buskin.

"Certainly not! Something very bizarre is afoot."

"Bizarre?" echoed Freddie, putting on a shocked expression.

Suddenly flustered, Buskin clearly couldn't decide how much to divulge. "Someone broke into my lodgings ...and, uh, *tampered* with my very rare and priceless specimens." Even as he spoke, he pointed a finger at her. "Has anything out of the ordinary happened in this house?"

"You might say so," Charles said calmly. "That's why we sent for you, Terrance."

As if on cue, Charles and Freddie both turned to stare at the stuffed finch lying in the middle of the desk. "When I came downstairs to work this morning, I discovered that," she said in her professor voice. Circling around to stand behind the desk, Freddie pointed apprehensively at the tiny bird. "I couldn't imagine what to think. It wasn't there when I retired last night ...and there is a label on its leg, dated the very day Anthony St. Briac went missing. The handwriting is *his*! Where the devil could it have come from?"

Looking as if he might be sick, Terrance Buskin went closer and picked up the magnifying glass from its usual place on the desk. "It cannot be," he said in a choked voice and peered at the label. As if forgetting that Freddie, Darwin, and Syms were all present, he shook his head and muttered, "There was no label. This is impossible."

"Mr. Buskin, have you seen this woodpecker finch before?" exclaimed Freddie.

Darwin took a step toward them. "We called for you because you were there that day. Only you would know if St. Briac captured this specimen on the day he disappeared."

In spite of the chilly fall morning, Buskin had begun to perspire. "Dash it, how can I possibly remember?"

"But you just said there was no label!" cried Syms Covington. "It's all mighty peculiar. Reminds me of that night on board the *Beagle* when you discovered the other stuffed finch in your hammock. Of course, we all knew Mr. St. Briac slept in that very hammock before he disappeared from the face of the earth."

At that moment, as if from the very soul of the house, a deep echoing voice accused, "Terrance Buskin, you lefffft me to die!"

Terrance went dead white, eyes bulging. "Did you hear that?"

Freddie, Charles, and Syms all looked at him askance. "What can you mean?" she asked.

"Didn't you hear? It was St. Briac!" Trembling, he collapsed in the nearest chair. "Speaking to me from beyond the grave."

"I didn't hear a thing," said Charles, and the other two shrugged and shook their heads.

"Syms, you know what I mean!" screamed Buskin. "It's just the same as that night on the *Beagle* when he left that finch in the hammock! Tell them! St. Briac is haunting me!"

"You lefffft me to die!" the voice boomed again.

Terrance flattened his hands to his ears, squeezed his eyes closed, and began to sob. "Stop, stop!" Opening one eye, he seemed to focus on the dead finch lying in the middle of the desk and let out a wail. "I was afraid, that's all. I didn't know what to do!"

"Drowwwwning ..." the voice proclaimed in haunting tones.

"God save me!" Buskin's face crumpled. "He's bloody *here*!"

"Water filllling my *lungs*! You walked away, Buskin ...left me ..."

Addressing the ghostly speaker, Terrance cried, "But, but, after you fell into the spring, there was nothing I could do. Even if I could have climbed down the treacherous side of that cliff, I can't swim. I would have drowned, too!" Buskin turned to Darwin and clutched at his sleeve. "You hear him, don't you? Tell him to stop, I beg you. There was nothing I could do!"

Darwin angrily shook his head. "I don't hear anything except *you*, Buskin! You have just told us that you left St. Briac unconscious, assuming he would drown in the water below. You are nothing better than a *murderer!*"

Even though Freddie and Anthony had already realized this truth, it was still stunning to witness Buskin's confession unfold before her. Following the lead of Syms Covington, she advanced to stand beside Charles Darwin, guarding against the possibility that Buskin might resort to violence.

"I panicked," he was saying. "And once I ran away, I didn't know what to do."

"Yet you kept the specimen bag Anthony asked you to hold," Freddie accused in angry tones. "You stole everything inside – including the notebook where he had kept all his observations, the same ones you pre-sented to the Geological Society as your own!"

"How do you know that?" cried Buskin incredulously.

As if on cue, Anthony's ghostlike voice called from within the walls, "*Everyone* knows …you are a murderer and a thief, Terrance Buskin! Admit to your crimes!" There was a brief, charged pause, and then the voice bellowed even louder, "*Admit, you coward!*"

"Yes! I admit it!" Buskin said brokenly, weeping. "It's all true. I did it. Now, I beg you, stop torturing me!"

Silence filled the library, then the bookcase across the room slowly swung open again and Anthony emerged. Freddie felt her heartbeat accelerate as Terrance Buskin struggled for breath, staring in disbelief, shaking. When Anthony came to stand over the chair where Buskin cowered, he looked at him for a long moment and made a sound of disgust.

"By Lucifer, what a sorry excuse for a man you are," Anthony said darkly.

"But – but are you a spirit?"

"Believe me, I am fully *alive*. No thanks to you." His voice was ice-cold, but Freddie sensed the deeper layer of pain. "Did you think I would allow you to get away with your cowardly deeds?"

As these new developments began to sink in, Buskin straightened in his chair. But when he tried to rise, Syms put a hand on his shoulder to hold him back.

"You'd be wise to stay right there," said Darwin's young assistant.

Buskin looked at them, one by one. "But ...did you all know that St. Briac was alive?" His pale blue eyes fixed on Frederica. "What of you, professor? Were you playing me for a fool all along?"

"Not all along," Freddie replied, longing to tear off her wig and false mustache and assume her real identity.

"None of that matters," Darwin intoned. "St. Briac survived and now we must address *your* fate, Buskin." Turning, he addressed Anthony. "Do you want to drop him off a cliff into the English Channel and walk away, leaving him as he left you?"

Terrance broke in, "Dear God, no, I beg you! I can't swim. Please, no! Listen to me." He tried unsuccessfully to grasp Anthony's hands. "My mother passed not long ago, and Papa has been floundering all alone. Allow me to leave London and return to live with him, far away in Blickling Corners. You'll never see or hear from me again!"

Anthony arched a dubious brow. "Where the devil is Blickling Corners?"

"Far away in Yorkshire! I've scarce been back since coming down to Cambridge all those years ago."

"If I agree, Buskin, it will only be because I am sick to death of even thinking about you." He pressed a hand to the side of his head, grimacing slightly. "I just want my life back, as it once was."

This declaration sent a chill down Freddie's spine. Whether Anthony meant to or not, he had let her know that he longed for a future without her in it ...for his life 'as it once was' was that of a bachelor rogue.

"That's all well and good, but I have a demand to make!" Charles Darwin said sternly. "St. Briac, before you allow Buskin to simply slink away, he must visit to the Geological Society and confess to them his crimes."

"What?" Buskin looked startled, then aghast.

Freddie perked up as she considered Darwin's plan. "Oh, excellent. That is a perfect punishment."

"Since the day we first met Terrance at Cambridge, he has been angling for acceptance by real scientists, hasn't he?" Darwin reminded a dubious-looking Anthony. "When the *Beagle* returned last month and he was granted membership in the Geological Society, it must have felt a grand achievement."

"Oh yes, no doubt," Anthony said harshly. "But Buskin falsely stood atop *my* discoveries to reach that pinnacle."

"Exactly!" Charles was nodding vigorously. "No prison could deliver a worse punishment than banishment from membership in the Geological Society. Buskin's speech would be erased from the records, and the attribution for those findings would of course return to you, St. Briac." Pausing, Darwin spoke directly to the cowering Buskin. "Finally, you would be barred forever from the halls of science. Even if you should creep back to London one day, everyone who matters in the scientific community would offer you the cut supreme."

Each point seemed to strike Terrance like a mortal blow. He grew paler by the moment, his shoulders hunched, head bowed, hands clenched.

"Yes. I understand," he said weakly.

Darwin turned back to Anthony. "Does this plan meet with your approval?"

"Indeed. It's brilliant."

"Right then. Syms and I shall take Buskin with us and keep watch over him until a meeting with the directors of the Geological Society can be arranged."

"And after that," Syms Covington chimed in, "I will take him myself to that place in Yorkshire. What's it called?"

"Blickling Corners," muttered Buskin. "I trust you'll allow me to return to my lodgings and pack my things?"

Anthony made a derisive sound. "Not before I visit there again and retrieve the rest of my specimens."

Freddie had drawn back from the men clustered behind the desk. Leaning against rows of books she had come to treasure, she watched as Syms hoisted Terrance Buskin to his feet, and started toward the entry hall. She was awash with a sense of triumphant elation, yet other bittersweet feelings began to tangle themselves in the mix.

This was what she and Anthony had been working toward, wasn't it? He had agreed that she might remain here to help him discover what had happened the day of his terrible accident. They had risked their very lives just last night, first breaking into Buskin's rooms and then dangling from the ledge outside in a driving rainstorm. And now that the villain had been exposed and would be punished, Anthony could finally come out in the open and resume his rightful life.

Freddie tasted tears at the back of her throat. They had reached a crossroads. Their shared adventure was at an end, and the time was at hand to chart a new course for herself ...alone.

The day was unseasonably warm, and the sun was high in a cerulean sky as Anthony made his way to Grosvenor Square. It felt exhilarating yet odd to remind himself that he no longer needed to hide. Since his accident in the Galápagos Islands and the myriad challenges that followed, Anthony had often feared he might never see London or his family again, never enjoy the decadent pleasures he had enjoyed as a bachelor. Now, walking openly along South Audley Street, he was surprised to see the slim, towering figure of an old acquaintance coming toward him.

"By Jupiter, is it you, St. Briac?" The Honorable William Everhard stopped on the flagstone path and blinked his large gray eyes. "Thought you'd perished somewhere in the Pacific!"

Shaking Everhard's hand, Anthony assured him that he was indeed alive, but when the other man inquired if they would meet at the gaming tables in St. James that night, he paused.

"Tonight? I'm not certain…"

"Egad, what was I thinking?" exclaimed Everhard. He paused to straighten the spreading collar of his fashionably fitted overcoat. "Of course, you would pine for *other* pleasures after so long an absence. But …had you heard about your favorite cyprian, Marianne Chambers?"

Anthony began to wish he had kept to the back streets, as before. "No. I only just returned."

Drawing him away from the other passersby, Everhard bent near and said in the manner of one who is delivering a juicy piece of gossip, "The fair Marianne wed old Hartstone five full years ago! He was smitten, devoted as a pup to her."

"Do you mean the *Earl* of Hartstone?" Even as Anthony spoke, the other man was already nodding, smiling broadly.

"Indeed. She is now a countess! Changed her ways, of course, but a leopard can't change all its spots, can it?" In the midst of sending Anthony a broad wink, he straightened to his full height and pointed out into the thoroughfare. "By Jupiter, look at that! You'd think I planned it."

With a sense of misgiving, Anthony turned his head and beheld a dark-green town coach, the Hartstone crest displayed on its door. It proceeded slowly down St. Audley Street, caught in the crush of hackney cabs, phaetons, gigs, and other vehicles. An elegant golden-haired woman gazed out the window, looking rather bored, but when her eyes lit on Anthony, she suddenly sat up straight and gaped in surprise.

As the coach disappeared into traffic, Anthony began to walk northward, toward Grosvenor Square. Everhard kept pace beside him, chuckling in a way that made Anthony want to plant him a facer.

"No reason to avoid her, old chap," Everhard exclaimed. "But wait, you wouldn't know. She's a widow! Hartstone keeled over dead at the opera just six months after they wed."

Anthony stopped to face the other man. "See here, I

have just returned after a rather difficult last year, to put it mildly. I want to postpone all conversations of this nature until after I've seen my family and sorted those matters."

"Right. Why didn't you say so?" Everhard slapped him on the shoulder. "I'll leave you to it, then. Goodbye!"

Continuing on to his grandparents' home in Grosvenor Square, Anthony wondered if he would ever feel like his old self. Before the *Beagle* voyage, he'd reveled in life as a London bachelor, able to juggle scientific pursuits by day with a libertine's nightlife that included gaming with his male friends and carnal adventures with willing beauties like Marianne Chambers. It had seemed idyllic ...but was that what he wanted for the future?

Having sent word to his family that he was coming, Anthony entered Raveneau House, and the servants led him to join them in the walled garden behind the house. It was a magical place that held many memories of his childhood, especially the years when they had lived in London, during his mother Mouette's marriage to Sir Harry Brandreth. For most of Anthony's childhood, everyone assumed that Harry was his father. It wasn't until long after Harry's downfall and death that he discovered he'd been the product of a brief affair between his mother and Justin St. Briac.

His true parents were now a happy, if tempestuous, couple. Yet who could blame Anthony for avoiding the commitment of marriage for himself? Since childhood, he'd felt a confusing ache when he probed his memories. Very little had been as it seemed.

Emerging now into the garden and seeing his family rise up at the sight of him, Anthony let go of the old sadness once again. He had years of practice at this, papering over the parts of the past that would never be right, but he had never found a way to transform them into something whole and happy.

"Oh, Anthony!" exclaimed his mother, rushing forward to wrap her arms around his chest. "I have ached to hold you properly." As her tears soaked through his cambric shirt, he returned her embrace. Waves of love welled up in him.

"Mama," soothed Anthony, patting her slim back. Over her shoulder, he saw his father standing nearby, his expression betraying more emotion than Anthony ever remembered seeing before. Something made him stretch out an arm in invitation.

"Papa," he said huskily, as Justin joined their embrace. "How good it is to be back, at last, with all of you."

Emeline rushed forward. "Oh, Anthony, you'll simply never know how desperately I've missed you. Being without my brother has been utterly unbearable! Like – like having a limb cut off."

"You always were the most dramatic child," he said fondly, holding her. "Haven't we already enjoyed more than one reunion scene?"

"Well, yes, perhaps. But it feels even more intense now that all the family is watching."

Anthony's grandmother, Devon, came forward for her moment in his arms. "You never seem to change, Grandmama," he marveled, inhaling her faint yet wonderfully familiar scent.

"Of course, I change." A radiant smile lit her face. "My hair has gone white in your absence."

André Raveneau spoke up from a nearby stone bench where he sat holding an ebony walking stick between his knees. "It is fortunate that your hair turned white, *ma petite*, or else everyone would take you for my daughter."

Daisy, who had been chasing shadows near the

garden wall, barked and rushed over to join the group. The door to the house swung open, and Arabella emerged carrying a tray laden with covered dishes and a steaming pot of tea. When the housekeeper beamed at Anthony, he gave her a wink.

"It is such a lovely day, I thought we might linger outside," said Devon.

The family gathered around a long table covered with a blue patterned cloth. As the others filled their plates with flaky chicken pie, slender green beans with almonds, and saffron rice studded with currents, Anthony looked around. To his surprise, he saw his cousin, Camille, on the edge of the group and went to embrace her.

"My God, Cam, you grew into a woman while I was away." He held her away from him and shook his head. "The last time I saw you in Cornwall, you were only fifteen years old ...crusading against the hunting of exotic birds for their feathers."

The dimpled smile she gave Anthony made him realize that Camille must be breaking men's hearts everywhere she went. Even as a child, she'd been exquisite, with tawny-gold ringlets and thick-lashed Parisian blue eyes.

"Indeed, I have grown older, but my determination to stop the feather hunters hasn't changed," she replied firmly. "But I came today to talk about you, dear cousin. I know my parents and sister, Louise, will be over the moon when they learn you are truly alive and back on English soil."

"I am eager to see them all," said Anthony, "including your little brother. Damien was barely walking when I left, but now he must be at least—"

"Six!" Camille supplied.

He blinked in mock disbelief. "Tell me, how fares dear Louise? During my years away, I wondered if my brother, Charles, might finally become worthy enough to beg for her hand in marriage?"

Camille ruefully shook her head. "My sister remains dedicated to her work hunting fossils with Miss Mary Anning in Lyme Regis, and as you doubtless have heard, Charles is in Rome, furthering his architectural studies. However, I do suspect that she holds a place for him in her heart. Perhaps when he returns to England, they will reunite."

Anthony nodded. "And what brings you to London?"

"I am hoping to meet with John Gould, the great ornithologist! I believe he is helping Charles Darwin examine and classify the specimens that were discovered during the voyage of the *Beagle*. My goal is to enlist his support for my urgent cause." Pausing, she put a hand on his arm. "Do you know Mr. Gould, Anthony?"

He gave a wry laugh. "We have met, and I hope to know him better very soon. Of course, I would be pleased to introduce you."

"Oh, thank you!" Camille threw her arms around him. "I could not wish for a better cousin!"

Luncheon, eaten *al fresco* in the golden light of the autumn afternoon, passed in a blur of animated conversation, laughter, and storytelling. Justin poured bottles of his best wine and Arabella served a glazed apple tart, made in the French style with paper-thin slices of apples.

As the afternoon sun began to wane, Anthony glanced over to see his grandfather watching him.

"Yes, Grandpère?" Anthony lifted a questioning brow.

"I was just wondering ...how fares your lovely stowaway?" There was that astute glint in his eyes again. "Have you put her off the ship, so to speak?"

Anthony hoped his grandfather couldn't detect his

telltale flush. "I suppose you are referring to Miss Redfield?" he replied warily.

"You know I am." After a long pause weighted with irony, Raveneau smiled. "I understand, of course, all too well. I once suffered just as you suffer now."

"Suffer?" Anthony flicked a bit of Daisy's fur from his coat sleeve. "That is putting far too strong a point on it, I think."

To Anthony's dismay, he saw his own father lean over, listening, before he exchanged a shrewd glance with Grandpère. "Anthony is descended from libertines, on both sides of his family. We doubtless could have predicted everything that is happening now."

"*C'est vrai!*" agreed Raveneau. "We had to learn those same lessons the hard way."

Justin St. Briac lifted his glass in a toast. "Torture of the sweetest kind."

As they touched goblets and drank, Anthony pushed to his feet, annoyed. "I will leave you two to the memories of your lost youth. For myself, I anticipate returning to the pleasures of my former life here in London. Gaming ...and so forth."

His face grew warmer still as the two men looked at each other and laughed.

"Good fortune to you, son," chuckled Justin. "Particularly in the realm of 'and so forth'."

Before Anthony could summon a rejoinder, his mother came up and slipped her hand through the crook of his elbow.

"Darling, I can see that you are eager to be off," she said, "but first, will you take a turn around the square with me?"

Agreeing, he bid them all farewell, keenly aware of how good it felt to know he could now return here and enjoy the company of his family whenever he chose. When he and his mother were outside, facing the green oval of Grosvenor Square, she stopped, reaching up to caress his rough cheek.

"When we thought you were lost forever, I had so many dreams like this. You would turn up unexpectedly to join us for a meal, piquet, or a long, lovely chat. We would walk together under the trees, and you would make me laugh. My dreams were so real..."

"Perhaps they weren't dreams at all, Mama. Some part of you felt the truth."

She sighed at that. "Perhaps." As they crossed into the square, where residents strolled on the garden paths, Mouette continued gently, "When you sailed away on the *Beagle*, you were two-and-twenty, just out of university. I realize that you are much older now, and you have been tempered by the harsh events of this past year. No doubt you don't wish to receive any guidance from your mama."

Anthony wanted to groan aloud, but instead he managed a tense smile. "I am listening."

"Darling, I would be remiss if I did not ask you about Frederica."

A part of him wanted to protest that she was right, he was a man now, and all of them should bloody leave him be. "Frederica is well," he said tersely. "I invited her to accompany me today, but she was busy with a project. Fossils."

"I see." His mother's plum-tinted skirts fluttered in the breeze. "I will be frank with you, my dear. I do not ask because of my own regard for her, which is quite real, but because I am concerned for her wellbeing."

"Have I not told you that she is perfectly fine?"

Mouette would not be deterred. "Sit with me so I can look at you as we speak."

Wishing he were elsewhere, Anthony joined her on a nearby bench. At this time of day, there were others walking nearby, chatting and laughing. But Mouette seemed to see none of them as she turned toward Anthony.

"I will not take very much of your time, son."

He wondered why it was that, when she called him 'son' he felt ten years old again. "It's fine, Mama."

"I won't ask what exists between you and Frederica. That is your affair. But whether you two have feelings for one another or not, she cannot stay under your roof any longer."

"I know that." Her plain words were the truth, of course. "I know!"

"When we contrived to have her live at your house, in disguise, none of us imagined that you might truly return. She remained because she needed a refuge, and you two also planned to bring that awful Buskin man to justice." Mouette smoothed a few errant black locks of hair from his brow, and her touch was soothing. "Now that you have achieved that goal and everyone will know that you are alive and back in London, Frederica must find another refuge. I know that you are wise enough to understand the reasons why."

"Yes, all right, I understand, but where can she go?" As he spoke, the familiar whirlwind began inside him. He thought of the moment he had left Frederica today in the library, unpacking another crate of specimens. In her eyes, he'd seen her uncertainty about the two of them. It was an uncertainty he shared. Entrapping Terrance Buskin had become an excuse for them to be alone together, living in secret under the same roof. Now, speaking to his mother, Anthony saw that they had both been playing with fire.

"Freddie has tried doing this her own way, in disguise, locked up with a lot of fossils," said Mouette, toying with the ribbons of her bonnet. "But it couldn't last, even if you had not returned to London. Really, it was no way for someone as lovely and charming as Frederica to live, was it?"

"Since you put it that way, no."

"There is nothing for it, I believe, but that she should come here and stay with us, undisguised. Theo will know his plot to force her to wed Baron Cobleigh is out in the open. He can hardly burst in and take her by force!"

Anthony rubbed the side of his jaw. "I don't see that your plan is sustainable either, Mama. Frederica can't live with my grandparents for the rest of her life!"

"I know that, of course." His mother rose and drew her cloak closer. "We shall launch her in society, and before you know it, she'll have a dozen offers."

"Offers?" he repeated coolly and stood to continue their walk.

"Yes! The Season has just begun, so it is the perfect time."

"The Season!" Anthony stared in mock disbelief. "Frederica maintains that she is on the shelf."

"That is a shocking thing to say! Why, I think Freddie has only grown lovelier this autumn, and she has an aura that no chit in her first Season could match. Men will find her irresistible, mark my words. They'll be entranced by her intelligence and forthright manner."

"I think you may be mad, Mama." Anthony heard the edge in his own voice, but continued, "Frederica is five-and-twenty, for God's sake."

"She will make her age a new fashion. Just watch." Mouette lightly cuffed his arm. "Before the cherry trees bud in spring, our Frederica will have so many offers, she will be free to choose a man who meets *her* requirements!"

CHAPTER 23

$\mathcal{W}$hen Anthony returned home at dusk, Quincy informed him that Professor Loudon had retired to his rooms.

"Mrs. Bell is feeling poorly, sir, and Meg went out for the afternoon, so the professor made up a tray himself. Alongside the pot of tea and cakes, he placed one of those horrible fossils." The butler shuddered at the memory.

Anthony handed the old man his hat and gloves. "I realize that we need to hire more servants, Quincy. Now that I am no longer in hiding, I know that time has come." He smiled at him. "I hope you will help me choose the new staff."

Quincy nodded soberly, but an approving twinkle brightened his eyes. "As you say, sir. First, you will need a proper valet."

"Not too proper, though, all right?"

"Understood, sir."

Anthony climbed the stairs, past his own rooms, and paused outside the blue bedroom that Frederica had made her own. He felt uneasy as it came to him that he had missed her that day. He'd been telling himself that what he wanted most was the freedom to come and go and do as he pleased, just as he had always done. Unconstrained! But lingering in the back of his mind, all day long, had been Freddie. It was disturbing to realize how often he had wanted to turn to her and share a speaking glance, hear her laughter, or listen to her frank opinion.

His mother's voice intruded on his thoughts. *Frederica will have so many offers, she will be free to choose a man who meets her requirements!* Frowning, Anthony reflected that it was true, she had been shut away, first taking care of her grandfather, and now hiding here, in disguise. Her horizons and dreams were very limited, and Anthony had taken from her an intimate gift that might well be expected by another man in her future.

No sooner did he raise his hand tap at the door than it opened. Frederica stood before him, her head tilted to one side. She was clad, once again, in the simple, flattering rose gown, and her long, shining curls were loose.

"I sensed you were there," she said, her voice tinged with excitement. "Come in. I have something to show you!"

Anthony hesitated. It was completely improper for him to be here, especially given what he had already done to her, yet when she gestured to him again, he followed her inside. He tried not to think about the big, inviting bed, tried not to imagine her naked, tangled in his arms.

"Look!" she exclaimed, pointing to the writing desk near the window. "I've just unwrapped more fossils from Punta Alta, and I'm quite certain these teeth fit into the jawbone you and Mr. Darwin thought could be a relative of the sloth. What do you think?"

Anthony advanced for a closer look. Laid out on a

piece of white cloth were four broken teeth and a long, narrow mandible. Intrigued, he sat down on the fragile chair.

"I wish I had my gloves."

"I brought them up with my own." She proffered a pair of his special, thin gloves and smiled. "Just in case."

"Thank you." Drawing them on, Anthony picked up the magnifying glass and long tweezers. He peered at the tooth fragments one by one, fitting each to the empty sockets on the jawbone. After several minutes, he murmured, "Amazing."

"Oh!" exclaimed Freddie. "You agree. I am so pleased!" She clasped her hands together in a way that made him long to draw her down onto his lap and kiss her. Thoroughly.

"Excellent work. You are gifted."

She beamed. "Yes, I believe so."

Anthony rose to his feet, utterly charmed, and stripped off the gloves. "Darwin will be very impressed."

"I hope one day he will allow me to help in his studies, at least until the British Museum agrees to employ women to assist in their research."

"They would all be fortunate to have you, my dear minx. Which reminds me, I've come to talk to you about your future."

It seemed he could hear her heartbeat accelerate. She licked her lips. "I see. Pray continue."

They sat down together on a cushioned bench against the wall.

Anthony drew a breath. "I visited my family today, and my mother had some very firm thoughts about you and your path forward." He suddenly felt very cold. "Mama said aloud what you and I both know. You cannot remain here any longer."

Freddie stared back at him intently, nodding, but said nothing.

"My mother believes that you could return to your true identity, under my Raveneau grandparents' roof. She thinks Viscount Redfield would now realize he cannot simply abduct you, since so many other people know your situation."

"Perhaps she is right. I am aware that I cannot stay here."

Her delphinium-blue eyes swam with emotion, but her chin was resolute. From a safe distance, Anthony reached for her hand. "Frederica ..."

"Have I not given you leave to call me Freddie?"

He nodded. "Freddie. As you might imagine, I have thought a great deal about what happened between us. Last night."

"So much has occurred since then!" She gazed into the distance. "The drama with Terrance Buskin, and all."

"Are you about to tell me you had forgotten about our ..." Suddenly his throat went dry. "Interlude?"

"I did not forget. But may I assure you again that our *interlude* did not shake the very foundations of my existence?"

"I am glad to hear it," he replied with a faint, wry smile. "I think."

"Oh, please do not misunderstand! I do not mean to imply that it was unpleasant." She blushed. "On the contrary."

"I appreciate that." A part of him wanted to laugh. "I was about to tell you that I have realized I should not have allowed it to happen. In the light of day, it is plain to me that I crossed a line. A very clear line! I lost my head."

Freddie sighed. "Stop that. We have already talked

about this, haven't we? I was not a young innocent whom you ravished!"

"But you were *innocent*. I took something very special from you, a gift that was meant for the man you marry."

"Fustian!" She waved a dismissive hand in the air. "You make it sound as if you were in charge of the entire evening and I was helpless. I chose to be there, with you." Her voice shook slightly. "Furthermore, all that nonsense about a *gift* sets my teeth on edge. This is still my body. It belongs to me; I'm certainly not making a gift of any part of it to a man. That includes you, sir!"

Anthony bit back a smile, nodding slowly. "I've never known a female like you."

"What a lovely thing to say. Thank you." She rose to her feet and smoothed her skirts. "Please don't waste another tiresome moment feeling guilty about last night. We both enjoyed it, and now the time has come for us to go on with our lives."

In his wildest dreams, Anthony hadn't imagined that Frederica would end up being the one to give that particular speech. "You're very cool about it."

"I have known you for many years, Anthony." As she spoke, he thought he saw a shadow pass over her face. "I was quite aware that you are a rake, or at least next door to one. I have no desire to protect my reputation. I don't want a husband, I want my freedom and the opportunity to do work I enjoy. But I am still a woman. I ought to thank you for allowing me to express my ... passions." She crossed to look out the window into the darkening garden. "You are no doubt about to embark on a very lively existence here in London. I naturally wish you all the best in future."

Was the minx dismissing him? Feeling rather stung, Anthony realized this had never happened to him before. Before he could decide how to respond, a soft knock sounded at the door. Freddie turned to look at him, biting her lip.

"Behind the drapes," he whispered softly.

Crossing to open the door, Anthony found Meg standing there, something half-hidden in her hands.

"You were not in your rooms, sir, so I thought you might be here, with Professor Loudon." As she spoke, the maid craned her head slightly to peer past him, her thin brows lifted.

"And?" he demanded.

"A visitor is waiting for you in the drawing room. 'Tis a *lady!*"

Anthony stepped into the corridor with her, closed the door, and took the card Meg proffered. With a sense of unreality, he focused on the ornately written name:

Marianne, The Countess of Hartstone.

* * *

FREDDIE EMERGED from behind the draperies and crossed to the door. She heard footsteps retreating down the corridor. Cautiously, she peeked out and saw that the hallway was empty. Voices rose from the downstairs drawing room that opened off the stairway, followed by a trill of female laughter.

Her heart raced with wild emotions that felt too hot to touch. Of course, everything she had told Anthony was true, but one important piece remained unsaid: she was in love with him. Admitting this, even to herself, made Freddie feel positively ill.

Her true feelings must remain a secret. Anthony had come home hardened after a lost, dangerous year, intending to reconstruct the adult life he had begun after university. The last thing he needed or wanted was a lovesick chit mooning about, especially since he was prone to feeling guilty about lying with her.

Tears stung Freddie's eyes, and she dashed them away. Even as she reminded herself of how it must be between them, she heard the feminine voice again, drifting upward from the drawing room. She ought to return to her room and close the door, but her feet would not take her there. Instead, Freddie tiptoed down the corridor. What were they saying? Of course, it was none of her affair, yet something compelled her to take a few more steps ...perhaps discovering the identity of this mysterious female caller. She passed Anthony's own rooms and came to the top of the wide staircase.

Leaning over the balustrade, Freddie could see past the landing to the hall below, glimpsing the partially open door to the drawing room. At least he hadn't shut himself in with the lady, but perhaps that was because he wanted to protect her reputation.

"Oh, Anthony," exclaimed the woman.

Unable to bear another moment, Freddie turned and rushed back to her bedchamber.

* * *

ANTHONY STOOD in the drawing room and stared down at his erstwhile opera-dancer-lover, Marianne Chambers. Of course, she wasn't *that* person now. In his absence, she'd been transformed into a deuced countess!

"My darling, I simply couldn't believe my eyes when I saw you today on South Audley Street," Marianne was saying in passionate tones. "I mean, everyone believes you are *dead*."

He smiled. "Yet you can see for yourself that I am alive. I was the victim of an accidental fall in the Galápagos Islands and, as a result, went missing, but of course I persevered."

Stepping closer, she peeled off one embroidered kid glove and touched his cheek with her bare hand. "I missed you desperately." Still a rare beauty, she was now tastefully garbed as befitted her new position. Anthony knew he ought to offer to take her cloak and ring for refreshments, but he couldn't quite bring himself to do it.

"Your adventures have only made you more magnificent," Marianne said, gazing at him from head to toe. "But darling, what has happened to your beautiful nose?"

He touched it reflexively. "It was broken during my fall. You don't like it?"

Desire darkened her green eyes. "On second thought, I adore it. It lends you an air of …roughness."

She stepped close enough for Anthony to smell her Parisian perfume and feel the heat of her body. His primitive self wondered if Marianne might be just the distraction he needed to stop thinking about Freddie. He tried to remember the things she had done to him in bed, and how he had lusted for her upon his return to London …before Freddie had appeared under his roof and turned his heart upside-down.

Just as Marianne reached out and let her fingertips trail suggestively down his waistcoat, a figure appeared in the doorway.

"Pardon me, sir!" boomed a gruff voice. A moment later, Freddie – in the guise of Professor Loudon – entered the drawing room. In outstretched hands, she held the rather grotesque mandible they had just examined upstairs. "Dash it, am I interrupting?"

Marianne blinked, startled and apparently speechless.

With a nod to Marianne, the professor spluttered,

"A thousand pardons, madame. I had no notion Mr. St. Briac was entertaining."

Anthony sent Freddie a warning glance before addressing the countess. "My lady, may I present to you Professor Frederick Loudon? He has been assisting me with the many specimens and artifacts I gathered during my years of travel." Turning to Freddie, he said, "You have the honor of meeting the Countess of Hartstone."

Freddie bowed so low that the fuzzy iron-gray spikes of her wig nearly touched Marianne's bodice. "I am indeed deeply honored, Lady Hartstone!"

Marianne took a step back. "A pleasure, sir."

Freddie had the nerve then to step between Anthony and Marianne, holding the jawbone up. "I hope I am not interrupting, St. Briac, but I did feel a sense of urgency to show you this quite amazing fossil."

Marianne wrinkled her nose and averted her face, as if the professor had just shown her a putrid eyeball. "Oh!"

"I have no doubt you share Mr. St. Briac's passion for fossils, my lady," Freddie enthused, peering at the countess through smudged spectacles. "We believe this particular jawbone may belong to a relative of the sloth who lived thousands of years ago. Would you care to examine it?"

The lady grimaced. "Not at this time, sir."

Freddie seemed not to hear her. Marching over to a carved tripod table, she reverentially placed the jawbone in the center and gestured to them. "Do come and have a closer look!"

"I fear I cannot," said Marianne, drawing on her gloves. "I have just remembered that I have another appointment." Turning back to Anthony, she murmured, "My dear, I hope you will come to see me so that we may enjoy a proper reunion." She gave him her hand to kiss and added, "Just the two of us."

"I will see you to the door, my lady," Anthony said. As they left the drawing room, he glanced at Freddie with narrowed eyes. She merely smiled back at him, her mustache twitching slightly.

By the time he returned from putting Marianne and her maid into the elegant town coach, Freddie and her cursed fossil had disappeared from the drawing room.

CHAPTER 24

$\mathcal{F}$reddie rushed into her bedroom, put down the ancient jawbone, and pressed both hands to her burning cheeks. Her true feelings must now be clear to Anthony! Why else would she behave so outrageously if not for love? She wanted to cry, but that was unthinkable. Instead, she ripped off her mustache and wig and began to undress.

Moments later, just as she stepped out of her trousers, a knock sounded at the door.

"Frederica?" demanded a familiar male voice.

Ignoring Anthony, she tried to decide if there was time to unbind her breasts and get back into her female clothing before he forced his way into the room. She began to work at the knotted linen strips.

"Open the door," he ground out. "I want to talk to you."

"I must decline. I don't care for your tone." The knot finally loosened enough for her to pull the strips off and release her breasts, hopefully for the last time *ever*. Standing there naked, she looked around wildly for her chemise and gown. If he should somehow manage to open the door, it seemed that the world might end.

"Frederica!" The doorknob rattled. "This is my house. I demand that you open the door."

She found her chemise and yanked it over her head. Next came the rose gown. Without assistance, Freddie couldn't possibly fasten the back, but at least she was covered. Pushing back her long, disordered curls, she marched to the door and threw it open.

"There. Are you happy now?" Challenging him before he could challenge her was the best tactic she could think of at the moment. "You nearly forced yourself in while I was completely undressed!"

His expression reminded her that he had seen all of that and more. "Let me help you with your gown," he said coolly.

This seemed a very practical notion. "Thank you."

Freddie turned her back to him and tried not to respond to the sensation of his deft fingertips brushing her skin as he fastened the small, flat hooks. Toward the middle of her back, Anthony paused and stepped close enough so that she could hear the intake of his breath. Her heart leaped, every bit of her aroused by the possibility of what might happen next, and heat blossomed between her thighs.

"Freddie," he said in a low voice. "Why did you do it?"

Her eyes stung. "I don't know."

"Yes, you do." Anthony put a large hand on each of her shoulders and drew her back against his chest. When he spoke again, his breath grazed her ear. Oh, how she yearned for him. "Were you jealous?"

"That is a very bold question," she managed to reply.

"But you can be honest with me."

"Well ..." His nearness was like a drug, muddling her senses. "I heard that woman, talking downstairs as if she were your lover, and her intentions were quite clear. I simply could not allow her to go further!"

"Right." He laughed softly. "You were jealous."

"Perhaps, a little," she admitted, incurably honest. "I am human, after all."

"So am I." His voice was husky.

Oh, my. Would it be wrong for them to make love again, one last time? Freddie was on the verge of turning in his arms and showing him exactly what she wanted, needed, when another unwelcome knock sounded at the door.

"Freddie! It is I, Emeline!" came the excited greeting. "You will be staying with us in Grosvenor Square. Isn't it the most exciting prospect? I've come to help you pack!"

Anthony quickly stepped away from Freddie and she felt his fingertips make quick work of the remaining hooks. Turning her to face him, he smoothed back her curls and gave her a rueful smile.

"I'm sure it's just as well. I can't be trusted alone with you."

With that, Anthony went to open the door and greeted his little sister with a brief, mocking bow. "Didn't our parents teach you to send word before arriving uninvited?"

Emeline laughed. "But this is your house, darling Anthony, and you have finally emerged from hiding. Surely you didn't expect me to stand on ceremony?" She entered the bedroom and looked around, brows aloft. "And speaking of propriety, what are *you* doing here, alone with Freddie?"

"Your brother just came to ask if he could loan me a traveling trunk," Freddie said as she embraced the younger girl. "I have just begun packing."

"I'll leave you to it then, ladies," Anthony called from the doorway. "I have work of my own to do."

When he had closed the door, Emeline looked at Freddie. "I suspect we are taking you away just in time.

I know Mama has been worried, knowing the two of you were alone together in this house."

Freddie felt her face growing warm. "Well, none of you need worry for me. I can look after myself."

"I am very glad to hear it! My brother can be a wicked libertine, you know. His many conquests will be all aflutter when they learn he is alive and back among them."

The fluttering has already begun ...Freddie thought, her heart aching.

* * *

IN THE MORNING, Frederica drank chocolate as she finished packing the last of her belongings in her portmanteau and small trunk. From a shelf by the window, she took down her precious volumes of *Principles of Geology* by Charles Lyell and *Views of Nature* by Alexander von Humboldt. Already hidden in the portmanteau was her well-worn copy of *The Wicked Highwayman*. With a pang, Freddie realized that even though the great romantic adventure of her life had ended, she could still escape into the pages of her favorite novel.

The moment she stood in the doorway to the blue bedroom and looked around for the last time was very bittersweet. The birds she loved were hopping in the tree outside the window, eating the bits of apple and raisin Freddie had regularly leaned out to place in the crotch of two big branches. Who would feed them now?

Walking down the familiar corridor, she paused to look in at Anthony's bedroom. During her early days in this house, she had slept there alone with what seemed to be his ghost. The walls were still lined with the evocative watercolors of nature that he had painted, and the great map of South America hung over the mantle. Across the room, the door to the dressing room stood open, reminding her of the day when "Professor Loudon" had been blocked inside with Anthony, and he'd slowly stripped away her disguise. It had been an excruciating scene at the time, but later they had laughed about it.

Freddie turned back to the hallway, unable to look at the bed where she had discovered not only the fulfillment of her own suppressed, sensual longings, but also the depth of her connection to Anthony.

Freddie sighed. *Admit it. You love him.*

Downstairs, she found Anthony already at work at his desk in the library. His black hair was in disarray and there was a pale blue smudge on his jaw.

"Good morning," Freddie greeted him in cordial tones.

"Ah." He looked up and gave her an intoxicating smile. "I see you are ready to go. I assumed as much because Mrs. Bell is waiting in the kitchen with her bags packed, clearly eager to escape this den of iniquity."

She laughed a bit shakily. "Well, it is time, isn't it. We all need to get back into the world."

"Indeed." Anthony paused, then reached into his desk drawer and brought out what appeared to be a piece of parchment, loosely rolled up and tied with a blue ribbon. Holding it out to her, he said, "It's just a little something I thought you might like."

Her heart hurt as she accepted his offering. "Shall I open it?"

"No, no, it's all ready to travel with you to Grosvenor Square."

"Thank you so much." As Freddie put the scroll next to her reticule, a sudden worry occurred to her. "Before I go, I must show you how I catalogued all the specimens I unpacked before your return." She came around the desk to stand beside him. "Do you remember how I organized the listings?"

"I trust you will instruct me, my dear professor," he murmured, seemingly amused.

"Yes, I will! Look here." Freddie opened the green, leatherbound logbook that she kept on one side of the desk. Moving her finger across the pages, she showed Anthony exactly how she had recorded each item, including a notation for the tags he had attached at the time of collection. "Do you understand?"

"I think so." He grinned at her. "I've been to university, you know."

Freddie decided to ignore this. "Look here. I have made special symbols for each type of specimen: plant, animal, rock, insect, and so forth." She pointed again at various entries on the pages. "And you will find corresponding symbols on the storage crates."

"Brilliant. You have a gift for organization that I clearly lack."

She couldn't resist the urge to reach out and move an errant lock of hair from his eyes. "If you become confused or you need me ..." Freddie's mouth was very dry. "To help with this matter ..."

"Yes." He nodded, and his gaze touched her lips for the merest instant. "I know where to find you."

"But of course, you will *not* need me," she asserted with a nervous laugh. "In fact, you will doubtless organize a system of your very own. One that suits you perfectly." Freddie took a step back. "I know you are eager to get on with your life again after so very long."

"I suppose." He looked pensive. "And you too are on the brink of a bright future, my sweet. I wonder which path you will choose."

She made a circle with her hands and pretended to gaze into a crystal ball. "I see the British Museum waiting for me, just around that next bend in the road."

At that moment, Quincy appeared in the doorway. When he caught sight of Freddie, he shook his head in amazement. "I must confess I have been in shock ever since you revealed yourself to Meg and me last night, Miss Redfield."

"I was growing very impatient with my disguise," Freddie said as she walked around to the other side of the desk. "Honestly, I'm surprised none of you realized the truth sooner."

"I'll own I may have had my suspicions," Quincy confided, smiling. "I've brought your things downstairs, Miss Redfield, and the Raveneaus have sent a very fine landaulet to fetch you. It is waiting now, just outside." He looked at the parchment scroll she carried. "May I take that for you?"

Instinctively, she held it closer. "No! Thank you."

Mrs. Bell trundled into the stair hall, looking expectantly at Freddie, her cheeks bright with color. "We should be on our way, mistress," she said, plainly relieved. "Now that you are once again clearly a female, it is imperative that we remove you from this house before someone sees you here with your *portmanteau* and believes the worst."

"Stuff." Freddie made a dismissive motion with one hand. "Of course, I don't care a fig for any of that, and in any event, I have been accompanied throughout my visit by you, Mrs. Bell, a very proper companion."

Quincy, who waited nearby, cleared his throat. "If I may be so bold, ma'm, I would assure you that my lips are sealed. And Meg's as well, but I shall remind her again when she returns from her errand."

Across the library, Anthony rose from his desk chair and came forward. "I would be a very poor host if I did not thank you ladies for all you have done to help me since my return to London." He bowed slightly to Mrs. Bell, then turned to Freddie.

When she extended her hand to him, he caught it up and kissed it. "It has been a great pleasure."

Her eyes swam with tears. "And now we must go."

Anthony followed them through the door, oddly pleased to see that Freddie carried his gift along with her reticule. Outside on the narrow bend in Charles Street that passed in front of his own house, the driver and a groom were loading the baggage. A curricle drew up behind the handsome landaulet and the driver made an impatient noise.

No sooner were the two women assisted into the equipage, than it began to roll forward. Anthony felt an uncomfortable pressure in his chest as he watched Frederica leave his home and his life, perhaps forever.

Just before the vehicle rounded the corner of Chesterfield Hill, Freddie leaned out her window and waved. Was something wrong? Perhaps she had changed her mind. Was she gesturing for him to rush to her aid?

Before Anthony could start forward, Freddie's clear voice drifted back to him on the morning air. "Goodbye!"

CHAPTER 25

*A*nthony stood for a full minute in front of the house, feeling oddly empty and wishing he had somewhere else to go.

"Sir?" Quincy called rather uncertainly from the doorway.

He turned and forced himself to smile and return inside. "What is it, Quincy?"

"Now that Miss Redfield is on her way, there is another matter I must raise with you."

Nodding reluctantly, Anthony followed the old man through to the stair hall and tried to think of an excuse to close himself in the library and open the brandy.

"Could it possibly wait? I have another—"

Quincy broke in, shaking his head. "I fear not." With that, he opened a door leading toward the kitchen and made a gesture inside. "This young gentleman appeared early this morning, insisting that he must speak to you."

Before Anthony could reply, a familiar face emerged through the narrow doorway. He blinked in disbelief. "Rafael?"

"Aye, sir!" The boy, who had dark, curly hair and an expressive face, spoke in heavily accented English. He threw Quincy a triumphant glance and added, "I did tell you he knows me!"

Anthony tried to get his bearings. Turning to the butler, he explained, "Rafael was a stowaway on board the ship that brought me from Brazil back to England. As I recall, his Brazilian mother recently died of a fever, and Rafael was determined to discover his English father here in London." He looked at the boy, whom he judged to be about a dozen years old. Speaking in Portuguese, Anthony asked, "I assume you have not yet found your father?"

"No, I cannot." The lad's large chocolate-brown eyes were sorrowful. "I have been sleeping among thieves by the river, sir. Today I come here to assume employment in this house."

Quincy grimaced. "I think not!"

Rafael glared back at the butler. "I do." When he next looked at Anthony, his gaze held a plea, but also charm. "I can serve you, sir."

"Perhaps …in the stables, for now." He looked at Quincy. "Ask Hobbes to show Rafael around."

In rapid Portuguese, Rafael argued, "I want to serve *you*, sir! Here in this house. Perhaps you need servants? I can do anything!" He sank into a low bow. "I beg you, let me try."

"No bowing! If you do well, you might be trained as a groom," Anthony said. "One step at a time. And meanwhile, you'll have a roof over your head and hot food to eat."

Rafael frowned, his mind clearly working. The momentary lull gave Anthony an opportunity to assess the boy. Under his soiled, dark breeches and coat, he wore a waistcoat of sapphire-and-silver striped silk, and he had applied a pomade of some sort to his black curls.

"I see that you admire my waistcoat!" said Rafael.

"Not particularly. I was actually hoping you didn't

steal it," Anthony replied ironically. "For now, we will have Hobbes give you one of the rooms in the mews, where you can have a hot meal and a bath. Next you must learn to speak English properly. We will look for a teacher for you."

"But sir, I must protest," complained Rafael.

"Be grateful I haven't sent you away," Anthony replied. "I can assure you, I have many other things to think about right now."

Quincy had been listening to this conversation with an expression of trepidation. "Pardon me, sir, but when you say 'we' who exactly do you intend will see to all of this?"

"I wouldn't trust anyone but you, my good fellow!" Anthony grinned and clapped the butler's bony back.

Sighing, Quincy nodded and turned toward the back of the house. "Come along with me, then, lad. We'll talk to Hobbes. I expect Meg to return soon, and she will give you some bread and soup."

Rafael allowed the old man to lead him off, but after a few steps, he stopped and sent Anthony an imploring look. "I beg you, sir, do not forget about me!" he called in urgent tones.

* * *

EMELINE HAD GATHERED with her mother and grandmother to welcome Freddie to the house in Grosvenor Square. Devon Raveneau graciously invited Mrs. Bell to come with her and meet Arabella, their housekeeper, promising that she would have a room of her own and assuring her that she needn't do any work as long as she was there.

When Freddie inquired after Justin St. Briac and André Raveneau, Emmie informed her that they had gone off to a select meeting at the Geological Society.

"It's something to do with Anthony and his terrible accident, I think," the girl added.

If Frederica weren't so dreadfully tired of her Professor Loudon costume, she might have considered donning it one more time and turning up at Somerset House herself to see what it was all about. Instead, she walked with Emeline and Mouette up to the lovely bedchamber where she had slept after escaping from her father's house. It all seemed very long ago!

As the trio came into the light-filled room, Emeline's gaze fell on the rolled-up parchment Freddie had been carrying ever since she left Anthony's home. "What's that you have?"

Freddie held it lightly in both hands, aware that both Emeline and Mouette were watching her. "A small token from Anthony."

"Aren't you going to open it?" prompted Emeline.

"Oh." Some part of her wanted to wait until she was alone, but *why*? It would certainly not prove to be a proclamation of his undying love! "Yes, of course."

Freddie untied the ribbon and handed it to Emeline. Slowly unfurling the parchment, she saw that it was a beautifully rendered watercolor of the very woodpecker finch she and Anthony had used to entrap Terrance Buskin. However, this small, olive-tan bird was not dead and stuffed, but alive on the page, perched on a branch. In its conical beak, it clutched a cactus needle, poking this tool at a seed to access its contents. Freddie's eyes stung as she realized the sky in the background was the same intense, pale blue as the smudge she'd noticed on Anthony's jaw that morning.

"What a plain little bird," Emmie observed.

When Freddie tried to speak, her voice sounded thick. "Yes, but this little fellow is one of the very special finches your brother and Mr. Darwin discovered in the Galápagos Islands." Reaching out, she touched a fingertip to Anthony's distinctively inscribed initials in the lower corner: ASB.

"Mama has some very exciting plans for you," Emeline was saying.

Mouette touched Freddie's shoulder. "Why not set down your things and let us enjoy a nice chat."

Moments later, a maid appeared with a tray of biscuits and a pot of tea, and Daisy the corgi waddled in to settle herself in a basket near the fireplace.

"I have plans as well," said Freddie firmly. "With your support, I intend to stand up to my father. I will make him understand and accept that I will not be bullied or forced to marry anyone. If he has created problems for himself, I should not be called on to solve them."

Emeline applauded. "Brava! And he will know we are all protecting you, so there's no point in trying to carry you off."

"Yes, that does sound like a perfect first step," agreed Mouette, pouring tea into fragile blue, gold, and red Imari cups.

"After that, I shall seek employment at the British Museum," Freddie continued. "I have some means of my own, and Mrs. Bell has agreed to join me in my lodgings and keep house for us."

Emeline blinked, intrigued. "Is that sort of situation really possible?"

"It may not be as easy as it sounds," Mouette said carefully. "If you and Mrs. Bell were going to a cottage in the country, that might be feasible, but living on your own in London as an unmarried woman—and pursuing an occupation ..." She made a doubtful gesture.

Freddie remained stubbornly unmoved. "Just because something is not commonly done, that does not mean I cannot do it. I have no wish to travel the common path."

Leaning back in her chair, Mouette took a bite of raisin-studded biscuit and regarded Freddie. "What does my son think about all of this?"

"Are you referring to Anthony?" Freddie stiffened slightly. "He understands that I have a mind of my own."

"Of course. You two are alike in that way." She paused and set down her teacup. "My dear, I believe that you are quite capable of carrying out your plan, but I would only ask that you first consider my ideas."

"All right. I am listening, ma'am."

"The London Season is just beginning, and I hope you will join us for the festivities." Before Freddie could protest, Mouette lifted a hand. "I know, you have already endured two Seasons when you were younger, and you have no patience for society. But I have a notion that, now that you are older and so self-assured, you might attract the attentions of a someone who would not only appreciate your exceptional attributes, but whom you might *like* as well." She seemed unable to suppress a smile. "I can envision a handsome gentleman gifted with intelligence, humor, and curiosity being drawn to you, dear Freddie. Someone with whom you could make a wonderful life ... and who would encourage your dreams."

Freddie blinked. "I fear someone has put spirits in your tea, ma'am. There is no such man in London." What she couldn't add was that, even if there were, her heart belonged to Anthony.

"I ask only that you remain here with us for a time and agree to attend a gathering or two as the Season gets underway. Perhaps we can bring Emmie along, so that she might glimpse the pleasures that wait for her next year, when she has her come-out."

"Oh, yes!" cried Emeline. "I should love that above all things. Do say yes, Freddie!"

"During this time, if you would like to begin making plans for the future you have in mind, you could do so," Mouette continued. Her blue eyes were warm, but there was a determined glint in them that reminded Freddie of Anthony. "What do you say?"

"You are very kind." She swallowed. "How can I refuse?"

"Excellent," pronounced Mouette. "As it happens, Lord and Lady Thurston are holding a ball just two days hence!"

* * *

THE NEXT AFTERNOON, Anthony was at his desk studying the massive green logbook when his father was announced. It was a pleasure to look up and see Justin St. Briac striding into the library with his customary arrogant charm.

"*Bonjour.*" He came around the desk to embrace Anthony. "I can imagine that it might be annoying to have me call on you uninvited. When my parents do this, I immediately suspect that Maman is plotting something."

"I am happy to see you, sir," Anthony said with a laugh. "I missed your bold utterances."

Justin grinned, an eyepatch of charcoal-gray silk adding to his striking appearance. "I had to get out of the house today. The women can talk of nothing except their gowns for Lord Thurston's ball."

Anthony nodded, taking this in. He considered inquiring casually after Frederica, but his father was far too shrewd not to perceive a deeper meaning behind his interest. Instead, Anthony raised the subject of yesterday's gathering at the Geological Society.

"I wouldn't have gone," Justin declared, "but your grandfather insisted that we must take your part, and of course he was right. Your friend Darwin was there, and Charles Lyell, who is now the president." He crossed to the cellaret and poured himself a small brandy. "That Buskin fellow will appear before the Society very soon to confess that he is a fraud, that the findings he presented were, in fact, yours. Then, I ascertain, he will exile himself in some distant village and promise never to return." Returning to the desk, he handed Anthony a small brandy and raised his own in a sardonic salute. "Unmerited mercy, in my opinion."

Anthony shrugged. "Buskin is a weak and cowardly man, Papa. It would be easy enough to call him out and do away with him in a duel, but to what purpose? I do not care to be stained by his blood."

"*D'accord.* I see your point."

Just then, Meg appeared in the doorway, her cheeks deeply flushed. "Sir, you have another guest!"

Before Anthony could reply, a deep voice echoed through the stair hall: "By Jupiter, you do indeed, young St. Briac! But I am no bloody guest!"

Meg went scurrying away as Viscount Theodore Redfield loomed up on the library threshold. His countenance was so threatening that Anthony pushed instinctively to his feet and came around the desk.

"Did we have an appointment, my lord?" he inquired while raking the older man with a cool gaze.

"What have you done with my sweet, virtuous daughter, you rake?" cried Redfield.

"I am not at liberty to discuss your daughter with you or anyone else."

At that moment, the viscount's eyes seemed to bulge as he spied Anthony's father. "You! How fitting that the pair of you would be here together, conspiring again, no doubt to ruin me!" He was breathing so aggressively that Anthony thought he might suffer an attack of apoplexy. "Do you think I could ever forget how you stood between me and my beautiful Mouette, the love of my life, and then broke into my home and *stole* my treasured painting?"

Justin's expression was icy. "I believe you mean to say that Anthony and I *retrieved* the painting that you had stolen from my wife."

"You are all scoundrels!" shouted Redfield, pointing at Anthony. "Do you think I don't know that you have hidden my gently bred daughter under this roof for weeks? Sleeping in your *bed*?"

Anthony felt his stomach knot at this. *Curse it.* "Miss Redfield is not in this house, my lord, and you are making wild accusations without a shred of proof."

"I have it from the lips of a witness." Redfield sneered. His chest still heaved as if he had run a mile, but his expression was contemptuous. "Frederica is *my* daughter. She must be returned to me." Swiveling to stare at Justin, his old rival, the viscount added, "And if she is not, you will owe me, *m'sieur*. I intend at long last to collect on our debt of honor."

With that, Lord Redfield stalked away toward the entry and, moments later, the door banged behind him.

"What the devil did he mean by that?" Anthony asked his father. "And who has told him about Frederica staying here?"

Draining his brandy, Justin shrugged. "I have no idea. He is mad, I think." He seemed then to consider this at greater length. "Not only mad, but desperate. Perhaps Lord Cobleigh no longer desires to marry Frederica, so Redfield is now hoping he can pressure me to pay his debts."

"Good God." Anthony dragged a hand through his hair. "I am glad she is safely out of this house."

"Your mother intends to make a fine match for

Frederica," Justin spoke with studied nonchalance as he drew on his gloves, preparing to depart. "Some discerning fellow who will recognize her worth, protect her from Redfield, and encourage her scholarly ambitions."

"Yes, I know." Anthony found that his breathing was impaired. "No doubt that would be best, for all concerned."

As they walked together toward the front door, his father inquired, "Now that you have resumed your former life, I suppose you are keeping late hours at your clubs …and other haunts?"

"You would approve if I were?"

"*Eh bien*. I carried on in that fashion until your mother cast her spell on me, when I was much older than you. Men are allowed to do this, don't you agree?"

Anthony sent him a fondly mocking smile. "You are as inquisitive as Mama."

This drew a sharp laugh from his father. "And you are very elusive."

"Everything I know, I learned from the master."

"If I thought you were exactly like me, I should have grave cause for concern," parried Justin. "Which reminds me, as soon as your mother has settled Frederica's future, we shall at last return to Cornwall. I like your Raveneau grandparents well enough, but I am a man who needs to be the master of my own home." He gave a self-deprecating laugh. "Fortunately, your mama likes that about me."

As they came into the entry hall, a small figure darted out of the shadows to open the door. It was Rafael. In barely twenty-four hours, the boy had already turned up more times than Anthony could count, finding endless reasons to come into the house.

"What are you doing here?" Anthony asked him with a trace of annoyance.

In halting English, Rafael replied, "You need a porter to open the door." For good measure, he bowed and swept one arm out to usher Anthony's father from the house.

"Who's that?" Justin inquired in an undertone as they went outside together.

Briefly, Anthony explained the situation. "I couldn't send him away. God knows what might happen to a boy like that alone in this city, especially with his limited understanding of English." After a moment, he added hopefully, "You don't need a Portuguese-speaking groom or even a stable boy, do you?"

"What, and deprive you of the opportunity to unravel yet another complication in your life?"

Anthony stood on the pavement and watched as his amused parent settled himself on the cabriolet's leather seat and took up the reins.

"Thank you for coming, Papa." Raising a hand in farewell, he added dryly, "I think."

During the hours before Lord Thurston's ball, Raveneau House was a flurry of activity. The women, including Emeline's cousin Camille St. Briac, were all gathered in Mouette's rooms, where they spent hours socializing as they prepared for the night's festivities.

Three ladies' maids were there to dress their hair and apply cosmetics. Arabella kept up a flow of tea and cakes followed later by savory *hors d'oeuvres* served with champagne. A footman delivered sprays of flowers to decorate their coiffures, but Camille forbade the use of feathers.

"It is barbaric," she proclaimed. "One of the only reasons I have agreed to attend this dull affair is so I can scold all the women who engage in this heartless pursuit of beauty at the expense of our splendid birds. Whole species will be eradicated if someone does not raise a hue and cry!"

Mouette exchanged glances with her mother. "Camille, I hope you don't mean to shout at anyone tonight."

"Will I embarrass you if I do?" she inquired. "Perhaps I should go in alone, so no one will know we are connected." Camille sent Devon Raveneau an apologetic look, and Freddie remembered that they were not directly related. Camille was the daughter of Justin's brother, Gabriel.

"Nonsense," said Devon. "You are quite right about the feathers. I daresay most people never think about the beautiful birds that are hunted and killed to provide ornamentation."

Across the room, Emeline reclined on a blue-striped chaise, clad only in a knee-length chemise. In her hands, she held Freddie's copy of *The Wicked Highwayman*, and appeared to be deeply engrossed in its pages.

Mouette approached her daughter with a silk shawl. "Put this around your shoulders," she said, then leaned closer to look at the book. "What are you reading?"

Freddie, watching from a distance, held her breath. When the curious Emeline had seen her unpacking *The Wicked Highwayman*, she allowed her to look at it but never imagined she would bring the novel out where her mother and grandmother might see it!

"Oh, Mama, it is the most brilliant story!" exclaimed Emeline. "Lady Caroline, the heroine, has been shut away in the country by her cruel uncle, and when he contrives to send her to London so that she might make an advantageous match, their coach is stopped by a wicked but exceedingly handsome *highwayman*!" Sitting up, she sighed and pressed a hand to her bosom. "He, of course, is the second son of a duke, in disguise."

"Of course," murmured Mouette, arching a brow.

"The highwayman abducts Caroline, carrying her off by *force* on his horse, and *then* ..." She broke off, glancing uncertainly toward Freddie, her eyes bright.

"And then?" Mouette leaned over to reach for the book.

At that moment, Freddie intervened, snatching the

novel out of Emeline's hands. Her cheeks felt hot as she faced Mouette. "It's just a silly romantic novel," she explained. "Perhaps I shouldn't have let Emeline read it. Now that I think of it, you might not approve."

Emeline pretended to swoon. "Indeed, it is very passionate."

"Do you imagine that I know nothing of passion?" inquired Mouette. Her penetrating blue eyes moved between the two young women. "I assure you, I could write a few romantic tales of my own."

Suddenly, Freddie was sorry she had ever taken the novel out her portmanteau. There was no explaining the carnal feelings it had always kindled inside her and were now clearly evoking in Emeline. "I think I should put this away."

Before Mouette could ask any more probing questions, Devon Raveneau waved to them from the dressing table. "Frederica, do come and allow Helen, my ladies maid, to dress your hair."

Grateful for the distraction, Freddie excused herself just long enough to rush to her own rooms and hide the novel away where it belonged, wrapped in an old chemise at the back of her drawer.

The next few hours passed in a flurry of activity. Freddie hardly knew what to make of the efforts to transform her into a great beauty. Even years ago, when she had her come-out while still living at home with Papa, he had not ordered her the new gowns and many fashionable accessories worn by other young ladies. At first, he had allowed her to visit the dressmaker, but soon enough his unpaid debts had caused Madame d'Amboise to refuse him credit. It had been just one humiliating episode in the terrible drama that had been her first Season.

Today everything seemed different. Freddie was older and wiser. She already had a clear plan for her future that had nothing to do with the London *ton*, and she was quite curious to behold her own transformation.

"This style is very much *au courant*," Helen confided as she pinned Freddie's luxuriant golden-brown curls up into a rather elaborate coiffure studded with yellow and cream rosebuds. The entire process took rather a long time, but at last the maid held up a mirror. "Miss Redfield, you look beautiful!"

"Oh my!" Freddie smothered a gasp. It certainly wasn't her style, but perhaps that was just as well. She would be relieved if other guests at the ball did not recognize her. "You have done a splendid job, Helen. Thank you."

Devon Raveneau came forward then, beaming. "We have a very beautiful gown for you to wear tonight. I hope you approve, my dear."

To Freddie's surprise, the door opened, and Madame d'Amboise entered. She hadn't seen the French dressmaker for several years, not since her first Season, when Papa had failed to pay his bills. Now, a smiling Madame came into the boudoir followed by an assistant holding aloft the most beautiful gown Freddie had ever seen.

"It is a great pleasure to see you again, mademoiselle," the Frenchwoman said warmly.

Frederica rose from the dressing table in her simple blue dimity *robe de chambre* and impulsively took both of Madame's gloved hands in her own. "How well you look!" It was true, for although the dressmaker's hair was now more white than chestnut, she was otherwise unchanged. She even wore the same sapphire-studded quizzing glass on a chain round her neck.

"How splendid to see you again, *ma petite*. I could not deal with your papa any longer, but I always held you in high regard. This gown ..." She kissed her fingertips, eyes dancing. "In this gown, you shall take your pick from all the eligible men of the *ton!*"

Mouette, Devon, Emeline, and Camille all gathered nearby, making rapturous sounds as Madame and her assistant helped Frederica to don the exquisite gown of golden silk with an overskirt of amber lace and gauze. The huge sleeves that had been in fashion were now much reduced, and a low, wide neckline exposed the tops of Freddie's shoulders. The creation fit her to perfection, hugging the high curves of her breasts and setting off her small waist.

"Never in my life have I seen such a magical gown," Freddie breathed at last. "Not even when my own mama was alive." Tears pricked her eyes. "I wish she could be here to see it."

Emeline clapped her hands. "Oh, Freddie, you look like a princess!"

Turning, she gazed at her reflection in the cheval mirror that stood nearby. "I am not certain I even recognize myself."

"It was high time that your own natural beauty was displayed to the world," said Mouette. She motioned to her own maid, Gwynn, who brought a small jewelry case. Opening it, Mouette withdrew a slim choker of emerald-cut diamonds and topaz with matching earrings. "They could have been made for you and your beautiful coloring."

Freddie touched the brilliant gems and sighed. "You all have made me feel very special."

"You *are* special," replied Mouette, stepping forward to embrace her. "It will be thrilling to take you openly into society and show your father that he cannot rule your life. It is my dream that this night will have a fairy-tale ending for you, darling Frederica."

* * *

IT WAS NEARLY eleven o'clock when Anthony arrived at Lord Thurston's ball. He was impeccably turned out in evening dress, his first extravagance since returning to London, and he had an idea that he looked just fine.

Perhaps even better than fine, he thought wryly, judging by the ladies' stares on his way into the grand ballroom. After greeting his hosts, who inquired like everyone else about his adventures with Darwin and the accident that everyone feared had taken his life, Anthony accepted a glass of champagne. The large room was lit by glittering chandeliers and scented with hot-house roses. Anthony stood alone for a time, drinking, and taking it all in …opulent chattering guests and too-loud laughter, the strains of the music, the heat emanating from the impeccably mannered dancers. It was certainly a far cry from the life he'd grown used to, exploring the world on board the *Beagle,* and then fighting to survive, to surmount countless obstacles in order to return home to England.

Across the ballroom, a striking lady raised her hand to him, and Anthony recognized his former lover, Marianne. It was odd to remember she was now Lady Hartstone and must be routinely invited to proper balls, routs, and assemblies. Even as Anthony inclined his head in reply to her wave, he was grateful to see another man claim her for the next waltz.

Just then, a voice piped, "Milord?"

Glancing over, he saw the top of Rafael's curly head. "What the devil are you doing here?" Against his better judgment, Anthony had been persuaded to let the lad act as his groom tonight. He gave silent thanks that he had at least made certain Rafael wore proper blue satin livery.

"After you left the carriage, I found something on the seat," the boy said in rapid Portuguese.

"Don't you know, you cannot come in here."

"But *this*." Rafael opened his hand to display a small purple velvet case.

Shocked, Anthony snatched it up. "Good God." He pushed it deep into his coat pocket.

"You see?" The boy cocked his head and grinned, adding in English, "You need me."

Anthony sent him a reluctant smile. "Go now. Stay with the equipage until you are summoned."

Alone again, he took a second glass of champagne and looked around for his family. Soon, he spied his parents and Raveneau grandparents, all looking splendid as they chatted with a lot of nobles considered by most to be dead bores. Emeline, clad in a new ball-gown, looked on as a besotted young dandy led her cousin Camille out for a waltz.

But where was Frederica?

Anthony would never admit it to anyone, but the real reason he had come tonight was to see ...Freddie. Just saying *Freddie*, silently, to himself, sent a surge of feelings through him.

He had tried to resist. Tonight, he'd gone to not one but two of his favorite clubs in St. James. His old friends had greeted him warmly, plied him with drink, and invited him to join them at faro and hazard tables. Anthony had played, winning a considerable sum, but the strident male voices and even the games grated on his nerves in a way he didn't remember from the past.

Yet, when he went home, that didn't feel right either. Restless, Anthony had finally gotten out the invitation his mother had sent round and changed into his evening clothes. It came to him that Freddie might need assistance but be unwilling to send word to him. Viscount Redfield was capable of all manner of villainy! Didn't Anthony owe it Freddie to stand by to rescue her?

Even as he had this thought, he caught a glimpse of

her. But—could that vision truly be Freddie? The slim, graceful female who waltzed in the arms of Sir Harold Alken was simply enchanting. She wore a gown that seemed fashioned of golden cobwebs, and her animated face was radiant. Frowning, Anthony disposed of his glass and made his way over to his family.

"Oh, darling," exclaimed Mouette as he drew near. "Look at you! Every female in attendance is staring. I think you must be the most handsome man in our family."

"I beg your pardon?" Justin interjected, expanding his chest.

Anthony's grandfather, who leaned on his ebony walking stick with a negligent air, laughed. "Justin, face facts. You and I must move aside to make room for the next generation."

At any other time, Anthony would have been amused by this interchange, but tonight he couldn't take his eyes of the young woman he now realized was indeed his own Frederica.

His mother sent him a meaningful glance. "Isn't she lovely?"

"Indeed, I would hardly know it is Freddie. But what about that old man who is dancing with her? Tell me he has a wife."

"Sir Harold isn't the least bit old! No more than five-and-thirty, and quite handsome, I think." She regarded him affectionately. "And he did indeed have a wife, but sadly Dame Philomena succumbed to a heart condition last year. Sir Harold is left to raise their twin sons alone."

Anthony took the bait. "What the devil are you suggesting, Mama?"

Her brows lifted. "Only that our Freddie is already very sought-after by the more mature, established men who wouldn't notice her if she were a green girl in her first Season." Pausing for effect, she added, "Observe the many gentlemen all around the ballroom, watching Freddie. They are dazzled, and rightly so."

"Are you quite finished?"

"Surely you are pleased for her success?" His mother blinked as if surprised. "One would assume so, given your long friendship."

He scowled. "Perhaps I would like to dance with her myself."

"Then you should have come sooner, darling. Freddie's every dance has been claimed."

* * *

"MY DEAR MISS REDFIELD," Sir Harold Alken was saying, "Will you consent to drive out with me in the park tomorrow afternoon? I have a very dashing new curricle I should like to show you."

As they turned smoothly with the music, Freddie could find no fault with her partner. He was attractive and kind, accomplished and prosperous. In fact, all her partners tonight had been very nice men, but of course, none of them were Anthony. When she thought of him, an invisible hand seemed to squeeze her heart.

"Sir Harold, you are very kind to ask, but I am otherwise engaged tomorrow." She softened this refusal with a kind smile.

Before he could reply, the waltz ended, and Sir Harold guided her back to her friends. Freddie saw with a sinking feeling that her next partner, a golden-haired young baronet, was already waiting there. At first, the dancing and male attention had been enlivening, but now her slippers pinched, and she found it increasingly difficult to make polite conversation with the long parade of admiring partners.

Even as she braced herself to greet the baronet,

Freddie felt someone watching her. Turning her head, she nearly gasped aloud, for standing off to one side, just behind Justin St. Briac, was Anthony. Her breath caught. Wide shoulders set off by a flawlessly tailored coat and black hair appealing windblown, Anthony met her eyes and arched one brow just enough to send a wordless message. As if in answer to his stare, her body responded, tingling, and heat pulsed between her legs.

"Thank you so much for that lovely dance," she managed to say to Sir Harold, hoping he would take the hint and go off to attend another young lady.

At that moment, the baronet, looking determined, stepped forward. "The next dance is mine, I believe, Miss Redfield."

Freddie saw Anthony coming toward them. His expression was coolly unconcerned, but she recognized the fire in his dark eyes. Her heart raced, and heat climbed in her cheeks.

Just as Anthony reached her side, a loud voice spoke from a distance.

"I see you are having quite the success, my girl!"

It was as if a chilly storm cloud had descended over the ballroom, blackening the moment. Freddie felt physically ill as she turned to behold the forbidding countenance of her father. Jaw thrust forward, he towered above her. Immediately she perceived that he had been drinking. Except for the day when she had been in disguise at the Geological Society meeting, she had not laid eyes on him since their last confrontation at Redfield House, the night she climbed down the tree and ran away to Grosvenor Square.

So much had happened since then, and Freddie had changed in a thousand ways, yet when she met Papa's furious stare, all her old terrors came alive in the pit of her stomach. Did he have the right to capture her there and take her away? At that moment, anything seemed possible.

"I have a new life, Papa," she said, proud to hear that her voice did not betray her inner turmoil.

"You are my *daughter*." He spoke the words as if he were God, handing down a commandment.

"See here, Redfield—" It was Justin St. Briac, moving forward, but before he could finish his sentence, Anthony stepped between the two men.

"Ah, I see you have come out of hiding, young St. Briac," Redfield taunted, his words slurred. "You are just the person I came to see tonight. Fancy finding you here with my own Frederica!"

"Say what you will and then leave us alone," Anthony ground out.

Freddie wanted to speak up again, but Mouette came up beside her and reached for her gloved hand, squeezing it. "Wait," she whispered.

As if realizing that the battle with Viscount Redfield was no longer his to fight, Justin stepped back and deferred to his son. It seemed that the eyes of every guest in the crowded ballroom were on their little group.

"I know what has been happening in your house, St. Briac," her father railed at Anthony. "You have been hiding my daughter under your roof, most improperly! You have sullied her good name so that no other man will want her."

Out of the corner of her eye, Freddie saw both Sir Harold and the golden-haired baronet move away from them. *Good*, she thought. *All of you men, just leave me alone.*

"If she took shelter with friends, it was to escape your threats," said Anthony.

Her father turned to glare at Justin St. Briac, and Freddie felt the power of his enduring resentment for the man Mouette had chosen over him. "Can you not force your son to be a gentleman?" he sneered. "Must I call him out?"

It was Anthony who replied, a hint of mockery in his voice. "Ah, but you are in a taking for no reason, sir. In truth, I am glad you are here, for I have been waiting for the right moment to ask your daughter an important question."

Freddie's heart leaped into her throat as he turned toward her, so impossibly splendid that she could scarcely believe he was real.

"My darling Frederica," Anthony said in a low, compelling voice as he reached into his coat pocket and produced a small, velvet box. With one hand, he deftly opened it and withdrew a tiny object that glittered in the light of the chandeliers. Then, to her utter shock, Anthony dropped down on one knee, looking up into her eyes. "Will you do me the honor of agreeing to become my wife?"

CHAPTER 27

Stunned and confused, Freddie stared at Anthony. For a moment, she felt dizzy, like a secret princess in a fairy tale who at last has won her prince. Was it possible that he truly loved her and wanted to give up the life he had planned to marry her?

"My darling," Anthony repeated firmly. This time, he squeezed her cold fingers. "Did you hear my question?"

It was, she realized, the only way out of this predicament. Her would-be oppressor, her father, was standing just feet away, poised to reclaim his right to direct her life. The London *ton* were all watching, and they had heard Viscount Redfield's loud insinuations about Freddie and Anthony. She was also aware that the beautiful Countess of Hartstone was present and doubtless observing more intently than any other guest.

Freddie saw only one clear choice. "I am quite overcome, sir," she said. "You do me a great honor, and I accept with pleasure."

The ring Anthony slipped on her finger was a round, brilliant emerald encircled with tiny diamonds. In the next moment, he rose to his feet in one smooth movement. His family were all offering their congratulations, but Papa stood back from the others, watching silently. What was he thinking?

As couples gathered for the country dance, Anthony took her hand. "Let me take you away from here so we can talk."

"Oh yes." Relief rushed through her. For a moment, she imagined them returning to his house in Charles Street. She would change into a simple gown and take the many pins from her hair, and they would sit close together in the library, talking, sipping wine, and ...

"Of course, we can't go home. Completely improper," Anthony said in a low voice, as if he had read her thoughts. "I will take you to Grosvenor Square."

With a pang, Freddie realized he was right. Even though they had been in hiding from the world, they had also enjoyed a sort of magical freedom to do as they pleased—together.

All eyes were on them now, and it seemed that everything had changed.

* * *

"WHERE ARE WE GOING?" Freddie asked as Anthony led her up a third staircase to a part of the Raveneau house she hadn't realized existed.

He held a small chamberstick in one hand, its flickering light dancing up the walls, and drew her along after him with his other hand. At the top of the stairs there was a landing that gave way to a wide, arched doorway.

"It's the ballroom," Anthony said. "No one ever comes up here, and it's far enough from the other rooms that we won't be overheard."

Inside, Freddie watched as he used the candlestick

to light wall sconces, and soon the spacious room was suffused with a quavering, golden glow.

"There is a bottle of Grandpère's best brandy. Would you like a small glass?" asked Anthony.

"Maybe just a tiny bit." She smiled, but her heart was beating fast.

He went to the cellaret near the piano and poured a bit for both of them, then they sat down together on a worn sofa against the wall.

"It's a lovely room," said Freddie. "Simple yet very graceful."

"We used to come up here for dancing lessons when I was a little boy," Anthony confided. "That almost feels like another life. My mother was very caught up in the *beau monde* then, married to Sir Harry Brandreth, who I thought was my father." He leaned back against the tufted blue upholstery and his entire countenance darkened. "Of course, I thought so! Why would any child believe otherwise?"

"Yes," she murmured. "I do remember a bit about that time, though I was quite young." More than anything, Frederica remembered the way her own parents whispered about Sir Harry's shocking disgrace and imprisonment. Because her father and Sir Harry had been lifelong friends, Papa had been determined to help Mouette get back on her feet, or at least that was what he had insisted to Freddie's mother.

"Our parents have lived ...complicated lives," said Freddie with a sigh.

"Ah, well," Anthony replied grimly, "that's a very nice way of putting it."

Her heart ached as she looked over at him, his profile harsh and yet strangely vulnerable in the candle glow. It was impossible to guess his thoughts, especially considering tonight's events and the emerald ring that winked on her wedding finger.

"I'm so glad you took me away from there so we might be private." She took a deep breath and turned to face him while removing the ring, certain that he had given it to her out of some misguided impulse to rescue her. "It was very kind of you to intervene so gallantly tonight at the ball, but now I must return this to you."

Freddie tried to give him the ring, but he would not open his hand. "Are you withdrawing your acceptance?"

"Anthony St. Briac, we both know you do not truly want to wed! You have been the best of friends to me—"

To Freddie's shock, he turned and lifted her onto his lap, his arms iron-hard around her back. "*Friends*? You know it is more than that, Frederica." His black eyes flashed. "Much more."

He bent her back over one arm and his lips slanted over hers, his tongue invading in a way that sent a spear of potent arousal directly to her intimate core. Freddie ached for him. If he would lift her skirts and take her right there on the sofa, she would submit without hesitation. Winding her arms around his neck, she returned his kiss, squirming a little in a way that made him smile against her eager mouth.

"I want to take off all your clothes and do wicked things with you," Anthony muttered, breaking their kiss and pressing hot kisses to the little pulse below her ear, then lower. Each touch of his skilled mouth was exquisite torture.

Freddie wanted to beg him to free her breasts. "Wicked?" she gasped.

"Deliciously so." His long fingers slid up under her petticoats, up her thigh, until he reached the split seam opening in her drawers.

"Is that why you asked me to marry you?" she managed to ask.

His fingertip trailed fire along the soft curls at the bare apex of her thighs. "So we could do wicked things?" His low laugh was pure seduction. "Ah, sweet, I can assure you that marriage is not necessary for us to indulge in such pleasures."

Freddie asked, aching, "Why, then?"

Their eyes met in the shadows, and she felt his hand slip free of her skirts. "To make your father go away."

Suddenly cold, she shivered, angry with herself for hoping for more, just as she had foolishly allowed herself to hope for words of love when they had lain together in his bed. Only in romantic novels did men like Anthony St. Briac surrender to true love. In real life, such men were inconstant, secretive, and restless.

Where was that bloody ring? Freddie fumbled and found it in the folds of her gown. "Please, take this back. I appreciate your good intentions, but it is mad to think we could marry when you are only being chivalrous. Such a proposition is doomed from the first." She sat up straight, looked at him, and tried to put the ring in his hand again.

"Frederica," Anthony said persuasively. "Don't make me take it back. Let us discuss this calmly."

She struggled with her skirts and rose from his lap. "All right, but do not touch me."

"I will endeavor to resist that temptation," he said solemnly. "You must agree, it isn't easy."

"I don't want to talk about that!" Heat rose in her cheeks.

He bit his lip and nodded again. "As you wish."

Adjusting the bodice of her ball gown with both hands, Freddie began to pace while Anthony reclined against the back of the sofa and sipped his brandy. After a moment, he offered, "You should know, I didn't just propose marriage on a whim."

She stopped. "What does that mean?"

He shrugged his wide shoulders. "We deal together very well, don't you agree?" A gleam came into his eyes. "In and out of the bedroom."

Selfishly, maddeningly, Freddie yearned for more. Yet hadn't she been the one to repeatedly deny any desire for love and marriage? Confusion pricked her heart. "That sounds rather like a business arrangement."

"Oh, I think we can make it much more enjoyable than that, don't you?" A suggestive smile touched his mouth. "But face it, my dear, you are in a corner—and in a way, so am I. Someone has informed your father that you have been staying in my house, both of us in hiding as it were. I suspect Redfield would not hesitate to lay waste to both our lives. After all we have been through together, Freddie, I don't want that for you."

Perhaps he did care for her? "Well, I certainly don't want Papa to make *your* life a misery either."

"There, you see? Don't worry." He patted the seat next to him and held up the ring. "Come back."

Reluctantly, Freddie obeyed, but kept a small space between them. Smoothing her skirts, she waited.

"I understand that you are hesitant. You have told me many times that you don't wish to marry, and you need to feel free," Anthony said. "It's understandable, given your experience with your own father." Pausing, he flashed a smile. "And of course, you are no ordinary female."

She nodded. "Thank you for saying so. I have ambitions, just as you do, and nothing will change those."

"My point exactly. I can give you security and a home of your own. You and I are alike in many ways, and if we must wed, why not to each other?"

Of course, this was quite true, but still his words "*if we must wed*" stung. A part of her wanted to refuse and make a graceful exit, but Anthony was right: she was in a corner. She couldn't stay with his family forever and if her father spread tales about her, there was no telling what sort of future she would face. It was already going to be difficult enough to pursue a career at the British Museum, but if they thought she was a woman of loose morals, it would be hopeless.

Slowly, Freddie nodded. "Perhaps you are right."

"Don't look so glum. We can make an unconventional marriage, unhindered by the usual constraints."

What did that mean? But Freddie couldn't bring herself to ask the question, to take a chance that he might perceive how much she really cared.

No, much more than that. *Loved.*

She stared as he held the stunning emerald ring between his strong, elegant forefinger and thumb.

"Shall we give it a go then?" Anthony's tone was casual, but he gazed at her in a way that made her feel as if she'd drunk too much Raveneau brandy.

"All right." Freddie watched as he slid the ring back onto her finger, strong emotions swirling inside her. "Yes. I will try."

"Excellent. And to demonstrate my good faith, I shall refrain from any wicked attentions until after our wedding." Leaning forward, Anthony touched his mouth to hers in a chaste kiss. Freddie's body instantly responded, but then it was over. "Now then, let us go back downstairs before my grandparents' servants add to the tales of our indecency."

"Yes, we should go. Your family will no doubt return home soon."

He rose and held out a hand to her. "I've just remembered that you have not met Rafael, the newest member of my household. He was the groom sitting up behind us when we drove here from the ball, but by some miracle he refrained from making himself known to you."

"That boy with the curly hair? He did give me a surprisingly friendly smile," said Freddie.

"Did he indeed? He refuses to behave as a servant." Anthony tucked her hand through the crook of his elbow and guided her out of the ballroom. "Come. Let us beg Arabella for a piece of the pear tart I saw cooling when we passed through the kitchen tonight. We will sit together, and I'll share the details of Rafael's colorful tale."

CHAPTER 28

*M*uch to Frederica's surprise, a notice of her engagement to Anthony St. Briac appeared in the *Gazette* and *Morning Post* just two mornings after the scene at the ball. Freddie had been finishing her eggs when Mouette sat down beside her at the dining table and showed her the newspapers.

"It seems he is indeed serious," Anthony's mother said, brows aloft.

"We had a little talk about it," replied Freddie. "For now, we will try."

"That is all very well, but I think you are past the point of simple 'trying', given these notices. You'll have to do it." Was there a note of doubt in her voice?

"Oh." Freddie nodded and smiled, but uncertainty swelled in the pit of her stomach. She thought of Anthony, who had reappeared among the *ton* for the first time at Lord Thurston's ball. Every beauty present had watched him with eager interest. He would now be the most sought-after bachelor in London if he were free to indulge in those pleasures. What was it Anthony had said? *We can make an unconventional marriage, unhindered by the usual constraints.*

"I think that yesterday he went to speak to your father," said Mouette as she began to eat her breakfast. "To sort out matters with him."

"Truly?" Freddie's stomach pitched again. "Oh, dear. I rather fear he may be doing this out of a sense of honor. Has he confided at all to you? His true feelings, I mean?"

Mouette broke off a piece of biscuit and handed it down to Daisy, who fixed her with an intense stare. "My son has a gift for hiding his 'true feelings' under a façade of casual charm ...something he cultivated during his rather bumpy upbringing. And I believe the dangers and trials of this past year have hardened him." She sighed. "All of which is to say that I cannot answer your question. I do think he is trying to do the right thing." Patting Freddie's hand, she added almost as an afterthought, "I rather suspect he has felt guilty all these years about the way he used his charms on you to gain access to the portrait hidden in your father's study."

"Indeed, he did use me very badly!" flashed Freddie, remembering that first awakening of her heart before she had realized Anthony's true intentions. She sank back now against her chair. "But surely, he would not *wed* simply to make amends for that transgression!"

"Oh no, I think not. You must pay no attention to me," she soothed. "Let us ring for more chocolate, shall we?"

* * *

THE NEXT EVENING, Anthony took Frederica on their first outing as an engaged couple. As they emerged from Raveneau House at dusk, she saw a curly-haired boy with a wide, impudent smile standing in front of Anthony's smart cabriolet.

"Hello, Mistress," he said in careful English, handing

her up with a flourish. "I am Rafael, and it is my honor to serve you."

Anthony sent him a stern, yet faintly amused look. "If you mean to remain as a groom, young toad-eater, you may not engage in conversation with my guests."

At this, Rafael should have silently bowed and removed himself, but instead he put up his chin and replied, "Yet I do not wish to be a groom, sir, as you well know. It is your valet I should be!"

"Not another word." Anthony threatened. He gestured for Rafael to climb up on the small groom's platform at the rear of the cabriolet. Although Freddie couldn't help liking the boy, she was relieved to see him obey.

Moments later, a blanket tucked around her legs, they set off.

"I apologize for the late notice, but Darwin came by to remind me that we're invited to dine at the home of Sir Charles Lyell and his wife, Mary," Anthony explained as he drove them down Park Lane toward Hyde Park Corner.

"As you know, Lyell's book on Geology is one of my prized possessions," Freddie said. "It will be thrilling to dine in his home ...but are you certain they are expecting me to come with you?"

"No, probably not, but Charles assures me they won't mind."

Anthony was momentarily diverted as he skillfully guided the cabriolet, drawn by one handsome gray, through a tangle of much larger coaches and carriages. Frederica saw her opportunity to change the subject.

"I heard from your mother that you had a meeting with Papa. Were you not going to tell me?"

He looked over at her and made a brief, dismissive gesture with the reins. "I would have, eventually, but I didn't want to spend any more of this evening talking about Viscount Redfield than was absolutely necessary. The fact is, I went round to see him so that I could formally secure his permission to marry you." Flicking a glance her way, he added, "That's the way it's done, you know."

"He doesn't deserve that sort of courtesy," Freddie pronounced. "He deceived Mama, keeping that portrait of your mother and spending more time with it than with his own family. And that says nothing at all about the way he has treated me, attempting to browbeat me into doing his bidding." To her horror, she heard her voice thicken with emotion. "Sometimes I think I hate him."

"Perfectly understandable," Anthony agreed calmly, and she felt very grateful that he didn't try to tell her she should not say such things about her own parent. "You're completely right, no doubt, but I had to smooth the waters with him. I don't want Viscount Redfield or anyone else spreading tales about us." Anthony paused. "Also, I wanted to find out how he learned that you were staying at my house ...which also meant someone must have realized you were not Professor Loudon."

"Did he tell you?" Freddie asked in surprise.

"Yes." They had come into Harley Street, and Anthony drew the cabriolet up in front of a handsome, three-story brick house but made no move to alight. "It was Terrance Buskin."

"Oh! Could he possibly be more despicable?" gasped Freddie. "It is horrible to imagine Terrance in league with my father! Thank God he will soon be out of London." She reflected over all the visits Buskin had paid to Anthony's house during her sojourn there. "I just do not understand how he could have known. He never gave me the slightest sign, and I do not think he could have been such a good actor."

"You're quite right, minx. It was Meg who went to

Buskin with the information, and I suppose he found a way to reward her. Perhaps she will go with him to Blickling Corners as his housekeeper, hoping for marriage in time."

"Meg!" cried Frederica, immediately thinking back to all the times she must have let down her guard as Professor Loudon when Meg had been nearby. "I find this shocking. People..."

"Yes?" He reached for her hand, and Freddie felt the warmth of his strong fingers through her glove. From behind the cabriolet's sheltering hood, Rafael cleared his throat as if to remind them to disembark.

"Oh, nothing. It's just I find it hard to predict when someone might disappoint me." She gave a little laugh. "It must be the reason why I like to lose myself in dead things like fossils."

For a moment, she thought he might close the small space between them and kiss her, but instead he only nodded. "You'll be able to talk of fossils to your heart's content tonight."

"Oh, I do hope so. I hope Mrs. Lyell won't take me away to see her needlework just as you men delve deepest into matters of geology."

* * *

CHARLES LYELL AND MARY, his wife of four years, warmly greeted both Anthony and Frederica. It seemed that Darwin had arrived at their house some time ago, for he had loosened his black neckcloth and had a book open in the parlor that he wanted to discuss with Lyell. Anthony knew that the two men had become fast friends since the return of the *Beagle*, and he was grateful to Darwin for including him in this exclusive circle. When they had spoken about it, Darwin remarked that Mary was a 'monument of patience' for enduring the long hours of geology conversation between Darwin and Lyell, so Anthony supposed Mary must be uninterested in natural science.

Their narrow, three-story home was cozy, warmed by a fire and redolent of the aromas of roast chicken, fresh-baked rolls, apples, and cinnamon. Anthony watched Freddie slowly relax in the company Charles Lyell, a Scotsman with a strong chin and twinkling eyes.

Midway through the meal, during which most conversation focused on the discoveries made during the *Beagle*'s voyage, Freddie smiled at the respected geologist and said, "I don't mean to interrupt, but I feel compelled to say that your book, *Principles of Geology*, awoke something in me that changed my life. Because I couldn't subscribe to the staid ideas about the earth being created in a few days and changes being wrought through catastrophes, I questioned everything. Your theory that our world has evolved through a series of very slow changes was absolutely thrilling to me." She paused, blushing slightly, and added, "When I was forced to leave my father's home, I took only three books, and yours was one of them."

Anthony turned slightly in his chair to gaze at Freddie as she spoke. She wore an off the shoulder gown of leaf-green silk and her caramel-hued locks were twisted into a simple chignon. Her entire countenance was glowing, and Anthony found her even more exquisite in that moment than she had been at Lord Thurston's ball. Pride and longing bumped together inside him.

"Oh my." Freddie broke off and looked over, as if sensing the intensity of his thoughts. "What is it? I am going on too long, aren't I?"

"Not a bit." On impulse, he reached out to graze her

cheek with his fingertip. Her skin was warm and soft as velvet.

"Ah, young love," Darwin murmured with a chuckle.

Across the table, Charles Lyell was smiling at Frederica. "I am honored to know that you have enjoyed my book so much that you've kept it with you, Miss Redfield."

Next to him, Mary's lovely doe eyes took it all in before she spoke. "How wonderful that you have a strong interest in geology. It will make your marriage so much richer, for these men are very passionate about science. Some wives might feel slighted, or even abandoned, when the next thrilling expedition calls them."

Incurably frank, Freddie asked, "How do you cope?"

"Oh, I go with Charles whenever possible. I have found a hundred ways to involve myself in his work." Looking over at her husband, she laughed softly. "If I were a man, I would join the Geological Society myself."

"Yes, so would I!" exclaimed Freddie.

"My wife is very modest," said Lyell. "In fact, Mary is a geologist and a conchologist in her own right. She catalogues my specimens, and when we travel, she sketches all the relevant geological structures and other noteworthy sights."

"The drawing lessons we females must endure have served me well," Mary said with a trace of irony.

"I have been cataloguing Anthony's specimens as well," Freddie told her new friend. "I have never found any project as absorbing as this one, not even the organization of my grandfather's extensive library."

"I should very much like to come and see what you've been doing," Mary rejoined. "I am always open to new methods. And it's possible that I might be able to suggest something you'll find helpful with your collections."

"Perhaps Mary has been able to travel with Lyell on land, for shorter distances," Darwin interjected, "but there's not a sea captain I know who would permit a lady on board a voyage like the one we made on the *Beagle*. Aside from the obvious distracting issues, females are thought to bring bad luck at sea."

This brought a shadow of uncertainty to Freddie's face, but before Anthony could comment, dessert was served, and everyone turned their attention to the inviting cinnamon-spiced apple pie.

* * *

BY THE TIME Anthony returned Frederica to Grosvenor Square, she was feeling tired but very happy. The evening had been a revelation. Never had she imagined dining with such exalted geologists as Charles Darwin and Charles Lyell, but perhaps best of all had been the discovery that Mary Lyell had felt free to pursue her own scientific ambitions.

Before alighting from the cabriolet, Anthony turned to look down at Freddie. He was so shockingly handsome that a part of her wanted to hide from his searching gaze, afraid to imagine so much happiness could possibly be hers. She longed to accept everything he offered, yet it seemed there must be an unseen pitfall lurking in his casual promise of an *unconventional marriage*. So many men took mistresses and excluded their wives from large parts of their lives. Was that what Anthony meant by *unhindered by the usual constraints?* When he had first used this phrase, it seemed an accommodation to her independence, but now she suspected just the opposite. How she wished her mind would stop circling back over his words, as if closer review would reveal the truth.

The only way to know for certain was to ask Anthony, and that prospect was far too daunting. Her own father's face flashed in her mind, and in the next instant she envisioned Mama, weeping when she thought no one could see.

"What worries you, minx?" he asked, taking her hand.

Freddie gathered her wits. "I suppose I am fretting about the conversation you had with Papa. He will no doubt make demands of you."

"You must not worry. Leave it all to me."

"I fear that he will ask you for money. He's desperately in debt, you know."

"You needn't trouble yourself on that account. Don't we have a host of other matters to attend to …such as our wedding?"

With that, Anthony drew her into his strong embrace and kissed her with a sweet, sensual tenderness that made her heart sting. Freddie wanted to believe it was love that infused his kiss, but even if he had said the words, she might struggle to believe him.

CHAPTER 29

The next few days were filled with wedding plans, largely overseen by Mouette. It seemed that she had a gift for designing not only homes, but also parties, and the dining room table was covered with her lists.

Freddie listened absently as Mouette and Devon discussed which flowers would be best for the bride's bouquet. Anthony had stated his desire that the wedding be held 'the sooner the better' and Mouette mused that a Christmas theme would be enchanting. Justin even came in at one point to suggest that they all travel to Cornwall so that the wedding might be held there.

As they talked, Freddie moved to stand at the window overlooking Grosvenor Square. The sky was lead-gray, the grass was brown, and the tree branches were all barren of leaves. In the middle of the square, Freddie spied Mrs. Bell sitting on a bench, all alone.

"If you can spare me, I think I will go out for some air," she said to the two women.

Heads together, they glanced up distractedly. "Of course, dear," replied Devon. "While you are out, do think about a church. Perhaps your family attended somewhere regularly, before your mother's passing?"

"Yes, yes, I will," Freddie replied.

Moments later, she was donning her bonnet and mantelet and escaping into the chilly afternoon. The sight of Mrs. Bell sitting alone, gazing across the square at Justmore House where she had been housekeeper for decades, tugged at Freddie's heart. Coming up behind the bench, she rested a hand on the old woman's shoulder.

"I imagine you must miss it," she said.

"Indeed. Whenever I see the new Lord Justmore emerge from the house, I do feel a bit sad." Mrs. Bell lifted her spectacles to dab at her eyes.

"Oh, yes, that is sad. It seems that a stranger lives in the home we loved." Freddie drew a ragged breath. "I miss Grandpapa very much."

"Sit down right here, beside me, mistress."

She obeyed, longing to put her arms around the housekeeper who had so faithfully served her grandparents and then Frederica herself. "I hope you will consider coming with me after Mr. St. Briac and I are wed. I should like it above all things, and of course, any assistance you could lend to running the house would be very welcome."

Mrs. Bell looked skeptical. "Perhaps. We shall see." She sighed. "I hope you are doing the right thing."

Her stomach pitched in a way that was becoming familiar. "What do you mean by that?"

The housekeeper seemed not to have heard. Following her gaze, Freddie looked through the leafless trees. The door to Justmore House had opened, and her father emerged. *Oh no.*

His rather shabby landau was waiting at the edge of the walkway, but Viscount Redfield passed it by without speaking a word to the waiting groom. Instead, he entered the square through an unlocked iron gate and strode directly toward them, a towering figure in his tall hat of black silk.

"I will go in, my dear," said Mrs. Bell.

Freddie wanted to beg her not to leave her, but of course she had to stand up to her father alone. She stood and waited until they were face to face.

"Hello, Papa."

"Ah, Frederica, I'm glad to find you here today. I suppose you are making wedding plans?"

To her surprise, he did not appear angry or aggressive in any way. Instead, he was smiling, holding out his hands to her.

"Actually, yes ..." A part of her expected some lackey of his to leap out from behind a tree and attempt to carry her off. "You aren't angry?"

"When you ran away, I was extremely afraid for your safety. To this day, I cannot fathom how you could bring such anguish to your own father." He sighed deeply. "And when Mr. Buskin called on me and informed me of your whereabouts as well as the masquerade you had been conducting, under the same roof as that known rake, St. Briac, I'll own I did feel quite angry."

There was a great deal Freddie could have said in reply, but she knew her father too well. He had tried more than once to sell her in marriage to the wealthy Lord Cobleigh, with no consideration at all for her feelings or wishes. No matter what he claimed now, that was the truth she must never forget.

"You needn't worry, Papa. I have my own future well in hand."

"Yes, I know, puss." Redfield smiled. "I've had a visit from your bridegroom. He was most reassuring."

For the first time, Freddie noticed the ruby stickpin in his cravat and the fine new suit of clothes he wore. A chill ran down her spine. "I'm glad to hear it ..."

"It's all rather absurd, isn't it? I wanted Mouette so much, it nearly cost me everything, and now you are going to wed her son!" He gave a sharp laugh. "Who would have thought it? Our odd, bookish Freddie, who could not garner even one offer during her Season, is now betrothed to London's most elusive rake." Sniffing, he added, "Even so, you are above him. You should have married a nobleman like Cobleigh ...but I suppose I must lower my sights."

Freddie forced herself to ask a painful question. "Papa, did Anthony give you money?"

"By Jove, of course he gave me money!" He smoothed his silk waistcoat with one big hand. "Paid my debts as well. Asked me to go away to the continent for a few years to give you some breathing room. Ridiculous notion, but I was happy to agree."

She barely heard anything he said after that first smug sentence: *Of course, he gave me money!* Oh, how could he? How could Anthony do such a thing without telling her, especially when she had asked him directly? Did he think he could keep it from her forever? A red mist obscured her vision as this new reality swept over her.

Perhaps she had been a fool to open her heart and trust Anthony.

Her own father had attempted to manipulate her life and future by selling her to Lord Cobleigh. Now, unbelievably, it was happening again, only this time Anthony had become the highest bidder.

* * *

IN THOSE CRUSHING moments after her father's shocking disclosure, Freddie's first impulse was to take matters into her own hands again and flee. Numbly, she told Papa goodbye, but couldn't bring herself to go back inside the Raveneau home. Lights glowed in the windows. She saw Emeline sketching in the parlor and Mouette and Devon in the dining room, nodding together over their lists. Upstairs, André Raveneau's study was illuminated, and she imagined him at his desk with Daisy curled nearby on her cushion. It seemed, if she tried to explain, none of them could understand the reasons for her hopelessness. Their lives were golden.

The only solution was to speak to Anthony, as soon as possible. Freddie could walk from Grosvenor Square to Charles Street in only a few minutes. Impulsively, she set out alone.

She thought of how tender and sweet Anthony had been the night they dined with the Lyells. Yet, he had been evasive about her father as well, and now she wondered again if that was how he intended to go forward in all areas of their marriage, doing as he pleased and using his charm to deflect her questions.

Freddie's pulse was racing as she turned the corner on Charles Street and approached the handsome butterscotch-tinted house where she had felt so intensely alive. Drawing near, she saw a portly man in a tall beaver hat on the front step, raising the knocker. Moments later, Quincy appeared and ushered the gentleman inside.

Her emotions in turmoil, Freddie had no desire to explain herself to Quincy or anyone else. She approached the front door and gently turned the brass knob, feeling fully justified in simply walking in. After all, as far as anyone knew, she would soon be Anthony St. Briac's bride, and this would be her home.

The entry hall was utterly still. There was no sign of Quincy, but Freddie heard male voices coming from the library. One of the men was Anthony, and no doubt he was conversing with the portly stranger. Her heart pounded in her ears as she stood there, straining to hear what they were saying. What would she do if Anthony suddenly came out of the library and saw her standing there, unannounced, eavesdropping?

She took a few more silent steps closer to the open doorway, afraid to breathe.

"Excellent, Captain Liggett," Anthony was saying. "I have dreamed of traveling to the Canary Islands since I was at university and Darwin talked of going there."

"We will be honored to have you join our expedition as our naturalist, sir," the other man replied. "The *Susannah* sails in March. I will keep you apprised of all the plans as they unfold."

"I look forward to it," Anthony said. "I do have one more request, however."

Freddie waited, her heart in her throat.

"What is that?" asked Captain Liggett.

"As I have mentioned, I will be married soon, and I don't want my wife to know about this voyage." He paused. "I must ask you to communicate with me in private, Captain, at least for the time being."

Freddie pressed a hand to her mouth and tears blurred her vision. As she turned to flee, a slight figure appeared near the stairway. It was Rafael, his sapphire-striped waistcoat bright in the gloomy afternoon light.

She stared at him and pressed a forefinger to her lips, imploring his silence, before running from the house.

* * *

"I HAVE BEEN IN WORSE SCRAPES," Frederica told Mrs. Bell when they were alone in the housekeeper's neat, cozy room at the back of the Raveneau home. "But there is only one solution to this. I cannot marry Anthony St. Briac. I began to hope he might be different, but it seems he is as duplicitous in his own way as Papa."

"Oh, I have feared you were making a mistake," Mrs. Bell said sadly, putting her arms around Freddie. The temptation to lean, weeping, against her soft bulk was strong. "Men of that ilk do not change their spots. And even if they *seem* to do so, it never lasts."

Freddie took a deep breath, reminding herself that there was no time for a discussion of Anthony's character. "I propose that you and I go away, as we should have done from the very first. Once the storm passes, we can quietly return to London and carry on with our original plan to take lodgings near the British Museum, where I shall pursue the vocation I have long aspired to."

Even as she spoke the words, Freddie wondered if it were still true. Now that Anthony had awakened so many other longings inside her, could she ever be satisfied with her solitary studies? And, as for the ramifications of withdrawing from her engagement to Anthony ...Freddie could not think about that today.

"We shall travel to my brother's farm in Sussex," said Mrs. Bell.

"It should be easy enough to manage on the Stage."

"Oh, no, mistress, I would never agree to you going by the common stage or the Mail. Not only are they far too crowded, but one never knows what sort of persons might be on board or what might transpire." She gave her white head a disapproving shake. "Do you remember Carter, Lord Justmore's coachman? He often comes out and speaks to me when I'm taking the air, and always begs me to call on him for any needed assistance. I will ask him to hire a post-chaise for our journey."

"Oh, yes, that's excellent," said Freddie. Feeling herself flush, she added, "On my way back to

Grosvenor Square, I obtained funds for our endeavor ...by selling the rare diamond ring Grandpapa left me. He always meant that I should use it to obtain my independence."

Mrs. Bell frowned but nodded. "We shan't need much until we return to London and set up a household."

"Let us depart at dawn." She had no plan to see Anthony until tomorrow, when he was expected at a birthday lunch for his cousin Camille. By the time he came, she and Mrs. Bell would be well on their way to Sussex, and he would have no notion how to find her.

Mrs. Bell patted Freddie's cheek. "Mistress, you show a brave front to the world, but perhaps it isn't as easy as you let on?"

For one dangerous moment, her chin trembled. "I will be fine." Although her heart was breaking, she would never say so.

* * *

AT SIX IN THE MORNING, the sky was still dark. Carter came into the mews behind Raveneau House and waved just once, their signal that it was time for them to depart. Although there would be no footman to ride up in back, Carter assured them that his best groom, David, would serve as postillion and deliver them safely to Sussex.

Since returning the previous afternoon, Freddie had managed to avoid Anthony's family by telling Emeline she had a headache. They were all so good. Mouette had even sent a note with Freddie's dinner tray, saying she understood how tiring it could be to plan a wedding and imploring her to rest.

While the household slept, Freddie slipped a letter under Emeline's door, explaining some of what had happened, but begging her friend not to betray her to Anthony.

I ask that you thank your family for all their kindnesses. I am so very grateful! But it was not meant to be, and how much better it is to understand that now rather than after vows are exchanged. Truly, neither of us is suited to marriage, and I suspect he only proposed out of a misguided sense of gallantry.

It would have been better for me to leave London in the beginning, before your brother returned. None of you need worry in the least. Mrs. Bell is with me, and we shall set up housekeeping together. I am depending on you, as my friend, to say nothing to Anthony! I certainly would not want him to feel he must engage in some reckless behavior like chasing after me.

When Freddie wrote those last words, she thought with a pang of *The Wicked Highwayman*, which was still in Emeline's possession. Her friend professed not to have finished the romantic novel but Freddie suspected that Emeline held onto it so she could review the naughty bits.

Following Mrs. Bell out through the servants' entrance into the dark, foggy garden, Freddie reflected that she would be well off without *The Wicked Highwayman*.

She had experienced passion on a grand scale, beyond her wildest dreams, with Anthony.

Perhaps too far beyond her dreams, for now it felt dangerous ...

* * *

THE SUN WAS SHINING when Anthony and Rafael arrived in Grosvenor Square. He found his parents in the drawing room, chatting with Grandmama while reviewing Mouette's extensive wedding lists. Emeline perched in the bow window, sketching, while their Raveneau grandfather sat across the room in his favorite worn leather wing chair. A book was open on Grandpère's lap, but he appeared to be napping.

"Ah, you've come early," said Anthony's mother, rising to kiss him. She glanced toward Rafael, who waited in the stair hall. "Who's this?"

"Rafael, my rather annoyingly devoted new servant." Very briefly, he explained how Rafael had come to England and eventually attached himself to Anthony. "Since Quincy is now alone in the house, I have succumbed to the boy's constant entreaties to serve as my valet or groom or footman. He insists on filling any or all positions, in fact."

"I see. How lovely." She lifted dark, delicate brows. "That striped waistcoat is quite a unique touch with his livery."

"He fancies himself a tulip of fashion," Anthony observed dryly. "But enough about that. I've come to see Freddie, not talk about Rafael."

"Of course, you have! Just grant me one favor, darling, and give us your opinion about the best location for your wedding. Grandmama and I have London churches in mind, but Papa thinks we all ought to travel to Cornwall and hold the ceremony there."

This entire subject made him want to elope to Gretna Green. "What does Freddie say?"

"Not very much. Frederica has been rather preoccupied of late." A cloud seemed to pass over his mother's lovely face. "I think she went out today with Mrs. Bell."

"Out?" Something made him seek out Rafael in the stair hall. No sooner did they make eye contact than the boy glanced away, apparently looking for something on the Aubusson rug. With a rising sense of unease, Anthony turned his attention to Emeline, but his sister appeared oblivious to anything that was being said around her.

"Emmie, where is Frederica?" he demanded.

A telltale flush stained her cheeks. "I couldn't say."

"What the devil is going on here?" he heard himself demand. Just then, Cedric the butler appeared bearing a letter on a silver salver. He saw *Anthony* written across the creamy paper in a hand he knew all too well.

Snatching it, he broke the seal and read:

My dear Anthony,

I've come to my senses. It had to be this way, before the plans advanced any further, for both our sakes. Thank you for your friendship and even affection, but I cannot marry a man who keeps secrets of any kind.

She had started to write *I will always* but crossed out the words with her pen. This infuriated him. What had she been about to say?

I wish you only the best in your future adventures. Please do me the courtesy of trusting my judgment and letting me go.

Kind regards, Frederica Redfield.

Kind regards! As if she were writing to her cursed solicitor! An irrational rage blazed through him. Stalking across the room to Emeline, he grasped her by both arms and hauled her to her feet.

"What is this all about? And where the devil is Freddie?"

Emeline shrank back in shock. "Have you gone mad?"

"I can see it in your face, brat. You know where she is. I demand that you tell me!"

Her black-lashed violet eyes flashed back at him. "Unhand me this instant or I won't tell you anything at all."

Out of the corner of his eye, he saw his father push to his feet, frowning. "*Arrête.*"

Anthony released Emeline and stepped back. "I would never hurt her and well she knows it. It's just that ...I cannot believe this is happening. Freddie refers to secrets I have kept, but what can she mean?"

His grandmother raised a hand. "Yesterday, when Mouette and I were discussing your wedding in the dining room, Frederica went outside to converse with Mrs. Bell. I saw them sitting together on a bench in the square." She paused as if weighing her next words. "It may not mean anything, but when I looked outside again, I saw Viscount Redfield standing with them, talking to Frederica who appeared quite animated."

"Freddie's father?" Anthony dragged a hand through his hair in frustration. With an effort, he forced himself to review his own meeting with Redfield, and then the brief conversation he and Freddie had about it. She'd asked if he had given her father money—and Anthony had deflected her question. Crossing the room, he sank into a chair opposite his family members. "I may have taken it upon myself to try to solve matters with Redfield. For God's sake, he is her father, is he not? And she will be my wife. If I have the means to settle his debts and make him go away ..."

Mouette winced. "Giving Theo money without discussing it with Frederica would be a terrible thing to do. If you kept it from her, much worse."

"But surely that isn't enough to make her run away!" he heard himself shout. "The Freddie I know would confront me, rail at me, but run away? Never!"

"There may indeed be more, but her feelings about Theo have very deep, difficult roots, I think. Broken trust leaves scars." His mother nodded to herself and added, "Even a very strong woman might run away if she thinks a situation has no real solution."

The truth of this came into focus for Anthony. He jumped to his feet and began to pace. "By Lucifer, I will find her! I will show her that I – I –" His throat went dry.

Justin, leaning back in the sofa beside Mouette, murmured, "*Eh bien*, say it. It will feel surprisingly good."

His heart gave a great thump. "I love her. I *love* her, and I must find her."

"Oh, that is wonderful," his mother exclaimed, her eyes agleam with tears.

"Spoken like a true son of mine," pronounced Justin with fond irony.

Mouette shook her head and laughed, "Oh no, you were a much harder case."

"Do not forget that Anthony is also André's grandson," Devon interjected. "Really, he cannot help it."

"Enough of this!" Anthony strode back over to his sister. "Where the devil has she gone? I must give chase immediately."

Emeline pressed her lips together before saying reluctantly, "I have been sworn to secrecy."

He felt as if his head might explode. "Stop saying that word! I am your brother!"

She looked over at their parents. "He's doing it again!"

Just then, André Raveneau cleared his throat from his wing chair in the far corner of the room. "Anthony, if you mean to give chase, you must do it with great flair, calculated to make Frederica realize that you alone can make her feel truly alive. At such times, more practical concerns are forgotten." Grandpère paused and reached down to pet Daisy, who had dragged her cushion close to the wing chair. "It is a pity Frederica hasn't run off with another man so that you might challenge him to a duel." He flashed a smile at his wife, and she blew him a kiss.

Anthony wanted to protest that his forthright

Freddie wasn't the sort of female who would succumb to such tactics, but what the devil did he know about the ways of true love? Very little apparently. "Thank you, Grandpère, for your sage advice. However, I must first find out where Freddie has gone." He looked around the room. "Surely someone can help me?"

"She is accompanied by Mrs. Bell, which means they have hired a chaise rather than travel by stage or the Mail," said Devon. "She would never allow her beloved mistress to sit among the rabble on a stage." Standing, she dusted off her hands. "I suspect they've had a bit of help, probably from a servant at Justmore House where Mrs. Bell was housekeeper for decades. I will go and inquire."

Anthony's mood swung from despair to hope as he embraced his grandmother. "How fortunate I am to have such an excellent family. Thank you." He looked around at the others, adding, "I will go home to organize my things and return here on horseback. Hopefully by then Grandmama will have discovered their destination and means of transport."

In the stair hall, Anthony found Rafael waiting expectantly.

"You need me," the boy informed him. "I will be your groom by day and manservant by

night. If you agree, I can tell you some things I know."

"Ah, very good," Anthony said sarcastically. "Blackmail."

"No," the lad replied firmly, "Persuasion."

Before Anthony could respond, he saw Emeline coming out of the library near the stairs. She held a very worn book in both hands, and when she drew near, she extended the volume to him.

"Freddie implored me to keep quiet about her current circumstances, but she gave me no instructions about this book." Emeline put the tattered volume in his hands. "It was her secret pleasure. You would be wise to read it …quickly."

Anthony opened the book and stared at the title page in disbelief. In bold, florid letters, it read: *The Wicked Highwayman: A Tale of Disguise, Deception, Romance, and Ravishment in Three Parts.*

Looking up, he met his sister's intent gaze. "You may want to read only Part Three. Those are the pages we love best." She blushed prettily before adding, "The ravishment!"

CHAPTER 30

"If the coachman is armed, we could both be killed," Anthony remarked to Rafael as they waited on horseback in a thicket of half-bare trees.

"Worry not. We are armed as well, and there are two of us," replied the boy.

"I do not care to shoot anyone as part of this supposed romantic masquerade."

Rafael made no reply to that. Opening a napkin filled with nuts and dried fruit, he offered some to Anthony.

"How can you eat at a time like this?"

"All will be well!"

Rafael had been spouting such platitudes ever since they rode south out of London. Thanks to Anthony's clever grandmother, they knew the exact location of Standish Farm, the home of Mrs. Bell's brother, and also the route into West Sussex given to David, the very trustworthy groom who had volunteered to deliver Mrs. Bell and Miss Redfield safely to Standish Farm.

After scanning Part Three of *The Wicked Highwayman*, Anthony had felt rather wicked himself as he planned Frederica's abduction. Rafael animated the plans with his own infectious excitement, but now that they were here, dressed in heavy, caped coats, tricorn hats, and black curtain masks, Anthony was having second thoughts.

"I believe highwaymen are a thing of the past, for good reason," he mused. "Perhaps they've all been hanged at Tyburn Tree."

Rafael seemed not to hear. "I hope only that we are on the right road. Perhaps you didn't offer the innkeeper enough coin."

Anthony made a derisory sound. Yesterday, when the two of them had made the necessary preparations and finally left London on horseback, he estimated that Freddie and Mrs. Bell had a seven-hour lead time. It was true that they could travel much faster than Freddie's post-chaise, but Anthony knew that she would not dawdle, just in case he came after her. He also lost time stopping at every coaching inn, seeking information about two female travelers.

This morning's stop at the Black Conqueror Inn had been a huge success, in spite of the wizened, bad-tempered innkeeper who had demanded another guinea for each nugget of information.

"The ladies be packing up now, bound for Standish Farm along South Downs Way, mayhap two hours west," the old man said at last. "No doubt they'll be along in a trice. D'you care to wait for them?"

"No!" barked Anthony, then caught himself and smiled. "That is, I will see my wife a bit later. I beg you, do not tell her I am back from the army. It's meant to be a surprise." He pressed two more guineas in the man's palm before swinging up onto Marcus, the chestnut gelding he'd purchased recently at Tattersall's. Almost as an afterthought, he handed more coins to the innkeeper and added, "Keep your best room for me, with freshly aired sheets. I shall return anon."

Now, waiting in the trees just beyond a bend in the

ancient roadway, Anthony steeled himself for what lay ahead. Too many things could go wrong. Frederica might be so angry she would never forgive him, or the postillion could fire his weapon before anyone discovered the wicked highwayman's true identity.

"I hear a carriage!" Rafael whispered excitedly in Portuguese. "Listen!"

It was true. In the distance came the sound of horse's hooves and an equipage rumbling and wheezing over the rutted road. As the sounds grew nearer, Anthony nodded to the identically garbed Rafael, secured his curtain mask, and tensed, waiting.

* * *

"WHAT'S AMISS, MISTRESS?" Mrs. Bell asked, watching Frederica in a way that made the interior of the post-chaise feel very tiny. "I hope you're not ill."

"No, not ill," Freddie murmured, though she was feeling deeply uncertain about her recent choices. Perhaps she had acted too impulsively, leaving London without speaking directly to Anthony. Yet, she had fully intended to confront him—until the moment he told Captain Liggett of his secret plans to sail off without her!

"I hope you have no regrets either," Mrs. Bell said firmly. "You are doing the right thing." She reached across and patted Freddie's cold hand as the equipage jounced along. "I vow you'll enjoy staying at Standish Farm. My brother has an oast house. Have you ever seen one?"

Before Freddie could reply, the horses suddenly whinnied, and the young postillion gave a frightened shout.

"Highwaymen!" he screamed.

"Oh, oh!" cried Mrs. Bell.

Freddie gave her a steady look. "Pray get down, ma'am. They doubtless are armed."

Even as the old woman tried to crouch lower, Frederica boldly slid closer to the dirt-smudged window and looked out. The post-chaise was rattling to a shaky halt in the middle of the lane, and she saw two masked, black-clad figures on horseback bearing down on them, pistols raised. Her heart froze with terror.

"Throw down your arms!" shouted the taller, broad-shouldered man who rode in front.

Freddie was shocked to feel an unexpected thrill at the sound of his deep voice, for the highwayman almost sounded like Anthony. *Don't be a goose!* She scolded herself. This was reality, not a romantic novel, and there was no telling what this villain might be capable of.

Meanwhile, David, the postillion, had taken his weapons from the saddle-holster and handed them over to the highwayman. He passed them to his smaller accomplice who continued to point a large pistol of his own at David.

"Don't shoot, I beg you!" cried the postillion in a quavering voice. "I've a new babe at home."

"I wouldn't think of it," came the highwayman's husky yet surprisingly cultured reply. "But I must insist on claiming your valuable cargo."

"But – but I have no cargo or valuables to surrender!" pleaded David.

"Oh, I think you do." The man's voice held a lazy note of amusement as he gestured toward the interior of the chaise.

To Freddie's horror, the highwayman brought his mount sidling near the equipage. Her heart pounded wildly. His tricorn hat was pulled low, and a mask obscured the bottom half of his face, but his glittering dark eyes bore into her through the window. There was no place to run or hide. Suddenly he was leaning down from his horse to twist open the chaise door. A blast of cold air rushed in, bringing with it Freddie's first clear view of the highwayman.

"Do not imagine that you can ravish us, sir!" quavered a pink-cheeked Mrs. Bell from her half-crouching posture in the far corner.

"Fear not, madame, I only wish to ravish one of you," he drawled. Pointing to Frederica, the black-clad man held out his gloved hand. "Come, my lovely."

"I most certainly will *not*," she said coldly, and moved farther away against the squabs. In that same terrified moment, Freddie felt a frisson of memory, a sense that she had been here before …in the pages of her favorite novel.

"Perhaps you wish to be taken by force?" he demanded, laughter in his eyes.

"I demand that you go away and leave us alone."

"My lady, that is impossible, for I have come today for the sole purpose of carrying you off with me." With that, the highwayman swung down from the horse, leaned in, and caught Frederica easily around her waist. His gloved hands were strong and sure as he cradled her body, and suddenly she wasn't afraid any longer.

For an instant, their eyes met and her breath caught as a familiar heat blossomed at her core. Was she going mad? "You are a villain," she exclaimed, panting a little. "I demand that you unhand me!"

"I will do so, love," came his cool reply, "but not until we are safely alone together."

Mrs. Bell began to wail as the highwayman lifted Freddie out of the chaise and onto the back of his black stallion. A moment later, he was behind her in the saddle, one powerful arm clamped around her middle.

"My partner will hold you here for one hour," the man told David, his voice rough. "This lady will not be harmed if you obey. Then, go on your way and say nothing of this to anyone."

"Oh, my poor, sweet mistress!" moaned Mrs. Bell.

Freddie looked back as the highwayman wheeled his stallion around. "Fear not!" she called. "I will prevail, as ever."

They had only ridden a short distance when her captor leaned down, his breath stirringly warm on her ear. "My lady, did you imagine you could hide from me? You are mine now."

"I belong to no man," she managed to challenge.

"Agreed." Over the wind, he called, "No man except me."

* * *

As THEY CAME into the yard at the Black Conqueror Inn, Anthony drew on the reins and the big stallion paused under a tree. Warm and supple, Freddie fit perfectly against his chest. Her face, still under the brim of her bonnet, rested in the crook of his shoulder. Was she sleeping?

The time had come for him to unmask, else he could hardly show himself inside the inn. "Frederica," he murmured.

Slowly, she opened her eyes and whispered, "How many times have I asked you to call me Freddie?"

"Clever minx." His heart swelled with love. "Do not say you knew from the first."

She looked up as he removed the mask. "No, though I'll own I thought I might have hit my head and the entire episode was a dream."

"Like a chapter from *The Wicked Highwayman?*"

Color washed her cheeks in a way that made him want to kiss her, right there in sight of the ostlers. "How do you know so much?"

Anthony laughed. "I'll tell you later. Will you come inside with me willingly?"

"I will come—to talk." Freddie closed her beautiful blue eyes, then opened them. "In truth, there are things I should have said to you before I left London."

"Just so."

* * *

THE INNKEEPER, who informed them his name was Blunt, bowed so many times to them that Freddie guessed Anthony must have compensated him well. The man had not been half so accommodating when she and Mrs. Bell had slept there the night before.

"We be honored you've brought yer wife, sir," Blunt said as they mounted the creaking steps. In a loud whisper he added, "The sheets were well aired, as ye bid, and the maid has just brought wine and a cold collation."

The paneled bedchamber was large, with two south-facing windows and a four-poster bed that appeared to date back to Tudor days. In the corner, a pair of rustic chairs flanked a small table. As soon as Freddie was inside, Anthony blocked the doorway so Blunt couldn't follow. He put more coins in the man's bony hand, ordered wine and food to be served later in the room, and closed the door.

When he had divested himself of the caped greatcoat and tricorn hat, Freddie saw her own Anthony standing there. Her heart squeezed as she tried to steel herself against his crooked grin. It might be true that she had been wrong to run away from London rather than confront Anthony directly, but that did not change the very real problems between them.

"How could you do this dangerous thing today?" Freddie demanded. "What if someone had been shot?"

"Our pistols were unloaded. I was determined that no one would be hurt, though I'll own I wasn't certain what your postillion might do with his weapons."

Her mind somewhat relieved, she pursued, "And what of poor Mrs. Bell? She will be terrified for my safety!"

"Ah, yes, poor Mrs. Bell, who has disapproved of me since the moment I returned from the dead." His lips twitched for just an instant. "Worry not. Rafael was instructed to explain all to her after we were safely away. I am even resolved that Mrs. Bell may join our household if you come back to me."

"It seems you thought of everything."

"With varying degrees of success." He sat down on the edge of the bed and began to remove his boots. "I made a plan, you know, for what would happen after I carried you off and brought you, a most unwilling miss, to this inn."

Freddie removed her own cloak and bonnet and hung them on a peg. "I assume Emeline must have shown you *The Wicked Highwayman*," she said, avoiding his gaze. "No doubt you intend to ravish me."

He shrugged. "I sense that it might not be a good idea. Not yet at least."

Walking closer to him, Freddie said, "It was very bad of you to carry me off today."

"Yes. Very bad." He bit back a grin. "Thank God it worked."

"And you told the innkeeper I was your wife?"

"I said so in order to bring you back here." Anthony took a step forward and caught her hand, drawing her closer. His demeanor turned sober. "Freddie, tell me why you left me. What were the secrets you mentioned in your message?"

"You know very well." Her pain flared again. "You paid Papa for my hand in marriage."

"You are twisting the situation!" Anthony protested, looking shocked.

"No. For years, he tried to use me, like a pawn on a chessboard. It was the torment I fought against the hardest, but you undid all my efforts in one conversation."

"I was only trying to do the right thing, for your sake. Viscount Redfield is your father, and I felt it was my duty to help him out of his difficulties once and for all—"

"There is no *once and for all*! This has been going on most of my life." She pulled her hand from his grasp and backed away. "Papa tried to manipulate Mouette for his own ends as well! You knew perfectly well how it was with him."

"That's why I intervened. I only desired to remove Redfield from our lives so you wouldn't have to see or think about him." He paused, and Freddie saw that his hard-muscled body was taut beneath his clothing. "I don't give a damn about the monetary cost."

"Well, I do!" Tears stung her eyes. "Don't you see, Papa cares more for money than his own daughter. When I learned – from his own lips – that you had *paid* for my hand in marriage, it was a terrible betrayal. You had an opportunity to tell me, but you very charmingly brushed my question aside." Freddie's cheeks were wet, an outward sign of the flood of emotions inside her. "I know I agreed to an unconventional marriage ...but deep inside I hoped we might have more. That night at the Lyells', I began to dream of a union based on friendship as well as affection, common interests, but that dream was poisoned by the secrets you kept from me, as if I was not worthy of your respect or confidence."

Anthony was by her side. She let him take her to one of the chairs where he brought her onto his lap. A part of her was steeled not to listen for fear she might believe him.

"My darling Freddie, I was wrong." The deep throb in his voice was very hard to resist.

"Wrong?" It was a word seldom spoken by any male of her acquaintance.

"I acted arrogantly, believing I knew what was best. I should have consulted you."

She blinked. "Are you just saying that so I will forgive you?"

Anthony brushed errant curls from her temple before touching his lips to the pulse that beat there. "When I read your letter, I saw the light. It couldn't have been more blinding if I'd been staring at the sun." He turned her in his arms and their eyes met. "I love you, Freddie. I think I fell in love years ago, but I ruined it then over that portrait, and I was too young and stupid back then to tell you that I'd been wrong."

Freddie felt dizzy. A fretful voice deep inside told her to hold back, to protect her heart, but she heard herself saying, "I love you, too. Oh, Anthony, I'm very afraid, but it is the truth."

"It's all right. Will you trust me?" He bent and kissed her deeply, convincingly. "We're together now. Anything is possible for us if we trust one another."

It felt as if her bones were melting. All she wanted was this man, body and soul, but she had been burned enough times to hold back. Pressing her palm to his broad chest, Freddie said, "Wait. You are going too fast. There is more I must say." She drew a ragged breath. "After Papa told me what you had done, I was determined to speak to you about it. I walked to Charles Street ...and when I arrived, you had a guest. I went inside alone."

She waited for him to react to this revelation, but

Anthony merely nodded. "I know. Rafael saw you leave and told me later."

"Anthony, perhaps you don't understand. I heard what you said to that man, Captain Liggett."

"What exactly did you hear?" he asked calmly, watching her face.

She swallowed. "You agreed to be the naturalist on his voyage to the Canary Islands in the spring …and you told him you didn't want your future wife to know, that he must communicate with you in secret."

"I did say that," Anthony agreed, a smile touching his mouth. "And just moments ago, I told you I loved you and asked you to trust me. My darling, can you do it?"

Freddie looked into his dark, gold-flecked eyes and clearly saw his love for her. It came to her that her fears grew out of her own father's misdeeds, not Anthony's. If they were to have any chance for a life together, she would have to step out on the ledge and take his hand.

Her heart was racing as she dug deep for courage and nodded. "Yes. Yes, I trust you."

Anthony caught her up against him, holding her so close she could feel the warmth of his hard body through her gown and chemise. "For those of us who have known betrayal and struggled to trust, that vow means more than any other." With that, he reached into his coat pocket and brought out the emerald ring Freddie had left behind. "I did this all wrong the first time, Freddie. Thank God we have a second chance. I love you and I want to marry you. I want us to spend the rest of our lives together, to travel the world and learn together, and raise a family." He paused, holding the delicate ring between his thumb and forefinger. "Will you take me?"

Tears spilled from Freddie's eyes and her voice shook as she answered, "Yes, oh, yes."

Anthony slipped the ring onto her finger and produced a handkerchief to gently blot her tears. Flashing a smile, he said, "Now that we are properly betrothed, I will explain about Captain Liggett."

Freddie felt suffused with a golden glow as he lifted her from his lap and stood. "Of course, I want you to be happy, to do the work you love ..." she said.

For some reason, this made him laugh as he crossed the room to take a folded paper from his saddlebag. "I am glad to hear it, my selfless darling, but I can assure you I would not go away without you."

Aching with love, she replied, "To be honest, I do not want us to be parted."

"And we shall not be. Come and sit with me." He perched on the edge of the bed and held out his arms to her. Freddie gladly went into the shelter of his embrace, watching as Anthony opened the paper. It seemed to be a list of names. "This paper lists all the crew of Liggett's small expedition to the Canary Islands. I borrowed it from him before I left London to chase you down."

Freddie followed his fingertip as it moved down the list, stopping on the tenth line. What she saw made her heart soar: *Anthony and Frederica St. Briac, Naturalists.*

"How can this be possible?" she whispered.

Lifting her eyes to his face, she saw him watching her, his handsome head cocked slightly. "It was meant to be a surprise. I couldn't think of any better wedding gift for my very unconventional bride."

A tide of emotion rose up in her. Turning in Anthony's embrace, Freddie twined her arms around his neck and kissed him with all the pent-up fervor she possessed. She sank her fingers into his thick, unruly locks and greeted his tongue as it invaded her mouth. On and on they kissed, his cheek rough against her soft skin, his long fingers deftly unfastening the back of her gown.

"I love you," she heard herself breathe. "It's like a dream."

She felt him smile as he kissed the tender column of her throat. "A dream come true, yes? And this is just the beginning, love."

Effortlessly, he drew down the front of Freddie's dress, freeing her arms and exposing her breasts, covered now by only a thin chemise. Heat coursed through her, settling between her legs and tightening her nipples. She reached out and caught his hands, bringing them to her breasts, thrilling to the sensation of his warm, possessive touch.

"So lovely," he marveled, bending to kiss her nipple through the fragile batiste fabric. His lips tugged at it for one long moment, a promise of what was to come.

"I am so looking forward to being ravished," Freddie murmured as she met his gaze.

He gave a low, seductive laugh. "I've read your novel, you know." With one hand, he drew back the covers. "The wicked highwayman was quite good at ravishing the heroine, but I promise you I can do much better."

"Oh, yes, I don't doubt it." Aching with need, Freddie fumbled at the buttons of his shirt. "Please do not delay."

She watched, her own desire building, as he stripped off his clothing to reveal the lean, muscular body she had fantasized about every night since going to stay with the Raveneaus.

"You're a very willing captive, my girl," Anthony teased as he knelt over her.

"Well, I must confess …I find your wickedness quite impossible to resist," she replied, running her hands down from the lizard tattoo on his neck, over wide shoulders to his hard, flat hips. Boldly, then, she caressed the aroused length of him and heard his sharp intake of breath.

"You will have to submit to me, you know," he threatened.

Their eyes met, smoldering. Anthony slowly drew her shift up her thighs and made a low sound. "No drawers?"

"I was in a hurry this morning." She felt herself blushing.

"How providential for me." One dark brow flicked upward.

Drunk with arousal, Freddie's head dropped back on the pillow. Each touch of his fingertips trailed fire up her sensitive inner thighs, and then his mouth followed, scorching. She moaned and let her legs fall open to him.

"Mmm," muttered Anthony. "So beautiful."

She felt feverish, all her intimate sensations heightened. Anthony touched her expertly, delving into the tender cleft, using his fingertip to circle the moist bud of her desire, then moving to slide inside her, inch by inch. Freddie gave a sharp gasp of pleasure. It was almost too much, but when she squirmed, he framed her hips with his hands and held her still.

"I'm going to taste you now," came his soft warning.

Freddie lifted her head off the pillow. "Oh!" A heated memory came of the day he'd crouched between her legs under the desk, and she had felt the erotic warmth of his breath *there*.

"At last," he murmured tenderly. His knowing tongue teased its way to her swollen, delicate peak, slowly exploring in ways that drove her mad. The throbbing began to build in earnest at her core. Stroking, suckling, harder, softer, Anthony brought her to the edge of the precipice, then moved away, until she could bear no more.

"Please," she whimpered, and reached down to grasp his hair and hold him against her.

Moments later, Freddie thought she would break into pieces as the tide swept over her in waves of excruciating pleasure. When at last the storm ebbed, she reached out for Anthony, needing him inside her, their bodies joined.

He rose up and kissed her deeply. Freddie tasted her own essence on his lips as she guided him to her entrance. He came into her with one long thrust, closing his eyes and emitting a low groan. Gradually he drew back before filling her again and again, and as she clung to him, sensations swirled through her that far surpassed mere physical pleasure. Dimly she heard both of them making sounds beyond words, their bodies joined in the timeless rhythm.

This is why they call it making love, Freddie marveled, even as another delicious climax surged up, hot and urgent. Trembling, she clung to Anthony's broad back, now damp with sweat, and felt the rasp of his unshaven cheek against her temple as he drew a sudden, harsh breath. He tightened his embrace just as Freddie sensed the warmth of his release deep inside her.

They lay entwined, still connected, and she closed her eyes, melting into him. The sensation of his slowing heartbeat lulled her. *Bliss.* Sometime later, Freddie awoke to find Anthony angling his body to gaze at her.

"This is what I have longed for, to wake to find you in my arms, the barriers between us broken at last." He cradled her cheek in his hand. "And I just remembered that I have something else to show you."

"Does that mean you are going to get out of bed?" Freddie protested.

Smiling, Anthony pushed up on one elbow and reached over to his saddlebag on a nearby chair. After a moment, he brought out a small velvet pouch and put it in her hands. Freddie couldn't imagine what might be inside. Pulling the cords open, she peeked in and saw the diamond and sapphire ring from Grandpapa that she had sold to finance her independence.

For a long moment, Freddie had trouble breathing. "I – I don't understand ..."

He was gazing at her with so much love, she felt dizzy. "When you left my house two days ago, Rafael followed and saw you enter the shop of William Newman, Jeweler and Goldsmith. He didn't realize the significance of your visit until later, when I discovered that you had fled. Before the two of us set off in pursuit, I paid Mr. Newman a visit and recovered your precious ring."

Freddie's voice was thick with tears. "Grandpapa gave it to me before he died, so that I might have means of my own and never be controlled by a man."

Gravely, Anthony replied, "I hope you never find it necessary to part with it again."

"Indeed, everything is different now," Freddie marveled. "I feel safe."

As he drew her back into his embrace, Anthony nodded. "My love, so do I."

EPILOGUE

SOMERSET HOUSE

January 4, 1837

"*O*ur own Charles Darwin, newly returned from the voyage of the *Beagle*, will speak today on the slow rising of the land mass of South America," Charles Lyell announced from the Geological Society lectern.

Anthony, who sat next to his friend in the front row, joined in the applause. It was an amazing feeling to be here among so many scientists who shared his passion for natural history. When he had arrived today flanked by his father and grandfather, they all came to greet him, shaking his hand, patting him on the back, welcoming him back from the grave.

And now Darwin was striding to the lectern. "Before I begin, I have the honor of introducing my friend and colleague, Anthony St. Briac. Earlier today I presented my mammal and bird collection to the Zoological Society, and it should be known that St. Briac played a key role in gathering those specimens. We all have been shocked by the ethical crimes committed by

Terrance Buskin, who not only plagiarized St. Briac's discoveries but was instrumental in his terrible accident. Fortunately, Buskin has been banished from our ranks, and from London itself, and St. Briac has a long and productive career ahead of him. I ask you now to welcome him back into our ranks."

The room erupted in cheers and applause as Darwin stepped aside and Anthony came forward. Standing at the lectern, he looked out at the sea of expectant male faces.

"Thank you all for that warm welcome," Anthony said. "There were many times during this past year when I wondered if I would ever stand on English soil again, let alone return to these meetings." He paused, caught off-guard by a surge of emotion. After a moment, he continued, "Before I sit down to enjoy our esteemed colleague Darwin's speech, I must thank someone. This person is unable to join us due to her gender but has contributed more to my scientific studies than anyone else."

As Anthony spoke, he glimpsed a slender gentleman with a large mustache hastening down the aisle. The man kept his head of chaotic gray hair bent, face obscured. Not until the bespectacled latecomer slipped into a chair between Anthony's father and grandfather did realization dawn.

Could this be? He wanted to laugh and shout her name: *Frederica!* However, since women were forbidden to attend meetings of the Geological Society, Anthony could only allow himself the most fleeting of smiles.

"That person who has worked tirelessly at my side since my return to London is my new wife, Frederica Redfield St. Briac," he continued. "Even before I returned, when all of you thought I was dead, she spent untold hours cataloguing and analyzing the specimens

I had sent home throughout the *Beagle* voyage." As he spoke, Anthony saw Freddie beaming up at him, and his heart turned over. "My wife is a scientist in her own right, and I look forward to the day when she and other capable, learned ladies may join our meetings." Polite applause followed this unexpected speech. "Again, I am grateful for your warm welcome today. I know we are all eager to hear Mr. Darwin's findings."

With that, Anthony made his way back to his chair as his old friend began to speak from the lectern. Lowering himself into the seat next to Freddie, he caught a whiff of meadowsweet and knew a powerful urge to turn, take the eccentric-looking professor in his arms, and deliver a passionate kiss in front of all the gawking Society members. The thought of this made his lips twitch.

Anthony's father, looking especially piratical in an eye-patch of smoke-gray silk, leaned forward slightly, and lifted both brows. "*Bien*," he whispered, and flashed a grin.

Freddie, meanwhile, dared to glance up at Anthony, her blue eyes full of mischief and love.

"I'll have a word with you later, Professor," Anthony said under his breath.

"Oh yes, please do," came her whispered reply.

* * *

"OUTRAGEOUS!" exclaimed Anthony when they all were back inside the library on Charles Street. Turning to his father and grandfather, he added, "Did you two know about this?"

André Raveneau, ever a compelling figure, lowered himself into a chair and smiled. "If you suppose either Justin or I could have stopped your bride from infiltrating that meeting, you are gravely mistaken."

Since Anthony and Frederica's small wedding the week before at nearby Grosvenor Chapel, they had reorganized the library. It now featured a second desk, pushed up next to Anthony's own, so that he and Freddie could work side by side. The thirty-fourth crate of specimens was open, and they were both eager to discover what it held.

Freddie herself was now perched on the edge of her desk, wig, mustache, and spectacles removed, swinging her trousered legs and smiling radiantly. On the wall behind the desk hung the watercolor of a Galápagos woodpecker finch that Anthony had painted for Freddie.

"What do you have to say for yourself, Mrs. St. Briac?" Anthony pretended to scold.

"Oh, wasn't that great fun?" Hopping down, she crossed to his side. "If they are going to continue to allow women to become Fellows of the Geological Society but bar us from meetings, what choice do we have but to take matters into our own hands?"

"*Frederica*," he warned with mock severity. "Promise me you will not turn up in disguise again without alerting me in advance."

Before she could reply, a knock sounded at the front door and Quincy passed by on his way to answer it. A few moments later, Mouette, Devon, and Emeline came into the library, bringing with them a burst of frigid evening air.

"We've come to see Freddie," announced Emeline as she removed her bonnet.

Leaning around Anthony, Freddie blushed a little as she put her hand in the air. "Here I am."

"Oh, famous!" Emeline exclaimed, laughing. "I see that Professor Loudon has returned."

"Just for today. I donned this costume one last time because I simply had to be there for Anthony's moment of triumph at the Geological Society," Freddie explained. "And I wanted to surprise him."

"*Surprise* me?" He pretended to be taken aback by this assertion. Looking at his mother, he added, "This minx appeared in her ridiculous male garb just as I was standing at the lectern, soberly addressing the entire audience of geologists."

Justin said, "It was one of the professor's finer moments."

Everyone began to laugh, including Anthony.

"I should go upstairs and change into a proper gown before dinner is served," said Freddie. "You'll all join us, won't you? We have a wonderful new Brazilian cook. Rafael found him on the docks."

As if on cue, the boy appeared in the doorway, resplendent in blue livery paired with his own sapphire-striped waistcoat. He gave an irrepressible grin before bowing deeply. "Dinner will be served in one-half hour."

When he had gone, Anthony answered their questioning looks with a wry shrug. "Today Rafael is a footman, but by tonight he could turn up as my valet. When he first came to me, I thought I was being generous offering him a post as stable boy. How little I knew!"

Freddie beamed. "Mrs. Bell says that Rafael's versatility has saved her from hiring many more servants."

"How fortunate," Mouette said. "Rafael will be able to help Quincy and Mrs. Bell watch over the house during your wedding trip."

Freddie had taken a few steps toward the stair hall, but now she stopped and looked back. "Wedding trip?"

"Of course! Mama, Emmie, and I were chatting today. We agreed that since you and Anthony did not care to have a real wedding celebration, it would be lovely to organize a romantic journey instead. We could make all the arrangements for you." Mouette came to Freddie's side, and Anthony could see that his mother was trying to ignore her male garb. "What about *Paris*? Delicious meals, new gowns, champagne, museums, strolls along the Seine..."

Laughing inside, Anthony closed the distance to Freddie, who seemed at a loss.

"It's very thoughtful of you," Freddie managed.

"An excellent idea, Mama," Anthony put in, "but I'm afraid we have other plans."

Now all eyes were on him.

"A different destination perhaps?" asked his grandmother, who had gone to nestle on Grandpère's lap.

"Rome?" ventured Mouette.

"Actually," he said, "we have been engaged to be the naturalists on a scientific voyage to the Canary Islands. We set sail in just a few weeks." He paused. "Both of us."

They were all staring now, speechless.

"Yes, that's right!" said Freddie, looking relieved. "Anthony meant it as a surprise wedding gift for me. Because he knows me so well, he understood that nothing could please me more."

Smiling fondly, Anthony drew her against him. "My wife is a very singular woman."

"I would not disparage the pleasures of Paris," Freddie continued, "but I must admit that for me, such diversions would be a trifle dull."

Emeline laughed. "I can see the truth in that." She sighed. "The Canary Islands! Adventure and romance together."

"I think so, too!" Freddie's cheeks were pink. "And now that we have the wedding out of the way and the Geological Society meeting is over, we can begin planning in earnest. Space is limited, so we must carefully choose our equipment and books. I am very eager to begin."

The library was momentarily quiet except for the

crackle of the fire as Anthony's family digested these plans.

"You two were very fortunate to find one another," Mouette said softly.

Anthony exhaled. "I can even be grateful for nearly dying on an island across the world, because I have been given a new appreciation for life – and love."

He bent to press his cheek to Freddie's soft curls, and she looked up at him, eyes sparkling with tears that told him she felt just the same.

1 – HIS MAKE-BELIEVE BRIDE(Justin & Mouette)

2 – HER IMPOSSIBLE HUSBAND (Justin & Mouette)

3 – HER SECRET ROGUE (Anthony & Frederica)

The Raveneau Family:

1 – SILVER STORM(André & Devon)

2 – HER HUSBAND, THE RAKE a sequel novella (André & Devon)

3 – SMUGGLER'S MOON (Sebastian & Julia

4 – THE SECRET OF LOVE (Gabriel & Isabella)

5 – SURRENDER THE STARS (Ryan & Lindsay)

6 – HIS RECKLESS BARGAIN (Nathan & Adrienne)

7 – TEMPEST(Adam & Cathy)

The Beauvisage Family:

1 – STOLEN BY A PIRATE: a novella prequel to CAROLINE (Jean-Philippe & Antonia)

2 – RESCUED BY A ROGUE BY A ROGUE (Alec & Caro)

3 – TOUCH THE SUN (Lion & Meagan)

4 – SPRING FIRES (Nicholai & Lisette)

5 – HER DANGEROUS VISCOUNT (Grey & Natalya)

Do you love audiobooks as much as I do? Most of my titles are now available in audio format, with special prices on Chirpbooks.com. You can listen to samples of my audiobooks here.

A special excerpt of the next book in this series is just ahead! And if you haven't yet read SILVER STORM, the bestselling romance of André and Devon Raveneau that started it all, you can download your copy now!

Once again, my heartfelt thanks for your support,

interest, and encouragement for my books. I welcome your comments and suggestions, and I hope that you'll write to me at <u>Cynthia@CynthiaWrightAuthor.com</u>. I promise to reply!

Warmest wishes,
~ Cynthia

I hope you've enjoyed Her Secret Rogue with Anthony and Frederica!

If you've been following this series, you have noticed that natural history plays a major role in the stories. The 1820's and 1830's were a fascinating time when amazing scientific discoveries were being made and many great naturalists were emerging, including Charles Darwin, who plays a major part in Her Secret Rogue.

If you are interested in reading more about Darwin and the voyage of the *Beagle*, you might enjoy my favorite research book, ODYSSEY, by Tom Chaffin.

During the creation of Her Secret Rogue, I was fortunate to visit London and stay in Mayfair, right in the heart of my characters' neighborhood! Armed with a walking guide and accompanied by friends Lynne Shear and Heike Conrad, we wound our way through the charming streets of Mayfair. It was great fun to explore Grosvenor Square and later discover Anthony's butterscotch-colored house on Charles Street.

If you'd like to see more of the images "behind the book" for Her Secret Rogue, I hope you'll visit its Pinterest page.

I'm now writing Camille St. Briac's story! When she gets serious about pursuing and exposing a notorious "plume hunter" she may be surprised by the outcome...

If you page ahead, you'll find an excerpt of THE SECRET OF LOVE, the 1808-set book where you'll reunite with many familiar characters. It also features the first tempestuous meeting between Justin and Mouette St. Briac.

Thank you, as always, for your friendship and support!
Warmest regards,

Cynthia

THE SECRET OF LOVE

RAKES & REBELS: THE RAVENEAU FAMILY, BOOK 4

PROLOGUE

LONDON, ENGLAND, SEPTEMBER 1804

"*D*arling Izzie, I beg you to reconsider your decision and come to Lady Kingston's reception tomorrow evening!" Mouette Raveneau exclaimed. "I shall be bereft if you don't attend. My betrothal to Sir Harry may have elevated my position in Society, but I vow that nothing shall ever alter the bond of our friendship." She was perched just-so on a gilded chair as the gifted artist, Élisabeth Vigée Le Brun, painted a portrait to celebrate her betrothal.

Lady Isabella Trevarre glanced over from her own easel, positioned next to the Frenchwoman who was her mentor. She felt her face growing warm, even though she loved Mouette as a sister. "I have told you privately that I don't care for parties."

"We could make you look lovely!" Mouette looked toward her mother, Devon. "Couldn't we, Mama? My gown of white muslin trimmed in silver could be altered by our dressmaker to fit darling Izzie! All she needs is a bit of… help."

Before Devon Raveneau could speak, Izzie held up a hand. "Madame Le Brun has asked that you sit perfectly still, Mouette. Let us postpone this conversation until later."

333

Izzie tried to will the hot blood from her cheeks. The thought of spending hours in the midst of London's *ton* made her insides churn, and none of Mouette's beauty tricks could transform Izzie from a duckling into a swan. She couldn't bear to hear more whispers from aristocrats who expected her to fit in among them, but always found her lacking.

They invariably began by pretending to be kind. Izzie had heard them sigh to one another about the loss of her parents, the Marquess and Marchioness of Caverleigh, in a carriage accident when she was just fourteen. Then the dowagers discreetly lifted their fans and whispered, "Tsk, tsk, but the poor girl has always been awkward and plain." They remarked that the only reason she'd had a proper Season was because of her captivating London friends, the Raveneau family. Even so, nothing had come of her launch into Society.

The whispers had grown louder now that Izzie's twentieth birthday had passed without a marriage proposal. "Such a shame she wears those spectacles," one noblewoman had murmured at a recent ball, just loudly enough for her to hear. "And she is far too... *robust*, especially for a girl with only a fine family name to recommend her."

But Izzie had no desire to waste time mingling in Society and even less to marry. The thought of marriage to one of the languid bucks one met at routs made her shudder.

No, she liked her life exactly the way it was. Her passion was reserved for her art; she vowed to devote herself completely to her craft. Every night before falling asleep in the Raveneau family's Grosvenor Square home, she gave thanks that Madame Le Brun, one of the greatest portrait painters alive, had consented to be her teacher. And every morning, she awoke filled with excitement to hurry off to the Frenchwoman's lovely apartments in Portman Square.

Madame had only lived in London for two years, and Izzie never tired of hearing her recount her glamorous, adventurous past. Because Élisabeth "Louise" Vigée Le Brun had been a friend and portraitist to Queen Marie Antoinette, she'd been driven from France by the bloody Revolution and had spent the last decade of the 18th century in Italy and Russia, painting portraits of aristocrats and royals, and being fêted at a succession of grand estates. Now that Napoleon Bonaparte had come to power in France, Madame Le Brun had returned from Russia, and her sense of adventure had demanded a sojourn in England, where she was greatly admired by society and her colleagues alike.

This lovely late-summer day was a special occasion, as Madame painted Mouette Raveneau in celebration of her betrothal. Izzie had so many reasons to be grateful to the Raveneaus, from the comforting warmth of their friendship after her parents' deaths to her current position as Madame Le Brun's student. It had been Mouette's father, André Raveneau, who had contacted his old friend Louise Le Brun and asked if she might be willing to mentor a budding young artist, Lady Isabella Trevarre. Madame had quickly taken her under her wing, later revealing that she had known Izzie's artist mother, long ago in Paris.

The morning light was soft and flattering in Madame's sitting room. The French portraitist, still fetching at nearly fifty years of age, tilted her head as she gazed at Mouette and strategically applied tiny dabs of oil paint to a canvas. Her silvery-brown curls were caught up in a striped turban and she bit her lower lip while pondering her creation.

Izzie sat nearby with a sketchbook, drawing her young friend with a pencil. When she glanced over at

Madame's canvas, she saw that the older woman had gone past Mouette's mannered pose to capture the hopeful light in her eyes. Izzie gave a tiny sigh. She knew that Madame Le Brun used special techniques, such as layers of glazing, to achieve the charm, luminosity, and emotional depth that distinguished her portraits. However, Madame also brought courage and vulnerability to her work, and a gift for reading her subjects. As her student, Izzie had witnessed this – but she felt nervous about attempting to develop that gift in herself. Like her own artist mother, Lady Charlotte Trevarre, Izzie was more comfortable painting landscapes.

"Shall we all take a bit of sugar in our tea?"

It was Mouette's delightful mother, Devon Raveneau, speaking from her place before a low table. A ray of sunlight streamed over her upswept rosy-gold hair as she poured hot tea into wafer-thin cups.

Before any of them could reply, an ear-splitting shriek filled the air. Mouette gasped in surprise, Devon nearly dropped the teapot, and Izzie smiled to herself.

"*Mon Dieu!*" Madame Le Brun's cheeks went pink with fury. "Don't pay any attention to that screeching parrot," she exclaimed in French. "My disagreeable neighbor refuses to move the monster's cage to another part of the house, no matter how I plead. I fear that the constant disruption will force me to change my lodgings again."

Devon Raveneau blinked. "A parrot? In London?"

"It is the most enormous bird you can imagine, with exceedingly long tail feathers. It was brought from the East Indies, and clearly the thing objects to being torn from its natural home." She paused and took a deep calming breath while mixing blues on her palette to match Mouette's scarf. "However, the parrot is not the only problem with this house. Would you be shocked to learn that there are people buried in the cellar?"

Even the obediently still Mouette turned her head at this. "How positively horrific! Was there a gruesome murder?"

"Oh, no, nothing like that," Madame continued, a twinkle in her eyes. "The previous tenants were diplomats from India. When their slaves died, they chose this cellar as their burial place. I suppose it has something to do with their religion, but I'll own that I do find it quite unnerving."

Izzie paused in her sketching and smiled at the Raveneau women. "Madame suspects that the Indian cook, now deceased, might be haunting the kitchen. There have been a few inexplicable accidents."

"I may have an explanation after all," the Frenchwoman amended. "I caught our kitchen maid drinking from a bottle of my best brandy yesterday. So perhaps there is an *earthly* explanation for the broken crockery and the guinea fowl that caught on fire."

As they all laughed, Izzie removed her spectacles and brushed off a speck of charcoal that clung to the right lens, silently thanking the parrot for steering the conversation away from tonight's rout. Now, if only Madame's faithful servant, Adelaide, would bring a tray of delectable petite madeleines to accompany the tea Devon Raveneau was pouring. Izzie's stomach made a little rumbling sound as she thought longingly of the buttery little cakes.

Mouette glanced over at her, brows raised, and Izzie blushed. Had her friend guessed her thoughts? She straightened her back in an effort to make herself look slimmer. As long as she could remember, she'd found comfort in food. And what was wrong with that? After Izzie had been orphaned and stranded at Florence Jarrett's horrid Academy for Young Gentlewomen, food had numbed her pain, her fear, her deep loneliness... and sweets never rejected her or abused her trust.

Mouette often urged her to think of her figure, so that she might attract an eligible suitor, but the very *thought* of romance made Izzie nervous. Only one man, a Frenchman she'd met six years ago, had ever inspired her to dream of romance, but Mouette scoffed at this fantasy. And perhaps her friend was right. What could she have known of true love at fourteen, and after one brief evening sitting beside him at dinner? Besides, Gabriel St. Briac was far too splendid for the likes of Izzie. True, he'd been charming and gallant, but in the way one might behave toward a young niece, and the table had been lined with other distracting guests, including Izzie's brother Sebastian, his new bride, Julia, and the entire Raveneau family.

She sketched more vigorously, scolding herself to stop thinking of St. Briac. No doubt he was long married to a sophisticated, slender beauty... with perfect vision.

No, it was Izzie's intention to follow Madame Le-Brun's example, making her own way in the world with her wits and artistic talent. It was the sort of independent life her own mother could have enjoyed if she had not become imprisoned in an abusive marriage to the Marquess of Caverleigh.

Just then, the bell inside the front door jangled.

Madame glanced up in annoyance. "Who can be bothering us?"

"Allow me to see who it is," said Devon Raveneau, looking relieved for a reason to get up and move around. "Adelaide is busy in the kitchen and I don't mind in the least. I should make myself useful."

* * *

THE DOOR WAS CRIMSON, a rather surprising color, since all the other doors to nearby residences in Portman Square were painted a shade of green so dark it looked black unless the sun was shining.

Gabriel St. Briac inspected the paper, inscribed in Élisabeth Vigée Le Brun's own hand. Confirming the address, he lifted the knocker again. Before he could release it, the door opened to reveal a very lovely petite woman with a cloud of dawn-colored curls. She widened her eyes at the sight of him.

"Oh, my! How very unexpected to see you again, m'sieur!"

"I might say the same of you, Madame Raveneau," he replied. Bending slightly, he reached out, caught her hand, and carried it to his lips.

"You must be in search of your countrywoman, Madame Le Brun."

"I am. We have an appointment." Looking over her head, he saw that Madame was standing in the middle of her sunlit atelier, a paint daubed palette in one hand and a long, delicate brush in the other. "Or perhaps I have mixed the dates?"

"Madame is painting a portrait of my daughter, Mouette, who will soon be married. Perhaps you recall meeting her when we were all together in Brittany a few years ago?"

'Of course..." As his gaze fell on the exquisite Miss Raveneau, he noticed the young lady sitting nearby, sketching. A spark flared in his memory. "How interesting that I should encounter the Raveneau family again, during my first journey to England after many years."

"*Mon Dieu!*" exclaimed Madame Le Brun. "I thought I recognized your voice. Was our meeting arranged for *this* morning?"

She had set down her palette and brushes and was

rushing toward him, arms outstretched. As they embraced, he caught a whiff of her scent, a mixture of violets and, inevitably, her oil paints.

"Yes," he murmured with a trace of irony, "So soon, I am here."

"How foolish I am. I forgot to ask Adelaide to mark our appointment in my book, so that she might remind me." A winning smile lit Madame Le Brun's face, and then she turned toward the young women. "*Mes amies*, I present to you the infamous and scandalously handsome Gabriel St. Briac. He is a smuggler, a corsair, and a libertine. Perhaps you have heard of him?"

* * *

IZZIE COULD ONLY BLINK. For a long moment, it seemed that her heart had stopped beating and she was unable to breathe. Could it be?

Gabriel St. Briac!

It seemed utterly impossible. She thought she must be dreaming until Mouette turned to stare hard at her.

"You must not swoon," the girl whispered before suddenly leaning forward to pinch Izzie's plump arm. "Sit up straight. Your prince has come!"

"Hush *up!*" Izzie felt hot blood rush to her cheeks. Helplessly, she drank in the sight of him. He was perhaps thirty years of age, and time had only heightened his good looks. St. Briac's dark-chestnut hair was wind-blown, his sculpted face was darkened by the sun, and a ready smile hovered at his mouth and lent a twinkle to his midnight-blue eyes.

Izzie caught herself on the verge of sighing aloud and realized he was looking at her. Warm blood flooded her face.

"M'sieur St. Briac," Devon was saying, "do you remember Sebastian's younger sister, Lady Isabella Trevarre?"

He came toward her, gazing directly into her eyes. She noticed that he was carrying a leather-bound case under one arm. "How could I forget that magical evening in Roscoff? Lady Isabella graciously shared my company when I dined with your family."

Izzie felt him take her hand. His fingers were strong and warm, as utterly perfect as he was. Daring to look up at his face, she suddenly feared she might be sick.

Right there, on his fine leather topboots.

"*Bonjour*, my lady," he said in a low, French-accented voice. It had a smoky undercurrent that made her feel that the two of them were all alone in the world. "What an unexpected pleasure to see you again."

Another wave of nausea filled her mouth with warm saliva. Somehow, she managed to nod and give him a brief smile. *Please, don't let me humiliate myself!*

To her relief, Gabriel continued speaking. "An unexpected pleasure indeed, and a coincidence. You see, I met your brother in Paris barely a fortnight ago."

"Sebastian?" she exclaimed. "In Paris?"

"No, no," he laughed. "Your eldest brother, the Marquess of Caverleigh. He was dining with Vivant Denon, the art connoisseur. When I stopped to speak to them, Denon introduced his lordship."

Izzie shook her head, too surprised to think of her own nerves. "That's not possible, m'sieur! George has been in exile in Italy for a full decade. We have always understood that he lives in Rome, shunned by polite society."

Devon chimed in, "He lost virtually the entire family fortune and was forced to flee his creditors. None of the family have seen or heard from him since!"

"Ah, well, perhaps I am mistaken," Gabriel said in an offhand tone as he took a chair next to Izzie. Glancing over at her easel, he raised his brows appreciatively. "My lady, I did not know that you were blessed with artistic gifts."

"Izzie's mother, Lady Caverleigh, was an accomplished artist," Devon said. "So you see, she was born with talent, and Madame Le Brun has been gracious enough to guide her."

He was nodding thoughtfully as he studied her sketch of Mouette. "I am very impressed. Do you paint portraits, Lady Isabella?"

"I fear I have no aptitude for portraits. Landscapes are my forte," Izzie replied, basking in his praise. "Thank you for your kind words. I am very grateful for the opportunity to study with a great artist like Madame."

Just then, Adelaide came in with a plate of warm madeleines. When she had set them down on a table, she turned to St. Briac.

"M'sieur, may I take your package?"

"No, *merci*. It is something I intend to show Madame Le Brun." Still holding the leather box, he glanced around the circle of clearly curious women. The amused gleam flickered again in his eyes. "But I have intruded at an inopportune time. Allow me to arrange a later meeting – "

"Oh, no, that would not be right," Devon protested.

"This is true, it would not be right. You and I had an appointment, Gabriel," said the Frenchwoman, looking contrite. "Why should you be inconvenienced by my forgetfulness? Can you not show me what is in your mysterious case while we all enjoy refreshments?"

"Or, let me take the girls into the garden," Devon said. "Truly, we don't mind a bit. No doubt you would prefer privacy, m'sieur."

"Absolutely not." He waved away this suggestion. "There is nothing for me to say that all of you cannot hear, but I must request that you keep this meeting confidential."

As he put a silencing forefinger to his mouth and looked around, smiling, Izzie thought she might swoon. Did the man have any idea of the effect he had on women?

"Of course, you have our solemn vow!" Mouette exclaimed, tugging her gilt chair closer to him. "It all sounds quite thrilling!"

St. Briac's attention was on Madame Le Brun. Slowly, he opened the case and lifted out a nearly flat, rectangular, linen-wrapped object, less than two feet in length. Could it be a large book? Izzie held her breath as he moved the linen aside to reveal a small, head-and-shoulders portrait of a man, in a frame of carved wood delicately painted with worn gold leaf. She saw that the man in the portrait had eyes both compelling and lively, a large nose, and a close-trimmed beard. He was garbed in a plumed hat and jeweled doublet, painted in muted shades of green and brown.

"What a striking piece!" Madame raised her quizzing glass and leaned closer. "Is it not King François I? I'll own, it does appear to have been painted during his lifetime. The frame alone looks to be three centuries old!"

St. Briac's gaze sharpened. "Yes, it is King François. My ancestor, Thomas Mardouet, seigneur de St. Briac, was a friend and companion to the king from the time they were boys. This painting has been passed down in my family with the legend that François gave it to Thomas and his wife Aimée as a wedding gift... and that it was painted by the great Leonardo da Vinci."

"It is a treasure," said Madame, staring intently at the portrait..

Izzie remembered the tale that St. Briac had told the long-ago night they met in Brittany, when he had dined with the Raveneau and Trevarre families. He had explained that his great-grandfather, Philippe, had been "misbegotten."

Because Philippe's father had been killed in a hunting accident, causing his pregnant mother to enter a convent, he had been raised at Château du Soleil in the Loire Valley, by his aunt, the sole heir to the St. Briac estates. Although Philippe could never inherit, he was sent into the world as a young man, in 1695. Armed with only the St. Briac surname, he made his own fortune in Brittany.

"How did this painting reach your branch of the St. Briac family?" Izzie asked, adding, "I remember the story of your heritage that you told us in Roscoff, m'sieur."

He gave her a heart-melting smile. "You are very tactful, Lady Isabella. And I am honored that you have remembered my humble tale."

"We all call her Izzie," Mouette interjected. "You should as well, m'sieur, because you are our friend."

St. Briac glanced from Mouette back to Izzie and wrinkled his nose slightly. "But no, you must be *Isabella*, a name of grace and intelligence. It suits you, my lady."

Her face flamed again. "You are too kind."

"I am merely stating a fact," he said, lifting a hand as if to dismiss the name *Izzie*. "As to the portrait... it was the one thing that my great-grandfather's Tante Marie gave him to take into the world as proof of his heritage. You may imagine that although my branch of the St. Briac family felt tainted by his illegitimate birth, we have been proud to own this portrait of the great king, painted by Leonardo. We have guarded it closely, for more than a century, regarding King François as part of the family." Smiling, he added, "We refer to the portrait as 'the King.'"

Madame Le Brun bit her lower lip. "Such a riveting

story. Would you permit me to look more closely at your treasure, Gabriel?"

"Of course." He put it in her hands, watching her face. "Do you doubt that it is authentic?"

"It is certainly very old," she assured him, then leaned closer to study it through her emerald-studded quizzing glass. "It may very well be a true da Vinci. We know that he traveled to France at the end of his life, to live next to Château d'Amboise, under the patronage of King François. Although he had nearly stopped painting by then, it certainly seems reasonable that he could have made this portrait of his royal sponsor." Madame fell silent, scrutinizing the old painting for long minutes. Finally, she looked up with a tentative smile. "I do see many hallmarks of Leonardo's style here. The colors are precisely the earth tones he favored, yet..."

"One of his protégés could have painted it," St. Briac finished for her.

"Possibly," Madame agreed. "Leonardo's faithful assistant Salaino was with him at Amboise, and this could be his work. Unfortunately, I am not expert enough to give you a definite answer."

Isabella found that she was holding her breath as she watched a shadow cross St. Briac's face.

"It wouldn't surprise me to discover that it isn't any more legitimate than our St. Briac name." Slowly, his customary smile returned. "Don't apologize. I really didn't expect that you'd be able to validate the portrait."

"Why then did you bring it to me?"

"As you know, my brother, Justin, and I have a shipping business, and I live much of the time in Roscoff." He lifted a brow and amended, "Well, I should be frank. We are smuggling agents. I am used to hiding valuable goods, and I found places to keep this painting safe during the French Revolution. However, now that

Napoleon's army has begun to confiscate works of art with terrifying, persistent efficiency, I resolved to bring King François to England."

"I have heard that Napoleon transformed the Louvre Palace into a great museum filled with works of art stolen from Italy," said Mouette.

"Indeed. The Louvre is now the Musée Napoleon." He frowned. "Denon, who I mentioned to you earlier, is the museum's director. He spends his days overseeing the trove of priceless masterpieces that have become the spoils of war."

"I am well acquainted with Vivant Denon," said Madame Le Brun. "Of course, I knew him in Paris before the Revolution, but we became better friends during my time in Venice, a dozen years ago. He was kind enough to act as my *cicerone* and guide, and although I know he has often sacrificed his principles to the prevailing political tides, his dealings with me were always amiable." She wore a thoughtful smile. "He commissioned me to paint a portrait of his intimate friend, the lush beauty Madame Marini, and I am particularly proud of it."

St. Briac looked doubtful. "I have nothing good to say about Denon, especially since he began to carry out Napoleon's plan to fill the Louvre with plundered masterpieces. I am determined that my painting of the King will not fall into his hands."

"Did you imagine that I could hide it for you?" Madame Le Brun asked as she put down her quizzing glass.

"You know me too well, Madame. Who would notice my humble painting in the midst of all of these?" He waved a hand to indicate the stacks of canvases arranged near the fireplace. "And I suspect that you have many more tucked away in a storeroom, yes? It would be easy enough to add this to the collection."

"Ah, your charm is quite irresistible, *mon cher*! I would love to help you, but I intend to return to France in the New Year and then what would we do?" As she spoke, the parrot next door began to shriek as if someone were trying to murder him.

St. Briac nodded and reached for the painting's storage box. "Of course, you are right. I should not have put you in this position, Madame."

Izzie sensed the pain concealed by his casual tone. Without thinking, she exclaimed, "I think that your portrait is a treasure. And I know the perfect place where it can be kept safe from Napoleon's henchmen."

"How kind you are. Where is this perfect place?"

"In the wilds of Cornwall! My brother, Sebastian, has a remote estate near Fowey." She beamed. "He used to be a smuggler, as you know, and Cornwall abounds with hiding places. No doubt Sebastian would be pleased to guard King François until it is safe for you to return him to France."

"That's an excellent plan," Gabriel St. Briac said warmly. "I already intended to travel through Cornwall next week, en route to France. I will rest for a night at Fowey and reunite with my old friend, Lord Sebastian Trevarre. He may have renounced smuggling, but I suspect he would still enjoy a bit of intrigue." A twinkle returned to his eyes. "No doubt his lordship will have just the place to hide King François away until Napoleon and his art thieves have been vanquished."

Madame Le Brun clapped her hands. "A fine scheme indeed!"

St. Briac gave Izzie a roguish wink and raised his teacup. "*Salut* to you and your friends, Lady Isabella. I am in your debt."

BUY THE SECRET OF LOVE on AMAZON

~ MEET CYNTHIA WRIGHT ~

Cynthia Wright is the *New York Times* and *USA Today* bestselling author of the two *Rakes & Rebels* series, 14 intertwining historical romances starring the irresistible Raveneau and Beauvisage families. She has also written beloved series set during the Renaissance in France, England, and Scotland, and in the 19th century American West. Cynthia has won numerous awards over the years, and Romantic Times Magazine hails her novels as "Romance the way it was meant to be."

Cynthia lives in northern California. She enjoys riding a tandem bike and taking road trips in an airstream trailer with her Colombian-born husband, Alvaro and their corgi, Watson. She is also devoted to her two adorable grandsons who live nearby.

You are invited to visit Cynthia's website (where you can sign up for her newsletter and peruse the Books Page):

http://cynthiawrightauthor.com/

You can join Cynthia's Facebook Reader's Group here:
https://www.facebook.com/cynthiawrightauthor/

View her "Behind the Books" boards on Pinterest:
http://pinterest.com/cynthiawright77/

YOU AND NO OTHER
OF ONE HEART
ABDUCTED AT THE ALTAR
RETURN OF THE LOST BRIDE
QUEST OF THE HIGHLANDER

* * *

ROGUES GO WEST
BRIGHTER THAN GOLD
IN A RENEGADE'S EMBRACE
THE DUKE AND THE COWGIRL

* * *

BOXED SETS

RAKES & REBELS: THE RAVENEAU FAMILY 1
(Silver Storm, Her Husband, the Rake)

RAKES & REBELS: THE RAVENEAU FAMILY 2
(Smuggler's Moon, The Secret of Love, Surrender the Stars)

RAKES & REBELS: THE RAVENEAU FAMILY 3
(His Make-Believe Bride, His Reckless Bargain, Tempest)

THE RAVENEAU FAMILY IN CORNWALL
(Smuggler's Moon, The Secret of Love, His Make-Believe
Bride)

RAKES & REBELS: THE BEAUVISAGE FAMILY 1
(Stolen by a Pirate, Rescued by a Rogue)

RAKES & REBELS: THE BEAUVISAGE FAMILY 2

(Touch the Sun, Spring Fires, Her Dangerous Viscount)

CROWNS & KILTS: COLLECTION 1 – CROWNS
(You and No Other, Of One Heart)

CROWNS & KILTS: COLLECTION 2 – KILTS
(Abducted at the Altar, Return of the Lost Bride, Quest of the
Highlander)

ROGUES GO WEST
(Brighter than Gold, In a Renegade's Embrace, The Duke and
the Cowgirl)

www.ingramcontent.com/pod-product-compliance
Lightning Source LLC
Chambersburg PA
CBHW010525100726
47903CB00011B/2903